C R DEMPSEY

Uprising

Two kingdoms, one wedding and the hangman's noose

This book was professionally typeset on Reedsy.
Find out more at reedsy.com

For Mena and Maya

Contents

Acknowledgement

Thank you to all my friends and family and all those who have helped.

Special thanks to: Mena - endless patience and support, Eoin - sounding board, inspiration, advice, answering random WhatsApp messages etc., Richard Burnham - support and advice, Justin Moule - support and advice.

Cover by Dominic Forbes
Editing by Mark Empy

1

The river

Eunan tumbled from the tower. Water exploded around his head. The pain, the pain! Water invaded his mouth. Panic! A light flashed above him, ripples left on a blue skin.

"Must swim towards the light!"

He flapped his arms but still sank, slowly, slowly. Panic! Water conspired with maternal memories to drown him in spirit, body, and mind. The survival instinct kicked in. What was weighing him down? He felt for his waist. The throwing axes. He would need them. He kicked as hard as he could. His lungs were shrinking. Panic! He kicked and flapped at the same time. Propulsion! He swam towards the light. He kicked and flapped again. He broke through the skin. He spat out the water from his mouth and bit the air. Lungs inflated, he slipped back into the water once more.

The tumultuous torrents propelled him towards the bow of one of the English assault boats. Eunan used his experience gained by growing up beside a lake. While his aquatic abilities saved him, his flailing arms and bobbing head became unwanted companions of the battle debris, trying to float away and make their escape. Bullets from the English boats pursued his flailing arms and rasped through air and water until they buried themselves in the river bed.

Eunan saw the lights and heard the shouts of angry men. He realised where he was, took a breath and dived into the murkiness, and swam under a boat. He hid until his breath betrayed him, a weak, so-called friend. He propelled himself forward, kicking against the bottom of the boat.

He swam as covertly as he could, peering over his shoulder to see if the English soldiers' attention had settled elsewhere. Enniskillen gave Eunan a parting farewell gift, for its blaze distracted the soldiers long enough to provide him with a brief opportunity to escape. The bitterness of parting sunk Eunan's heart to the pit of his chest. So many men had died horrible deaths, yet he, possibly the least deserving, still lived. Yet it may have been for a reason. He endeavoured to carry on, if not for his own sake, then for the memory of his dead comrades who would want him to live and avenge them. He turned from Enniskillen to make good his escape. Too late! The bow of a boat rammed straight into the side of his head! He lost consciousness. The bow drove Eunan's body beneath the hull and discarded his body to float downriver with the other debris.

* * *

Odin sat and stoked the fire. He positioned himself where Eunan's father once sat as if he were him. He gazed outward over Upper Lough Erne, and he wished he was not there, as if he were Eunan. The village burned around him. Flames licked and kissed the houses, trees, and grass. Any love that may have once resided there instantly became ash. A circle of stakes surrounded Odin's fire, and skewered onto each stake was the head of one of Eunan's friends or relatives who had died in the village's various destructions. But Odin held the best for himself as he poured his mead into Eunan's mother's skull until it overflowed its sides. Odin picked it up from the temples and downed its contents. Loki and Badu emerged from the fire and sat down beside Odin. Loki picked up the skull of Eunan's father and Badu, the small and delicate skull of Eunan's sister. Odin poured and they drank.

"How bodes war and chaos?" Odin asked.

"Our host lives, but our blood flows out onto the river, and we don't know whether he will meet death," replied Badu.

"His time will come, but not yet. The bad blood still gushes through his veins. There is much entertainment for us to enjoy yet!"

The Norse gods laughed as they slammed their skulls together and toasted once again. Fire devoured the village.

* * *

Water no longer flowed over Eunan's face. He awoke, half spat, half vomited. The pain of both smooth and jagged hardness penetrated his body. He opened his eyes to a blurred outline and a mouth that made no sound. His senses gradually recovered.

"Eunan?"

2

The prisoner

Seamus was confused. All he could see of the man who stood before him was chain mail, a helmet, and a sharp axe. But where there should have been a face was leather, embedded by round holes for eyes, nose and mouth. Confidence exuded from the man's every stride, and intimidation from every hole in his mask. Seamus raised his axe.

"I am an old and experienced Galloglass, prepared to fight to the death. Whoever comes before me had better be prepared to die if they take me on!"

"Oh, I'm ready to take you on alright! Don't you recognise me, Seamus?"

Several more men emerged from the stairwell and stood behind the masked man. Seamus squinted. The fresh faces were vaguely familiar.

"I'll make you an offer, far more generous than the offer you made me," continued the man. "The captain of this castle has already surrendered. If you surrender now, my boys and I won't chop you up and feed you to the fishes. Well, not just yet. Do you want to die a senseless death or take your chances with me?"

Seamus looked at the man in the mask and his henchmen and

estimated he would not get out alive. He made up his mind.

"I like a man who is willing to negotiate, and a Galloglass is always willing to take a risk."

Seamus threw down his axe. Two of the men who had emerged from the stairs grabbed Seamus by the arms and hauled him over to the masked man. The man stared into Seamus's blank face.

"You don't remember me, do you?"

Seamus did not react.

"'Tis always better if you know who you're negotiating with!" and the man removed his helmet and handed it to one of his sons. He revealed a leather mask, which was a lattice of neatly stitched together brown leather strips. He undid the string at the back of the mask.

His face was a patchwork of pink and scarlet, volcanic fissures of pain that melted into each other, the eyes hollow, their bags slid down to his nose that bled across his face. Even Seamus winced as he tried to pick which colour patches were the rawest. Seamus may have once known who he was, but he did not recognise him now.

"I preferred you with your mask on, as I'm sure did your former lady. Why are you showing me your face? Why not skip the courtship and kill me?"

"Because you did this to me!"

Seamus looked at him sceptically and tried to remember. He came upon a guess.

"Shea Óg O'Rourke?"

"It took you long enough, but you didn't stay to admire your work when you did it!"

"Well, there'll be no one doing any admiring until you put the bag back on your head. I told you, you should have pledged."

The shaft of Shea Óg's axe burned with friction.

"I'd smash your skull right now if you weren't worth the bounty the English captain is willing to pay for bringing the leaders to him alive."

5

"I like a man whose pragmatism can make a mere morsel of his morality!"

"After telling the English about you, I'm sure I can get paid and smash your skull in all at the same time."

"You can save your tall stories for the whores when you try to bargain them down from doubling their price because of your face."

One swift blow to the stomach from Shea Óg had Seamus gasping for air.

"You won't be so smart when you see what's in store for you. Bring him down to the courtyard."

Shea's sons administered blows to the body and head to ensure Seamus's compliance. They dragged him down the stairs. Seamus opened his eyes again when they threw him to the ground. In the corner of the courtyard, the Irish soldiers who had surrendered sat under the English guns. In another corner, their wives and children crouched, crying out for the protection of their fathers and husbands or, failing that, for the mercy of the English. The English soldiers and their Irish allies collected the rebel dead and wounded from the castle in two piles. Nonchalance ruled their allocation, for each pile was to be cast into the river from the castle walls as a warning to potential rebels that may be planning to resist in the lower lough.

Captain Dowdall stood in the centre, a totem to victory. His uniform was a little dusty but nothing compared to the blackened, blood-stained uniforms of his men. The soldier buzzed around him, returning for his approval when they had completed the latest task in the destruction of the rebels.

Seamus was groggy now from the beatings administered Shea Óg to him and the bruises to his lower body as they dragged him down every stair and over every obstacle. Shea Óg saw his chance. His sons threw Seamus in front of Captain Dowdall, and a random bucket of slops dumped upon Seamus to encourage his revival.

"I caught this renegade on the roof swinging his axe."

"Why are you bothering me with him? There are quicker ways to get him off the roof than to drag him down!"

"I apologise, captain, but I'm here to collect my reward."

"I pay the same for bodies. Why do you drag this breathing 'Mac' and 'O' before me to make your claim?"

"Don't you recognise him?"

"Who's he supposed to be?" Dowdall shrugged.

"One of William Stanley's most trusted men! An officer and a confidant of that foulest of renegades."

"Well, this would be a grand prize for the Lord Deputy. If only we could verify it was true. Do you have any proof or plan to run away once the coin settles on the palm of your hand?"

"See my face. He did this to me! It was supposed to be a lesson from the Maguire, so Seamus could brag how he deformed me to frighten any other loyal subjects. Well, I had the last laugh. A man came to me who said he knew his handiwork from his time in the Netherlands, and there was a large bounty on his head from the Crown. He said he'd pay handsomely for any information that led to his arrest, more for him alive than for the body. So why don't you give me a small cut of the reward now, and I'll send the man to you?"

"Do you take me for a fool?"

"No, no sir! I take you for an astute gentleman who is about to celebrate a glorious victory. If the coward Maguire hadn't hidden his cattle, you'd be a rich man too. I know you want to make an example of all the rebels, but this one is worth way too much money."

"I haven't time for this. You guard the prisoner and get this gentleman with more money than sense to come here and offer the reward. I set sail for Lower Lough Erne by the end of the week. So if we haven't struck a bargain by then, I'll shoot this prisoner myself. Be off with you, and when you come back to see me wear another mask.

7

Surely you can make a better one than that monstrosity!"

Captain Dowdall dismissed Shea Óg and called his sergeants over to converse about the reconstruction of the castle. Shea Óg resentfully took his prize. He got his sons to haul Seamus to the camp outside the castle so no one would steal his prisoner from him.

3

Sanctuary

The figure placed Eunan's head on his knee with such gentleness that Eunan's water-numbed skin barely registered the movement. He created a cascade of water from his flask onto the palm of his hand and then softly into Eunan's lips and mouth. Eunan had rarely befriended gentleness and boiled over with mistrust, opened his eyes and brushed him off to fight his fits of coughs and splutters. Rolling over onto his elbows, he wiped his face and looked at his Good Samaritan.

"Arthur!!" he croaked with relief, for in his state, his defensive tension was exhausting.

Arthur paid back his smile with interest.

"The luck was with you when the river took you in her torrents."

"Luck deserted me long ago if she was ever acquainted with me!" and Eunan lifted himself to his feet.

"You've got the affliction of youth upon you, always aspiring after something else but not realising what you've got until it's gone."

"Enniskillen is gone, my village is gone, Fermanagh is gone. Soon the Maguires will follow!"

"Don't be so downhearted. Sure, look - you still have your axes!"

Eunan reached for his side pouch, and sure enough, the three axes given to him by Desmond were safely wrapped up inside.

"Now, isn't that a bit of luck for you; the man who's got nothing? Sure, when you get back to the war and throw them at someone's head, you'll have brains on them too. Why so downhearted? Speculating to accumulate, that's you! You're acquiring things all the time. Come on, let me help you up. Desmond is waiting for us in the house on the other side of the island."

"Desmond is here?"

"Yes, and he'll be glad to see you. Now come on."

Eunan's body was a bag of aches and groans and moved like a man quadruple his age. But Arthur took pity on him, offered him a shoulder and helped him up and off the rocky beach. They climbed the small hill and looked over the lake. Bobbing bodies and debris blighted their view.

"They did that on purpose to frighten us," said Arthur. "Pushing the bodies from the castle downriver. But it won't work. We know we're safe out here on the islands."

Eunan turned away, for he could dwell on his defeat no more.

"We can't live here forever, but we can for now. Let's go find Desmond," and Arthur led Eunan away.

The island was small, and it took them five minutes to cross it. The island was not the first one Eunan encountered as he floated up the lake. Hugh Maguire supposedly occupied Devenish Island. The island was an obvious target for the English, working their way downriver since the island commanded access to the lower lough. However, Hugh Maguire had created a formidable defence. Desmond had chosen somewhere far more discrete; a little hideaway that you would sail straight past unless you had a specific reason to go there.

Arthur led Eunan to a compact cove, surrounded by trees, facing out onto the lake. It was the perfect hideout. Desmond sat on a rock with a large stick pointing over the lake, and its string looped carelessly around so that the end tickled the waves. Eunan's heart lept. He would have run to greet Desmond, but his legs were jelly and had spent most of their energy crossing the island. All he could manage was to give out a faint croak.

"Come, he'll never hear that. You need to rest yourself."

Arthur turned toward Desmond's back and cupped his mouth.

"Master, come see who has come to visit!" he shouted.

Desmond looked over his shoulder as if this exertion was all the energy he was prepared to spend. That was until he saw...

"Eunan!"

Desmond dropped his stick into the lake to float off into oblivion, and the fish were spared their lives for a couple of hours at least. Desmond hobbled over the smooth stone shore with all the speed his legs and grip of his shoes would grant him. His exertions were not in vain, for the embrace was true, and the words of welcome exuded a warmth rarely expressed by either of them. This time Arthur became the physical crutch for both as the three-legged horse hopped towards the little stone house that was the sanctuary. There were three chairs and a table in the house's shadows, all donated by the trees of the island. Eunan flopped onto the most comfortable looking of these and Desmond, only momentarily, grimaced as he had the grace to give up his favourite chair for his dearest guest.

"Here, let me take these," said Arthur as he undid the axes pouch from Eunan's belt. "I'll fetch you some clothes. I doubt they'll fit, but they'll do 'till we get your rags clean. I'll see if anyone else has some spare clothes the next time I visit the other islands."

"Thank you, very kind," mumbled Eunan.

Arthur came with some spare clothes, and Eunan picked them off his arm one by one and changed.

"Now my duties as a clothes rack are complete. I hope you like

11

fish, for its fish with everything around here! My speciality is fish with fish, but recently I've been venturing into fish with grass," smiled Arthur.

"He's not joking!" exclaimed Desmond.

"I prefer to feast from the field than dip my stick in the water," said Eunan.

"A strange sentiment for a man who grew up beside a lake," said Desmond.

"But you'll make do with it, for you'll need your strength for the war all the same," added Arthur.

Arthur picked up Desmond's bag and sighed into its emptiness.

"Well, we won't be relying on Desmond's stick for our supper, for it has barely had its strength tested by little mouths tugging on the line."

"I've far better skills than my fishing, that's for sure!" laughed Desmond.

"None of which are any use to us on this island! Since when has arguing politics with a trout turned it into dinner? It looks like I'll have to do the fishing as usual," said Arthur as he turned to fetch his rod.

Eunan's smile overcame the tiredness on his face, and he turned to his mentor.

"Desmond, I have missed you."

"Don't ruin a pleasant reunion by getting all sentimental."

"The Maguires need you!"

Desmond saw Eunan could barely keep awake.

"Sleep before the conversation turns serious. I want to know everything, but you need strength and a clear head to tell me. Arthur, take him and put him to bed. We'll eat and talk when you're ready."

Eunan attempted to protest, but Arthur's kindness was overpowering and the lure of a comfortable bed overwhelming.

* * *

"Get up, sleepyhead!" and Arthur shook Eunan awake.

"Where am I?" Eunan cried, but he remembered and relaxed again upon sight of Arthur's face. "Is it time to eat? The feast of the marriage of Hugh Maguire could barely dent my insatiable appetite!"

"It has been time to eat many times since you laid down your head, and Desmond couldn't wait for you! You've slept for two days, but I have spent those two days well. I have fetched your new clothes, food from the field, and an axe worthy of a warrior of your stature. I suggest you bathe so your smell does not put us off eating the modest meal I have prepared. Then I'll look at your wounds, and then you can eat. Only when your stomach is full and your mind is at rest, can you discuss the woes of the world with Desmond. Now, let me help you up and bring you to the lake."

Eunan deflated into the comfort of kindness. He followed Arthur's instructions, and he soon dangled his feet in the lake, dressed in new clothes, with a full belly, and his wounds tended and wrapped. Desmond came to join him. Desmond set his fishing line into the lake and listened to the stories of Eunan's adventures and what he had found out about himself since they last parted. He listened and did not interrupt. At last, Eunan finished and sought his reaction and words of wisdom. He composed himself.

"I knew of this man you speak of, Seamus MacSheehy, briefly in my time in the Netherlands and the distant past in Fermanagh. He is a man of great cunning and skill, and I hope you have more of his traits rather than those of his brother. You are young and impulsive, and I fear he may lead you down the wrong path. Since you ask, I will give you my advice.

"Forget Seamus. If he survived, he has probably now fled. Forget your childhood, and the priests and the knights of St Colmcille, and how those priests scarred you with their bloodletting, which they claim will cure you. It won't. Trust me. I've done it all. It is all in your mind, and until you resolve it within yourself, it will burden you forever. The worries of the world are significant, without you weighing yourself down with a view of the past that exists only in your head. You can, and need to be, a great warrior for your clan. Hugh Maguire needs you more than ever now.

"I'm vaguely familiar with your father, Cathal, but more familiar with the O'Cassidys in your region. However, I have news for you. The spies that watch Donnacha O'Cassidy Maguire for me, tell me that a certain Captain Willis organised the raid that led to your father's death. I don't know how Donnacha came across the information, and he is not averse to spreading poison and lies. Don't follow the path of pursuing revenge. It will cloud your judgment and distract you from your actual mission.

"I am also familiar with your mother, and it's your mother's family that you should pursue. She was an O'Cassidy Maguire, whose father married her off to your father for some mysterious reason, especially considering the O'Cassidys were on the ascent. She was a cousin to Donnacha O'Cassidy Maguire, with whom you're very familiar. If you are as serious as you say you are about helping your clan, the best way you can do that is to become the O'Cassidy Maguire. Ride south to Derrylinn and stake your claim to the title. The incumbent is your mother's brother, Cormac O'Cassidy. He is a turncoat and a cheat. Barely a bullet had left Captain Dowdall's guns and embedded themselves in rebel flesh or the walls of Enniskillen when he turned and declared for Connor Roe.

"However, Cormac O'Cassidy is a powerful and connected man, and the O'Cassidys have a potent influence on the Maguires. Therefore, you must use stealth and guile to achieve your aims. But with war comes opportunity, and, if you are clever, your time will come.

"But we can talk more about that later. You are going nowhere until you are fit and healthy. Why don't you relax and we might do a little fishing to pass the time? If the English try to attack this lake, it'll be a long time before they make it up here."

"I'd like that."

"Now, why don't you relax or make yourself useful somewhere else. Your shadow is distracting the fish!"

Eunan laughed.

"Try to catch enough for all of us this dinnertime. I'm famished!"

"Don't you go taking anything Arthur says about me seriously. Now go get some rest."

Eunan got up and set about exploring the tiny island. It had not much of anything except a peaceful silence. Eunan went to the opposite side of the island, to where Desmond and Arthur were. He looked out onto the lake and tried to pick out Devenish Island. Dark clouds gathered both over his head and in his mind.

He felt his blood boil in his arms. He berated himself for being weak, for letting his father die, for letting Hugh Maguire fall under the spell of Donnacha O'Cassidy Maguire, for letting Seamus live, for the fall of Enniskillen Castle.

"May a curse be on all those who have done me and my family ill. May this bad blood that runs through my veins be good for something, and that thing be vengeance!"

He heard Desmond and Arthur's voices from behind the trees on the other side of the island. He calmed down, and as the adrenalin of his bad blood receded, he deflated and was once more overcome by tiredness.

He lay down on a grassy knoll that overlooked the stony shore. He looked up at the sky and examined the white fluffy clouds that had taken over the sky since he last looked, and wondered when the next rain shower was coming. His mind drifted back to his youth, but he banished the flashes of anger and think back to the idyllic times he spent in Enniskillen the last time he paid attention to clouds. He was soon in blissful sleep, waiting for the next rain shower.

4

The promise

Shea Óg sat his prize beside the fire so he could keep his eye on him. Shea Óg's sons had badly beaten Seamus, but on Shea Óg's orders, they spared his face. Seamus hung his head, bound hand and foot, and starving. Shea Óg and his sons feasted on the beasts from the Maguire's fields and ale stolen from the Maguire cellars while Seamus looked on.

"Do I get a last supper? Surely you'll get more money for me if I'm fit and recognisable?"

"You! Shut yer face! Or I'll come over and smash it in for you!"

"Easy, Sean," said his father. "Our reward will be with us tomorrow morning. The man who offered us good money for Seamus is on his way. So there'll be no killing going on tonight."

Sean cursed and sat back down again. Seamus thought it best to be quiet for a while. Shea Óg and his sons sat and drank and became increasingly rowdy. Seamus became increasingly more hungry.

"Can you throw a bit of that meat my way? If I look scrawny and ill, he may take pity on me and dull his desire to kill me and offer you less."

"It would give me just as much pleasure to kill you myself as it would to take that man's money," roared Sean over his shoulder.

"But if you did that, you'd be straight back to starving in the middle of a bog when the English discard you, which they will."

There was silence. Sean slammed his spoon into his bowl as if a crooked penny had dropped.

"You know what? I think you're right! So why don't you come over and have some of our stew!"

Sean ran over and grabbed the bound Seamus and dragged him towards the fire. A pot bubbled suspended over the fire.

"No! No!" cried Seamus, for he recognised the look in Sean's eye.

"Who's the big man now?" and Sean pulled Seamus up, grabbed him by the hair and pushed him towards the pot.

The stew bubbled beneath him. The bubbles popped and singed his face, and the heat repulsed him. He hadn't eaten in days, and the waft drew him back. He felt faint as his resistance weakened and the violence of Sean's pressure intensified.

"No! No!" cried Shea Óg. "As much as it would please me to avenge myself by doing to him what he did to me, we have mouths to feed. We need to replace the cattle he stole from us, and we can't do that without selling him. We'll get nothing for him if you mangle his face, and he can't be recognised."

"I recognise him! I'll say it's him!" and anger surged from red face to red fists.

"No, Sean, let him go."

"Damn him to hell!" and Sean threw Seamus backwards and kicked him in the ribs.

"You're not getting any food for that," he shouted as Seamus squirmed on the ground.

Sean sat down, and Shea Óg put his arm around his shoulders.

"We'll get paid, and get suitable revenge for my face, mark my words!"

Sean shook him off and flopped back into his former seat. They ate in silence.

* * *

A feast laced with ale topped off the exhaustion of a day of battle and cast a slumber across the English camp. All was calm until a fleet of foot messengers ran amongst them.

"The captain has summoned the prisoners! The captain has summoned the prisoners!"

"Ha!" shouted Shea Óg as he jolted upright, shook off the ale, and pointed at his prisoner.

He smelt a modicum of revenge in the humiliation of his captive.

"Bring him! Let Seamus see what happens to the enemies of the English."

"Don't do it on my account," replied Seamus. "I've seen it all before."

"Ah, sure, then do it for us," said Sean. "We've only seen our father's face being shoved in a pot of boiling water. We want to increase our torture proficiency."

Shea Óg's sons picked up Seamus and dragged him across the Irish allies' periphery camp to the English campsite; the hollering and gunfire echoed in the air as guidance.

When they arrived, the first order of business was to cast Seamus to the ground, leaving him with Sean and his freshly sharpened axe for company. The second was for Shea Óg and the other sons to explore the camp. All the roads in the camp led to a large circle within which burned the celebratory fire. To one side lay the dejected Irish prisoners and those English soldiers who were unlucky in drawing lots as to who should perform guard duty. Captain Dowdall stood to the side to avoid being the centre of attention, enjoyed a drink with the other officers, and left the soldiers to their own devices. The looted vaults of the castle would provide the merriment tonight.

The drink had stripped away the English soldiers' stress and inhibitions, and they turned on the prisoners with a cruel thirst for vengeance. A drunken sergeant who stumbled from the crowd announced himself as "James Eccarsall esquire, loyal servant of the Queen and scourge of these Irish scoundrels."

The soldiers met his stumbling, exaggerated bows with cheers and laughter. Sergeant Eccarsall's reputation in the camp was such that several soldiers lined up behind him, for they knew that the prime entertainment was about to begin.

"Ladies and gentlemen! Traitors and loyal subjects of the Crown! To what do we owe our victory today? Well, of course, there was the cunning of our excellent Captain Dowdall!"

The Captain nodded, raised his mug and smiled in approval to the cheers of his men.

"But we had a little secret, didn't we?"

"Yes!" and the soldiers laughed and scorned the unsuspecting prisoners.

"Now we still have many of these Irish traitors still alive, don't we?"

"Not for long," bayed back the soldiers.

"Oh, don't be so cruel. We have to introduce them to the man who served them up to us on a platter, don't we?"

"Yes!"

"Bring him here."

Two soldiers escorted a young man with the darting eyes and quivering body of a frightened rabbit. They stood him beside Sergeant Eccarsall.

"Here he is, ladies and gentlemen: Connor O'Cassidy!"

"Hurray!"

The Irish survivors, bound and sat to the side, said nothing. Some of them recognised Connor O'Cassidy and deposited the remains of their saliva in the mud at the mention of his name. The English soldiers cheered.

"We caught this man with the messages of the traitor Hugh Maguire, carrying the plots and conspiracies against the Queen to other gullible Macs and O's. He readily gave up his messages and begged us for a way he could make up his previous connivances to his beloved Queen."

The soldiers jeered.

"So what did our goodly traitor do? He showed us the secret way into the castle. That's what he did. And when we got there, what did we do? Massacred all the treacherous Macs and O's!"

"Hurray!"

"So here is your reward, oh loyal servant of the Queen. Here in this bag are your thirty pieces of silver which I'll tie around your neck!" and the sergeant held up a bag of coins for all to see.

"Hurray!"

The sergeant tied the bag around Connor O'Cassidy's neck.

"I...didn't...you forced me to..."

"Now, don't be so modest. I know you wanted to give all to Queen and country. But subjects who have given such service should accept their just rewards. So kneel before the representative of the Queen!"

The sergeant unsheathed his sword, and two soldiers came behind Connor O'Cassidy and pressed down on his shoulders until he knelt. James Eccarsall gently placed the blade of his sword on both of Connor's shoulders.

"By the powers vested in me, I dub thee, Sir Connor Cassidy."

The English soldiers roared with laughter.

"Arise, Sir Cassidy, let us dispense with those savage marks of the O'."

The soldiers behind Connor O'Cassidy hooked his arms and lifted him to his feet.

"Now, for your service to the Queen, you can have any of the lands of your former brethren. Tell us, what lands would you like?"

"I don't want to take anything that does not belong..."

"Don't worry about that! You don't have to pick now. Once you decide we will section off your land nice and neat so that when the English settlers arrive, they'll take all the traitors' land, but not yours. But what you do need is some peasants to work the land for you."

Sergeant Eccarsall walked over to the Irish prisoners, stood behind them and expanded his arms out wide, as if offering them to Connor.

"So, what do we have here? Take your pick, Sir Cassidy. There are plenty of peasants to choose from. Lazy ones, fat ones, liars all. But we'll soon starve them into submission so they'll work for you. All they have to do is pledge their loyalty to the Queen. Then they'll receive a plot of land, a sum of rent to pay both yourself and the Queen, and they can live. So who's first to pledge?"

The English jeers submerged the rebel silence. Sergeant Eccarsall walked back to Connor O'Cassidy.

"They must be a little shy. They don't want to break rank in front of their former comrades."

Sergeant Eccarsall turned to chide the prisoners.

"The rebellion is over. Enniskillen burns around you! The Maguire is now a fugitive, a wild dog hiding by himself in a wood. Save yourselves. Accept her Majesty's pardon, pledge to the Crown and accept your place. Now, who's first?"

The Irish prisoners bowed their heads again to escape the sergeant's attention. Finally, Sergeant Eccarsall ran out of patience.

"If you will not volunteer, then we are going to have to volunteer you. Men, bring me the first prisoner."

Two guards grabbed the nearest prisoner to them and threw them in front of Sir Cassidy.

"Now then, kiss the hand of your new lord, pledge allegiance to the Queen, and you can go free," said Sergeant Eccarsall.

The soldiers grabbed the wrist of Connor O'Cassidy and thrust it into the face of the prisoner.

"Kiss his hand!"

Another soldier came behind the prisoner and forced the prisoner's head forward.

"I'll never pledge for that traitor!" the prisoner croaked, and what little saliva he had struck Sir Cassidy's shirt.

"Nobody insults a knight of the realm like that," and Sergeant Eccarsall plunged his sword into the prisoner's chest.

"Send him back to the Maguire," and the sergeant waived the body away.

The guards dragged the dead man's body into the dark.

"You two, come. Fetch the next prisoner," and Sergeant Eccarsall selected two new soldiers and directed them to stand behind the prisoners.

The sergeant chose his next victim and forced him to kneel in front of Sir Cassidy, bow his head and kiss his hand.

"What's this?" James Eccarsall exclaimed.

The man turned away in shame. A wet ring rapidly expanded around the prisoner's groin.

"What!? We can't have this," roared the sergeant. "Cowards, go straight back to the Maguire!"

The guards dragged him into the dark, ignoring his cries for mercy. Everyone heard one final short sharp cry, and then a substantial plop of something heavy being dropped into water.

Shea Óg had returned to protect his prize. He leaned in behind Seamus.

"They are literally sending them back to the Maguire. But you won't get to die so easily."

Seamus jerked his head away from Shea's foul breath. By the end of the evening, Sir Cassidy had enough residents for his first tiny village.

* * *

Excessive drinking created voluminous amounts of urine, which the sergeant diligently made his fellow soldiers collect in buckets. The soldiers returned the recycled vaults of the Maguire with interest to his wretched soldiers. Seamus found his temporary and accidental solace on the shoulder of a comrade, violently wrenched away when the liquid hit. The prisoners began to wretch the moment the smells penetrated their nostrils.

Captain Dowdall stood before them, and the sun glistened on his fresh uniform as it bypassed his cruel smirk. His men around him appeared as monsters to the bleary-eyed rebel prisoners, dirty faces and clothes, the scrawny beards of men in the middle of a campaign, the sideward stagger of those not yet sober enough to hold their weapons straight. Yet, they were hulking, leering monsters all the same, and they could whip the prisoners lives away in one flash of hungover temper. Captain Dowdall was neither impressed by the state of his men, the tools with which to fulfil his orders, nor the tatters hulks of men he held prisoner, for they encumbered his progress. However, he had more pressing matters. He called his men to attention. The guttural barks of his sergeants echoed his articulate shout. The men made the best line they could, given the night before.

"We need to leave a small garrison here and move onto the lower lough," he said as he addressed his men. "Sergeant Rogers, take fifty men and string up the prisoners in the town. Kill any that resist or cannot walk. Make sure the peasants can see the hangings. Sergeant McGregor will continue the castle repairs with the rest of the men. We leave in three days."

"What about the prisoners we promised to Connor O'Cassidy, sir?" said Sergeant Rogers.

"What!? Are you drunk on duty, sergeant? You didn't take that seriously, did you? String them up in the town as a warning to the rest of the Macs and O's. We have neither the time nor capacity to herd a bunch of prisoners behind us!"

"Yes, sir, at once, sir!" and the sergeant ran away with such an enthusiasm to fulfil his orders, hoping with his endeavours being so impressive, the captain would not remember the previous conversation.

The English soldiers broke their rickety lines and descended on the Irish prisoners. Most prisoners offered little resistance and could walk. The remaining few met a sword's blade for the last time.

The soldiers came for Seamus, for Shea Óg was no longer there to protect him. They bound Seamus hand and foot and raised a sword above his head. Seamus clenched his eyes shut as if for the last time. He felt his legs turn to jelly. Prayers came to his lips but remained incomplete. The sword descended, and he heard it cut into something, but he felt no pain. His arms fell to the ground, and his upper body felt such relief. He was free. If only for a moment.

"Get up, or the sword fills your chest."

Seamus obeyed and joined the column of twenty survivors in their march out of the castle and into the town. Their heads were bowed, their bodies mostly stripped, their minds substantially broken. The soldiers went to fetch Connor O'Cassidy, but Captain Dowdall intervened.

"No! Not him. He stays in the castle for now. I've got other plans for him."

Seamus turned his head to see Connor O'Cassidy being taken away.

The column reached the town, and the soldiers searched the streets for prominent wood beams sound enough to hold a hanging man. Their hangovers impaired their judgment because for every man that was dangled successfully from a rope and succumbed to gravity despite their struggles, the next man would splutter and cough and turn scarlet and would not die. Instead, they would 'send him to Jesus' with a sword penetrating his side until it reached his heart, or the sergeant would order them to cut him down and have another go. The young man to be hanged before Seamus refused to slide easily to death at the hands of his hungover tormentors and was cut down three times before being shot by an impatient sergeant.

"You next!"

The sergeant pushed Seamus down the street and along the way tested the solidity of the house beams with his sword. He was finally satisfied by a wood beam that intersected two lanes, where a body would hang in prominent display. The sergeant smiled, for he was running out of traitors faster than he was running out of streets to display them in.

"Up there!" he said, addressing his men as he pointed to the beam. "Cast your rope up there!"

The soldiers secured the rope, tied the knot, and placed the noose around Seamus's neck.

"We would ask you if you wanted to say any last prayers, but we don't want to encourage any papist blasphemy now, do we?" and he smirked at Seamus. "Stand him on the bucket, boys, and then haul him up!"

"No!"

Everyone turned to see Sean O'Rourke at the end of the street, raising his hand in the air as he bent over and gasped for breath. He had arisen from his drunken slumber to find his father's prize had gone. As much as he wanted to see Seamus dead, he did not want to be responsible for his clan's continued poverty.

"That man is the possession of my father! He captured him, and he has a price on his head. Captain Dowdall promised us his ransom money as part of our payment for our support!"

"Well, you're too late. The captain told us to execute all the prisoners, all except the prime traitor O'Cassidy. If the captain had any deal with you, he didn't tell us about it. So string him up, boys!"

"No, do not touch that man! The Crown wants him!"

Sergeant Rogers turned towards the voice that came from the other end of the street. The silhouette of a one-armed man on horseback stood before him.

"Are we going to get on with this hanging or what?" Seamus pleaded with the sergeant, for he felt the man on horseback was a past that he did not want to catch up with, and he would rather die quickly. The man on horseback came out of the shadows to reveal his captain's uniform. Shea Óg buzzed around his feet as if an irritating insect.

"That man is mine!" said the captain. "Release him to me."

The sergeant hesitated but realised he had little choice, or it would be his neck in the noose.

Shea Óg patted his pocket and smiled towards Seamus. The deed was done.

5

Back at the castle

The pain of the floorboards on Seamus's knees was almost unbearable. However, it was more bearable than to give any of his enemies the pleasure of seeing him in pain. He was back again in Enniskillen Castle as he waited for his unknown fate.

Shea Óg was elated. He sat in the shadows waiting for instruction from his masters. He got half his money up front, and the rest was due on Seamus's demise. Was he getting paid to watch Seamus die? He could not believe his luck.

Captain Dowdall's mood was entirely on the other side of the spectrum, for he had just received news of his defeated soldiers from their raid on Devenish Island, and he raged around his room. He poured over maps, barked at his sergeants, and dictated pleading letters to Dublin and the governor of Connacht, stating that Fermanagh was almost conquered, but he could not fully subdue the Maguires without more men.

The other mysterious English captain who paid for Seamus sat and ate. His clothes were dirty from a long ride, and he was tired and hungry. His only words to Seamus had been "I have got you now" before Shea Óg came buzzing around asking for his money. He pushed his empty plate into the middle of the table and took a long drink. Before he had even finished...

"Are we going to hang Seamus now?"

The scorn in the captain's eyes was visible even in the dimly lit room.

"Seamus MacSheehy will meet his fate all in good time. Meanwhile, I'm sure Captain Dowdall has some tasks to keep you gainfully employed?"

"Only if he knows how to flush those snakes out of the lower lakes," replied Dowdall.

"I'm sure I could think of something for a suitable amount of coin!" said Shea Óg.

"You need to show your loyalty to the Crown and do things for the good of the realm, not dance at the gleam of a shiny coin!" said Captain Dowdall.

"I take the example of Lord Deputy Fitzwilliam seriously."

"You Irish knaves need a far better role model!"

The other captain turned to Seamus.

"Men, bring him to the roof. I wish to speak to him alone."

Shea Óg turned in horror.

"But if he dies..."

"Let go of your prize! You'll be paid in good time. Don't wear out your welcome by being tiresome."

Shea Óg nodded and cowered back towards Captain Dowdall and let Seamus leave the room.

The soldiers escorted Seamus to the roof.

"Leave us," ordered the Captain.

"But sir! He is only bound by hand!"

"I shall put him down with a swift slash of my sword should he be so foolish as to try anything. Do as I say."

The men left and positioned themselves out of sight on the stairwell, for they did not share their superior's confidence.

Seamus edged over to the wall, so at least he had death as an escape route. The captain smirked.

"You don't remember me, do you?"

"I have met many an English captain, mainly with an axe in my hand. But I don't remember you."

"I can't have changed that much. We both served together in the Netherlands. Don't you remember?"

"You must've been a spy, for I only served the Spanish Crown!"

"There is no need to lie to me. None of your compatriots are here to dub you a traitor. We both know you served under William Stanley."

Seamus paused. He knew being caught in Ireland and being recognised as a compatriot of William Stanley was a death sentence. Unfortunately, Seamus lived under the shadow of several death sentences and had yet to work out which sword loomed over him.

"I was a mercenary for the Spanish, but what makes you think I served under him?"

"Because I was one of the few officers that remained loyal to the Queen and country when the cowardly traitor gave Deventer to the Spanish. Do you not remember me? I am Captain Williamson, and I have sworn to track down every Irish traitor from Deventer who sets foot on Irish soil and hang them from the nearest tree!"

"You must have mistaken me for someone else. Many Irish served in the Netherlands, and I'm surprised you can tell them apart. But why make such a fuss about me? Why save me from the rope?"

"We'll get to that. But I know who you are, and we have met. You may have never served under the English, but yet you caused us so much damage. I was there that night in Deventer. I was one of the few non-Catholic English officers serving under Stanley. He argued so bitterly against his commander Sir John Norris, all it needed was a little worm from the Spanish to have him turning coat. You were that little worm."

"You have a vivid imagination! Even if you believe your own story, that makes me even more likely to be swinging off the rafters in Enniskillen town."

"You had infiltrated the ranks of the Irish units in the English army, leveraging the sympathies of your fellow Munster men."

"Even more foolish for you to go recruiting in lands you've just destroyed. That's the harvest you get when you sow bitter seeds."

"You whispered in Stanley's ear to revolt and turned to the Spanish. In the bitter fighting that ensued between him and what few loyal men we could gather, we had to take to the river and flee."

"That still doesn't tell me why I am still alive?"

"Stanley's men are drip-fed back to Ireland to both encourage and lead an insurrection!"

"I left the Netherlands years ago."

"Yet here we are!"

Captain Williamson walked over to the other side of the roof while monitoring Seamus.

"Come over here and look into the courtyard."

Seamus gave the captain a mistrustful glace but knew he did not have a choice.

"Look down in the courtyard below. Tell me what you see."

Seamus looked at Captain Williamson.

"Go on, look. If I wanted to kill you, I would have let you swung from the rope last night. Look down below and tell me what you see."

Seamus peered over the edge of the wall and pulled back after the shortest of views.

"People."

"I know that! What sort of people? Who are they? Look down and find the answer to what I'm looking for as if your life, or maybe someone else's, depends on it. Only give me an answer when you know what it is."

Seamus looked over the edge again. He studied all the people in the courtyard, who they were and what they were doing.

"It looks like you are rounding up all the refugees from the castle and the surrounding areas. Why are you showing this to me? I'm a mercenary. What do I care for the locals when I know I will not get paid?"

"A mercenary you may be, but you have a heart and decide certain things for yourself. Look again and tell me when you have the answer."

Seamus looked in the courtyard again. It was the same mass of faces, the same expressions of apprehension and despair. This time he noticed that the Irish lackeys were searching through the crowds and separating some people, be it for they were rebels or for the settlement of some feud or grudge whose cause had been long forgotten. The soldiers reopened the castle gate, and a flood of refugees rolled into the courtyard. Seamus then saw Shea Óg and Sean. They waded through the crowds of people searching for someone. They came upon a group near the gate. Shea Óg looked up towards Captain Williamson and smiled. He pointed towards the cluster, who were attempting to obscure themselves with hoods and scarves. Captain Williamson smiled.

"You may have your answer soon."

Shea Óg and his sons swam through the crowd at several angles, so there was no escape for their victims. They had them surrounded, and fear created a circle around them as those that were not part of this group separated themselves. Shea Óg walked up to his prey and tore off their hoods and scarves. Seamus grimaced.

"Now it is time to begin our negotiations," said Captain Williamson.

"I want to see her first."

"You already have. I don't want you to go all soft on me before you start your mission."

"Let me say goodbye. If I know my wife and my men's families are safe, they will help me in whatever connivance you would have me do. You can spare me a couple of minutes before we talk!"

Captain Williamson lent over the wall and signalled to Shea Óg. Seamus saw the disappointment in Shea's nodding head. There would be no killing today.

"Men! Bring him to the basement!"

* * *

Seamus stood with only his hands bound in a cell at the bottom of the castle tower. The guards shoved his wife through the opened door and slammed it behind her.

"I'm so glad to see that you are alive," and Seamus held up his bound hands, for he sought her tender touch.

His wife knew his meaning, and she embraced him.

"I am surprised to see you here," she said. "Given the bodies around the castle and the bodies of once good men hanging from the trees, I'm surprised they did not kill you on sight!"

"I fear they have a worse fate for me, one where I wished they'd killed me instead. But that is for the future. I must bargain my life for yours. Once I make the bargain, what will you do with your life, my love?"

"I don't want you to sacrifice yourself for me. Let us die here together! Surely you must have a blade? Cut my throat first and then finish yourself, and we shall leave this wretched world to its feuds and endless spirals of revenge."

"Rags on a man don't have many uses and makes concealing a weapon increasingly more difficult. Go south to Munster. See what has happened to your family. They may have made some recovery there. Forget me. Whatever they have in store for me ends in my death. You have two Galloglass to protect you. Go far away from here, as far as you can get! If I live, I will find you."

The butt of an axe slammed against the door.

"Start finishing up in there, lover boy! If you try anything when we come in, we're going to slice your sweetheart in two."

Sean and his brother slowly opened the door and grabbed Seamus's wife. They smiled as if their eyes were windows to all the evil deeds they would like to do to his wife in revenge for their father.

"Don't touch her, or you'll answer to Captain Williamson!"

"Ha! You changed your tune pretty quick."

The door slammed, and she was gone.

They left Seamus for several hours to contemplate what could happen to his wife if he did not cooperate.

* * *

Thud! Thud! Thud!

"Stand back from the door!"

"I sit here waiting for my food. Whatever your dastardly task is, it requires energy, so I must be fed!"

"You can eat this," and the last thing Seamus saw was the butt of an axe swinging towards his face.

The cool breeze and several slaps revived him. The light was now fading on the rooftop, and Captain Williamson stood, supporting himself on his elbow on the other side of the roof.

"Now you have seen your motivation. I'm sure you'll be more amenable to my offers."

"Speak of your offers, and we shall see what I can do for you."

"It should be quite easy. All you have to do is swap sides. You are a mercenary, after all."

"If only it were that easy!"

"Let me continue my tale from the Netherlands, and you shall see why my mission so fits a man of your skills, flexible morality and deftness with dagger, axe or gun!"

"You talk me up so much. You'll only increase your disappointment!"

Captain Williamson ignored Seamus's sarcasm.

"You followed our unit after the battle of Zutphen and you whispered in the ears of Rowland York and the traitor Stanley. You served with the Irish brigades in the Spanish army, and your deception was that your Irish soldiers were going to defect to us! Meanwhile, unbeknown to the loyal officers of the garrisons of Zutphen and Deventer, you were planning the ultimate double-cross. So when the double-cross came, they executed many loyal and faithful soldiers of the Crown, hanged, or best died when trying to make their escape. When I fled, I pleaded to track down every Irish wretch that ever tried to return home to cause trouble and hang them from the nearest tree. I have dreamed for years of capturing you and watching the life squeezed out of your neck!"

"But you still haven't answered my questions. Why am I still alive, and why are you bothering to blackmail me with the life of my wife?"

"Because we hear there is a bigger prize than you coming back from the Netherlands. Even bigger than you! One prize that I would even risk seeing you escape for if I could get them."

"Which is?"

"Hugh Boye MacDavitt!"

"MacDavitt!"

"Yes, MacDavitt! Your commander in the Netherlands. We revile and loath you, but he is a much greater threat to us than you are. You are a cunning, devious, bloodthirsty mercenary, but you do not have MacDavitt's military prowess. The rebel confederacy would be much more powerful with his organisational and training skills. That is why we want you to kill him for us!"

Seamus shook his head.

"That is the stupidest thing I have ever heard. Just throw me over the side and into the river and get it done with!"

"But I also have personal reasons for sparing you for MacDavitt."

"Which are?" Seamus did not want to know but knew he would find out anyway.

"This!" and Captain Williamson waved the stub of his left arm at Seamus. "I sought the Queen's revenge against the traitors, and MacDavitt stabbed me in the arm. I was too injured to fight and was forced to flee. The wound went septic, and the doctor had to take it. From that day onwards, I swore revenge on MacDavitt, and now, you can deliver it for me!"

"How am I supposed to do it if no one knows where he is?"

"Ha! It will not be easy, but we know how you can do it."

"More to the point, why would I do it?"

"Because we have your wife and the families of your men. If you refuse to do it or double-cross us, we'll make such examples of them, their legend will never be forgotten on these shores."

"So how am I supposed to do it, and how do I know you won't double-cross me?"

"Don't worry about that. I have a plan. I have thought of everything."

* * *

The next day Seamus rode out of the castle in front of a body of men. Shea Óg and Sean O'Rourke rode beside Seamus. Six other Irish veterans from the Netherlands rode behind. They ducked to avoid the hanging body of Dáithai MacCabe, the ex-Maguire commander of the castle, as he hung above the castle gate.

6

The cry of the Maguire

"Must you go so soon?" said Desmond. "Your wounds have barely healed. Your pale skin still betrays the trust you put in those priests. I fear for you when you go back out there. You're still young and naïve, and they'll eat you alive."

Desmond put his hand on Eunan's shoulders, the most fatherly hand ever to be placed there. Eunan glanced at Desmond's sorrowful eyes and felt a pang in his heart, the ache of a stranger to his modest, controllable, emotional range. Once he had identified the strange feeling, Eunan's shell hardened to repel this intruder. He moved away. The emotional exposure unnerved him more than any swinging axe because, with an axe, he could evade, but with raw emotion, he could only run away. He had to be strong. He was going away to war. How could he fight the enemies of the Maguire if he blubbers when he is leaving his friends? He must be strong and true, like the blades of his Maguire throwing axes. If they bent when faced with friction, he would surely be dead.

"You worry too much and overthink things," Eunan finally replied once he was a safe distance away.

Desmond knew him too well. A quivering boy in the body of a man, trying to steady himself. A boy who thought the path to adulthood was to have an axe in his hand and the threshold when he found someone to use it on, a boy crying out for guidance, a sense of belonging and some unconditional love. Desmond braced himself for rejection, but knew he had to try.

"You think too little. You get caught up in a whirl of emotion and then lash out. Stay longer. The war will still be there when you're ready to leave."

"It's too late. I must get ready to leave now," and Eunan pushed his three Maguire throwing axes securely to his belt. "I need to get a good supply of expendable throwing axes, for I think there is going to be much demand!" he laughed to break the tension, but Desmond was having none of it.

"If you must go, you know you are always welcome here, and be safe from whatever."

"Thank you for everything, Desmond," and Eunan embraced his friend's bulk.

Arthur smiled from behind his master's back.

"I have so much to thank you for, too, Arthur. Not least, if you hadn't fed us, we'd have starved on this little island!"

They both laughed and embraced. Eunan placed his spare clothes and battle-axe into the small boat Arthur got for him.

Desmond knew he had lost him for now, but hoped he would see sense and return soon. He sighed and stood on the shore by Eunan's boat. Desmond had seen many a young man he had got close to in their training go off into the world seeking battle, but this was one of the most emotional. He hid his feelings, for he knew the boy was weak and had no wish to exacerbate this when he was about to go off and fight.

"If you want the Maguire and some action, head for Devenish Island. That is the first place the English will attack if they haven't already," said Desmond.

Eunan gave Desmond a nervous smile.

"I know how to get there. I'm sure I'll be intercepted by the Maguire's men long before I arrive."

"Good luck, and come back!"

Eunan got in his boat and rowed. The island seemed like home. Eunan felt as if a sadness propelled him over the tiny waves of the lake. No one had waited and watched him leave before. Well, no one who wanted him to stay. His parents would look to make sure that he had gone.

Desmond and Arthur waved from the shore. They stayed until he was out of sight. Both were more than a little downhearted.

"Do you think he'll come back?" asked Arthur.

"I hope so," replied Desmond, and he slapped his friend on the back. "I didn't think he'd make it back last time, so there is hope yet. It's almost time to prepare for dinner. Don't you think so?"

* * *

Devenish Island was an obvious place for the Maguire to hide. The family's historical shelter, their traditional burial ground, and the Maguires had patronised the Augustine monks and their three churches on the island. Hugh Maguire calculated the English had neither the boats nor sufficient soldiers to launch a full-blown assault it would take to overcome his Galloglass or the small fort on the island. If they did, his blood would soak into Sour Hill, and he would join his ancestors in heaven and become another glorious chapter in the annals of the Maguire. The time-honoured sanctuary on the upper lake will be the Maguire's magnificent last stand if need be.

Eunan's oars dipped steadily along into the stillness of the lake, giving him swift but silent propulsion. He passed by islands large and small, wooded and bare, inviting and uninviting, and felt prying eyes upon his tiny craft. But the words of Desmond had left a resonance, even when Eunan spied Devenish Island up ahead. He paused to think.

"I'll think of three good reasons I should help the Maguire in his hour of need and three reasons I should heed the words of Desmond and wait until I've healed. To whoever I can assign the wisest option, I'll row in their direction. One, the Maguire needs me, but I am not ready. Two, if the Maguire dies, the rebellion dies with him. But I could flee north and bring Desmond and..."

No sooner had he looked away from his potential destination of Devenish Island than the boats of the Maguire surrounded him. Three boats pulled up alongside him and pointed their weapons in his face before they recognised him. All four boats cried with delight, and Eunan clasped hands with his comrades, for his small craft was too shaky for him to throw his weight to one side for a full embrace.

The boats led Eunan to the south side of Devenish Island's jetties, where small boats departed along the lake to either patrol, fish or bring in supplies. It occupied the lower lough entrance as if a giant plug to stop any force from progressing further. If Captain Dowdall were to make any excursions northwards, he would first have to take Devenish Island.

The extended hand of a friendly monk helped Eunan onto the island. Eunan felt the moist hand, saw the tension in the monk's eyes and the worry etched upon his face. However, the monk was kind enough to bless Eunan, even if it felt like an apology, as if he was there to meet his death.

The island's fields and dirt tracks were a flurry of activity as the monks gathered what provisions they could and hid them in their storerooms. Eunan resisted the local monastery's lure and forgiveness for his various sins and lapses, for he felt strong enough to bear the weight of the sin to come. He went straight past the watchtower, the only place on the island so far with the presence of soldiers of the Maguire. Maguire's men led him from the tower to the wooded half of the island. The wood was diminutive but perfectly formed, neatly hemmed in by the north of the island's narrow pebbled beaches. It provided cover to hide men and boats under which they could bombard any enemy shipping that may pass along it. The guides led Eunan along a narrow path to a small house nestled in the wood where they told him the Maguire was hiding. Familiar faces of the MacCabe Galloglass warmly greeted him. One of the Galloglass went inside the house to announce his arrival. Hugh Maguire himself rushed out to embrace him.

"It is good to see you, my friend! Come in. We have much to discuss."

Eunan embraced Hugh Maguire both as a friend and a leader to the rebellion. Hugh led him into a sparsely decorated room that could only tell a tale of neglect, with a couple of chairs, a table covered in writing paper and a couple of small maps. The inkpot looked as if it were as desperate for ink as the words it formed. The stack of letters was a forlorn cry for help, laid as they were beneath a bare dagger, waiting to be sent to their recipients. There were neither tapestries on the wall nor a hearty meal waiting for Eunan, just the cold bare walls to remind him of the loss of Enniskillen.

"This is the hiding place of the Maguire. It is not much, but I would be so much easier to find if I hid out in a palace!"

Hugh shrank before him with every word uttered as an excuse. Eunan nodded and tried to mould his facial expressions to wax, for he did not want to show the pity he felt for the Maguire and further demean him.

"Where are the others?" asked Eunan, as his throat went dry and his brain barren as he tried to remain calm. Hugh's crimson cheeks were his first reply.

"To what others do you refer? Most of the lords and gentry of Fermanagh turned coat upon the fall of Fermanagh and swore loyalty to Connor Roe. Some fled to Tyrone and Tirconnell, but I am hopeful they will return when I take to the field again. My Scots and Galloglass left when they saw that I no longer had the means to pay them. It is a bitter lesson to learn, but it is partly down to me thinking that mercenaries owed me their allegiance. I am the Maguire, but such esteem only works on the Maguires or lesser clans, and then when I have a wall of Galloglass at my back. Even the Maguire must have full pockets to command the respect of the north. But I have fifty of the finest MacCabes here, guarding the island. They stayed loyal, for they are familiar with the bobbing fortunes of the Maguire. My younger brother, entwined in my fate as he is, has gone to seek rabbits for our supper. If we can prevent the fall of Devenish Island to Captain Dowdall, I am confident that I can take once more to the mainland and rally the men of Fermanagh back to my cause."

"You will always have my loyalty, until I can swing my axe no more!" said Eunan, and he clasped Hugh on the shoulder. Eunan also knew his fate was entwined to the Maguire.

"Thank you, Eunan. You have always served my family well."

However well the words were accepted, the clasp on the shoulder was not.

A horn sounded from a distant part of the island. A Galloglass entered the house to translate the horn's meaning for those who did not know or sought to hide from reality.

"We must go, lord. The attack has begun!"

"The English are upon us! Let us go to the boats!" and Hugh gestured towards the door.

He picked up his pistol and his axe and blessed himself while he was bent over. After steadying his nerves and composing himself, he went out to his men. The Galloglass made a semi-circle around him and awaited his orders. He turned to Eunan, who had followed him out.

"I will attack the English in our boats when the opportunity arises," and Hugh waved to the Galloglass to follow him. "You take the other men and defend the island. I will await your signal."

Eunan grabbed him by the forearm as he turned to leave.

"Be safe, my Prince. Don't let the pride of Fermanagh fall today."

"Thank you for your concern, but the men will fight all the better for the Maguire leading them. The island must not fall. Good luck!" and Hugh pulled his arm away from the indignity of a lesser man placing his hand upon him.

Eunan then saw the men that remained after the Galloglass departed. Some eager young men, barely older than himself, armed with bows and axes, stood before him. Their only attribute was their eyes that burnt with enthusiasm.

"Where are the MacCabe?" Eunan cried.

One boy pointed to the backs of the men that ran after Hugh Maguire.

"Is this it?"

The boy nodded to Eunan.

"Where are all the warriors?"

The boy shrugged. Eunan cursed.

"Come on then. We've got an island to defend!"

Eunan ran through the woods with his band of boys behind him. When they emerged from the woods, they found the rest of the island deserted. The monks and priests hid in the stone buildings of their village. Five MacCabe Galloglass who manned the watchtower came to join Eunan, leaving just one man to watch the river. He was soon gainfully employed as he hollered at the sight of the English boats coming down the river.

"What do we do, lord?" asked the boys who stood in front of Eunan, naively the only visible presence on the island.

"Come, let us hide in the village and allow them land. Then with our axes and arrows, we will drive them back into the water."

They snook down to the village edge and made use of what cover they could find. Those boys that had bows set out their arrows, so they were within easy reach and took sight of the jetties to ensure they were well within their ranges. Eunan bent and hid and wished he had his old axe. He hated the poverty of waiting with an axe that wasn't his to defend an island for which he felt nothing. His pride and anger could well up and provide him with a shield for almost any situation, but all he felt was nervous adrenalin. Duty - a Galloglass could not choose when and where he wanted to fight but was at the beck and call of his master. It was his duty.

An older hand of bitten nails and a coating of Devenish clay placed itself upon Eunan's shoulder.

"Three ships will be here before you know it, filled with English conscripts. Probably a hundred men."

"If enough of them die when they hit the shore, they'll surely turn back," replied Eunan.

"One can only but hope," and the Galloglass left to take his position. Eunan couched down in his hiding place and waited.

The boats slowly rowed up the river. Eunan prayed for his rescue by vessels of the Maguire while he attempted to banish the memories of the fall of Enniskillen. The boats moored at the island jetties, and men came onshore. Eunan leapt from his hiding place and raised his axe.

"Let us vanquish our enemies with the CRY OF THE MAGUIRE!"
"THE MAGUIRE!"

The boys of Fermanagh sprayed the jetty and surrounding areas with a shower of arrows and then fired individually. Eunan and the Galloglass charged towards the jetties. The English soldiers on the shore dived for cover while the soldiers on the boats hesitated. The sergeant bellowed at his men while the ends of muskets poked over the boat and laid down some counter fire. It was the boys from Fermanagh's turn to waiver. Eunan continued his charge. He was almost upon the English.

"For the MAGUIRE!" screamed Eunan, and he swung his axe at the approaching enemy. The Maguire arrow cover was much diminished, and the English sergeant inspired his soldiers to follow him and they cast their doubts into the waves and reinforced the men on shore. Eunan and his five Galloglass found themselves heavily outnumbered, their only ally was the chaos of battle. Eunan swung his axe. It sliced through flesh. Swords swung at him only to be deflected away. His axe hit a skull, and it showered him in blood. Eunan heaved it out with spurts of blood all over his arms and face his only reward. He swung again. The next victim was an arm, not fully severed but enough to send the soldier howling to the ground. But Eunan grew tired. One of his Galloglass fell. The barrage of arrows supporting him from the sky grew thinner. Another Galloglass fell. More English soldiers jumped to the shore while their comrades in the boat reloaded. They aimed at Eunan and the remaining Galloglass. The belltower blared its warning horn.

"The Maguire is coming!" came the shout.

The battle froze. Everyone looked to the river, and sure enough, two boats appeared on each side of the island.

"Retreat!" came the call from the English boats. The soldiers grabbed whatever they could and made for their crafts. Eunan was too exhausted to follow them, but tried to scavenge what few fallen muskets were still on the field. The boys ran to catch up with Eunan and the remaining three Galloglass. They cheered, but Eunan knew they had got lucky. The English escaped in their boats, but it did not matter. The Maguires had a victory to tell their brethren and rally them back to the cause. Hugh Maguire did not pursue his beaten enemy. His boat rowed back to shore. He landed and went straight to embrace Eunan.

"You came and saved the Maguires! You can have whatever you wish for when the war ends. Whatever you want."

At that moment, Eunan was just glad to be alive.

7

Derrylinn

It had been weeks since the attack on Devenish Island, and Captain Dowdall thought better of launching another large-scale attack on the lower lough islands. His men had raided as far as Belleek but skirted along by the northern shores, for they were not foolhardy enough to expose themselves on the lough. The captain had mounted guns on riverboats and could command the river up to the lower lough. They cut Fermanagh in two, but mounted guns could not make up for the power of geography. They could not get past the key strategic stronghold of Devenish Island.

Hugh Maguire sat in the safety of his lodgings. His quill bobbed with the delight of a man who had won a glorious victory, or so said the words on his letters, which oozed a persuasiveness seldom seen merely days before. He employed all possible levers, duty, greed, destiny, even immortality through a bard's melody. He distributed each lever with discernment, emphasising the lever most likely to work on the designated recipient of each letter. His letters were sometimes coarse, sometimes brief, for he was a man of action, a wielder of a sword, not a pen. He missed his linguistic warrior, Donnacha. His diplomatic bard seemed to do more with his well-selected words than Hugh could ever do, evoking the Maguire's mythical power, the manipulation of the past, and, if all else failed, there was the time-honoured lever of threats. Hugh finished his lesser letters, and he impatiently waited for messengers to deliver them and also for the signal from his father-in-law, Hugh O'Neill, that he should return to the field. He did not have to wait long.

A small boat rowed across the lake to be intercepted by a patrol boat of the Maguire. The soldiers identified the messenger and sent him straight to their master. Meanwhile, Eunan trained the boys who had performed so bravely in defence of Devenish Island in the fields of the monastery.

"Come quickly, the Maguire summons you!" cried a messenger between breaths after running to fetch him.

Eunan hurried his way through the forest to the little house. Hugh's mood made once tiny rooms as colossal as a castle.

"My father-in-law has unleashed raids right across the north: from Connor Roe to Marshall Bagenal, let our enemies in the north quiver!"

Eunan clasped him on the shoulder. He had not learned his lesson.

"That is splendid news, lord. When do the Maguires get their revenge and set forth for Enniskillen?"

Hugh freed himself from Eunan's grasp, his mood only slightly diminished.

"When we assemble our forces, we are to march north and meet Cormac MacBaron. Then we can free Fermanagh! But first, my friend, I have something to ask of you."

"Whatever I can do to help, please ask."

"Go to the mainland and reassemble the nobles and men of Fermanagh and when you are ready, send for me, and we'll set out together and join the O'Neill."

"What about you, lord? The men would rally all the quicker if they could see you."

"I need to go to Tirconnell to speak to Red Hugh. Our allies grow strong and please do not let me down if I promise them a Maguire army!"

"You will lead the finest body of men ever to fight for Fermanagh when you return," Eunan boasted.

"Thank you, my friend. A boat awaits you, so make haste."

Before the hour was through, Eunan was on a boat headed for the south side of the lake from which he would get a horse and set forth for south Fermanagh with a heart full of energy and courage.

* * *

Eunan spent the next two weeks searching every forest or mountain that he knew loyal men of the Maguire would hide, waiting for the call. He quickly found Seán Óg Maguire, Hugh's trusted commander, and they agreed that Seán Óg should set forth to an assembly spot just south of Belleek, where Eunan would direct the men he found on his travels. Seán Óg eagerly agreed and sent Eunan on his mission with a hearty embrace to warm his way.

As Eunan tread through forest, bog and field, most people he met recognised him, and most were more than willing to set forth towards Belleek. He showed those who proved more reluctant or sceptical, a letter with the Maguire's seal and poured forth whatever decorative words he considered apt to grease the persuasion. Eunan stretched the bounds of his imagination to convince the illiterate, especially those with no respect, or even contempt, for the seal of the Maguire. But he soon learned that the appeal of greed or vanity could be just as effective as appeals to more honourable motivations.

Eunan had spent so much time on his horse and met so many steadfast warriors of the Maguire that he soon had a posse of men to assist him. One such illiterate was Óisin, who seemed especially motivated by the calls of the Maguire. He was of similar age to Eunan, but opportunity would only carve out the role of common forest bandit, not that of an emissary for the Maguire like Eunan. However, as with Eunan, he was a youth of boundless energy, looking for a cause to absorb it all. Óisin's passion was not stirred by calls of patriotism or calls to defend the Maguire or the motherland but he was enthused by the potential for riches and glory. However, in Eunan's mind, it took all kinds of men and motivations to form an army, and as long as he could fight, the Maguire would be happy. The Maguire had employed Seamus, after all.

Eunan and his small band of adherents travelled all over south Fermanagh, where the call of the Maguire had a more subdued response, and he soon found himself on the outskirts of Derrylinn, the seat of the O'Cassidy Maguire. He remembered what Desmond had told him, and decided to tread cautiously. Eunan had only been there as a boy and never visited or met his uncle. He heard of him, but very little of it was from his parents. Derrylinn was a small but prosperous market town, a reasonable size for south Fermanagh; it was a stop on the road to Enniskillen or Lisnaskea for those seeking the genuine power of the Maguires. Armed men roamed the small, winding streets. Eunan could not tell their loyalty so he got directions to his uncle's farm on the edge of the town instead.

* * *

He rode out of town with his men, only to run into a blacksmith near the farm holding. The smith bashed out the share of a plough, moulding the end so it would furrow a deep gorge in the rich Fermanagh soil. Eunan's past weighed heavily on his shoulders, and his supposed bad blood pulsed through his veins and preyed on his mind. How much did his uncle know? Did his uncle know that he even existed? There was only one way to find out, and it terrified Eunan right down to his bones. However, he had an idea and brought his horse to a halt opposite the blacksmith. The man ignored him. Eunan felt humiliated in front of his men and slammed his fist on what appeared to be the shop front.

"Blacksmith, I need a battle axe, forged from the finest O'Cassidy steel, that will slice a man's arm off with me only having to exert the effort of lifting the axe over my head. The blade will stand between the O'Cassidy and his enemies to protect the good folk of the O'Cassidy clan. Can you do that for me?"

The blacksmith did not look up from his work.

"I am sorry, lord, but I am only in the employment of Cormac O'Cassidy. He has me working for his fields and his oxen. Only he can instruct me to stop from my tasks."

Eunan nodded. He did not know how to respond to such reason, but some of his men were not so easily put off.

"Do you know who you are speaking to? He may be an O'Keenan Maguire, but he is the finest young warrior in all of south Fermanagh. He has returned to claim his O'Cassidy heritage, and you should be honoured to be asked to equip him before he goes into battle to protect you from the English. What do you say now you know who he is?" said Óisin.

The blacksmith rested the share on his anvil and stopped bashing.

"I would say that the O'Cassidy Maguire is situated only a mile from here and if you want my time, request it from him. This young man may be the most famous man in Fermanagh, but I have never made his acquaintance and care not whether he stands for Hugh or Connor Roe. I merely beat metal for my master. Please, converse with me no more, for if I continue, the share will be ruined and break in the soil."

The young man went for his sword, but Eunan had spotted the armed villagers coming for them.

"Easy there, Óisin. We come in peace to raise men for war, not to start one."

Eunan remounted his horse.

"You may as well prepare my axe, for I will be back with my uncle's permission, and he will be angry if you do not obey him."

"I will wait for my master's word before any work begins."

The blacksmith continued his work. Eunan saluted him and left before the armed men arrived.

"Just wait until my uncle finds out how disrespectful he was to me," said Eunan to Óisin.

He knew he had to regain the men's respect given this humiliation.

"If only he knew you had the Maguire's ear," replied Óisin. "Then you would get your axe."

* * *

Eunan's nerves began to tingle, and his hand shook. He stuffed his hand back in his pocket.

"I am a warrior of the Maguire. I slay all my foes. I am not afraid of my uncle. He should be afraid of me!"

Eunan expected the gush of an out-breath to be replaced by a steely belief in his abilities. It did not work. He was out of breath and out of confidence. He quivered on his horse like a little boy taking his first ride. His fragile ego had been dented when the blacksmith had never heard of him. He could not banish the memories of his childhood from his mind. But he needed to recover his composure to be strong when facing his uncle.

"He could be a man of cunning, your uncle," said Óisin, seeing that Eunan needed distracting.

"Why is that?"

"He timed his defection to Connor Roe to perfection. There is barely a kernel out of place in his fields while the English have ravaged all the surrounding lands. You'll have to keep your wits about you."

"Every blade of grass in Fermanagh seems to conceal a viper," hissed Eunan.

News of Eunan's arrival appeared to have travelled fast as three MacCabe Galloglass waited for them on their approach to his uncle's house.

"State your business here," shouted the central Galloglass, as he signalled for them to stop.

Eunan brought his horse to a halt.

"I come as a messenger from the true Maguire, Hugh of Enniskillen, head of all the MacCabe Galloglass to receive a pledge of allegiance from the O'Cassidy Maguire."

"The O'Cassidy Maguire does not tip his hat to any old group of armed men that come across his land. Leave, for if you remain, it will be to your ultimate detriment!"

"I'm sure your master would not like to deliver the body of his nephew to Hugh Maguire; should his men be so fortunate to overwhelm that said nephew?"

The Galloglass adopted a more aggressive stance.

A man walked out of the house.

"Let him in. Let him in. Do not spoil this beautiful day by spilling blood in the garden."

Eunan looked up, for he recognised the voice of Donnacha O'Cassidy Maguire. He dismounted and greeted him. Donnacha only invited Óisin and himself into the house.

The wealth of the land reflected throughout the house. Instead of bountiful brown soil, there were floors of boundless oak beams, the golden kernels by silver plates and ornaments. The blue skies were wooden beamed roofs, the rivers and lakes by beautiful tapestries and the wide variety of trees by ornaments from far-off lands beyond

Ireland's shores. It was the first time Eunan had seen such luxury in a private house. Donnacha led him into the drawing-room, where his uncle sat, smoking a long pipe. A small man lacking the stature of a warrior, but his fine clothes told of a man who made a weapon of his brain and exuded power through his wealth. His uncle looked at Eunan with a knowing contempt and took another toke from his pipe.

"We were expecting you some time," said Cormac O'Cassidy. "We have watched from afar your lofty elevation from an unknown boy from a small village to, look at you now, one of the most respected warriors in the Maguire clan. The most surprising fact of all is you did it without a victory to your name!"

Eunan ground his teeth.

"Devenish Island?" could only tumble out as a croak.

"Uncle, why would you greet your sister's son with an insult? Don't mind him," said Donnacha. "He has no manners. That's why nobody will let him into their courts."

Cormac threw himself out of his chair.

"State what you want, boy! You didn't come all this way in your dusty clothes and battle axe for a family reunion."

Eunan swallowed, but his mouth was dry. His nerve had deserted him. He felt again like the little boy who everyone hated.

"I have forgotten my manners. Get him a drink," cried Donnacha, noticing Eunan's distress.

A man-servant came with goblets of ale for everyone. The break gave Eunan time to think. He lubricated his larynx and summoned what mental strength he could.

"I am here to enlist your support for Hugh Maguire to recapture Fermanagh and free the Maguires from the tyranny of the English."

Cormac and Donnacha looked at each other.

"Do you see any tyranny here, boy?" replied Cormac O'Cassidy, who began pacing around him.

Cormac reached into his pocket and held up a bag of coins.

"Does this look to you like the contents of the pockets of a man who is oppressed? My new line of business to the Pale is doing very well, thanks for asking! Why do you come to me, the remains of your family, with promises of war and destruction? Your own family is dead because of your foolishness. Why do you want to wipe out the rest of us? You should have listened to your father in one of the few wise things he ever said. Let other people fight other people's wars. We are perfectly happy with the rule of Connor Roe Maguire from the senior branch of the family. He has promised to steer us away from the destruction of war and protect us and our assets. Even the great Cúchonnacht sold out to the English when it suited him. Now my servants will feed you, and you can have your precious axe you tried to force my blacksmith to make. You can even take a memento of your mother if you can find one. But if you ever darken my door again, you'll be treated as an intruder. Now be gone."

Insulted, Eunan's jaw stiffened.

"Is this the same for you, Donnacha? Hugh Maguire's chief adviser?"

"I dispense advice to Maguire and O'Cassidy Maguire alike. The path to destiny is not always clear."

"You can keep your food, but I'll take your axe. Just pray you'll never meet its bitter blade!"

Eunan stormed out of the house with Óisin running behind. Eunan mounted his horse. The servant ran behind him.

"Wait! The O'Cassidy Maguire wants you to have this bag of your mother's things."

Eunan looked down at the bag, and his lip curl said everything he could not put into words.

"Your mother would want you to have them," the man pleaded.

So Eunan snatched the bag and rode off without a word.

* * *

Eunan gathered his men, and they rode back to the blacksmith. The share was no longer on the anvil; an axe blade occupied pride of place. Eunan dismounted and walked over to the blacksmith, but he was not first to speak.

"I received your uncle's instructions. I'm to provide you with the finest O'Cassidy axe, and then you'll be gone."

Eunan boiled with rage at being addressed so. But something caught his attention out of the corner of his eye. He turned, and there before him was a sight that warmed his eyes and melted his heart. Her long black hair shone in the sunlight, and her piercing blue eyes stopped him in his tracks. She was everything Eunan's wife RÓisin wasn't. Eunan's tongue deserted him. He could only but stare.

"She is the O'Cassidy Maguire's daughter. Beautiful she may be, but she'll bind you to unending troubles," whispered the blacksmith.

"Is my axe finished yet?" snapped Eunan.

Óisin noticed that the woman caught Eunan's eye.

"Have you finished the axe of the O'Cassidy Maguire's finest warrior yet?" he exclaimed, ensuring the young woman was within earshot.

Eunan nervously glanced at the young woman and saw that Óisin grabbed her attention. So distracted was he that he dropped the bag of his mother's things. Out of the bag fell an emblem of an Irish wolfhound. Eunan picked it up and saw the swish of her blue dress coming towards him. He fumbled to pick up the wolfhound emblem. She was almost beside him.

"And don't forget to put the wolfhound emblem on the lip to show I am a warrior from the O'Cassidy Maguires."

The blacksmith looked at Eunan.

"But it's not…"

Óisin touched his scabbard. The blacksmith turned to Eunan

but saw that the young woman standing beside him absorbed his attention.

"Of course. Please pass the emblem, and I'll embed it in the axe."

Óisin slapped him on the back. Eunan handed the emblem over his shoulder, and Óisin passed it to the blacksmith.

The young woman stood right beside Eunan, whose tongue was in deep freeze.

"I heard a great warrior visited us, but my father never told me when you were coming. Are you going to stay with us?"

"I'm afraid I've already been..."

Óisin decided such patter was unworthy of a warrior of Eunan's stature and interjected.

"Unfortunately, war calls the noble warrior Eunan Maguire away. He needs to serve the people and protect their lands."

"Is that right? Beautiful lands like these and their maidens need protecting," said the young woman, as she smiled in Eunan's direction. "When you have finished fighting whoever you are fighting, come back and visit me and see how well you have protected me."

"I...I... Have to go fight, and then I can return."

"Good! Come back and visit me, Caoimhe O'Cassidy Maguire, in the big house you've just come from and tell me about all the battles you have won and all the cattle you have gained."

"I... I will. I'll come as soon as I can, Caoimhe."

"Good. I look forward to it!"

She walked towards the house and looked back at Eunan, and smiled and laughed. Eunan could not take his eyes off her. He snapped out of it and saw his men staring at him and smirking.

"What?"

"Shall I plan our next visit to Derrylinn?" asked Óisin.

Eunan scowled. His shattered nerves now possessed him.

"Where's my axe?" he barked.

He could at least take his frustrations out on someone. Derrylinn had chewed him up and spit him out.

8

Return to Tirconnell

A ll was not well with Seamus's motley crew of renegades, cutthroats, and traitors. "When do these godforsaken, bog-ridden, windswept, mountains end?"

"Shut your face. You'll be drinking on the tit of a whiskey bottle before the morn."

Such scornful comments did not mould together a band of brothers united under any cause.

It was a cold, rainy day in hell, for Seamus was now reliant on Shea Óg to impose discipline and motivation on the men. He would normally have taken on those duties himself to imbue their loyalty and prepare them for the hardships of war, but he felt himself to be their prisoner; to reprimand them would be to open himself up to their wrath. Seamus had said little since he left, merely providing directions when Shea Óg was lost. His predicament was still to sink in fully. He was used to dealing with men of dubious reputations and intentions since they often made the best Galloglass, but this lot seemed to be a special class of moral degenerates. They appeared to revel in the competition of telling tales of their low deeds to see who was the most depraved, as they craved their new companions' approval. How Captain Williamson expected this lot to kill Hugh Boye MacDavitt was beyond him. Unless, of course, they were all here just to ensure that he did it or kill him if he did not.

"We'll be in Donegal town in a few hours," said Seamus. "There'll be miscellaneous low life crawling around looking for coin for a kill, but you lot are special. Let me do the talking, and I'll find us somewhere comfortable to settle in."

"I always knew you could be agreeable," said Shea Óg.

"Maybe this once, but don't bet your life on it!" and Seamus rode ahead so that he was alone.

On the outskirts of Donegal town, they met a MacSweeney Galloglass patrol who recognised Seamus. They escorted him and his men and directed them to a campsite on the outskirts of the town. Coin and livery were in short supply since Red Hugh had recruited more mercenaries than the population of south Tirconnell could comfortably support. He was wise enough not to test the depths of the local population's tolerance. The men of the O'Donnell allocated them some tents, and when they had settled in, Seamus wanted to see who else was in the camp.

"You're going nowhere without one of us," said Shea Óg, pointing to Sean.

"You can't babysit me forever," said Seamus. "I'm well capable of looking after myself."

He walked off.

"It's you, 'taking care of us' is what I'm worried about. I'll go with you."

The thought of 'taking care' of Shea Óg and Sean brought a faint smile to Seamus, which he could barely hide. But they had barely walked a couple of paces when Seamus noticed how the camp's other residents looked at them.

"You'll put people off talking to us with that bag over your head," he said.

"May it remind you that doing this to me will always be on your soul," replied Shea Óg.

"You may find yourself foolish to assume I have a soul!" replied Seamus.

Seamus and Shea Óg set off to explore the campsite. They walked and, as they did so, were surprised by the number of different clans assembled, mainly from Connacht and Breifne. Some MacSweeney Galloglass stopped them, for they recognised Seamus. They directed them to a tent at the gate of the camp occupied by administration scribes of the O'Donnell and guarded by MacSweeney Galloglass. There, the two men registered themselves and their men, and the scribes assigned them to an O'Donnell leader. Seamus saw warm faces and Shea Óg weird looks.

"Seamus! I knew you'd come back!" exclaimed the Galloglass constable who sat in the centre of the muddy tent, the host of many a Galloglass boot.

"I knew you'd need me!" and they hugged like long-lost comrades.

"Have you brought some men with you?"

"Oh, just some assorted low life."

"Like him? What happened to his face?"

"We argued about how ugly he was, and now he's a sore loser!"

The constable laughed. Shea Óg made a fist hidden behind his thigh.

"So who have you brought with you, Maguires?"

"Not this time. I served in the Netherlands with the Spanish army. They are all ex-veterans. I have an extensive number of contacts and would like to rally returning veterans to the O'Donnell cause."

"We need all the experienced soldiers we can get. I'll make sure the O'Donnell hears of your arrival."

"Thank you, my friend. I look forward to being of service to the O'Donnell again."

They shook each other by the forearm, and Seamus and Shea Óg left.

"I may get him to put an axe through the back of your head one day," said Seamus.

"Not if I tell him first what a traitor you are. It's a pity I've come so far just to ruin your cosy relationship with the O'Donnell."

"That's if you live long enough!"

"You're in no position to make threats," and Shea Óg grinned as if he had to remind him who had his wife. Seamus ignored him.

"Let's go back and see what these vagabonds you've lumbered me with have got up to. I've got to uphold my reputation and the O'Donnell's trust to fulfil my mission."

"Don't worry, Sean will take care of them," and Shea Óg slapped Seamus on the back.

"Refrain from touching me, or I will send your hand back to your captain, and he can sew it on to his missing arm."

Shea Óg scowled and walked behind Seamus.

They arrived back to see Sean O'Rourke sitting beside a fire, stuffing his face with two of the other men.

"The rest of them have fucked off. Don't know where, don't care!" and Sean continued eating.

Seamus fumed.

"Well, we'll just have to go find them, won't we?"

"You can; I'm not their Mammy," replied Sean.

"I'll go with you," said Sean Og, determined not to let Seamus out of his sight.

"Go look over there," and Seamus pointed to the other side of the camp. "You don't have to follow me everywhere. You're not my shadow!"

Shea Óg grunted but obeyed. He disappeared towards some large fires in the distance, which loud, drunken men surrounded. Seamus walked in the other direction. He wandered past the many campfires he encountered, giving a cursory look for his men, as he thought he did not want to find them. Seamus thought of his wife and his men's families and how he was going soft in his old age. His mind wandered to the stars above his head, to a time when his heart was not a shrivelled prune, and he was young and naïve. A bit like Eunan.

"I hope the boy is still alive. He is a gullible fool, but so was I, once! Now I'm just an old..."

A goblet to the face and a shirt decorated with ale brought him back to reality.

"If I find the fucker who threw that!" he raged at a campfire full of revellers.

A man staggered towards him.

"Seamus, ya 'oul fuck! Sit down and have a drink with us!"

It was one of Shea Óg's men he picked up in Enniskillen.

"Look at the state of you! Go back to the camp. We'll deal with this in the morning."

"Fuck you. I don't take orders from you. You take orders from me! I served with Captain Williamson for years. Don't you come here ordering me about, or I'll tell everyone here that you're in the pocket of the English."

No sooner than the final 'sh' breathed its way into life on a stale alcohol breath through yellow, broken, crooked teeth than Seamus's axe swung. The axe cut through the air and lodged itself in the man's nose and skull in one swift arc. The man spat as blood gurgled from his face. It took more than a jolt for Seamus to remove the axe. The men at the campfire froze. Seamus pointed his dripping axe at them.

"No one calls Seamus MacSheehy a traitor! No one! If I hear anything that this dead drunken fool uttered being repeated, I'll do the same to whoever spread those rumours. Have you all got that?"

The men nodded.

"Good! Now enjoy your drink while you can and let no more be said of this."

As Seamus turned, he saw the man's body twitch, and a groan came forth from the gurgling pit of spewing blood.

"This is more mercy than what you've ever shown," and Seamus brought the man's unhappy stay on earth to an end as his axe severed the head clean from his body.

Seamus walked back towards his bed and contemplated his actions. What would Shea Óg do in response? Would he report this back to Captain Williamson? Would they kill him and sacrifice their chances of killing Hugh Boye MacDavitt because some drunken mercenary got killed in a brawl? No, of course they would not. He thought of Dervella and the last moments they spent together in that Enniskillen jail. Seamus vowed he would do whatever was necessary to free her, but he was no longer afraid of the consequences of his actions. He no longer cared what happened to Captain Williamson's men.

* * *

The following day a horrid smell climbed up Seamus's nostrils. His dreams turned to hell, and the devil appeared before him, welcoming him in for all his blasphemies and the countless number of sins. He awoke to a leather mask in his face.

"Only four came back!"

"What are you on about? Fuck off, and don't get in my face first thing in the morning."

Seamus sat up. "Do you ever take that thing and wash it? Surely the whores, who make you do them from behind so they don't see your mask, complain about the smell?"

"I've got used to their premium rates, much in demand these days due to all the lowlife men. Speaking of lowlifes, only four came back."

repeated Shea Óg.

"What do you care? They're probably unconscious under a bush somewhere. Oh, it's hard to get reliable traitors these days!"

"Or they're lying in a bush after getting an axe in the back of the head! How come I found some of them, and you didn't?"

"Because you're so much better at sniffing out shit unless your sense of smell has been destroyed, having your nose trapped under a mask all day. Fuck them and fuck you! Don't push me, Shea Óg. We're at least quits by now. You may have my wife, but I still have a limit!"

Shea Óg sat down. He glared at Seamus.

"When are you going to see the O'Donnell?"

"When I'm good and ready, that's when. Why don't you settle down here with Sean? Maybe wander are the camp and see if you can meet some nice O'Rourkes that don't think you are traitors? You just leave the rest to me."

"Can I go with you?"

"So, you're asking me, can the traitor with the leather bag on his head walk into the court of the O'Donnell and remain inconspicuous? I'd rather postpone my execution for a little while longer thank you very much. You stay here and make sure our other guests don't cause trouble or give the game away. I'll sit and wait until I'm summoned."

Seamus lay down, put his feet up on a log and waited, ignoring the growing intensity of Shea Óg's glares.

* * *

Several days later, Seamus found himself once more in the court of the O'Donnell. Spirits were buoyant, especially from those who had built up years of resentment from the actions of the sheriffs of the Crown and were eager for war. Alongside the lords of Tirconnell were leaders of clans from other northern parts of Ireland's. Seamus embraced the few that he knew and introduced himself to some others. They reserved the warmest embraces for those returning veterans of the Netherlands who had assembled in Tirconnell no matter what part of their Ireland was their destination when they first returned. Many knew him as a friend or by sight, but definitely by reputation. Some lords of northern and eastern Tirconnell looked less than happy to be there, but the fixers of the O'Donnell gave them extra attention.

Red Hugh finally arrived after making everyone wait. He entered from the back of the room, escorted by Eoghan McToole O'Gallagher and Tadhg Óg O'Boyle and ensured to shake the hands of everyone he thought was important as he made his way to his seat. The room went silent.

"Lords, friends and allies of the O'Donnell clan, let me welcome you. Many of you are here from Connacht and other traditional areas of tribute to the O'Donnell clan, and let me tell you, the O'Donnell will support you in your bid for freedom from English oppression. We will soon march south and free all your lands, and all those loyal to the O'Donnell will be amply rewarded!"

"Hurray!"

"But first, we must turn to assist our allies, the Maguires, and help free their lands from the English. To do that, I will send my trusted Galloglass to aid in the relief of Enniskillen."

There was a widespread cheer from the room, as many of the Maguire clan had fled to Tirconnell.

"But to my dear brother-in-law, I give command of the O'Donnell forces poised above Sligo. Niall Garbh is a great warrior of the clan, as were his forefathers before him."

Red Hugh went down onto the floor and embraced his brother-in-law. The show of unity raised the atmosphere in the hall.

"Now go all and prepare for the oncoming war!"

The floor cheered and broke down into groups. Red Hugh tapped his Niall Garbh on the arm.

"It is time we spoke in private and put the past behind us."

"Everything is led by the past. You cannot change it," insisted Niall Garbh.

"Yes, but it does not have to lead us. The O'Donnells may acknowledge the past, but they must set their future, their agenda. Come, let us talk in private."

Niall Garbh scowled.

"Come! Did I not give you my sister?"

His brother-in-law followed him into the back room. Red Hugh smiled, hoping to appease his fellow clansman.

"Niall, you are a great warrior, one of the best the O'Donnells have. We both must work together to make us the greatest clan in Ulster and Connacht before the Spanish king sends his armies. To do that, we need you and your men out there fighting with the rest of the O'Donnells."

"The title of O'Donnell should have gone to me, son of Conn, grandson of Calvagh."

Red Hugh threw his hands in the air.

"We have done all this, raised support, fought battles, split O'Donnell blood. You married my sister to solidify your place in the O'Donnell hierarchy. Whatever claim you have is in the past. What I am asking is that you stake your claim for the future! The stronger the O'Donnells are when the Spanish king comes, the more spoils there will be to split between us. Why settle for some land on the River Foyle when there is the whole of Connacht to conquer?"

"If they come. Promises are like little butterflies, they may look pretty, but when you try to catch them, they fly away!"

"I would not have permitted my sister to marry you if I didn't want to build a bond of trust. Am I not going to have a feud with my sister, am I? To be a proper Irish lord, you need to be flexible. You leave the politics to me, and I will leave the fighting to you. Agreed?"

Niall Garbh hesitated.

"If you're not with me, you're against me. I have hundreds of mercenaries outside the town spoiling for a fight. Don't make me send them north. Let us once and for all unite the O'Donnells and crush our enemies!"

Niall Garbh hesitated, realised he had little choice and embraced his brother-in-law.

"That's right. Let bygones be bygones!" said Red Hugh. "My mother has returned to Scotland to recruit redshanks. Many thousands of them are waiting to join us. We need to raid to raise the money and cattle to pay for them. That is your first mission. Raid into Connacht and bring back as much riches as you can carry. Now go prepare your men, for war is nearly upon us."

Niall Garbh's demeanour raised at the prospect of looting and fighting. He would leave his claim to rest for another day.

* * *

Several days later, the O'Donnells reconvened in the court. Disquiet had spread amongst certain leading O'Donnells about the prospect of war. They were nervous about the route they thought the Red Hugh was following, for they thought it would lead to their doom. When he entered the room, his brother Ruaidhri stood up before his older brother.

"What are your intentions, brother? Years of war have left deep scars. Be it the scourge of the English sheriffs and their mercenaries or the wars of the O'Donnell succession. Every family has borne the death of at least one son, and all it has done is increase the decline of the clan. Do you propose to bring us to war once more? Should we not consolidate and heal? Or at least wait for the Spanish king?"

"War will not wait until we are ready. The English will not rest until they have destroyed the O'Donnells, We are at war whether you like it or not!" Red Hugh exclaimed, and he got out of his chair and waved his arms to appeal to his clansmen for support.

"We either live with the axe on our hands or die with the English as our masters! There is no peace, only war."

Red Hugh's father lifted his frail bones and addressed his fellow O'Donnells.

"Ruaidhri is right. We are not ready for war. We need a time of peace to recover our strength from years of strife."

Red Hugh would not stand for such subordination, especially from the nearest and dearest. He rose to his full height and lifted his chin.

"Lords, we once more see past our differences and can stand united. I cannot speak against my father. I owe everything to my mother, but yet, I see the power of the O'Donnells united before me. The kings of Ulster, just like the days of old! Speak out, my clansmen, and tell me what you wish to do?"

Everyone looked around the room. Neither Tadhg Og O'Boyle nor Eoghan McToole O'Gallagher wished to speak out against the former O'Donnell. Since niceties did not impinge upon the consciousness of Niall Garbh, he was ready to show the world what a great warrior he was. Niall Garbh stood beside his brother-in-law.

"We are the O'Donnells, and we fight for the glory of the O'Donnells. There is no peace without freedom!"

Niall Garbh looked around the room. He raised his fist.

"There is no peace without freedom!"

Tadhg Og O'Boyle raised his fist.

"There is no peace without freedom!"

Eoghan McToole O'Gallagher raised his fist.

"There is no peace without freedom!"

Soon the entire room was chanting with their fists, nodding in the air.

"There is no peace without freedom!"

Red Hugh sat back in his seat and smiled.

* * *

Hugh O'Neill called the lords of the north to a secret conference in Tyrone. Hugh Maguire left Devenish Island under cover of night for the first time since January. Red Hugh and his most trusted commanders came, along with all the prominent O'Neill lords. They were all whisked into the heavily guarded castle in Dungannon, where they were treated to a feast and wine before O'Neill brought business before them.

"Comrades! We have seen the fall of Enniskillen and how the traitor Connor Roe has sold out his clansmen to become the English lord of Fermanagh."

"May we burn his lands to the bare soil!" cried Hugh Maguire.

"We'll get to that," said O'Neill. "The Crown has sequestered me to restore order in the north and to controlling the actions of our dear Red Hugh."

The room cheered, and Red Hugh raised his glass with a beaming smile.

"The Crown has also ordered the removal of Lord Deputy Fitzwilliam..."

"Hurray!" and the men slammed their cups on the table.

"But Fitzwilliam does not want to go. Therein lies our opportunity. Whilst he squirms on his hook, and the new lord deputy lies powerless in the wings, we'll rid the north of collaborators with the English. Raid their lands! Steal their cattle! Burn their crops! Besiege Enniskillen!"

"Hurray!" the lords cheered, and beat the air with their fists.

"Red Hugh and I will go to the Irish Council to 'negotiate'. The rest of you breathe nothing of this plan to anyone but make the north ungovernable."

The lords cheered and made endless toasts.

O'Neill eventually took Hugh Maguire aside.

"I am sending my best man and brother, Cormac, to help relieve Enniskillen. I will also take care of Connor Roe. Fermanagh will be united again! Put a call out to the men of Fermanagh to prepare for war."

"If you do that, you'll have the allegiance of every Maguire in Fermanagh."

"Here's to the freedom of the north!" and O'Neill slammed his cup into that of Hugh Maguire.

"The freedom of the north!"

Cups were filled and filled again to match the elan for the next toast. The evening gradually slid into a blur.

9

March on Enniskillen

Eunan and his men rode to the woods south of Belleek to assemble with the rest of the rebel Maguires. He had his new O'Cassidy axe tied to his back, with its wolfhound medallion embedded in the cheek. But he could not get Caoimhe out of his mind. He rubbed the wolfhound medallion for luck. The visit to Desmond had done him good. He should recast himself as an O'Cassidy, follow his mother's line and take over south Fermanagh. Cormac O'Cassidy would soon be disposed of as a traitor when the lords of the north marshalled their armies, freed Enniskillen and set their sites on the Pale, and the Spanish king's fleet would envelop the oceans…

"Eunan! Stop thinking about that girl! We're almost here," shouted Óisin.

"You're lucky to have so tolerant a master," growled Eunan. "Many another would have flung his axe at you for being so cheeky."

"You'd want to be not so distracted when someone flings an axe at you."

Eunan waived his jesting away.

"It's been a long ride. Let's find the Maguire."

Eunan and his men rode on.

They were soon stopped by guards who recognised Eunan. They directed him to the main camp and from there to Hugh Maguire's tent.

"Eunan!" exclaimed Maguire, "you have done the Maguires and myself proud with all the men you have raised."

"I'm glad to be of service, lord. I see the MacCabes have returned."

"Never underestimate the Galloglass nose for sniffing out their master's ability to pay. Once they realised the Maguire herd of cattle was safe in the hands of Hugh O'Neill and not robbed by his lesser lords, they came back."

"I hope the men I found prove more loyal. I searched the whole of Fermanagh, except for the lands under Connor Roe. Men came forth on the words that the Maguire will return, but my kinsmen, the O'Cassidys, contributed nothing. Even more surprising considering Donnacha was there."

"I'll take care of Donnacha. The O'Cassidy helps us in far more ways than is obvious. They will come. But meanwhile, the Maguires will march on Enniskillen and meet with Cormac MacBaron and the O'Neills before we retake our town."

"That is glorious news, lord. When do we march?"

"At first light tomorrow! We have over five hundred men, and the English will flee before us."

"I will embrace that day! But first, I will go to the campsites and reacquaint myself with the men."

Eunan left and roamed through the forest and picked his way past all the groups of tents from all the various septs. It was just like the stories of old, when the Maguire calls; the Maguires come running.

* * *

The following day they set out for Enniskillen. There was no sign of the English, and no opposition blighted their march. The Maguires waited in the woods south of Enniskillen, unwilling to reveal their intentions without their better-armed allies. Word reached Hugh Maguire that Cormac MacBaron had entered Fermanagh and was waiting for the Maguires. Hugh and his men abandoned camp and went to meet him.

Eunan's heart leapt at the size of Cormac MacBaron's camp. This was no raid, for the size of the force suggested Cormac MacBaron was here to stay. The Maguires found somewhere suitable, with enough room to hold all the tents, graze the horses and set up camp. Cormac invited Hugh, Eunan, and several of the other Maguire lords to his tent. Once inside, Hugh clasped Cormac with delight and relief.

"Greetings from the O'Neills! My brother has kept his promise," bellowed Cormac.

"Indeed, he has, my friend! Indeed, he has!" replied Hugh.

"I have brought some of the finest shot, pike and horsemen in all of Tyrone. My brother burns the north free of its English landlords and their Irish allies, and we are here to do the same."

"When do we lay siege to Enniskillen?"

"In time. But first, we must isolate it from England and its allies. I am here to fulfil my brother's plan," and Cormac rolled out the O'Neill battle maps. When they left the tent, Hugh Maguire and his lords embraced and grasped hands. The rebellion had restarted.

The next day, the two armies set out from their camps. They made straight for Connor Roe's territory, and they devastated his lands to such a degree they thought it would knock him out of the war. The MacMahons destroyed Monaghan to add to Connor Roe's isolation. The O'Neills and their allies then turned their attention northwards. They either took the pledges of any lords that had not come out for Hugh Maguire, or else they ruined their lands. They lay lands bare in a twenty-mile radius of Enniskillen and the armies set about creating defensive earthworks along the River Erne's narrower parts by planting stakes in the river to cut off Enniskillen of re-supply from the upper lough and Connor Roe. The Maguires and Cormac MacBaron had no cannon for a quick retake of Enniskillen Castle, so they made their camps and settled in for a siege.

News of the devastation of Connor Roe and the siege of Enniskillen quickly spread. The wavering Maguires of south Fermanagh then declared for the Maguire, which caused the numbers in the Maguire camp to swell. Then one day, as Hugh, Eunan, and the leaders of the Maguire hunched over a roughly drawn map of Enniskillen and its surroundings, Donnacha O'Cassidy Maguire entered the tent. Behind him strode a man a couple of years younger than Eunan, but old enough to hold an axe. Hugh greeted Donnacha as if he were a long-lost friend.

"I knew you'd come when the time was right. South Fermanagh has declared for me?"

"When you removed the darkness of Connor Roe, they saw the light, lord."

"That is excellent! The Maguires have risen again," and Hugh punched the air. "And who have you brought as the assistant that cowers behind you?"

"I cower behind no one, good lord," and the young man made himself known.

"Before I put an axe through his impetuous head, please tell me who he is?"

Donnacha scowled at the boy.

"The badly mannered boy who embarrasses me is my nephew, Cillian O'Cassidy. Despite his rudeness, I don't think the fragile alliance of south Fermanagh would survive an axe through his head. When you meet him again, his manners will be impeccable as I remind him that nobody usurps the Maguire. He asks for your forgiveness, doesn't he?"

The boy stepped up on cue.

"Please forgive me, sir. My nerves got the better of me from being in such exalted company."

"It is best you be quiet in the future, should you ever be in my tent again. How many men do you bring, and who is their commander?"

Donnacha stepped in.

"The boy has one hundred warriors from south Fermanagh, all ready to do their duty."

"Hmm, we don't need badly armed men who run at the first volley of shot. Who leads these men?"

"Er, the boy does, lord!"

"No, we cannot have that. We need experienced commanders."

"I will lead them!" cried Eunan. "I am from south Fermanagh. The men will respect me."

"No!" cried the boy.

Donnacha pushed him towards the door.

"Lord, please reconsider. The O'Cassidys are headstrong and independent. They would rebel at being put under an inexperienced commander they don't know."

"The O'Cassidys sway in the wind like a head of barley every time Connor Roe comes calling. They need to be led by a loyal commander from their region, like me," replied Eunan.

"Say no more, Eunan. Donnacha, step aside. I will place the O'Cassidys under Eunan, and if they run like the wind back to south Fermanagh at the first sign of trouble, then Eunan will be to blame, and you won't have to bring a dead boy back to your cousin."

"But lord.."

"Don't say too much, Donnacha, or I may remember your absence when I was alone on Devenish Island!"

"I will take my leave to go persuade my clansmen of the wise nature of your idea," and Donnacha bowed as he backed out of the room.

"Take Eunan with you. They may as well meet him sooner rather than later."

* * *

Donnacha walked in front of Eunan, not bothering to look behind. He would merely cast a "this way" over his shoulder, not caring if Eunan was in earshot every time the route twisted in the town of tents. Cillian parted ways with Donnacha, but Eunan was too far behind to figure out why.

The camp collapsed into indiscipline the further they got from the centre. The journey started in the neat rows of tents of the MacCabe, which exuded professionalism as they surrounded the central hub of the tent of the Maguire. There, pathways out to the individual septs and bands of mercenaries twisted and meandered out to both desirable and undesirable destinations. The end of this seldom trodden spoke they set out upon led to the shantytown of the O'Cassidys, possibly the least professional segment of the camp.

There was no semblance of organisation or structure in this landscape of wilful neglect and ineptitude. Some men had tents, some covered their carts with blankets, but there seemed to be a distinct lack of suitable accommodation for the youths drifting around. Some men had brought decent armour and weapons with them, but Eunan mainly saw bows and pitchforks. Anguish took hold of Eunan, for he barely saw a soldier amongst them.

"How could such a rich man as my uncle send such a rabble to the Maguire?" exclaimed Eunan.

"They're your rabble now," replied Donnacha.

Some men stood to attention when Donnacha was going to address them. Most continued what they were doing before, such as drinking, engaging in horseplay or organising where to forage for food.

"Well then, you may as well start by calling them to attention."

Donnacha stood aside to show Eunan was in charge now.

"MEN!" Eunan exclaimed. "COME LINE UP FOR YOUR CLAN! THE MAGUIRE NEEDS YOU!"

A couple of boys looked at him and laughed, but carried on their horseplay. Several other men and boys paid him casual attention, as if he could be a source of entertainment.

"You'll get nowhere by appealing to their sense of loyalty or patriotism. Do you give up yet?" said Donnacha as he looked at his nails.

"PRESENT YOURSELVES, MEN, FOR INSPECTION BY THE MAGUIRE!"

The force of Eunan's tone drew more attention to himself but as more of a curiosity than a figure of authority.

"Shall I get Cillian now?" asked Donnacha.

"And what would he do?" barked Eunan.

"I will do you this one favour, not for you, but because I am hungry and wish to return to civilisation. Besides, the Maguire always does the best food."

He turned to the O'Cassidy rabble.

"Boys," Donnacha said calmly, "the Maguire sent this man to train and lead you as a replacement for your clansman, Cillian. Not a word of this must make it back to the O'Cassidy, for I do not know how he would bear the insult, and I know you all still want to get paid. This man has ample amounts of food, drink and tents for you. After he has provided, the training will begin. I leave you in the capable hands of Eunan Maguire."

Eunan's face dropped, for he had none of these things for the wall of toothless grins, boyish naivety, bad breath, and assorted odours of the countryside that now surrounded him. It was as if the O'Cassidy had gathered up all the never-do-wells on his lands and sent them off to be a burden on the Maguire. But they were his burden now. Donnacha laughed.

"Good luck!" he said as he waved over his shoulder and walked towards the Maguire's tent.

* * *

Eunan tried to close his eyes on a disappointing day. Failing to evoke any feeling of patriotism or loyalty to the Maguire in that mob of human waste collapsed his soul. It was as if he were a boy back in his village again, holding out his hand, trying to prise out some feeling of friendship from his contemporaries who would shun or laugh at him or both. It was as if he was at the bottom of the same pit of despair, never to claw his way out. But he needed to get it together. He was no longer a child but a warrior of the Maguire. He needed to think of them as a bunch of raw young boys that needed to be turned into warriors like him.

But the Maguire was right. These men owed more allegiance to a bottle of mead than any boy like Cillian, never mind the Maguire. Not even with his men, and Óisin to provide a spine would they stand and fight. Being their commander seemed a quick way to lose a hard-won reputation. Worry kept him awake until tiredness eventually overwhelmed him, and he drifted off.

* * *

Eunan found himself in the forest, a familiar place by sight and touch. He moved forward towards where he thought his village used to be. The light formed a bubble that surrounded him, for the more he moved forward, the more it seemed to hem him in and follow him.

Eunan reached for his belt. His trusty Maguire axes were no longer at his side. The air in his bubble, loneliness and vulnerability all weighed on his shoulders. He came to the edge of the forest, and before him was the well that was his mother's grave. A light drew him towards it but he resisted every step. Something pulled his foot off the ground, floated it forward, and then drove it down into the ground, where he found himself over the well. He looked down below into the blackness and the faint echo of falling debris. From behind he was surrounded by a wall of bad breath and missing teeth belonging to the men of the O'Cassidy. They laughed and poked him with little sticks shaped like weapons. Closing in, they forced him further and further back until they pressed him against the exterior wall of the well. He leant back to get away from them, but they trapped his legs. The men seized his legs and flipped him backwards. He was failing.

Eunan landed on his back, on the ground. It was completely dry, unlike the familiar well of his village. He looked upwards, and the walls were sheer and the sky unreachable. Beside him was a hole in the wall. It was the only means of escape. He braced himself, crouched down and crawled on his belly for several minutes through dust, stone and debris, coughing every couple of meters. He bled from his elbow and his knees, coated in dust and small stones. But at long last, he made it to a circular room. As he dusted himself off, suddenly he saw before him was his mother on a stone altar. She was dressed in the funeral garb of Maguire nobility, a green flowing dress and around her the pride and beauty of the plants of Fermanagh. Beneath the altar was dried firewood, completing the funeral pyre. Caoimhe ran crying from the shadows and threw herself on his mother's dead body. Caoimhe wailed as if his mother were her own. Eunan walked towards her and reached out.

Cillian O'Cassidy emerged from the shadows and stood between Eunan and the altar with an axe rested on his forearms. Eunan tried to get past him, but Cillian kept moving to block his way. He tried to push past, but Cillian shoved him back and squeezed the shaft of his axe. A hand placed itself upon Eunan's shoulders.

"One man stands between you and your mother and the woman of your dreams. Put an axe through his head," a whisper came in Eunan's ear.

Eunan turned his head and saw Seamus.

"Put an axe through his head!" and Seamus nodded in the grim-faced Cillian's direction.

Eunan's veins bulged.

"Put an axe through his head!"

"I…I have no axe."

"Here, take mine. Now put an axe through his head."

Eunan looked at Cillian, whose face did not move.

"Put an axe through his head!" commanded Seamus. "Do I have to tell your father?!"

"M-my father?"

Eunan looked at his forearm. His blood began to boil, and the bubble protruded out of his veins.

"Yes! Your father! Here he comes now!"

Cillian O'Cassidy now gripped his axe shaft with both hands.

"Now what were you told, boy? Put an axe through his head!" came a roar from the shadows.

A ginger giant emerged, covered in his mother's blood, and ran at Eunan. Eunan tried to run, but Finn came from behind and crouched down and tripped him. His head hit the ground. The bad blood boiled over and exploded from his arms. Eunan screamed into the ceiling of his tent.

10

Second siege of Enniskillen

Several months of stability passed by in Tirconnell. Red Hugh concentrated his time sending delegations to Scotland to hire mercenaries, training his men, and gathering together rebels from Connacht and Leinster and directing them to take up residence in his lands. The news of the siege of Enniskillen spread like wildfire across the north. Hugh Maguire lit the beacon of rebellion, and it drove potential recruits from all over Ireland to Tirconnell, eager for action. Red Hugh, determined not to disappoint, prepared his men for war.

* * *

In the meantime, as one of the favoured men, they provided Seamus with coin and livery. He took up residence in a small house on the outskirts of Donegal town, much to the anger of Shea Óg, who had to make do with the squalor of the camp. Heaped upon this burden, Shea Óg also had to hold together his rabble of misfits and ensure that Seamus delivered Hugh Boye MacDavitt. Seamus tried to prise out news of his wife back in Enniskillen from any source but Shea

Óg to no avail. He grew more anxious about her welfare, so he put aside his better judgment and sought Shea Óg.

Shea Óg sat beside a modest fire, trying to suck the last of the meat off a poor unfortunate rabbit that in its fatal error made a burrow beside a camp of hungry, drunken men. He was so engrossed that he did not see Seamus coming.

"Have you made yourself at home in the land of the O'Donnell's yet?" asked Seamus over Shea's shoulder.

Shea Óg turned his head.

"You haven't lost your sense of humour, you lazy shite. Another two have disappeared, and we don't have a single corpse to show for it. You'd better worry about your wife! I need to report back soon, and I can't be telling them the men are mysteriously dying," but the talk of his men's demise did not stop him from stripping another piece of meat off the rabbit with his teeth.

"And how do you do that?" asked Seamus.

Shea Óg could smell weakness even over the waft of the rabbit.

"Wouldn't you like to know?" he turned to Seamus, his attention now fully settled on their conversation.

"Well, I wouldn't want yourself and Sean getting killed, not until I get my wife back."

"You've heard the news of the siege of Enniskillen. She'll be a long time gone to the security of Lisnaskea and Connor Roe." Shea Óg smiled. "Our leverage will be safely hidden away."

Seamus cursed and got up to leave.

"Well, when you write your report, you can tell them that the O'Donnell has assigned me to Connacht, and there's no sign of Hugh Boye MacDavitt. So they'd better keep my wife well until he shows up."

"You'd better not be lying to me, Seamus MacSheehy."

"If you'd brains, you'd be dangerous. Don't be getting yourself killed in some stupid drunken brawl or the like. I want my wife back!"

"Good day to you as well," and Shea Óg turned his back on Seamus, returning his full attention to the rabbit bones.

Seamus cursed again before setting off back to Donegal town. Asking Shea Óg had only increased his anxiety.

* * *

The borderlands of Ulster had become a dangerous place for the servants of the Crown and their allies. Besides the Blackwater Fort, three isolated garrisons in Cavan, Monaghan, and Enniskillen protruded out as rocks in the turbulent sea of rebellion. The Maguire roamed free in Fermanagh, except for Enniskillen, and bands of warriors from the north's minor clans terrorised the countryside. Red Hugh O'Donnell had by now openly joined the rebellion and arrived outside Enniskillen with his finest soldiers that had not yet departed to Connacht with Niall Garbh.

He rode into the camp like a proud peacock, eager to brandish his axe in the anger of war, and was directed straight to Hugh Maguire's tent. Hugh and Cormac MacBaron were hunched over maps, planning the siege as he entered.

"I have arrived with my warriors to lead the attack. When is the assault?" Red Hugh roared as he extended out his arms to his allies.

"My friend!" and Hugh Maguire ran to embrace him.

Cormac MacBaron did not look so impressed, and ignored the invitation. He had no desire to be usurped as army commander. He wished to move swiftly to business.

"We have to squeeze them until they squeal. Then we can attack. There'll be no assault, for the only way to take the castle without filling the graveyards is with siege equipment, and we've none of that."

"Well, I am here now," said Red Hugh with contempt for caution. "I will survey the castle tomorrow. Hugh, can you assign me a few of your men to show me how the English got into the castle to take it in the first place?"

Cormac was not one to be ignored.

"Hugh O'Neill has given me explicit orders not to assault the castle. The O'Neill is not ready for war."

Red Hugh squared up to Cormac MacBaron.

"Well, the O'Neill isn't here, and I am the O'Donnell. We assault if I say we assault!"

Hugh Maguire stood between them.

"I will give you some of my best scouts tomorrow. You may change your mind once you survey the castle, Hugh."

"Are you saying the Maguires can't take back their castle?" asked Red Hugh.

"I'm saying the English are well dug in, and we have time to starve them out. I'm sure you'll agree once you inspect the castle."

"We'll see! Send your men to men at first light. My men and I will set up camp on the other side of the river."

Cormac MacBaron bowed to him.

"I'll take my leave and inform the O'Neill of your arrival."

"You go do that!" and Red Hugh stormed out.

* * *

The next day Hugh Maguire arrived at Red Hugh's camp with several of his best scouts. Red Hugh gathered his military advisers and bodyguards. They mounted and rode out to a nearby hilltop to survey the land. Seamus was a trusted adviser. Hugh Maguire rode alongside Red Hugh as he surveyed the landscape.

"If you look at the moat and walls of the castle, whatever holes or secret ways existed before, the English first exploited and then neutralised them. There's no way in, except over a pile of dead bodies."

Red Hugh turned to his entourage.

"Well, men, is there any way in?"

"Hugh Maguire is right. Better to starve them out," said Seamus.

Hugh Maguire recognised the voice and cocked his head back to check it was Seamus.

"Glad to have you back with us!" said Hugh Maguire. "Few can say they survived the siege of Enniskillen."

"Aye, few can. Nobody wants to take her more than me, but we need to preserve our men, for the English will want to give battle soon. If we sit here and besiege the castle, they will come to us. Therefore, we can pick where and when we want to fight them. So I say let the siege continue."

"You won't get wiser than that from me," said Red Hugh. "My men will build earthworks and let us wait for the English to attack. In the meantime, I will send emissaries to Scotland to recruit redshanks. We'll need all the men we can get. Let us set off back to camp."

They turned their horses and set off. Hugh Maguire rode up to Seamus while they were mid-journey.

"I'm glad to see you're still alive!"

"No one is more glad than me, lord."

"Why did you not come back into my service?"

"When I escaped from the castle and fled Fermanagh, Red Hugh gave me sanctuary. The O'Donnell wants me to organise veterans from the Netherlands to train and fight with his armies."

"We could always do with your help here. Eunan is in the camp. I'm sure he would be delighted to see you."

"All in good time. However, lord, I have a favour to ask of you."

"What is it?"

"They captured my wife and the families of my original Galloglass when Enniskillen fell. Have you heard anything about them?"

"You are the only survivor of Enniskillen that I know of, but if I hear anything, I shall pass it on to you. Now I must ride with Red Hugh, but we shall speak again."

* * *

Red Hugh and his men settled in for a long siege, but the rebels' actions had not gone unnoticed in the Pale. The lord deputy ordered a relief force in Cavan of six hundred men and forty-six horse to relieve the siege and resupply Enniskillen. He put Sir Henry Duke and Sir Edward Herbert in charge. They had the services of such veterans of Fermanagh as Captain Dowdall, who previously took Enniskillen and Captain Humphrey Willis, the ex-sheriff of Fermanagh, whose actions were one of the leading causes of Hugh Maguire to rebel. They set out on the road to Enniskillen, but the Irish rebels were soon aware of their movements.

* * *

Another axe missed its target. This time it did not even shave the wood on its side.

"What am I supposed to do with you? Who trained you?" cried Eunan as the O'Cassidy boys just stared at him, for they had by now developed thick skins from his berating.

Donnacha and Cillian O'Cassidy looked on and smiled.

"I'm sick of all of you! Just leave me, and we'll start tomorrow morning again," said Eunan, throwing up his hands in exasperation.

The O'Cassidy boys sloped back off to the camp to find some alcohol or other mischief.

"What are you looking at?" Eunan growled at Cillian. "If you don't train, Donnacha will have to send your corpse back to your father."

"They don't like having some impostor imposed on them pretending to be their leader," said Cillian O'Cassidy.

"Well, it's an insult to God and the Maguire, including your father. For all the wealth he had on his farm, he could have hired a few Galloglass for the cause instead of sending us these useless idiots."

"Are the boys not a sacrifice enough?" replied Donnacha. "The O'Cassidy land will change hands so many times before Hugh Maguire has the sense to sign an agreement with the English. There is no point in antagonising the future winner of the conflict and throwing away all that money and all that life. The boys are here to learn how to fight, and it is you, my dear sir, who is doing the insulting by the poor job you are doing of training them!"

"I never figured you for a traitor," shouted Eunan.

"No, you always figured me for a wise man, but you are too deaf to hear my wise words. Train the boys, play your silly war games, but they will settle this when the Queen gets her cattle and coin."

"You can play your silly politics all you like, but an English army is marching towards Enniskillen right now. They are coming from Cavan, so they will march right through the O'Cassidy lands and then give battle. Every man must be prepared! These boys will die on the battlefield, and you'll have to bring their bodies back to the O'Cassidys whose lands will have been pillaged by the English army. Then you can play your politics."

"Don't get over-excited! The O'Cassidy boys can run as fast as any other man. As soon as the English army appears, the army of the Maguire will melt away. Why don't you spend your time better and go look for Seamus, who has returned to the camp?"

Eunan went silent, the thunderstorms in his brain etched on his face. But he remembered the words of Desmond, to forget about Seamus and concentrate on becoming the O'Cassidy.

"First things first!" he exclaimed. "Cillian, you train the men, and

I'll be back in several days."

Donnacha smirked, for he thought he knew how to pull Eunan's strings. Within the hour, Eunan, Óisin, and several more of his reliable men were on the road to Derrylinn.

11

The crossroads

Eunan and his men rode for the imagined lives of his brethren: the O'Cassidys. Derrylinn's prosperity was now its downfall, for the same road that brought it wealth now brought it the English army. Eunan arrived at the town to see its limbs were as sluggish as before. No evacuation, no preparation. He knew he had to act. He went to the blacksmith, where he got his new axe. The blacksmith was engrossed in the flaming metal wrapped around his anvil. No sign of panic for the imminent arrival of the English. Eunan sought attention by slapping his hand down the blacksmith's rough-and-ready counter.

"I've kept my promise and am here to return the favour you did for me. Pack your things and come to Enniskillen. Men of your skills are in high demand and will be well rewarded by the Maguire. The English army is but a day's march away and will destroy everything in its path," Eunan shouted at him over the rhythmic banging of the hammer.

The blacksmith stopped hammering.

"Kept your promise? But you are here! You reneged on your promise. You said you would go and never come back. All that follows you is destruction!"

"Quit babbling, old man! I am going to the O'Cassidy's house and will see you on the road to Enniskillen. My men will protect you. Goodbye."

"The road to Enniskillen?" the blacksmith shouted after him. "Captain Willis is there with his men. There is no escape that way."

That name stopped Eunan in his tracks. He turned, both in mood and stance.

"Where is Willis? Tell me now!"

"Up there beyond those woods, on the crossroads to Enniskillen."

He jumped on his horse and pointed his axe toward the crossroads.

* * *

Eunan crouched beneath the cover provided by the bushes and trees and tried to contain the urge to leap out and confront Willis. He had instantaneously recognised him from the siege of the church. He barely looked a day older than when he saw him last.

"If I knew then what I know now, I could have sabotaged Willis's negotiations at the church, and my father would have been partly avenged. By God's bones, I'll not let this fresh opportunity pass."

He reached for his throwing axes and cursed for the simple solution did not avail itself, for he was out of range. He turned to the crouched Óisin, who was beside him.

"If you go around the front and lay a covering fire of arrows and prevent their escape, I'll take the rest of the men and confront Willis."

"Do you hear yourself?" replied Óisin. "They outnumber us two to one! They're English regulars, not mercenary scum from the Pale. We'd be dead in minutes."

Eunan looked him straight in the eye.

"I didn't take you as a coward!"

The words lit the anger in Óisin's eye, and he raised his axe to signal the men to follow him. Eunan quickly learned how to manipulate Óisin's combustible ego. Several minutes later, the hail of arrows attacked Captain Willis and his men, who took to the woods as Eunan had predicted. The English ran for a couple of minutes until they realised how few arrows were coming after them. Captain Willis halted his men, and they returned fire. This time it was Óisin under pressure and his turn to retreat. Eunan had laid his ambush, but seeing that the English had stopped, he assumed Óisin had engaged. He could not let Willis escape a second time, nor let Óisin take the glory of what should be his revenge.

"THE CRY OF THE MAGUIRE!" and his men followed him out from the cover of the trees.

Eunan had much ground to cover before he let out his rebel yell, but it was a time for haste, not sense. Bullets quickly honed in on the rebels' shouts, and one by one, they fell while making up the ground to engage. Soon only three rebels remained.

"TAKE COVER!" Eunan ordered.

The bullets stopped. He heard the distant cracking of sticks and branches, waiving to his men to retreat. The cracking noise got nearer. Eunan looked out from behind his tree.

"RUN!"

It was his turn to be the hunted.

He directed his men to split up as they ran in three different directions. The English gave up on none of them. Eunan ran as fast as he could back toward Derrylinn, hoping to run into Óisin along the way. The first of his men tripped and fell into a gorge. His pursuers made their way down the muddy slopes to fish him out of the river below. They felled the second with a bullet, and the soldiers retrieved him as well. Eunan was now alone, running in the woods, with bullets whizzing past his head. He ran as fast as he could but could hear the English gaining on him as they caught his comrades, and more soldiers turned to hunt for him. Eunan ran until his feet hurt and his face stung from running into twigs and branches. He saw a chink of daylight between the trees. It was not far now. Surely the English would not be brave enough to chase him out into the open? He looked back behind him. The soldiers were still gaining on him. Just a little more to go... THUD!

Eunan awoke to the point of a sword held by the uniform of an English officer.

"I thought that since you Macs and Os lived in the forest, you'd have learned to avoid the trees."

Another voice laughed from somewhere behind the officer.

"Don't worry, we'll spare you the disgrace of hanging you in your own home. We'll hang you in the town instead," said the officer.

The other voice laughed until the air was filled with a swish, and the laugh became a gurgle. The officer turned to see his soldier collapse with an arrow through his neck.

"Run while you still can, Englishman!" came a voice from the woods.

The English officer looked around him, saw no one, and then took to his heels.

Óisin came out from the bushes and picked Eunan up from the ground.

"That was Captain Willis! You could have got my vengeance!"

"Yeah, and then we'd both be dead in the woods. Come on, I've got your horse."

* * *

Eunan rode towards the O'Cassidy's house. He left the remains of his men on the outskirts of the grounds, cursing himself for throwing their lives away with nothing to show for it. But he still had a chance to redeem himself and rescue his clan.

"Óisín, you come with me. The rest of you, if we are not back by the time the sun sets over those trees there, come and get us," instructed Eunan.

The men nodded while their horses pointed northwards, as if they may need to make a quick getaway. Eunan saluted them and prayed that their loyalty would still be intact when the sun went down.

Grimacing as he rode his horse towards the house, he knew he had to hold his nerve much better than he did the last time. He needed to be strong enough to overcome his uncle's inevitable resistance. Such strength and fortitude may even impress Caoimhe. Such pressure merely increased the weight on his young, muscular shoulders. Such strength in limb was not matched by a similar strength in mind.

Eunan approached the house to see that no preparations were being made for the English. Treachery or negligence? He flung himself off his horse and ran to the house to find out.

"Where do you think you're going?"

A pointed sword blocked his path.

"I must warn the master of the impending arrival of the English army. He must evacuate now," he pleaded with the snarled face of the grizzled Galloglass.

"You'll do no such thing! The master knows what's coming and has many a dealing with Captains Willis and Dowdall. He also knows what to do about your interference."

Óisín dismounted from his horse.

"Put your sword down now or have my axe cleave its way through your thick skull," and Óisín strode with grim purpose towards the Galloglass.

Men gathered at the front of the house, armed with whatever came to hand.

"Let him in," cried a female voice, and Eunan saw Caoimhe once again.

The men backed away, and Eunan walked past them. But he only had eyes for Caoimhe. She secretly grabbed his hand.

"Whatever happens, don't let my brother die," she whispered in his ear.

Eunan smiled and squeezed her hand. Several more Galloglass appeared at the door to escort him.

* * *

Cormac O'Cassidy prowled the room like a cornered ferret. Gone was whatever politeness or curiosity was there before. The sight of Eunan gave direction to his fury.

"I thought I told you to leave and never come back?"

"I came back to warn you, to save you and your family," pleaded Eunan.

He glanced over to Caoimhe to see if she was impressed, but she had melted into the background of the crowd of men that followed Eunan into the room.

"I don't need saving. I don't need warning. A rumour tells me you've taken control of the O'Cassidy men sent to help Hugh Maguire? You've no right to do that. Your mother may have been an O'Cassidy when she was born, but she certainly wasn't one when she died!"

"Don't you speak ill of my mother!" and Eunan squeezed the shaft of his axe.

"Did no one disarm him when he came in? What do I pay you Galloglass for?"

"Why weren't they sent to join Hugh Maguire?" and Eunan pointed accusingly at the Galloglass.

"Are our sons and the sons of my clansmen not good enough? How much blood must the fields of Fermanagh absorb before this young

Maguire is satisfied?"

"You may as well have sent me a bunch of frightened rabbits, except they won't run so fast."

"Our boys are only carrying on a great Maguire tradition, running at the first sign of trouble. How do you think the Maguires have survived for so long to sing their songs of glory to themselves?"

"The O'Cassidy boys won't run when I've finished with them!"

"That's because they'll all be dead. But let me reconsider, for I would like my son back, preferably alive. If you can bring my boy back alive and those of my fellow clansmen, I will suitably reward you."

"What does suitably reward me mean?"

"I will give you what you most desire in the world: to be acknowledged as being from clan O'Cassidy. But once I do you must agree never to darken our door again."

"What about the English?"

"Leave now with your men and return our boys to us. Then you will be an O'Cassidy free to roam the earth as long as it is not south Fermanagh!"

"What if I refuse?"

"My men will cut you to pieces, blame the English and then I try to retrieve my boy."

Eunan looked around the room, and four heavily armed Galloglass jutted out their chins, straightened their backs, and fondled their sword grips.

"I reluctantly accept," for Eunan realised there was no other way out while remaining alive.

Caoimhe smiled, which was of little consolation for his submission.

"Oh, and avoid the town on your way out. The English are stringing up some rebels they found in the woods."

Eunan turned, and the anger boiled in his eyes.

"I thought you might not be able to help yourself. My Galloglass will see you off my land."

They surrounded Eunan and led him to the door.

He walked out of the O'Cassidy house to mount his horse. Óisín pointed down the road. In the distance, Eunan could make out the first elements of the English army.

"Come. We must warn Hugh Maguire."

"Not so fast," said the Galloglass constable. "We want you off this land without causing us any trouble."

"As much as it pains me to abandon my men, I must warn the Maguire."

"If it's any consolation, your men are already dead."

Eunan paused, pained.

"So be it. Enniskillen is my destination. Are you going to hinder me from getting there?"

"If it is the quickest way to be rid of you, then no."

"Tell your master I'll be back to claim my inheritance when the English are defeated."

"So I won't have to set the noose upon the old oak tree any day soon them?"

"Good day. May God hasten the day you join the ranks of the army of the Maguire!"

"May God give you the sense never to come back here again!"

Eunan ignored the man and mounted his horse. He and his men rode away from Derrylinn as fast as the wind would carry them.

12

Ford of the biscuits

Eunan and the remains of his men made it back to the camp outside Enniskillen, and the guards on the perimeter directed Eunan straight to Hugh Maguire's tent, where a war council was taking place. All the captains and high-ranking clansmen from the Maguires, O'Donnells, O'Neills, and the minor clans were there. Spirits were high, and defiance lingered like the chill in the air, steadfastly stating its existence even though it was mid-August.

The O'Neills had with them a guest, Pablo Blanco, a military aide sent from the king of Spain. Cormac MacBaron ensured Pablo had worn his Spanish army uniform and stood proudly beside him, a subtle hint if one were needed, that the O'Neills were the dominant clan.

The tent was too small to accommodate all the clan chiefs and their constables, so the men of the lesser clans had to make do by peering into the tent from the adjacent ground. They listened eagerly to hear if they would fight this day.

Eunan tried to slip in behind the Maguire captains while looking for Seamus. There was no sign of Seamus or Red Hugh O'Donnell. He settled in behind the front rank of Maguire captains, who stood to one side of the table in the centre of the tent.

Hugh Maguire stood by the table and conversed with Cormac and Pablo until the appropriate moment came and he stepped forward to take charge of the proceedings. There was an excited quiver in his voice.

"Good afternoon, chiefs and warriors of the north. The English once again attempt to invade our lands but we will defy them!"

The gathered men cheered as Hugh poked the table to punctuate his speech.

"Our scouts tell us that the English left Cavan on 4th August…"

"They have already reached Derrylinn!" said Eunan, pushing past the front ranks of Maguire captains to make himself known.

"How do you know this?"

"I have come from there. I was trying to get the O'Cassidys to evacuate."

Hugh nodded in appreciation.

"Thank you, Eunan. Our scouts have reported back the strength of the English army and we have decided to attack. Cormac Mac Baron and I will take charge of the army. Pablo Blanco and the scouts of the Maguire have found us a suitable ambush spot, so come forth Pablo, and tell us your plan."

Pablo strode forth from behind Hugh and unrolled his maps on the table. With the revelation of the details, the Maguires and O'Neills smiled as one. It seemed the perfect ambush.

* * *

At the end of the meeting, Eunan waited behind to speak with Hugh Maguire. Donnacha O'Cassidy hovered around in the background, curious to know what he had to say. Hugh finished speaking with Cormac and Pablo and turned his attention to Eunan.

"Have you seen Seamus, lord? I wish to speak to him before the battle begins."

"He has returned north with Red Hugh. They are expecting a thousand redshanks from Scotland. Seamus appears to have done well for himself and earned Red Hugh's trust. He is apparently in charge of recruiting ex veterans into service for the O'Donnell. So prestigious a role that Red Hugh insisted Seamus come with him to meet his Scottish contacts."

Eunan struggled to rein in his contempt.

"No matter the scenario, he always seems to thrive."

"An admirable quality we should strive to achieve, especially in the battle to come. Are your O'Cassidys ready?"

Donnacha jumped in.

"The O'Cassidys are ready to serve! My young nephew Cillian O'Cassidy has trained them well."

"The O'Cassidys will be present and correct, lord," and Eunan glared at Donnacha, who did not flinch. "They will help set a trap for the English."

"Good," said Hugh. "I look forward to your tales of glory when we celebrate our victory."

* * *

Eunan lay in his tent, barely able to close his eyes. Tomorrow would be the first time the farm boys and spoilt O'Cassidy children would see combat, and he was responsible for their performance. Eventually, the exhaustion of the day got the better of him, and he nodded off. But the kindness of sleep eluded him once more.

He walked on the road to the O'Cassidys house. The road was straight and narrow, and the trees on either side closed in on him. Dark clouds rumbled in the sky, the rumbling thunder giving notice of the lightning to come. A whisper hung around Eunan's ear.

"Where are our boys? Where are our boys?"

He looked around, but no one was there. He proceeded forward, and the road narrowed and pointed towards the house.

"Where are our boys? Where are our boys?"

The earth cracked but did not shake. Eunan broke into a trot. Hands broke out of the ground along the side of the road: some had axes, and some had spears, some had farming implements, some hands had none.

"Where are our boys? Where are our boys?"

He turned, and Seamus was beside him. Seamus strode aggressively towards the house, axe in hand.

"You've got to take what is yours! Put an axe through his head! What would your father think of you?"

They got nearer the house.

The skeletons of the boys dug themselves out of their graves. They fell in behind Eunan, and they marched on the house. Eunan saw a female figure come out of the house, being pursued by Cormac O'Cassidy. He strode forward and recognised his mother. She was crying and could not see him. She ran into the woods. The skeletons of the boys chanted, "you're not an O'Cassidy, you're not an O'Cassidy."

Cormac ran over to him, his arms flailing like a scythe. "Get off my land! You're not an O'Cassidy!"

Eunan's bad blood boiled.

"Take what is yours! Put an axe through his head!" said a voice harsh and shrill.

Eunan's bad blood bulged in his arms and felt like some ghost of the past took control of his arms, and he saw his axe blade fly through the sky, over his head, and down towards Cormac.

He would get no more sleep that night.

* * *

Eunan got up and spent the rest of the night sat beside the fire, turning over in his mind whether he should save the O'Cassidy boys or how much they would disgrace him on the battlefield that day. Moreover, what would Hugh Maguire think? At dawn, he visited the tents and roused his men for the day ahead. They eventually fell out of their beds, be they in tents, carts or under the stars, and assembled with their collection of substandard weapons and occasional armour. Cillian O'Cassidy rolled in last.

"Alright boys, form a line," cried Eunan.

The line formed slowly, and he counted how many men were left.

"Seventy-nine."

Eunan sighed. Some boys had run home early, but he needed to motivate those that remained. He braced himself, stood before his men, and puffed his chest out.

"Now we have been given an important mission today. We need to channel the English into the main trap, so we must force them toward Enniskillen. So all you've got to do is harass the enemy and withdraw if they counter-attack. Each of you take three javelins and distribute the bows to the best shots. Don't disgrace me or the O'Cassidy name today."

"My father will richly reward any of those who enhance the O'Cassidy name on the battlefield today," shouted Cillian from the side.

Eunan fumed at being undermined but said nothing. Old wounds from his trips to the priests began to itch.

"Follow me. We need to take up our positions," and he led the way to the hills.

* * *

On the evening of 6th August, the English army - made up of a core of experienced English troops who had served in Ireland for many years and the main section of the force who were Irish volunteers and conscripts mainly from the Pale - camped three miles south of a ford on the Arney River. The Maguires constantly harassed the camp that evening as Eunan sat in his own camp contemplated how his men would perform the next day.

The next morning he found himself on a hill with Óisin, observing the English army as they set out from their camp. He knew what he had to do, but could his men perform their task? The English pike shot and horse meandered through the valleys below along the narrow road, encumbered by their extended baggage train full of supplies for both themselves and the garrison of Enniskillen. Eunan rode back to his men, positioned on another hill further back, to get them into position.

The English army snaked its way up the narrow, shallow valley. The ford ahead was the most obvious place for an army of size to cross, but it was surrounded by high ground. Boggy ground on both sides of the road both to and beyond the ford placed the advantage firmly with the attacker. However, the English commanders were confident that their troops would prove superior in quality and weaponry than the Irish rebels should the rebels be foolhardy enough to launch an attack. Eunan's men held their positions and let the main bulk of the army pass them by.

The English started to cross the ford, only to be stopped in their tracks by volleys of Irish shot coming from the high ground ahead of them. The entire column juddered to a halt at the shock of being attacked in such a vulnerable position. Eunan knew it was his time to strike. Hugh Maguire and his forces, together with Cormac MacBaron and the O'Neills, charged down from their hiding places on the high ground that the English army bypassed to get to the ford. Once they slammed into the back of the English, Eunan leapt out from his hiding place. He let out a shout: "the cry of the Maguire!"

His faithful men, who had been with him before his visit to Cormac O'Cassidy, followed down the hill with a selection of the braver O'Cassidy boys. Cillian O'Cassidy surveyed the battlefield, and those who followed "the cry of the Maguire". Seeing that lesser lights of the O'Cassidy clan were charging down the hill after Eunan, he decided he had better follow, if only for family pride. Opposite the O'Cassidy charge, the English shot hastily set up their guns as the pikemen turned and set up their formations. The charging O'Cassidys released a volley of javelins and arrows before retreating out of the effective range of the shot. Eunan was elated, for he saw some of the enemy fall, but none of his own.

"Again!" he shouted.

But as soon as they were in range to throw their javelins, they found themselves in range of the guns, and the first O'Cassidy boys fell.

"Come on! Throw your weapons!" Eunan exclaimed.

But the boys started to run. The shot had gained their sight now and picked off the O'Cassidys as they ran.

"Retreat!" and Eunan waved them back up the hill.

He saw something he recognised as he walked up the hill and reached down behind a bush. He picked up Cillian O'Cassidy by the hair.

"Come on! You can't hide there all day!"

Eunan laughed, and Cillian cursed him, but followed him up the hill nonetheless.

Eunan reached the top and surveyed the battle. The pike of the Maguire and O'Neills had mauled the rear of the English army and forced it up the valley. The pressure of the compacting army forced the English pike at the front over the ford, which forced the Irish shot back. The English army was now a shambles and forcing its way across the ford for that was its only escape route. Eunan knew he had to act, or the battle would be gone. He raised his axe.

"The cry of the Maguire!"

But there were few to hear his cry. He charged down the hill with about twenty men towards the remains of the enemy. The O'Cassidys discharged their missiles and then ran up the hill again. However, Eunan was determined the battle would not pass him by, no matter how encumbered he was by the O'Cassidys. He charged the English stragglers with Óisin and his handful of steadfast men. He swung his axe, and his wolfhound emblem soon dripped with blood. However, his enemies abandoned both their weapons and their baggage, and Eunan was too tired to chase after them.

"Victory!" he cried as he raised his axe, inadvertently soaking himself in his enemies' blood at the same time. But there were none there to celebrate with him, for his compatriots had descended like crows upon the baggage train of their fled foes. They would feast heartily tonight.

13

Hunting for rabbits

When Eunan got back to the Maguire camp, it had erupted in celebrations. The Maguire sent messengers to all the clan leaders of the north, whether friend or foe, to tell the tale of the rebels enormous victory. It was bittersweet for Eunan. As much as he had taken part and slain a few of the enemy with his own hand, the O'Cassidys were a cowardly disgrace which, as their leader, he should take responsibility. However, Óisin embraced his glum shoulders and poured alcohol down his reluctant throat. Eunan soon felt the alcohol in his belly and caught the joy in the air, and soon, he too became a reveller.

He rose at midday the next day, shook off the pain in his head and searched the camp for O'Cassidys. He regretted not agreeing to a specific number of O'Cassidy boys he had to return before Cormac officially recognised him. In his immediate surroundings, he counted twenty. Most of them were hungover but bore no scars of battle, for they ran away the first chance they got. They surprised Eunan by having the gall to come back to the camp and not run straight home. He ordered them to stay put, for he would berate them later for their cowardice when he had gathered together as many as he could reasonably find.

Eunan searched the campfires of the officers and the nobles of the various clans, for there lay the best pickings for hungry boys. Every time he came across a renegade O'Cassidy, he redirected them back to the campsite. He finally came to Hugh Maguire's tent, where Hugh hosted the other leaders to plan the campaign. There he met an animated Donnacha O'Cassidy.

"Here's your war hero, lord, the captain whose men ran away!" exclaimed Donnacha.

"What am I supposed to do with a load of turncoat cowards? They were waiting to run since they arrived," roared Eunan.

"And this is the family you do so much to join."

"The sooner Hugh Maguire does away with that coward Cormac O'Cassidy and his crony Connor Roe, the sooner Fermanagh will be united against the Crown."

"Oh Donnacha, don't goad him so. You use up so much of your credibility defending that useless cousin of yours whose only interest is lining his pocket. We won the battle, and Eunan is no coward, as I have seen many times myself. If you continue this path of sowing seeds of discontent and ill will, I may have to go to the islands and find Desmond MacCabe," said Hugh Maguire, unwilling to have his mood deflated by such bickering.

"I apologise if I caused you any offence, lord. But I have to face my clan and explain how their boys died whilst running away," replied Donnacha.

"It's because their fathers train them to be rabbits!" exclaimed Eunan. "But they'll be better the next time we face the enemy."

"I expect it, Eunan. You can always go south and recruit your own men if you wish to give them a bit of spine. The men you and Seamus brought with you acquitted themselves well."

"The men of south Fermanagh will acquit themselves much better the next time, lord. You have my word."

Eunan bowed and left the tent. The next day, he rode south with Óisin.

* * *

In the meantime, William Russell arrived in Dublin and officially took up his new role as lord deputy. He was greeted by news of the defeat at the Ford of the Biscuits and was told of the army's subsequent retreat to Sligo. In addition, he was informed that Enniskillen had remained unsupplied. Russell contemplated his first move. As a distinguished veteran of the Dutch Revolt and having formerly served in Ireland earlier in his career, he quickly decided that the only way to end this revolt was to crush it and organised another relief force for Enniskillen.

A week later, Hugh O'Neill rode into Dublin and presented himself before Russell and pleaded for terms. The lord deputy granted an audience while continuing to organise a relief party for Enniskillen. Meanwhile, the lords of the north took advantage of the time generated by O'Neill's ploy and took in their harvests.

In launching an expedition to relieve Enniskillen, Russell took an alternative route. On the orders of O'Neill, the column met no resistance even though on their way to Enniskillen, none of their scouts ever returned. When Lord Deputy Russell arrived at Enniskillen, the rebel army melted away, and the O'Donnells and O'Neills retreated to their respective territories, and Hugh Maguire returned to the woods. Given the lack of opposition and the previous pleadings of O'Neill, Lord Deputy Russell considered the rebellion over. He left a garrison in Enniskillen and discharged some of his Irish soldiers. In return, O'Neill and O'Donnell agreed to a truce with the lord deputy and made a series of submissions to the Irish Council to negotiate a more permanent peace.

* * *

The clouds darkened, and the rain beat down upon Eunan's head. It had been a long time since he cast his shadow on the entrance to his old village. He had tried to avoid it as he rode around south Fermanagh for weeks, visiting every village and clutch of houses except for it. The inhabitants restored some fields, houses and fortifications, but it was a far cry from the once prosperous village Eunan remembered from his youth. The locals soon recognised him, and the women shied away and went to fetch the men from the fields. An older man, similar in age to what his father would be if he were still alive, approached him.

"What are you doing here? Surely your curse has done us enough damage and has moved off somewhere else?"

"Shall I remove his insolent head?" said Óisin as he squeezed the grip of his sword.

"No," Eunan sighed. "He was once a friend of my father. Do you speak for the village?" as he again addressed the man.

"They'll listen to me far quicker than you!"

"I am here on behalf of Hugh Maguire. I need able-bodied men willing to fight."

"You destroyed our village with your last plea for men. What makes you think that any'll volunteer for you now?"

"Just spread the word. I'll wait here for as long as it takes to get my answer."

"I'll ask, but don't wait too long."

Eunan went to the lake to water his horses. He left Óisin in charge as the horses drank and went to have a look around. The burnt-out remains of his parent's house were still there. Somehow, when he looked at it, the remains were distant, as if they didn't belong to him. He felt he was an evil and cursed cuckoo who landed in the nest to cast out all the other eggs and watch the children die as they splatted on the ground. His parents had taken him in, for they did not know what they were doing. The cuckoo destroyed everything.

The man from the village returned to end Eunan's daydreaming.

"We've got some recruits," said his father's former friend.

Around fifteen years of age, with rags on their back and sweat of the fields on their foreheads, two young boys smiled enthusiastically at Eunan.

"If that's it, they'll have to do. You can be horse boys until you learn how to fight. Now let us leave, for this place is bringing me down."

"Don't let me stop you," and the man from the village turned his back and walked away.

Eunan hung his head as they trotted out to the road to Derrylinn with their two recruits.

Eunan and Óisin called into other villages along the way, but he could only entice young, naïve boys, the likes of which rendered by his village, to heed the call of the Maguire. None of the villagers said a word to them. The villagers' faces said never to come back, but the weapons of Eunan and Óisin meant they were not brave enough to say it.

Whilst Eunan was recruiting in south Fermanagh news came that Connor Roe submitted to Hugh O'Neill. Upon hearing this, he almost fell off his horse, not knowing if he should be delighted that his nemesis had finally succumbed or to be angry that he was not there to avenge RÓisin. His men made merry that night even though such celebrations were frowned upon in the village because of their old allegiance to Connor Roe. Eunan fell into despair: how could rounding up ten farmers boys that would run the first time a gun was pointed at them be considered a success? Seamus wrung out of the same population ten passable Galloglass, the deaths of who their fellow soldiers would at least mourn, instead of cowards more passable as rabbits than men.

Óisin grabbed him for a drunken embrace.

"We can catch up with your girl, ya miserable wretch. But this time, we're not getting thrown out by her father!"

"He should be a bit more receptive this time now his protector is gone."

"I think he won't be able to deny you're an O'Cassidy anymore. Once we get some decent men and a few victories under our belts, he'll even have to let you marry his daughter!"

"Let's not get carried away with ourselves. He still has powerful friends."

"Nothing a little axe wouldn't fix. You've got to take what you want. You're Eunan Maguire!"

"You don't know who Eunan Maguire really is. No one does!"

"Stop being so miserable and just have a drink."

"Not tonight. Leave me to my thoughts this evening. Then we'll ride to Derrylinn with a clear head."

"You'll never have a clear head," and Óisin wandered back to the campfire.

How right Óisin was, for Eunan had not a wink of sleep, for during the breaks where he practised addressing Cormac O'Cassidy in his head, he figured out what to say to Caoimhe.

14

The tale of an axe

Nothing was right for Eunan Maguire that morning. His clothes stank; he was a failure as a son, warrior, and leader; and the stale bread was, well, stale. He bit into the heel of the bread and was overwhelmed by a feeling of protectiveness for his remaining teeth. The bread became fuel for the fire.

"Nervous, are you?" asked Óisin.

Eunan just snarled.

"You have the upper hand. Connor Roe will no longer protect him. If he resists, tell the Maguire. Then whatever he has denied you, we can come back and steal!"

Eunan glanced over at his farm boy recruits. For some, the glamour of going off to fight had not lasted but one night.

"What about them? If we take them with us, the O'Cassidy will smell weakness. If we leave them here, they will all have gone home within the hour. I can't go back to the Maguire empty-handed. His patience is far from endless."

"I could stay here? Can you face the wrath of your uncle with only your axe for company?"

Eunan sprung to his feet and grabbed his axe.

"Of course I am alright! How dare you suggest otherwise. Wait here. I will be back before nightfall."

Eunan untied his horse and mounted him.

"Good luck," said Óisin, and he waived to his friend.

"It is the O'Cassidy to who you should wish luck. Begin their training within this idle time you have been granted."

As Eunan rode away, the anger dissipated. But into the gap seeped fear.

* * *

The horse slowed to a trot, then a walk, and came to a stop outside the O'Cassidy house. The finest house in south Fermanagh, draped in autumnal reds and browns of the ivy that clung to the brickwork, and the leaves on the branches of the large oak trees were a picture of prosperity. But to Eunan, the house was a giant looming tombstone, protruding from the ground as if a festering sore blighting the landscape. Across this tombstone was emblazoned the names of his mother and father and all those who had died to maintain this illusion of prosperity. The fertile lands of Fermanagh demanded much blood.

As he rode up, the fields beside him were being harvested, and he could have sworn that he recognised some boys working there. But all that waited to greet him was the crevassed and worn face of his uncle's Galloglass constable.

"Did my master not tell you to stay away?" he said as he passed Eunan's horse along to the stable boy.

Eunan took a deep breath.

"No, he never said that to me. He said that if I protected the lives of his boy and the other O'Cassidy sons, he would declare to the world that I am an O'Cassidy."

"That is selective hearing, or dreaming, or both!"

Eunan employed selective hearing.

"I look forward to riding with you to join Hugh Maguire, for you can no longer hide behind Connor Roe."

"Your cockiness will be your downfall. But the time for jesting is over. Come inside. My master waits for you."

Even the corridors of the house closed in on Eunan as they led him to Cormac O'Cassidy. Each step forward, more leaden than the last. The fineries of the house glared at him to tell him he was an alien and did not belong. There was not even a smile from Caoimhe to provide a light amongst the claustrophobic gloom. She looked at the floor, not even acknowledging his entrance into the room.

There were papers strewn carelessly across the desk, pollution in the considered order of the room. Even the Galloglass guards had an angry twitch on their stony faces. Cormac leapt out of his chair upon sight of Eunan.

"I suppose you're here to gloat, are you, with the demise of my protector? Do you think the world will now fall to its knees before Hugh Maguire? The only unknown is how much destruction must befall Fermanagh before the Crown crushes your beloved leader. You foolish boy, coming here to destroy everything, chasing some dream of your mother that never existed. You want to become an O'Cassidy so much because you destroyed the O'Keenans and what you had. I don't think you know it, but your mother left here a disgrace and married beneath her. Having an offspring such as yourself is what she deserved for what she did."

"Don't you speak about my mother like that!" and Eunan went for his axe, only to be met with a bristle of sword points marking the distance between himself and Cormac.

The anger in Cormac juddered to a halt, for something had caught his eye.

"Bring me his axe. I wish to see it," he instructed.

The soldiers picked up on his curiosity.

Eunan gripped his axe and positioned to defend himself, noting where his adversaries stood. The fear fell away, for violence was more familiar to him. Cormac waived this adolescent defiance away.

"If I wanted you dead, I have more than enough coin to have it done long ago. Just hand over the axe."

The constable held out his hand, and Eunan paused and then gave him the axe, shaft first. He handed it to Cormac, who worked his finger through the joints and embellishments.

"This is fine workmanship. Where did you get it?"

"From your blacksmith."

"I'm glad to hear I'm getting my money's worth."

He flipped the axe and broke into a knowing smile.

"What's this emblem here, this wolfhound?"

"It was amongst my mother's belongings. I hoped you could tell me!"

Cormac laughed and handed the axe back to the constable.

"You are more of a sentimental fool than I thought, grasping at any object that may remind you of your mother with no idea of its true meaning. Maybe if I tell you what dream you are trying to reclaim, then I will be rid of you?"

The look of expectation that Eunan failed to suppress showed to Cormac he was on the right path.

"Constable, clear the room, disarm Eunan, and I will tell this sorry tale that will hopefully free us all from the chains of the past and me from the moping and whining of this boy."

The constable did as instructed, and Cormac sat down in his seat by the fireside.

"Sit, Eunan. Make yourself comfortable for your last time here."

"I'd rather stand," growled Eunan, who did not want to appear weak.

"So be it. Let us begin.

115

"My father, Domhnall O'Cassidy was an ambitious man who had his eye on becoming the Maguire himself, even though he was not from either of the main Maguire branches. The O'Cassidys were, and still are, a minor family of influence in the Maguire hierarchy. But he would not let his low rank constrain him.

"He had two children, Fiona and me. His brother had several children, and one such child, Donnacha, showed exceptional promise. My father used his influence to get Donnacha a posting and an education in the court of the Maguire in Enniskillen. The O'Cassidys were on the rise.

"When we reached our teenage years, it was time for our father to make his move. He used the influence he built up with the Maguire and arranged for Fiona to marry one of Turlough O'Neill's sons. It was a very important engagement that my father had to work hard to arrange and put up considerable sums of both coin and cattle, since words and deeds alone did not suffice. It would have been the making of the O'Cassidys in the court of the Maguire and the pinnacle of my father's life's work. However, she succumbed to 'love', and the object of her affections was none other than Teige O'Keenan, a young man in the employment of my father as a Galloglass and your father Cathal's brother. My father feared the cancellation of the wedding and that the scandal would be the permanent ruin of the O'Cassidys and the undoing of everything for which he had worked. However, he loved his daughter and trusted her to see reason, so he forbade Fiona from seeing Teige again. She had none of it, ignored my father's wishes, and continued her romantic liaisons in stables and amongst the shadows. Fiona denied having anything to do with Teige when confronted by her father. But when his minions felt both loyal and brave enough, they would whisper in his ear rumours of his daughter's continued dalliances. The day of the wedding came near, and my father was determined that his daughter should respect his wishes and do her duty for her clan. He sent some men to deal with Teige.

"Teige was a handsome young man with a silver tongue, an eye for pretty but naïve young ladies, and a life dedicated to being a fop. A believer of fate, a consumer of drink and a hopeless risk taker should also be added to the list of his character flaws. He also had a devoted younger brother of a firmer moral standing, potentially linked to not being blessed with his brother's looks, who clung to his every word. Cathal got wind of his brother's peril and went to warn him. Teige made his belief in love a servant to his belief in fate as he used to make his decisions by tossing a wolfhound emblem. The wolfhound meant that he would pursue passion; the harp on the back meant that he would flee and leave Fiona to her fate. On the toss of that emblem, the ambitions of the O'Cassidys died.

"Teige came back for Fiona and persuaded her to flee with him. They intended to make their way to Dublin port. Cathal was to go with them halfway and at that point they would split and Cathal would lead the pursuers in the wrong direction. However, they were caught before Cathal could execute his part of the plan by Maguire's men, who were sent to retrieve her. They captured him trying to buy horses. Though he initially escaped, his pursuers followed him back to where Teige and Fiona were hiding. Teige died in the ensuing sword fight. Cathal survived and was dragged back to Enniskillen with Fiona. Fiona was with child and miscarried in Enniskillen after the delegates from Turlough arrived. The O'Cassidys were disgraced, and Fiona was cast out of the family. Cathal Maguire agreed to marry her to save some face for both families. Nonetheless, I still believe it is because he thought he would never get a woman so beautiful as my sister, so he took advantage of her fallen state: either that or guilt, because he caused his brother's death.

"The opportunity for Domhnall was gone, and Donnacha was shunned for years and eventually clawed his way into his current position.

That emblem you have in your axe is the same one Teige O'Keenan tossed in the air to decide whether to run away and marry Fiona. His bad luck is now enshrined in your axe, bringing death and misfortune."

Cormac rose from his chair and moved in for the emotional kill.

"Now, let me be frank with you, for I do not want to either see you or to have this conversation again. Our boys were a disgrace in that battle, but your cause is as false as your dream about your mother and not worth dying for. The English will come and rattle our cages but will leave if you pay them their rent quick enough, and you do not have the misfortune of getting a corrupt and greedy sheriff. We told our boys to run, and they did. You got a few of them killed, which was not our arrangement, but I will overlook that to be rid of you. I grant you your wish. I recognise you as an O'Cassidy, the boy of my dead sister. You can use the O'Cassidy name if you wish, but I banish you from our lands and commanding our soldiers, be they boys or men. I place a bounty on your head of fifty cattle for any man that slays you on O'Cassidy land; however, out of respect for my dead sister, you have until sundown before the bounty takes effect. It has taken me most of my life to claw the O'Cassidys back into a position of influence, and all my good work will not be ruined by you. Now begone with you! Men, throw him out!"

Before Eunan could protest, he found his face in the dirt of the courtyard outside the house and his horse roaming freely, searching for the exit.

"Take your bad luck with you!" and the Galloglass constable threw the wolfhound axe onto the dirt after Eunan.

Eunan picked himself up, retrieved the axe, got his horse, and rode off without another word.

15

The Reunion

Hugh O'Neill used bribery as both a lever and lubricant to get what he wanted, and his consistent use of it through John Bath was one of his more masterful displays. Bath was a merchant who could get whatever you wanted in almost any quantity if you were willing to pay the right price. Smuggling was not beyond him. It was his speciality.

O'Neill's agents were regular visitors to his office in Dublin. Towards the end of 1594, they gave Bath a rather sizeable sum of money to buy as many guns and ammunition as possible for the northern rebels. He readily agreed and sent his agents across England, Scotland and the continent to arrange purchase and shipment.

O'Neill's agents waited and watched the coastlines of the north for either the ships of the Spanish or the vessels of John Bath. In the winter of 1594, only Bath's ships arrived, but O'Neill's money was well spent. O'Neill took the lion's share of the guns and ammunition, as it was through his connections the operation was organised. Besides, he had paid for most of it. Red Hugh took the next largest share, but because it was not equal to that of O'Neill, he took it as a slight against himself and the O'Donnells. He also saw it as a sign that

O'Neill considered him the junior partner. Hugh Maguire and the other lesser lords in the confederacy were grateful for what they got. The Spanish survivors from the Armada and the Irish veterans from the continental wars set about turning traditional Galloglass into modern pike and shot.

* * *

Rebellion stirred once more in Wicklow. There had been a continuous low level of aggression from Fiach MacHugh O'Byrne and his loose alliance of Irish Catholic clans ever since the end of the Desmond Rebellions. But in 1594, the violence escalated, and the lords of the Leinster alliance conscripted men to fight.

That winter Lord Deputy Russell was in a strategic bind. The increased tension in the island drained his resources, for he had to distribute a large part of his fighting men to garrison various parts of the country. This left him with near 1,100 men. Since he estimated that the lords of Ulster had about 5,000 men at their disposal, including what Scottish mercenaries they could raise, Russell could only contain an ever-escalating rebellion.

However, Lord Deputy Russell saw the threat of the loose Leinster alliance and decided it was time to take action. The rebels were numerically weaker than the lords of the north, which made his decision easier. Russell first served in Ireland in 1579 and spent several years fighting O'Byrne and the Wicklow rebels. Indeed, he had been rewarded with lands around Carlow, Kildare and Dublin for his excellent service. During his service it had been ingrained into him that to pacify Ireland you first needed to pacify Wicklow; then Leinster and the rest would follow. Indeed, when he served the Queen in her foreign wars, he wrote a treatise on the subject.

Lord Deputy Russell waited until early 1595 to strike. On the assertion that O'Byrne was assisting the rebels of the north, he marched into south Wicklow to drive O'Byrne out of his home in Ballinacor.

The perpetual rebels of Wicklow, led by O'Byrne, then entered a secret alliance with the northern rebels. They had acted as a distraction to the crown forces when otherwise they would have focused attention on the rebellion in the north. Russell had had enough and concentrated all his forces to destroy the Wicklow rebels. O'Byrne appealed to Hugh O'Neill for help.

* * *

In late 1594, rumours reached O'Neill that the Queen was about to send veterans from the Brittany campaign to Ireland, soldiers far superior to the recruits the Crown conscripted in the Pale. Emboldened by the receipt of his new cash of arms, the positive flow of assurances from Spain, and the offence he took at the unprovoked attack on O'Byrne, he decided it was time to join the rebellion. In February 1595, he ordered his men to attack the fort on the River Blackwater.

The fort was intended to temper the power of Turlough O'Neill in the 1570s and 1580s and stood on the river beneath Lough Neagh for nearly twenty years. It comprised two towers on either side of the Blackwater River; on the eastern side was a square fort made of earthworks and a wooden wall. In February 1595, there was a garrison of only fifty men, but it could accommodate two hundred in the housing facilities within the fort and double that for the housing surrounding the fort.

O'Neill had not turned his attentions to the fort since he viewed any attack would provoke a violent response from the lord deputy. But if O'Neill was to enter the war, the fort had to be taken as it was in the middle of the O'Neill lands and within striking distance of his capital, Dungannon. In previous years, he isolated the fort and made it hard for the garrison to gather provisions. However, if he was to escalate the rebellion and show his hand, the fort had to be taken.

Art MacBaron led the assault on the fort early in the morning of 16th February. Fifty men advanced under the pretence of taking two prisoners to the fort. The guards noticed the men were acting suspiciously and preparing their weapons for firing. In reaction, the garrison shut themselves into their towers. With the rebels showering them with a hail of fire, the garrison ran out of ammunition after several exchanges. Only when the threat of burning down the towers with the garrison still inside did they finally surrender. The O'Neills destroyed the Blackwater fort. Hugh O'Neill had joined the rebellion.

* * *

A week later, a party from the northern lords was intercepted by the Wicklow foothills. Upon being detained, their leader forcefully defended his perceived right of passage.

"I'm not an English spy. Hugh O'Neill and Hugh O'Donnell have sent me. I know Fiach MacHugh O'Byrne for a long time, right back to the days of the Desmond Rebellion. I've roamed these mountains many a time, being offered shelter by the O'Byrnes on each occasion. You tell Fiach that Seamus MacSheehy is here. Then you'll see!"

"Do you know how many traitors have tried that line with us?" said the leader of the O'Byrnes.

"Yes, but none of them was Seamus MacSheehy. Tell your master it is I. Then you'll see."

"Do you have anything to identify that Hugh O'Neill sent you?"

"I have a letter, but it is for Fiach's eyes only."

The man stuck his hand out to take the letter, but Seamus did not move.

"You'd have to kill me, but I wouldn't like to hand the letter to Fiach with bloodstains on if I was you. Be a good boy and go to your master to see what to do next."

The man went for his sword, and Seamus grinned. Another of the O'Byrnes placed his hand on the man's arm to stop him from drawing his sword. He glared at Seamus but went to confer with someone behind the trees who Seamus could not see. The man came back and nodded at the men surrounding the party from the north.

"You'll wait here under guard. We should soon receive back word if Fiach knows you. If he doesn't, we'll cut your throats."

"We'll make ourselves comfortable over here," said Seamus, pointing to a soft looking patch of grass beneath a large tree. I hope you're not going to get us to sit beside the graves of all those other Seamus MacSheehys you claimed you've had to kill?"

"You're very cocky for a man who's surrounded. Maybe we just might slit your throats before we find out who you are?"

"You could try to do that, but you would not like to put me to the embarrassment of having to explain to Fiach why I had to kill his men? Fiach and I are like this," and Seamus held up his crossed fingers for the man to see. "You'd better be hospitable to me, or else he'll cut your throat!"

The man considered going for his sword again, but he thought better of it and spat and cursed. The two parties agreed on an uneasy truce while waiting for confirmation that Seamus and Fiach were so close.

A day later, Seamus and his men were brought before Fiach in his well-defended hideout deep in the southern Wicklow mountains. Fiach had answered that he knew a Seamus MacSheehy but thought the one he knew was dead. He instructed them to bring the strangers and he would decide whether they lived or died.

* * *

Fiach warmed himself by a fire with his sons. It was cold in the Wicklow mountains, with only a brief respite from the sea breezes in the valleys or woods. One of the younger men threw another log on the fire to share the heat of the blaze with his brethren. They sat in a circle in the woods, unafraid of the light a fire may create, for no Englishman or Pale lackey would dare climb the mountain slopes to ambush them. These were their mountains, and the English knew it.

Fiach was a large man and required several blankets to keep the heat in his old bones and several bowls of stew to satisfy his hunger. But he was used to it. Ever since his earliest memories he had been a rebel in the mountains with sparse periods of truce where he could take up residence in his castle at Ballinacor. The warmth of his castle was a distant memory that evening. But laughed and drank with his sons until one of his captains came and interrupted him.

"Lord, the strangers that claim to be from the north, are here."

Fiach turned his full attention to him.

"Did they bring the letter from O'Neill?"

"We did not see evidence of such a letter, lord. They will only give it directly to you. One of them claims to know you."

"You did not see evidence of the letter? What if all they have for me is a dagger?"

The sons of Fiach rose as one at the mention of a dagger.

"Send them in. I will never know until I meet them."

They ushered the supposed emissaries from the north through the crowd. Fiach's sons placed their hands on their scabbards. But when Fiach saw the men enter, he leapt from his seat and cried out: "Seamus!"

He ran towards his old friend, nearly knocking Seamus over with the bulk of his body and the strength of his embrace.

"Seamus, my old friend! Where have you been all these years? I heard you were in the Netherlands leading the good fight there!"

Seamus could not help but smile as he looked at his friend after such a long time.

"The Netherlands has been and gone. I've been up north for years, finding myself some gainful employment. But I've come all this way to see the Wicklow bear!"

"Well, there's always been gainful employment and a welcome for you down here in Wicklow. Come meet the family and my men before we catch up properly."

Several young men stood up from around the fire and smiled at Seamus in respect for the esteem their father held him in. Fiach slapped the shoulders of the first, a young man in his mid-twenties, of stocky build and much experience, revealed by the grey hairs nestled in his beard.

"This is Turlough, my son and heir. Was he up to your knees when you last saw him?"

"It has been so long I can barely remember, but he certainly takes after his father now! Come here to me."

Seamus held out his arms, and Turlough readily accepted his embrace.

Two younger men, barely out of their teens, smiled behind their brother. Their boyish faces hid their years of experience of being mountain rebels.

"These are the two youngest, barely babes, when you last saw them?"

"The sorties of the English prevented me from getting to know them better the last time. Hopefully, I will make up for that this time," and Seamus hugged them as well.

"I don't want to bombard you with too many faces. You must be tired after your long journey."

However, another man wished to press his hand into those of

Seamus. He eagerly shook Seamus's hand.

"This is Walter Reagh Fitzgerald, a noted outlaw and scourge of the English," said Fiach.

"Good to know you," said Seamus. "We need all the good men we can get."

An eager youth came, stuck out his hand, and presented himself to Seamus.

"This is Uaithne O'More, son of Rory. We've brought him up as our own since his father died."

Seamus took the young man's hand.

"I knew your father well. He was a great warrior and rebel. If you are half the man your father was, the English'll be running back across the water in no time!"

Uaithne smiled, almost embarrassed at the mention of his father.

"He's run a very effective campaign in the province, burning the English lords and settlers alike out of their homes. A great man to have on your side," said Fiach as he slapped Uaithne on the back.

Seamus smiled at the young man, intrigued at how the life of this young rebel would play out. However, his eyes drifted to a woman who was smiling at him. Fiach invited her forward and wrapped his arm around her waist.

"Lest we forget, my dear Rose! My wife, my rock, she has been beside me all this time. Death or the weight of knives in my back would have taken me long ago if it was not for her."

Rose gave a knowing smile, for she remembered Seamus well.

"Hello, Seamus. Glad to see you are still alive."

Seamus bowed. "I'm all the better for seeing you, Rose. You're still way too good for this renegade!"

"Someone has to steer him back to the righteous path!" she laughed.

Fiach pointed to a prized place beside the fire, where the smoke rarely blew.

"Sit down and eat and tell me all about why you're here. We have so much to catch up on."

Seamus sat with his old friend, and as the fire burned and crackled, they exchanged stories starting from the time they last met, what had happened to them, and people they knew. But something was troubling him. In all his years as a Galloglass, he had learned to read a man or a room, and a fireside was no different. Fiach sat at the most prominent place, with Seamus beside him as his guest. Rose sat to the other side of Fiach, but beside her were her two sisters and their husbands, the younger sons of Fiach.

Rose O'Toole was Fiach's current wife, a woman he married when he needed to strike an alliance with the O'Tooles in 1573. However, she bore him no children. Fiach's heir was Turlough O'Byrne, Fiach's eldest son from his first wife, who he had divorced. Fiach had another two sons from his original marriage, which Rose arranged for them to marry her younger sisters. The O'Byrnes and the O'Tooles were constantly at odds with one another since the former was the rising power in Leinster. Seamus noticed the O'Byrnes sat with the O'Byrnes, and they looked to Turlough O'Byrne, while the O'Tooles sat with the O'Tooles and Rose and the other sons. Rose was determined that the husbands of her sisters would take over from Fiach when he died.

Fiach loved his wife dearly, and she was one of his most politically significant allies. However, he wanted to keep his family and the loose set of allegiances together while also maintaining his marriage. By his reckoning, as long as they all had a common enemy, the O'Byrnes would not implode.

On Seamus's other side were Turlough, Uaithne and other young men from various Leinster clans. The two sides barely mixed much beyond exchanging pleasantries. But Fiach was the glue that bound this fragile alliance together. Seamus had to find out how weak it was to see how much Red Hugh could rely on it.

He leaned over to whisper to his old friend.

"Why are we eating here in the mountains when we could gaze at the starry night in Glenmalure?"

Seamus hit a sore point as Fiach stared at the sky as if for motivation.

"Christmas had barely formed a memory when the lord deputy and his Dublin lackeys came upon me. It took little cattle and coin to turn the heads of some of my clan to turn and lead my enemies to me while I lay unsuspecting. They snook through the forests with their daggers drawn, but the good Lord wished to spare me to fight for him another day. By chance, a patrol heard a drum, hit a single time and probably an accident, and rushed to the castle to raise the alarm. I bless that drummer boy, but I am sure he now hangs from a tree. I had barely time to grab my weapons and some clothes before I was a destitute renegade stalking these here woods."

Seamus put his arm around his friend's shoulders.

"The lords of the north will support you. Red Hugh has sent me to repay you for your kindness in assisting in his escape from Dublin Castle. Here, take this letter. The two great Hughs of the north have signed it. Red Hugh told me they would support their great ally, but alas, I have not read the letter."

Fiach took the letter and broke the seal. He smiled at its contents.

"Ah, sure, what else could I have done? No point in dying a lonely old rebel up a mountain when there's so much chaos I can cause!"

Seamus laughed.

"That's the old Fiach I know! But we've got to be wily in our efforts and give the lords of the north time to consolidate their positions and contact the Spanish king. Once they are sufficiently in place, they can take the war to the English."

Heads turned at the mention of the Spanish. Seamus unknowingly had stepped onto contentious ground.

"You're not falling for that 'ol chestnut, are you? These days it's the Spanish king who will save us. Yesterday it was the Pope and the Spanish king, or was it the French, the Spanish or the Pope? Whatever it was, some powerful king from faraway was always going to come and save us and give us all our land and rights back. We've even had some Spanish emissaries here barely a year ago. Boy, they can make some lavish promises. I said I'd start digging them a graveyard by the sea, for that's as far as they'll get, and at least their souls will have a pleasant view as they float off to heaven. They didn't find that funny at all. A Spanish invasion! As if that's going to happen?" laughed Walter Reagh.

"We all know how your family has been burned out these last couple of years," replied Fiach. "But King Philip is a devout and righteous man. If he says he will do something, I believe he will do all in his powers to do it. Instead of drowning in our cynicism about what has not worked previously, we should offer a prayer so that God can help King Philip to help us in our time of need."

"We would if we could, but we're not all good devout Catholics, are we?" spat Turlough as he stared at the O'Toole sisters.

"Don't speak to my wife and your stepmother like that!" barked Fiach. "That's enough squabbling and cynicism for this evening. If you can't enjoy yourselves in peace, go back to your tents and sulk. We have a formidable foe to fight tomorrow, so don't waste this evening fighting with each other. Come on, Seamus, let's go."

Fiach picked up his drink and signalled to Seamus to come with him for a walk in the woods.

"They just don't want to listen to the shepherd," moaned Fiach as he strode quickly, trying to shake off his anger.

Seamus put his hand on his friend's shoulder.

"I know how difficult it is to deal with family, especially when they won't do what is good for them, even though it is standing in front of them. You've got to be strong."

"I'm getting too old to be strong all the time."

"You're not that old, well, not yet!"

"I am surrounded by headstrong, impetuous youth."

"Where do you think they got that from?"

They both laughed.

"Come on, it is time to go back now," said Fiach. "If I'm not there to break up the fight, Lord knows what will happen. They're all armed, you know!"

The two men laughed again and turned around and went back to the campfire. They returned to their seats by the fire, but most of the family members had left. Fiach held his head in his hand and his drink in the other.

"I can't trust anyone, not even my family. Traitors perpetually surround me."

Seamus slapped him on the back.

"I thought you'd be used to that now, being an Irish lord. Fight the English to the front and go home and get stabbed in the back by your brother."

"I like the way you can joke about such things!"

"How did you get to be so naïve as to pour your heart out to a Galloglass, the ultimate heartless prostitute lusting after gold, cattle, and war? We stand back and look to see who is offering the most money before we pick our side. But you've lasted this long and still have the charms of Rose to help you renew any frayed alliances. Your sons may argue between themselves but will fall into line once the English come."

"I'm sorry to burden your weary mind with my perpetual problems. I should try to be more cheerful considering I haven't seen you in such a long time."

"Well, try, try your best. Now have another drink. It's supposed to be a reunion!"

Fiach held out his empty cup, and a young boy charged with keeping cups full ran over and obliged him.

Seamus remembered he had brought ten men with him, including two of Shea Óg's lot, and wondered where they were. They must have disappeared when Seamus started talking to Fiach. After the mood grew brighter and he exchanged more stories and ale with Fiach, Seamus leaned in.

"I think I may have picked up a couple of spies on my way here. I need them dealt with quietly."

"Say no more. You point them out, and they'll disappear without even a hint of suspicion on you."

"You're a good friend, Fiach."

"They'll regret the day they ever set foot in Wicklow. We're well used to dealing with spies in these parts!" and Fiach winked. "Have another drink," and Fiach and Seamus slammed their mugs together.

* * *

Seamus awoke the next day, the night of re-acquaintance and celebration weighing heavily on his weary body, especially his head. He got out of his tent and walked out into the campsite. Fiach was in a fine mood and just as Seamus had remembered him. He may have been getting old, but he could still party as hard as any of his sons. He also kept his ability to fight off a hangover and still maintain a decent level of conversation. Fiach wrapped his hand around Seamus's shoulder.

"Look how we decorate our trees around here."

Seamus followed Fiach's finger to the trees that hung over the valley. Fiach did not lie: from the trees hung two of Seamus's former companions and two other men he did not know.

"There's a Wicklow welcome for traitors. I hope you're not offended, but they would have you decorating the streets of Dublin, and the Queen's coin would nestle warmly in their pockets."

The eight remaining men of Seamus's company looked on, furious and frightened, for they had not suspected their comrades were traitors and supposed they could have been randomly singled out and hung. Seamus nodded reassuringly at them and beckoned them to stand down.

"I trust your nose for sniffing out traitors, and had suspected these men myself," said Seamus to Fiach in front of his men. "My men and I are in your hands, and, as emissaries for Hugh O'Donnell, we have faith that you will treat us well."

"As long as you serve the Confederacy and not the Crown, you are welcome guests here in Wicklow."

The tension was then diverted elsewhere.

"Lord, lord, Russell burns the O'Toole land to the north!" cried a boy as he ran towards Fiach.

"Catch your breath, boy, and give me the news," demanded Fiach.

"The English beast, Lord Russell, gave the O'Tooles an ultimatum. Swear loyalty to the Crown or burn. Half their lands burn, and the people are taking to the hills!"

"Damn him!" said Fiach.

The news attracted other members of the family and leaders of the group.

"We must save the other O'Tooles," exclaimed Phelim O'Byrne.

"We must hit the bastards back hard, where it hurts," exclaimed Walter Reagh as he punched the air to vent his frustration.

"Nobody hits anyone without my express permission," shouted Fiach. "Phelim, organise a band of men and go to the foothills and see that all the O'Tooles you can find are led to safety until the English go. Turlough, take some men and find out the plans of the English. I have some things to discuss with my old friend, and I do not want to be disturbed."

Fiach signalled to Seamus, and they sat by the embers of one of the previous night's fires. The conversation soon turned to the strategic situation. Fiach took a stick and drew a crude map of Wicklow in the dirt. He explained he was isolated in the Wicklow mountains with a loose alliance with the O'Tooles, Kavanaghs and O'Mores. These families were themselves splintered in their allegiances to the O'Byrnes and the Crown. Munster and other harbours of rebellion had long since been pacified in the Desmond Rebellions. Fiach's head sank.

"I fear I'm trapped up here, waiting to be hunted and killed like some hated fox that raided the chicken coup."

"Don't worry, my friend," and Seamus slapped him on the back. "I am here with the authority of the northern lords to strike a bargain."

"I am grateful that they consider that a man in my position still has something to offer."

"Red Hugh is forever in your debt for assisting his escape. However, nothing in this life is for free."

"Tell me, what do I have that is of value to exchange?"

Seamus leant in to whisper to Fiach, but Redmond O'Byrne wrenched them from their scheming.

"Walter is gone! Walter is gone! He's taken twenty men and horses with him."

An inflamed Fiach flew to his feet.

"What do you mean, he's gone? Where? To do what?"

"He said he was going to get revenge on the English for raiding the O'Byrnes!"

Fiach spat and cursed. Seamus tried to calm him down.

"You would have done the same in your youth."

"I am no sorry youth anymore! Do these fools not learn?" howled Fiach.

"Where has he gone?" Seamus asked Redmond. "Was he drunk? Will he just saunter back here in a couple of days when he's found some more ale?"

"Do you remember when I was telling you about hotheads that take after me?" interjected Fiach.

"Yes?"

"It's not always hereditary!

16

The Bargain

Paranoia possessed many a renegade who had taken to the hills in hiding, and Fiach MacHugh O'Byrne was no exception. He feared that Walter Reagh's foolishness would see him captured, and as Walter bargained for his life, he would exchange it for those of his former comrades even Fiach's head. It was a typical end for most of Leinster's would-be rebels, a tantrum rebellion, and they would pass the hangman's rope along to his former friends for a small grant of land as a tenanted farmer under an English lord. Fiach realised that his own head in a noose or at the end of a pike would buy much forgiveness and a rich settlement for anyone who wished to cash in their friendship. Therefore, he sought the safety of the hills.

Seamus joined Fiach and his men as they retreated to the heights of the Wicklow hills, for he had yet to complete the mission assigned to him by his master. They made their way to one of the many abandoned camps the O'Byrnes had dotted around the hills. There was food aplenty, and once they set up their campsite, the men dug up old weaponry they buried for such occasions. They presented the treasure to Fiach, who unwrapped the bundles with the glee of a child at Christmas.

"You'll find many a relic from the glorious battle of Glenmalure around these mountains, for we killed so many English as to keep us in arms for life," bragged Fiach.

"Unfortunately, old weapons," said Seamus as he tried to let his friend down gently. "More use for sentimental remembrance than an instrument of death. Those guns look like they'd kill the shooter far quicker than any Englishman."

"Well, that's why you're here, my good friend," and Fiach smiled at Seamus. "I've got to fight to be a reasonable ally."

Fiach distributed the weapons to the refugees that fled the onslaught of the English in the foothills. His general whereabouts were well known, so many an unarmed man seeking revenge for his losses would climb the hills and declare his allegiance to any band of armed men that accosted him in the hope they would spare his life and take them in. Fiach also organised the camp, established patrols in the mountains, and sent out messengers and spies to gather information.

A day of planning began, and Seamus shared an evening meal with Fiach and his sons. He sat back and observed the conversations, and asked pertinent questions. He established Fiach had about one hundred trustworthy men that were proficient with axe, bow and sword, and, depending on which part of the Wicklow mountains he was in, a variable number of outlaws, potential turncoats and farm labourers that could pelt the English with a hail of missiles. Fiach could organise successful ambushes in terrain he was familiar with, raid English land, but did not possess the strength to face the English out in the open. The fighting capacity of the O'Byrnes had considerably diminished since Seamus was last with them. He could see that his friend was potentially in trouble, and the lords of the north would have to prop up their ally considerably until he could renew the Leinster alliances of old and become a force again in the rebel Confederacy. Fiach's real value was how many English soldiers he could occupy as they tried to hunt him down. However, Seamus's masters had demands of their own, and nothing was for free.

It was time to talk business, yet he did not want to embarrass his old friend and make him feel like he was being used. He would have to guard his thoughts and release his words with consideration, not always a strength he could rely upon. Seamus raised the subject of their potential bargain, and Fiach was eager, so the Wicklow native sent his sons away so he could talk with Seamus in private.

"Fiach, I'll have to make my way back north soon, and yet we must make a bargain for the northern lords. They wish to create a haven in the Wicklow mountains for veterans from the continent landing in the south and then establish a safe route to the north. However, these veterans will be in demand among their own clans, and I am conscious of your need for seasoned men to assist you. The northern lords plan to sweep south when the Spanish king arrives. How many men do you need for your resistance to remain viable?"

"Two hundred could tie down double or triple that number of English soldiers that would otherwise head north, but, I'll know as soon as I get Ballinacor back. My castle will need a garrison, but that pig-headed son-in-law of mine who took twenty of my men is a blow. I'll wait to see if he brings them back, or I find they're all decorating trees. My boys Turlough and Phelim have a bit more sense."

"I'm glad to hear it. However, you may need to survive here relatively unaided for a couple of years because the northern lords are waiting for the Spanish king's army. Our archbishops plead with him for aid whenever the opportunity presents itself, but the war with England and the Dutch Revolt otherwise distracted him. When they come, I don't think the king will land anywhere near Wicklow, so you'll have to survive until the rebels from the north can come down and relieve the pressure from you. In exchange, the northern lords promise weapons, men and strategic coordination."

New hope swelled in Fiach at the sound of these promises made by a trusted friend. Few modern weapons had made their way to the mountain rebels, except those captured from dead English foes. With help, he could rejuvenate his alliances.

"I'll gladly take their weapons and whatever veterans they can spare if all I have to do is happily nod along with their plan."

"That's the spirit. You can join the nodding donkeys of the minor lords in the courts of the O'Donnells and O'Neills!"

"I prefer to be compared to a bear, or like my name, a raven!"

"As long as it's not a hedgehog with a spike through your head."

"You haven't lost your sense of humour. When do you have to return up north?"

"I only have a couple of weeks here, depending on what happens. Young Red Hugh has big plans to take the fight to the English and restore the O'Donnells to their former glories."

"There's a recipe for an early grave!"

"We were young and foolish once. You got wise though and left the foolishness to the young!"

"They are so much better at it than me. It takes up so much energy having to work back from your mistakes."

"Speaking of mistakes, what happened to that son-in-law of yours?"

"My men have gone to the Pale to find out. That is the easiest place to go when seeking revenge. Let's see what the foolish boy does. But never mind that. Let us seal our bargain."

They shook hands and made the deal. Fiach poured the drinks and raised his cup to toast their bargain, only to be rudely interrupted by Fiach's son, Redmond.

"Father, Turlough has left and joined Walter Reagh."

"I take back what I said about my sons being sensible," said Fiach to Seamus.

* * *

Time passed slowly in the camp as they waited for news of Walter and Turlough. It took several days to travel the relatively short distance from the Pale, for the spies had to evade the patrols in the Wicklow mountains and the Pale. Two made it back and were sent straight to their master.

Fiach sat outside his tent, honing tree branches into spikes for the various mantraps they set in the hills. Seamus busied himself with Phelim, mapping out the local hills to select the best places for their traps and potential ambush spots.

"Fiach, the men have returned from the Pale," said a trusted lieutenant who escorted the spies to the hilltops from the valley below. "They have news!"

Fiach feared they would tell him his firstborn was dead. But as leader of the clan, he had to put on a brave face.

"Well, speak! If you have valuable news, the sooner you tell, the sooner I act!"

"Walter Reagh and his men set fire to Crumlin in revenge for Ballinacor falling into the English's foul hands. The lord deputy released the calvary after them, but Walter escaped to the Wicklow foothills and has not been seen since."

Fiach gripped the insides of his eyes and the side of his nose with his thumb and index finger.

"Bloody fool! He'll bring the might of the English army down upon us, and we have but eighty fighting men."

"What of my son Turlough?"

"He is with Walter."

"Shall we search for them?" asked Phelim.

"If we shelter Walter, then we become targets," said Uaithne, who had come when he heard the spies had returned.

"We are targets anyway, but at least with us hiding in the hills, they may have given up," replied Fiach. "Now he has humiliated them. The new lord deputy has to put on a show of force for the Queen and the Pale. They will hunt Walter and Turlough down until they find them or kill all of us. We need to hide, and if they come, they come. We don't look for them. Have you got that?"

"Yes, lord."

Seamus looked at the spies. He recognised one of them but could not tell from where. The man did not show that he knew him, so Seamus stayed silent. Later that night, as Seamus closed his eyes to sleep, it suddenly came back to him. He had to speak to that man as soon as it was light.

17

The Spy

Seamus could barely sleep, for he needed to find the man he recognised. He dragged himself from his tent at first light and searched the camp and surrounding hillside. He soon found the tent. As Seamus stood over the spy's empty tent, he was approached from behind. A broken twig gave away the man and his intent.

"I'd be careful what you do with that knife," said Seamus as the spy tried to hide the weapon behind his thigh. "You'd be surprised at how quickly I could disarm you, and your knife would then stick out of your neck. But I recognise you. You served in the Low Countries. It seemed you had reached a new low once you came back to the mother country."

"Captain Williamson wants to see you. He warned me that his men have a habit of quickly ending up dead when they meet you. It's like you don't give a damn about your wife and your men's families."

Seamus held himself back from going for the man.

"What do you know about the whereabouts of my wife?"

"As I said, Captain Williamson wants to see you. He is in the comfort of the Pale where you must go."

"If he wants me to go to the Pale, why don't you just get it over with and just kill me now?"

"He wants Hugh Boye far more than he wants you! Now think of an excuse to go to the Pale, for we'll never evade the patrols of Fiach in his mountains. Once you have an excuse, volunteer me to go as your guide."

Seamus thought about it for a second but then considered that he had not much of a choice to make if he wanted to see his wife again

"What's your name, traitor?"

"Art O'Toole."

* * *

News reached Fiach that the English had cleared forests around Ballinacor to create a fort that would garrison and control the valleys of Wicklow. Furious, he brought Seamus and his two younger sons to spy on the English. They took up their positions in the mountains above Glenmalure.

"How can they defile my home!" Fiach growled. "They are making themselves a fort to control my beautiful valley. The good men who died in the great Battle of Glenmalure will roll over in their graves to see our lands desecrated."

"We've got to entice them out and ambush them in another valley, father," said Redmond. "Then we can drive them out of Wicklow for good!"

"We can but try, but I fear they have too many men."

Fiach returned to his camp, and that night sent a supposed traitor back to Glenmalure, claiming to know where Fiach and his sons were camped and how they could be taken by surprise.

* * *

News came that Lord Deputy Russell had moved out from his camp in the foothills of the Wicklow mountains, and was making his way south, spreading his men over a broad front to flush Fiach out. Fiach had spent most of his life as a rebel of the mountains, so this approach was nothing new. He went to get Seamus, who was sitting beside a fire talking to Phelim.

"Come on, Seamus, let's go. The English are coming. We need to find a suitable spot to ambush them. Anyway, we've got two spies to leave out for them as well," and Fiach winked at Seamus.

Seamus was keen to make plans to return north, for he was tired of living life on the run.

"Can you introduce me to any veterans you have here that I've not previously met?"

"What? And have you steal all my best men? You northerners have a cheek coming down here and asking for that."

"I'm no northerner, as you well know! The alliance is made because we share men and resources and allocate them to where they will do the most damage to our common enemy."

"Ah, friend, I'm only pulling your leg. You can save your speeches for your recruitment drive. We need to go. You can meet them all at the next camp. We certainly have had a few arrivals, mainly heading for the Pale. A few stories from us telling them they'd more than likely be hung then embraced, and they soon took to life in the mountains!"

Seamus packed his things and joined the march to the next camp. Fiach invited him to join himself and his sons at the head of the column. They reached the top of the mountain, and Fiach pointed down the valley from where they had just marched.

"What do you see?"

Seamus tried to pick something out from the beauty of the forests amongst the rolling valleys or the pronounced tops of the mountains with granite sprinkles on top.

"Is that Dublin in the distance?"

"Your eyesight can't be that good! No, look at the clouds of dust. That's the English army marching to their doom. See over there? Those little specks by the mountains? That is their spies showing them the way," Fiach laughed and slapped Seamus on the shoulder. "Just like the good ol' days!"

* * *

They walked for the rest of the day across valleys and mountains, penetrating deeper and deeper into Wicklow. The more they advanced, the further away the English were. The O'Byrnes seemed oddly jovial about their newfound predicament. It was as if the English army chasing after them had renewed their self-importance and pride again. Fiach seemed especially delighted.

"Come on! Hurry up, Seamus! I roam these valleys planning the perfect ambush, and they keep falling into them! Such glee! I have to teach my sons every inch of the mountains before the Lord takes me away from them."

"With all that you've seen, I surprised that more butchery would captivate you so."

"Was I born a butcher or butchery imposed on me?" Fiach laughed and extended his arms, showing his colossal bulk. "What is an old rebel like me supposed to do? They'll get me in the end, but not before I've taken way more than my fair share of them! Come on, Seamus, surely you feel the same?"

"I'm old and would have left this life behind long ago if it would let me. Let us set this trap and hope to be left alone. Then I can get down to my proper business."

"Mark my words Seamus. The real action will start in a couple of days!"

"I was to remind you that the northern lords would support you and raid from the north."

Fiach laughed.

"Even better! We can stab them in the back as they run back to Dublin! Such glee!"

"I'm glad you still find the slaughter of battle so exhilarating."

"It breathes life into these old bones. Come on, let's go set this trap."

They made double quick time to the next valley, pitched their tents, and waited for the dawn to come.

* * *

The next day, Lord Deputy Russell made his way along the narrow paths of the Wicklow valleys. The spies he captured told him where Fiach would hide, and he was eager to engage. Marching into the valley, Fiach watched on from the hilltops and laughed.

"You don't know how many times I've looked along this valley and wished for the day that I could pull off an ambush."

Seamus laughed back.

"They'd run out of men long before you could pull off all your planned ambushes!"

"Well, they should be in place for our attack in about an hour. My sons have already taken the liberty to cross over to the other side of the valley to assume their positions. Since you've come all this way to take my veterans, you may as well make yourself familiar with them now. Come this way."

Fiach led Seamus through the forest trails and over to the next hill. He took the opportunity of every break in the tree cover to glance over to the valley floor to ensure the English were advancing to where he wanted them. Seamus examined the English soldiers as they poured into the valley.

"Fiach! Fiach!" he hissed towards a nearby group of trees.

Fiach scowled as he stuck his head around the trees. He waved Seamus over.

"What's so important that you'd risk giving us away?" Fiach said when Seamus crouched down beside him.

"They're not your normal layabouts from the Pale," and Seamus pointed to the flags and uniforms of the troops. "They're the Brittany veterans that Hugh O'Neill's spies picked up that were supposed to be coming over. We're no match for them!"

"Speak for yourself. I never took you as a coward!"

"And I never took you as being a fool! They have at least two hundred men, proper English soldiers. We have only eighty. Let us call off the attack and disappear into the mountains. There'll be no victory for us here today."

"This is a beautifully prepared ambush. They have fallen almost exactly into our trap!" howled Fiach.

"Then I suggest that if we hit them, we do it fast, give them a fright and then melt away."

Fiach slammed the tree he hid behind in frustration, for he knew Seamus was right.

"Ok. We attack and then disappear."

Fiach signalled to his men, who made bird calls that rung around the valley. He raised his arm, and they slammed a volley of arrows into the English ranks in the valley below. They quickly reloaded and let loose another volley. However, the English ranks did not break, nor did they retreat. Their shot formed skirmish lines and returned fire. Most of the bullets lodged in trees but were effective enough to drive the rebels out of range with their bows. Seamus ducked behind a tree.

"This is pointless. We should retreat. The only way we are going to land a blow is to charge them. But if we do that, we'd probably lose most of the men."

Fiach grimaced at the thought of defeat. But he knew Seamus was right.

"Retreat!" he called, and his call was echoed by the similar calls of others through the valley.

The rebels fled back into the forest.

* * *

Despair scratched away at the soul of Fiach as he was hunted throughout the Wicklow mountains by a determined enemy. He could not risk an engagement, for he did not feel that the critical mass of men needed to sustain him would survive. Seamus realised they were in danger as long as Art O'Toole stayed with them, and he needed to meet Captain Williamson in the Pale. He went to speak to Fiach.

Fiach was busy dictating letters to fallen lords of Munster, trying to temp them back into the fray and into an alliance with him. His previous letters had failed to find a receptive audience. He turned when he saw his old friend approaching.

"Have you heard anything from the lords of the north? Have they struck at the Pale yet? Are reinforcements coming?"

"I have had some news from the north. Hugh O'Neill attempts to negotiate for time, and he made submissions on your behalf. His allies carry out raids, but they are more of a threat of force than any attempt to engage the Crown's soldiers. It is best that you cling on, for the pressure will build on the lord deputy to stop chasing you around the mountains and subdue the north instead."

"If only I had the strength to hold on. I am old. Too old to be shivering in the hills when I could be in my warm home of Ballinacor."

"They are not the words of my friend. You grow tired. We should talk when your spirits have returned."

"You came to me, and you usually only try when you have something to say. What is your plan?"

"I hear veterans are hiding in the Pale, for they do not know how to make the journey north and evade the English soldiers. They also claim to know English spies that have entangled themselves amongst the rebels. I want to go to the Pale and assist them."

"If that is your mission given by Red Hugh, then you must fulfil it. Take some men who can get you into the Pale and return with good news."

"I will, my friend, I will."

18

Back on the island

Eunan rode back to where Óisin and the raw recruits were camped. He leapt off his horse before it had even come to a halt. Óisin saw his urgency and went to see what was wrong.

"What did your uncle say? I have news…"

But Eunan brushed straight past him, threw his axe on the ground, and dived into the tent he shared with Óisin and some of the men. There he slept until morning, except for occasionally getting up to relieve himself. No one dared climb into the tent to disturb him. Óisin resigned himself to sleeping under the stars.

The next day, Eunan emerged and started hunting around the makeshift camp for food. He thought he remembered a hunk of stale bread in some bag he put somewhere. Óisin noted he was now awake and appeared in a slightly better mood than the night before. It looked like he could approach.

"Hey, you look as bad as I slept. Did things not go well?"

Eunan looked around the camp and noticed the distinct absence of most of their recent recruits.

"How well did it go for you?" he said with a contemptuous glance.

"Well, a few of them returned home to their mothers. At least it will save us from burying them after their first taste of action," replied Óisin, trying to inject some humour into the conversation.

"Take them north to meet up with the Maguire. I have private business to attend to," said Eunan, his face a slab of granite as he continued to search for the elusive bag.

"Do you want me to come with you?"

"No. I have to do this alone. Is there any food left?"

"No, that's what I meant to tell you. Whatever food remained was stolen by deserters."

"Damn them, damn the O'Cassidys and damn this blessed ground." Eunan went to his tent and retrieved his axe. He turned to Óisin.

"I'll be back. I don't know when, but I'll be back. Have some men waiting for me in the camp of the Maguire when I return. All I have left is the goodwill of the Maguire, and I don't want to let him down."

"I will do my best, but when will you return?"

Eunan had already turned his back to him and mounted his horse. He was soon dust in the distance.

* * *

After a long ride, Eunan arrived at Lower Lough Erne and went about hiring a boat. It did not take long for him to find a ferryman among the houses dotted along the shoreline.

"Leave the horse tied up there," said the ferryman, pointing to some fencing by his house with a healthy selection of grass alongside. "I'll look after him while you are on the lake. Where would you like to go?"

Eunan sat at the back of the boat and could not answer. He looked at the axe head and the wolfhound emblem that was a sign of the O'Cassidys.

"The wolfhound for Desmond and the blank side for the priests. Here

goes nothing!" and he spun the shaft of the axe in his hands and let it fall.

The toe of the bit of the axe lodged itself in the boat's floor.

"Mind my damn boat!" the boatman cried.

"It'll all be included in your coin!" and Eunan dismissed him with a wave of his hand and returned his attention to the fallen axe.

"Well, I never would have counted for that result!"

The sun caught the eye of the wolfhound on the axe shoulder, and the resulting glint momentarily blinded Eunan.

"I suppose the wolfhound calls it! Boatman! Go to the right of Devenish Island and head for the islands on the north side of the lough. I'll give you more directions when we get there."

"Right it is!"

Eunan sat back and relaxed somewhat for the first time on his journey.

* * *

He felt weak as he was rowed back towards Desmond. The physical resulted from him crossing Fermanagh so many times for the Maguire. But duty had its burdens. Eunan dipped his hand in the water and let it wash over his wrist. His mind drifted with the water and he thought that life was simple when he was a boy and lived by the lake and yearned for those times once again. However, selective memory was not one of Eunan's mental strengths. The demons of his fathers soon subsumed the dotted islands of mental sanctuary in the supposed simplicity of his youth.

Several voices in his head pecked away at him with relentless negativity. A warrior like him should not have to go back to his teacher every time he ran into trouble. He should be able to deal with the O'Cassidys himself and take back his mother's legacy. Why does

151

Seamus have to bail him out of everything? He was no better than either of his fathers and a lost cause like both. But the closer he got to the island, the more he spiralled down. Feeling for his axe, he stroked the haft and was reassured.

"It's the island over there on the right, towards the centre of the lough," Eunan told the boatman.

They got near the island and veered to the right by the cove where Desmond lived. Arthur stood on the rocks and watched the boat pull in. He looked delighted to see Eunan and called to the house for Desmond. Desmond hobbled out, stopped to make sure it was Eunan, and hurried down to the shoreline.

"Not dead yet?" asked Desmond, as he held out his hand to haul Eunan ashore.

"All their arrows and bullets bounced off my thick head!"

"That'd be right! Are you hungry?"

"Famished!"

"Lucky we got Arthur then, isn't it!"

Eunan gave the boatman his coin and said he would return to collect his horse in a couple of days. Desmond invited Arthur to take Eunan's bag.

"How long are you staying?" asked Desmond.

"Until I am rested in body and in mind," came the reply.

"That's nice," said Desmond. "At least we have the pleasure of your company for a few days."

"And I, the wisdom of yours!"

"Oh, it's like that, is it? I'd better get Arthur to fetch a good supply of ale."

Desmond led Eunan to the house, little changed from his last visit, and they sat outside on their wood stump chairs and rested their drinks on the large wooden table. It was just like old times. Eunan let out a sigh, as if lava escaping the confines of a volcano, and some of his tension was finally released.

"That bad is it?"

"Worse!"

Arthur brought out the food, the best meal he could prepare with the resources he had. Eunan beamed in gratitude.

"I have not seen such a meal since I saw Cormac O'Cassidy feasting before me on one of my previous visits."

"So he didn't invite you to eat?" asked Desmond. "Going well, is it?"

"I fear I have stumbled into the unknown. There is some story between my uncle and my mother that he dangles over me, but I have only heard his side and cannot untangle fact from fiction. He said he would recognise me as an O'Cassidy as long as I never darkened his door again. He has no loyalty to the Maguire, only sending him cowardly boys that run away whenever a musket is pointed at them. Donnacha is the same slimy beast as before. My cousin is a spoiled, useless coward."

"Well, you didn't think they were going to invite you in for a feast and give you the keys to their house when you showed up, did you?"

Eunan's face sagged like a pathetic dog.

"Oh, you did."

Desmond pushed his empty plate away and sat back on his stool.

"There are so many things in there that it is hard for me to talk about in the one conversation. Ireland has always been an unruly state under the English. The two kingdoms cannot not and will never live in harmony. There's always an unhappy warlord somewhere going into rebellion, and the English have to weigh up which is the best solution: to kill or to bribe. Alternatively, some English gent on the make with no morals and no thought for the native Irish is always on hand.

"I have observed the politics in the north for most of my life. I was lucky enough to exert some influence, even if most of the time it was merely an illusion to flatter my ego into thinking I was important. Most other lords see it in the same way. This is some petty rebellion that when the English work out the Maguire's price, the Maguire will fold. It explains why the O'Cassidys do not want to commit themselves. If they commit themselves to either, they risk being on the losing side, losing their lands, or even their lives. They see you as a young upstart, a foolish trouble maker who will throw away everything they have built for the sake of some story you can tell your ego. That is why they reject you. They hide the story of your mother for fear of the damage it could do them.

"Forget the O'Cassidys. Build your own following, recruit your own men, hire your own Galloglass. In Ireland, might is power. Heed my words, but first, we drink, and we'll return to these subjects over the coming days. Arthur! Bring some more ale! We are dying of thirst out here!"

Eunan hanged his head but held forth his mug.

"Nobody said it was going to be easy nor if you would even win," said Desmond. "But you should do what you feel is right. If you roll over to the English, you'll end up working on some farm, and you'll be fortunate if it is your own."

"To the point, no matter my feelings as always."

"Now is no time for feelings. It is a time for common sense and pragmatism. You must look at your actions and say to yourself: how will this propel me forward? How will this help me in the long run? Where do I need to position myself? Who are my enemies? What are their weaknesses? What is the path to victory?"

Eunan yawned.

"You make it sound all so easy."

"It will make more sense when you are rested and have a more positive frame of mind. Get some rest, and we shall talk in the morning."

Eunan put his mug down and held his head in his hands.

"You are right, as usual. Things will look better in the morning. I must remind myself of the low point the Maguire found himself in on Devenish Island and where he is now: in command of an army and besieging Enniskillen. I will leave you now and not dwell on my follies."

He placed his mug on the table, got up, and left while Desmond remained and poured himself another ale.

* * *

Eunan got up the next day to find that Desmond was already waiting outside for him.

"Come on then. Show me what you've got," and Desmond threw Eunan an axe.

"Hey! I've just woken up, and you're an old man!"

"I used to lead the Maguire MacCabe Galloglass if I haven't told you a thousand times already."

"I've just got up."

"Nobody is going to wait for you to get ready. Look!" and Desmond brought his axe to hover just above Eunan's head.

"Look, you're dead, and I didn't even have to try!"

"I'm in no mood for this. I came here to talk, not play rebels and the English with you."

Desmond threw his axe aside.

"Ok then, let's sit beside the lough and talk. We've got to get you ready, or else your war might decide to run away from you."

Eunan glared at him but went and sat on the stumps beside the lough. Desmond joined him.

"So, how do we get you out of this pit of despair?"

Eunan sighed and looked to the heavens.

"I feel like a pawn in some giant cosmic game. I just get moved around by God or whoever sets me up for more pain as some kind of joke. The tale of my mother has ripped away my soul, and my yearn to fight. I fear the Maguire will be both defeated and humiliated, and we will end up under the yoke of the English. All of this is just for nothing. Why should I even try?" and Eunan took out one of his throwing axes from his belt and threw it at the nearest tree.

His frustration did not follow the flight of the axe but festered within him.

"You are in a pit, aren't you?" and Desmond tried to reassure him by placing his hand on his back. Eunan felt the warmth and was comforted by the affection.

"If I take action, I fear my bad blood will overcome me."

Desmond was incensed.

"Now that is enough with that nonsense. What kind of self-respecting priest would fill your head with such tripe? I know you've had a lot to overcome, but look what you've achieved? You have the ear of the Maguire. You're on the cusp of potentially the most significant rebellion in God knows how long. You just had a glorious victory over the English, and the uprising gains recruits every day. The Maguire may even get himself into a position where he could dictate some terms!

"You dwell too much on the past, and it keeps you a prisoner in your mind. All the people you obsess about are dead, except Seamus. Your village is burnt to the ground, and you have distant relatives that want nothing to do with you.

"But war brings destruction and change. You need to set yourself up as being the beneficiary of this change. By being at the Maguire's side, you do just that; getting your own band of warriors and Galloglass, you do just that. But coming here sulking and crying, you destroy everything you work for. You've got to be patient and pragmatic. The time will come when you can smash the O'Cassidys, but you have to take your opportunities. Instead of obsessing about Seamus, use his cunning to advance your own agenda. If you find yourself in a situation, ask yourself, 'what would Seamus do?'"

Eunan looked down at the waves lapping in upon the shore.

"Oh, I know Desmond. You are so right. That's why I came. I am weak. Why do I need to come back and seek such reassurances from you?"

Desmond squeezed his hand into a fist.

"You may be weak, but you can change. Learn from the past. Become the warrior I know you can be! Become the warrior the Maguires need! Become the lord of south Fermanagh! You can do it. I have faith in you!"

Eunan lifted his head and saw the resolution in Desmond's eyes.

"Are you feeling brave enough to attack me with the axe again?"

* * *

Two months later, Eunan packed his things again. He placed his bags out in front of the house and joined Desmond for one last home-cooked meal. Arthur brought out the food that he had spent several hours preparing. He went to the mainland to hunt rabbits, especially for this meal. Both Desmond and Eunan vocally appreciated his efforts, but the meal was over, and it was time to go.

"Are you going permanently this time?" asked Desmond, with a hint of mischief.

"You stayed long enough this time. You may be lucky to have my presence on your little island once more!"

Eunan smiled as he squeezed the victuals given to him by Arthur into his bag.

"Don't forget all your little axes. You should have plenty of people to throw them at when you get back to playing soldiers."

Eunan just glared at him.

"It's all muskets and pikes these days if you hadn't heard."

"Oh, but a person of your position doesn't want to get involved in all of that. You sit on your horse, do a bit of yelling and point your axe in whatever direction you want them to go. You've got a much better chance of surviving and profiteering from all the dead bodies."

Eunan smiled at Desmond.

"It may be presumptuous of me, but I assume this was not in the lessons for your Galloglass when you were in charge of the MacCabes for the Maguires?"

"I save all my most honest lessons purely for the benefit of you, Eunan! Now I trust you are feeling better? Jump in your little boat. Your war won't wait for you for too long."

"Goodbye, Desmond! Thank you for helping me," and Eunan hugged his friend.

"Remember what I said. If all else fails, ask yourself 'what would Seamus do?'"

"Hmm, why has my life sunk so low?"

"Just get on the boat and wave goodbye."

The boatman sent by the Maguire waited patiently by the shore. Eunan turned and waved.

"It will not be long before I return!"

"Don't return until you are lord of south Fermanagh!" shouted Desmond in reply.

19

The Pale

Seamus and Art O'Toole picked their way through the Wicklow mountains, passing the many English patrols sent to look for rebels, and found themselves in the lowlands of the Pale. Art was a brilliant guide to add to his skills as a spy, and Seamus thought it a pity that he would have to kill him later. They waited until nightfall before approaching the walls of Dublin. As ever, Art had the ingenuity to get them past the gates, and soon they were walking through the streets of Dublin.

"Where are we going first?" asked Seamus.

He had seldom been to Dublin, and it was easy to get lost in the windy streets.

"To see Captain Williamson."

"But if I see him and he has us followed, we'll give away the location of the veterans?"

Art shrugged.

"What do you care? They're dead anyway. You work for us now."

Seamus imagined cutting Art's throat and pulling out his tongue but knew he had to play along for now.

"This way," said Art, and he pointed towards the quays.

Seamus could see the vast hulks of the merchant ships in the pale moonlight that brought prosperity to the Pale. Beside them in the next quay were the military ships that brought over the English soldiers from Brittany who were chasing Fiach and his men around the Wicklow mountains.

Then there were some gallows in a square in front of the quays. A sign hung for all to see.

"Here hang traitors to Queen and country who fought for the Spanish and dared return. Cursed are their souls!"

"Is this the way, or did you just want to show me the hangings?" said Seamus.

"It is the way. It is much easier to hide in the quays, for it is full of transient strangers."

"I hope to be one of them."

Art smiled and led Seamus through the shadowy back streets, and a flash of Seamus's axe blade from under his cloak put off any shady character who paid too much attention to them. Seamus was not nervous, but if he was going to have to use his axe, he wanted to plan out an escape route first.

They came to a tavern of ill repute and no discernible name. The shadows barely hid the drunks and beggars that sought the darkness for refuge or subterfuge.

"Surely the captain could have got better accommodation than this?" muttered Seamus.

"He hasn't invited you to a party," replied Art.

"It is certainly one I wouldn't like to attend."

"Come this way," and Art led him down an alley beside the tavern.

Two men stepped out of the shadows, lifted their coats, and drew their swords. They ordered Seamus to drop his weapons. He looked at Art.

"They are the captain's men."

Seamus handed Art his axe.

"I want that back when I leave."

"This way."

The two men opened the door to an adjacent house and ushered Seamus in. He glanced at them as he walked past. He was already thinking of his escape route. Another man came out as they tried to enter. He tried to hide his face, but Seamus thought he recognised him.

"You'll be meeting my axe later," Seamus muttered to himself.

He found himself in the living room of an ordinary house, absent of any apparent dwellers. Captain Williamson warmed himself and his remaining hand by the fire, and two of his bodyguards sat and ate at a table on the opposite wall. Both were armed with swords. The two men who invited him in shut the door behind Seamus as they guarded the entrance. He was now alone.

"Sit, Seamus. Have some food. I'm sure you're hungry after your journey," and Captain Williamson pushed a stool with his foot towards Seamus.

"No thanks. I didn't come here to socialise but to enquire after my wife. Where is she if you are here?"

The captain smiled and let the blanket wrapped around his shoulders fall to the floor.

"Art, the food invite also applies to you." Art smiled, for he did not need a second invitation and went to the table and helped himself.

Captain Williamson got up and walked around Seamus.

"You are a man with a formidable reputation. When you contact my men, they end up dead!"

"You should consider who you hire and don't go for the ones of worst repute and weakness of mind. If the first thing your men do is get blind drunk, then it is no wonder they end up dead. Shea Óg and his son, Sean, still live, or did when I left Tirconnell. God knows they don't deserve to!"

"Deserve does not exist while you still walk the earth."

"You see fit to employ me, if only by blackmail, so you must see something good in me or else I would be dead."

"You know Hugh Boye MacDavitt and are trusted by him. You have the moral flexibility to betray him. That is as far as my admiration goes."

Seamus saw the steel in his eyes. The captain's lost arm had been more than amply replaced by bitterness. But Seamus realised he still had some leverage.

"So, where is my wife? Is she here? Can I see her? How do I know she's still alive?"

"She is safe. Once you deliver Hugh Boye MacDavitt to me, dead or alive, she will be released along with the family members of your men."

"But how do I know she is still alive?"

The captain reached into his pocket.

"Here, she wrote you this. I made her write the date and the latest news about the northern uprising at the end to prove when she wrote it."

Seamus looked at the piece of paper in his hand as if the words were from the devil himself.

"Take it! It is the only proof that you will get as to whether she is still alive."

He took the piece of paper and read it slowly.

"This means she was alive a month ago. If she was nearby, then you could have got something written yesterday."

"It is chaos out there if you hadn't noticed. Now that we have proved she is alive, where is Hugh Boye MacDavitt? Our spies in the Netherlands last saw him a month ago."

"Maybe he eloped with my wife since they were both seen around the same time!"

"You don't want to stop co-operating, otherwise we may have to chop her up slowly and deliver you the parts to prove she's still alive!"

Seamus went cold.

"I do not know where Hugh Boye MacDavitt is or if he has stepped foot on Irish shores. I have certainly not seen him in Wicklow."

"Then what are you doing there? It is no good to me if you are there."

"I have to follow Red Hugh's orders. I am no good to anyone if he does not trust me or hold me in his confidence."

"I have plenty of spies. I don't need another one. What are you going to do for me while we wait for Hugh Boye MacDavitt?"

"Our agreement is purely for Hugh Boye MacDavitt. That is it!" spat Seamus.

"We shall see," and Captain Williamson gave a cynical laugh. "Art will look after you while you are in Wicklow and try to remain inconspicuous. Try not to kill him!"

Seamus glared at Art, and Art gulped. He took a step towards Captain Williamson, and the men went for their weapons.

"I will tell you when Hugh Boye arrives. However, to find him, I must meet my wife first, where ever she may be."

"If you provide us with accurate information, you shall meet your wife as a prelude to her being released. Now it is time for you to go."

Art finished his food and went towards the door.

"I need my axe back," said Seamus. "You never know who'll you'll meet on the back streets of Dublin.!"

"My men will escort you to the quay and give it back to you there. I shall make contact again soon. Anything you need to tell me, you can relay through Art."

Seamus spat on the floor and left.

20

The veterans of Dublin

Moonlight drenched the dreary streets of Dublin, but Seamus was glad that at least he got his axe back. Art cowered away from him, because Seamus was armed again. However, Seamus had no intention of plunging the axe in Art's head just yet, for he still needed him.

"Where are these veterans hiding, the ones you keep telling me about?"

"I can take you there," mumbled Art.

"We need to take them back to Wicklow with us tonight. I don't want them to meet you this evening, and for the captain's men to send them off to their maker tomorrow."

"That's impossible. We'd never evade the increased patrols because of the attack on Crumlin. We'd all be hanged!"

Seamus leaned towards him.

"Giving up Hugh Boye MacDavitt, the ablest Irish military man alive, is impossible, but I can do it. What motivations do you need to do what I ask?" and Seamus flashed his axe blade from beneath his cloak.

Art lifted his quivering hands to protect himself.

"I will bring you there. I will try, but it depends on how many of them there are."

"I'm sure you can manage it if you put your mind to it. Now lead the way!"

Art pointed towards some alleys leading away from the quays.

"Remember, I have my axe. If you lead me into an ambush, you'll die first!"

"My orders are to keep you alive," said Art, trying not to choke on his words.

They ventured through the darkness, and Seamus reached for his axe since the clamours of the slums at night was enough to intimidate anyone. However, the noises were more afraid of Seamus than he of them. Art led him to a dilapidated house, where the dim light was rapidly extinguished at the sound of approaching footsteps. He rapped on the door with the faintest of knocks that the dwellers would still hear inside. The door creaked open.

"Deventer!" Art whispered.

The door opened, and the candles were re-lit. The fresh candlelight illuminated the faces of three pale, emaciated and frightened men, their faces having never met a razor in months nor their faces any cleansing water. Their clothes had disintegrated into rags. Not much charity penetrated the house since the hangings began. Seamus stepped inside and surveyed the room.

"What beggars den have you brought me to Art? How many of you men of skin and bone will I have to kill before they overwhelm me?"

"This is no ambush," said Art. "These are your veterans."

"Veterans? They are beggars!" exclaimed Seamus.

"No sir!" said one man, who summoned the courage to speak. "We all served in the Netherlands for the Spanish king and all stowed away in various ships and came back through England. We want to go north, but the English are hunting veterans, so we had to hide out here. Very few people know we are here because of the enormous price on our heads. Better to starve in here than hang down by the quays!"

Seamus turned and took Art by the arm.

"These are not fighting men! Why did you not just toss them to the captain and take the reward?"

Then it dawned on Seamus.

"I know why we are here! These are not fighting men. They are a burden. We take them in, and they are unfit to fight; they slow us down and make us easier to catch. Nice try. I should tell them of your plan and let them tear you apart with their bare hands! At least they could take out one of the enemy before they die."

Art grabbed Seamus's arm.

"No, you can't do that, I beg you. I will help you bring them down to Wicklow and make sure they have somewhere safe to hide. Please don't let them kill me."

"Ah, a cowardly spy, the worst kind! How do I know you are not leading me into a trap?"

"Why would the captain want you killed? If he did, he could have easily had you killed in the house!"

"Then we must leave this evening, preferably now."

Art panicked.

"I have been in Wicklow for months. I know nothing about the frequency of patrols. What is the easiest way out...?"

Seamus stuck his face in Art's.

"Why don't you ask your good captain? I'm no good to him if I am hanged trying to escape from Dublin."

Art looked around for a way to escape, but the veterans rallied to Seamus's cause, since he was their only means of escape. Art relented when he realised he had a narrow path to survival.

"Ok then. Let me go now, and I'll see what I can arrange."

"Don't be long. The sooner we go, the better."

Seamus stood out of the way of the door and let Art leave. One veteran approached him.

"Are you going to place our lives in the hands of a known traitor?"

"The streets of Dublin are full of danger. I search myself for a means of escape, but fear we are at the mercy of traitors. I bid you farewell and only open the door to Art or I."

With that, the dark and cold swallowed Seamus, and the veterans locked the premises, hoping and praying for their salvation.

* * *

A knock came upon the door several hours later. The men cowered and hid.

"It is I, Seamus. Let me in."

The men hurried to oblige.

"Any luck with a plan to escape?" asked one soldier.

"No. I have found out that ever since Crumlin burned, the city has been crawling with patrols. I am not familiar with the city and fear we would be hanged by morning without Art."

"But he is a traitor!"

"He is a traitor that wants to keep me alive."

"Why?"

"The less you know, the longer you'll live."

"Well, from what you've told me, I will not live long, so you may as well tell me."

Seamus put his hand on the man's shoulder and squeezed.

"We need fighting men with your experience, and I would have put myself in a lot of danger only to have to kill you if we escaped. It is better that you did not know. But remember this. I am a sworn enemy of the English, so do not doubt my loyalty."

A knock came on the door. Seamus felt for his axe shaft, and the men shifted to the shadows of the room.

"Deventer."

Seamus nodded towards the door, and one man opened it. Art stuck his head through the door and waved at them to come out.

"There is a small boat for us at the docks, but we must leave now before the light."

Seamus nodded his approval, and the men gathered their things. They hid in the shadows of the alley while Art and Seamus checked that the path to the docks was free of patrols. The latter took this chance to find out why they had been the recipients of such good fortune.

"Captain Williamson supplied a boat and told the local patrols to look the other way. I said I'd see you all right, didn't I?"

"We're not on the boat yet!"

The street was empty, and Seamus waived the men forward. The moon sat tall in the sky, unencumbered by clouds. It omitted a cold light, a dull illumination for men with steel in their blood. Seamus and the veterans cast long shadows as they ran across the street before hiding in the darkness of the side of a merchant ship as Art searched the dock for their boat.

"This way," he whispered.

A mysterious man sat in a boat at the bottom of some steps and waited for them to board. Seamus's axe glinted in the moonlight.

"You, off the boat if you want to live," and the man quickly departed on Seamus's threat.

"Do you know Dublin bay?" said Art as he witnessed Seamus destroy his plan. "Because I certainly don't."

"No mystery passengers. I have a hard enough time sharing a boat with you!"

The five men got in the boat as quickly and as quietly as they could.

Seamus gave instructions. Art and the strongest of the veterans took an oar each. The boat was pushed off the side of the pier and hugged the shadows of the merchant ships, only allowing enough room for their oars to operate with barely a full range of motion. The oars slid into the water, and then Art and the soldier gave a big heave before returning to the calmness of delicately plucking the oar from the water again. It was slow going but necessary, for not even the seagulls bothered with their small craft. They reached the end of the docks and saw Howth out in the middle of Dublin Bay.

"To the right!" exclaimed one soldier who had not taken part in the rowing.

"How do you know?" asked Seamus.

"I used to live in Dublin."

"How come you had nobody to feed or look after you? Surely your family felt guilty with you so emaciated?"

"I didn't want to put them in danger knowing I was there. Once we saw how returning soldiers were treated, we went into hiding."

"Right it is," exclaimed Seamus.

Dublin bay was virtually empty at that hour of the night.

"We need to be out of the bay before dawn," said Art. "That is when the fishing boats will enter."

"Hug the coast until we reach Dalkey Island. We then cross the next bay. After that, we can look for somewhere to land near the mountains to ease our escape," said the soldier from Dublin.

"How long will that take?" enquired Seamus.

"We could be there by the evening."

"Too long. We need somewhere to hide for the day. Any ideas, Art?"

"We could moor up near Dalkey Island. After that it is more or less open seas where we would easily get spotted in the day."

"But surely now that we're out of sight of the walls and towers of Dublin, we're just another small boat of fishermen? I say we keep moving," said the soldier with the oar.

"So we've no food, and we're vulnerable out in the open. I say we rest up. Moor the boat when we reach Dalkey Island," instructed Seamus.

* * *

Dawn broke, and they pulled their boat up in a small harbour opposite Dalkey Island. The fishermen preparing their boats turned a blind eye to their arrival when they paid handsomely for some bread and water. Seamus asked for somewhere to rest, and they were directed to an abandoned house down by the shore where the five men lay down to rest.

When he woke up, Seamus found Art had disappeared. The three veterans were still asleep. Sean O'Toole, the soldier from Dublin, was the first to wake.

"The traitor is gone now," Seamus told him. "Now we can talk."

"Why do you trust him?"

"I don't, but I could see no other way out. Now tell me, why are you three starving in a shack in the slums of Dublin when you could escape or at least go on the rob to feed yourselves?"

"Hugh Boye MacDavitt and the other Irish leaders in the Spanish army sent us here to work out the best route to get back into Ireland. Previously, ex-soldiers used to return one at a time and land near their place of birth or where their clans were. That was easy at first if you were from the south or the east. Then the English put such large bounties on our heads that even our neighbours would turn us in, for they were offered the equivalent of a year's worth of earnings, a year of a good harvest. Who could turn that down? Some tried to sail around the island, but it is difficult in a small boat in treacherous waters. Many men drowned.

"Some came through England as Ruaidhri did, but most either got caught or lured away by the multitude of distractions in England. Others tried to go through Scotland, but the best warriors got distracted and got employment as mercenaries.

"But the leaders in the Netherlands want to send back larger parties and eventually come themselves. They sent us to work out the best route for landing a group of men from where they could make their way up north. As you can see from the state of us, we were not too successful."

"Our paths cross, and our stars align," said Seamus as his heart warmed to Sean's story. "I served in the Netherlands, probably before your time, for William Stanley and the Spanish. I served with Hugh Boye MacDavitt and await his return to Ireland. Because of my connections, Red Hugh O'Donnell has given me a special task to assemble all the continental soldiers I can find and either get them to serve the O'Donnell or train his men. That is why I forced Art to bring me to see you where we will go first to Wicklow and then to Tirconnell. I need to get you fit and assess your skills to see how you can serve. Are you willing to come with me?"

"That is why I came back!" Sean said proudly.

"So when is MacDavitt going to return?" asked Seamus.

"As soon as he can arrange safe passage. Hugh O'Neill has invited him back to act as one of his military advisors."

"I am trying to organise a route through Wicklow where veterans can get the protection of Fiach MacHugh O'Byrne before making their way up north. It's much more secure than going through Dublin or the Pale. I plan to organise a series of safe houses so men can stop off along the way as they travel north."

"That is what we need."

"We can also smuggle men into Ireland through sympathetic merchants. So they should be able to land in most parts of Ireland."

171

"There are so many Irishmen that I know want to come back and fight. They just need to be assured that it is safe to land on these shores."

There was a knock on the door. Seamus looked at Sean O'Byrne and nodded to him to open the door.

"Deventer!"

Sean opened the door to Art.

"We need to think of a new password," said Seamus.

"Look, I have brought back food," and Art opened his jacket to reveal two loaves of bread.

Sean snatched a loaf out of Art's hand and devoured it. Art woke the other two and handed a bottle to Sean after seeing him struggle.

"Take this before you choke," he said before turning to Seamus.

"We can leave at the first sign of darkness. There should be cloud cover tonight, which will make us less conspicuous on the water."

"Are there any soldiers about?" asked Seamus.

"No. Mainly fishermen. There is a little town nearby, but there is no need to go there and seek trouble."

Seamus gave the bread to the veterans and, after a while, left himself to seek sustenance and some air. He saw a hill nearby. It had a commanding view of Dublin and its approaches from the north side, the bay and the sea to the east, and the hills of Wicklow to the south. They were not far away. After a couple of hours in the boat, they could slip back into the mountains. He went back to the house via the little harbour, where he bought more bread and ale. This time he ate along with everyone else. The colour was coming back into the cheeks of the veterans. The food and fresh air did them a world of good.

Darkness set in, and they set out for the harbour. The clouds thickened the sky, but the moon would periodically peer out and illuminate the earth, catching out all those who were not asleep. The veterans had full bellies and sufficiently rested. They pushed the boat out into the sea and rowed under the shadow of Dalkey Island. To their collective horror, a large ship was anchored in the middle of the bay so rowed closer to the shore to avoid being detected. The lights twinkled upon the ship.

"Up oars! Let us drift upon the tide, so they do not see us in the moonlight," whisper Seamus urging his fellow travellers to be silent.

The tide dragged them slowly south, while all eyes remained on the ship. A smaller boat was cast off the side of the ship, and distant figures boarded.

"Should we row and try to escape?" asked Sean.

"We don't know if they've seen us yet," replied Seamus.

The small boat set off towards the shore with three oars to its port and starboard. It set off at a good pace towards the coast. Inadvertently, the fugitives thought it was heading straight for them.

"We need to escape now," pleaded Art.

"Why would an English vessel send men to shore in the dead of night?" asked Seamus. "We can't outrun them to Wicklow, so we may as well stay hidden here in plain sight."

They sat and watched the boat and prayed that the moon would disappear behind the clouds. The boat headed straight for the shore.

"Let us pull onto the shore and hide from this boat and wait. It is now obvious they are not coming for us," said Seamus.

"All the better reason to escape," said Art.

"I am the ranking officer here, and I say let us pull up on the shore!" hissed Seamus.

The men obeyed and dipped their oars quietly in the waves, heading for the pebbled beach. The front of the boat soon wedged in amongst the small stones. They crept out of the boat, hid behind it, and watched. The other vessel rowed steadily to the shore.

"They don't look like they are English sailors," said Sean. "Maybe they're smugglers."

"With a boat that small, they can only smuggle people," replied Seamus.

"So why are we hiding here and not making our way to Wicklow?" said Art. "Smugglers are usually heavily armed."

"Patience. My guts tell me there is something interesting going on here, so we wait."

The other boat pulled up onto the shore. They counted eight men in the boat. Four got out and looked along the beach as if they were waiting for someone. They were heavily armed, as Art suspected. They waited for about ten minutes, and Seamus could see agitation on their faces. Then one of them spotted something moving behind Seamus's boat. The man pointed his sword, and they went to investigate.

"We are going to die if we remain cowering behind this boat!" and Seamus stuck his head above it, drew his axe and advanced towards the men.

Sean nudged his fellow veterans.

"Come on, then!"

They walked behind Seamus.

"Who goes there?" he said.

"We've more swords than you. What is the password?" said one of the mysterious men.

"What password?"

The leading man raised his sword.

"Zutphen. It is Zutphen," and Sean stood beside Seamus and faced the men.

"Where were you? We sent messages to you but got no reply."

They all walked back to the boat from the ship.

"We were trapped in Dublin. We couldn't communicate with anyone. They were hanging any veterans they found on the streets."

Seamus glared at Sean, demanding to know what was going on. Sean shrugged his shoulders to show that he did not know, but that he should play along. The man signalled to the boat, and the last four people disembarked.

Seamus and Sean stood before the men in front of the boat. Seven armed men formed a semi-circle around them, and they faced the last man who remained with a hood that hid his face.

"Are you what is being smuggled?" asked Seamus.

The man stood and threw back his hood.

"Hugh Boye MacDavitt!" Seamus exclaimed.

"Seamus MacSheehy? Have you not gone to hell yet?"

21

Escape to Wicklow

The moonlight shone on Hugh Boye's face and caught the angles of his cheekbones. He ushered his men forward onto the beach so he could get out of the way of the lapping of waves around his feet. His boots were not what they were when he set out from the Netherlands. Once Hugh Boye was static again, his men reformed their defensive circle with the added benefit to Hugh Boye that it broke up the chilly wind but did nothing for his feet.

He was a man of slight build and pale complexion, only some of which could be attributed to having just completed a perilous sea journey. The few remaining hairs on Hugh Boye's head were combed together to provide as much coverage as possible, a man with a fading grip on his youth and a large concern for his image. But his efforts with his hair just made a plaything for the wind. Sean noticed the well-kept beard that climaxed at a point at the end of Hugh Boye's chin. Sean reckoned it must be the height of fashion on the continent, but would stick out a mile in Ireland anywhere except the Pale. That had to go. But it would not be his struggle to persuade Hugh Boye to do it.

From what Sean could make out from beneath his cloak he was well dressed and ill-prepared for hiding out as a fugitive. Sean had heard of but not met Hugh Boye and was well aware of his reputation for being difficult and vain. All the evidence he could make out in the moonlight reinforced that view. However, his men crowded defensively around him as they obviously held him in high repute. However, Seamus occupied their attention, for they did not know whether to consider him a threat. Sean felt it his duty to break the tension, not least so they could get off this cold, moonlit beach.

"You know each other?" asked Sean of Hugh Boye.

"We go back a long way, a long way," said Hugh Boye.

Sean sensed respect, some animosity, but not much friendship. Seamus stuck out his hand and Hugh Boye took it.

"You could have met far worse than me at some bay in Ireland. Do you know the price on your head?"

"It had better be high, for I don't come cheap. Few Irishmen have been lucky enough to gain the skills that I got from learning from someone as proficient on the battlefield as William Stanley himself."

"At least I know I won't have to talk you up when I introduce you to people!"

Hugh Boye was confused.

"Surely they would have heard of me already?"

Hugh Boye considered some more.

"Why would Hugh O'Neill send you to fetch me?"

"He didn't. Do you know where you are?"

"Well, I'm hoping it is the Mourne mountains, for I am sick of travelling. The weather on the seas was terrible. We got waylaid by a storm and then were pursued by the English. We lost our bearings in the stormy seas. It was decided that I should land here as the ship was damaged and could not outrun the English any more."

Seamus shook his head.

"You are so wrong. They are the Wicklow mountains, and above us is Dublin. We need to hurry and try to reach the foothills before morning and hope Fiach's scouts find us before the English do."

Hugh Boye ignored being told he was wrong.

"My men will get my things, and then we shall set off."

The men took three large chests from the boat. Seamus strode over and waved them away.

"You can put them back on your ship! We're going nowhere with them."

"But they have all my possessions, instruments and maps!" Hugh Boye protested.

"The English will have a great time going through these trunks while we swing from the trees above them. I am not sacrificing my life for your fineries."

Hugh Boye boiled with rage.

"I am not going anywhere without my things!"

"You went soft when you were indulged by the kings of Spain. Put them back on the ship or bury them here. I don't care. We're leaving now, and they are not coming with us."

Hugh Boye's men absorbed their master's anger and pointed their swords towards Seamus's face.

"We only take orders from MacDavitt, not some cheap cattle rustler from Munster."

"Then you may as well dig your own graves as you bury the chests because as soon as the light comes, we're not getting off this beach."

Both sides stood off against each other in the moonlight. Finally, Sean tried to break the deadlock.

"Seamus is right. We have to travel light when we go into the mountains, or we'll never make it."

Hugh Boye did not reply, so Seamus decided they had to compromise as time was short.

"Take whatever we can carry and leave the rest here. Once we are secure in the mountains with Fiach, we can send some men to fetch them. I cannot make you a better offer than that."

Hugh Boye looked at him and finally relented.

"Let me take some things for us to carry, and we can hide the rest."

"Art, you take three men and hide the chests. I will set off towards the hills with Hugh Boye."

"But you don't know the way."

"I am going to head for the valley entrance and stick by the coast. By the time we get there, you should have caught up."

Hugh Boye nodded his agreement, and Art knew there was no more to be said.

* * *

They travelled until dawn, and the foothills of the Wicklow mountains were still in the distance. Hugh Boye insisted they wait while Art caught up, for he did not want to lose track of his baggage. Seamus found an old abandoned house to hide in, and the two veterans from Dublin went out to find Art and the rest of Hugh Boye's men.

Those that remained found some chairs and other comforts of home and settled in to wait for Art to return. The men from the Netherlands were well provisioned and shared their rations with Seamus and Sean, who expressed their appreciation. Hugh Boye sat alone and ate off a rickety table but it was the only table in the house. However, barely had they digested their food than Hugh Boye wanted to get down to business.

"What is the situation in Ireland? What have I got myself in for?"

Seamus stopped Sean from answering, for he knew Hugh Boye well from the past and thought he knew what he wanted to know.

"The main rebellion is in the north, led by Hugh O'Neill and Hugh O'Donnell. They have forced most of the minor lords of the north that had not already joined them into an alliance with them. The Irish lords in Connacht are weak, but it is a tinderbox. Leinster is pacified, except for the Wicklow mountains. The English did a terrific job in suppressing Munster during the Desmond Rebellions so there is hardly a stir out of her these days. Whatever rebellious spirit is left could only be revived when the whole of Ireland is in flames."

"So the assessments I have received are relatively accurate. Many on the continent want to see Ireland free, be it for religion or see the English beaten. The problem is that Ireland is low on the Spanish king's list of priorities since he has so many other things to worry about, not least the Low Countries. What forces do the rebels have at their disposal?"

"Galloglass, mercenaries from Scotland, some shot and pike for the O'Neills and the O'Donnells. The lesser lords have farm boys with axes mostly and some small amounts of Galloglass."

"So they have not progressed since I left?!"

"That's why they want you so bad."

"Do they use modern battle tactics? I heard they won a brilliant victory over the English."

"Their skill in the ambush will be a trip down memory lane for you. If they took the field to fight a straight battle, they would be slaughtered."

"So, more or less, I have to start from scratch?" said Hugh Boye with more than a hint of anger.

Seamus looked puzzled.

"I thought you would have guessed that, no matter what you were told before you set out."

Hugh Boye looked out the window and wondered if he had made a mistake.

"And what of my clan, the O'Dohertys?" he said, turning to Seamus again.

"Once again, loyal servants of the O'Donnells."

Hugh Boye slumped into his seat and held his hands in his head.

"I thought I had given up this rebel life to grace the finest battlefields of Europe! I thought I had come here to create an army!"

"You have, but you didn't look to see what materials you had to do it with. I can always bring you back to the boat?"

Hugh Boye rose and stared out the window again, but his wounded pride just rebounded back to Seamus off the walls.

"No, I have given my word, and I am a patriot. I am here to help free my fellow countrymen. I shall think myself lucky to be cast back into my youth again at my tender age, something that many men wish for when they think they can take their older brains and forget about the hardship you could once endure because it was exciting."

"Well, you'll certainly be cast right back to your youth when you become an outlaw in the Wicklow mountains."

Hugh Boye turned around, his face visibly drained.

"What!? When can we go north?"

"As soon as the English stop trying to hunt down Fiach MacHugh O'Byrne and I can establish a safe route north."

"So I could die in an obscure valley in Wicklow, and my journey will have all been in vain?"

"The same could be said for any field in the Netherlands."

Hugh Boye turned to the window again for he wished to hide his disappointment.

"You always were a brutal man, Seamus MacSheehy."

"And that is why my masters have always liked me so much. I get the dirty jobs done."

"I remember, I remember."

One of Hugh Boye's guards knocked on the door.

"Art O'Toole has returned."

Art followed the guard into the house.

"I assume my baggage is safe?"

"No one will find it, for Fiach will send men to fetch them when we meet him in a day or so," said Art.

"Can we depart now?"

"Give me a few hours to scout out a route. Then I'll come back for you."

Art turned to leave.

"I'll come with you," said Seamus.

* * *

Art worked his way through the forests on the foothills of the Wicklow mountains, with Seamus walking in his footsteps. Art tried to remind Seamus of the bargain he had struck.

"It is the easiest way," Art explained. "You can claim he was ambushed, Captain Williamson will be happy, and you get your wife back. Sure have you listened to him complain? He doesn't want to be here anyway."

He did not see Seamus grimace behind his back.

"Keep walking. Does Captain Williamson know he is here?"

"No. I couldn't leave him a message with Hugh Boye's men with me. However, he knew of our escape, so I'm sure he had us followed."

"Hmm, that would have been quite hard, considering we took to the sea on a relatively clear night. But I'm sure Captain Williamson is nothing if not thorough. So we've got to assume we're being followed."

"You've also got to assume that he has your wife and will kill her if you try to double-cross him. He's already deeply suspicious since so many of the men he sent to watch over you have died."

"You're still alive!"

Art gulped.

"That's because you still need me."

"It's all about trust."

"And you trust no one!"

Seamus laughed and changed the subject.

"Where are the safer parts of the hills?"

"We need to penetrate a little further, and then we'll get an excellent view of what is around us."

They climbed hills for a few more hours until they reached the peak of a particular mountain where they stopped to rest. Both were exhausted from the strains of the last three days.

"Look," said Art. "We can see north Wicklow from here and south Dublin as well."

"My sight is not what it used to be; some say punishment for my sins, but I say because of old age. What do you think?"

Art gulped again.

"Let me tell you what I see, and we shall find out if it is the same?"

He did not wait for an answer.

"The hills roll beautifully into the lowlands of the Pale. It is easy to see why any man would fight for his freedom when he sees this view."

"How much coin and cows have they paid you to sell your brethren to their deaths? They died for such views whilst you sold it and your soul for the English coin. Tell me how the battlefields lie. I don't want to hear such frivolities."

Art was insulted, but he continued, for he felt he had no choice.

"There are several forts in the south Dublin Pale. We can expect them to have many patrols that would go as far as the foothills. The main body of the Lord Deputy's army appears to be in central Wicklow, but we can expect that supplies are going to go along the principal routes that are the least susceptible to ambush. If we stick to the tops of hills, we should make it back to Fiach's camp."

"How soon should we run into Fiach's patrols?"

"We should be into friendly territory over the next hill or two. The

English are still not strong here. What we need to avoid are the patrols and the O'Byrne faction that are sympathetic to the crown."

"Show me," and Seamus waved him on.

They climbed up the next hill and gazed down at the valleys below.

"Which way is the safest route to Fiach?"

"Around those mountains, sticking down by the sea. It is too obvious travelling down towards Ballinacor. That is where the English are concentrating their forces."

"Good. Let's go back and get Hugh Boye."

They travelled for a distance before Seamus had more questions.

"Can we set off straight away when we get back?"

"It would be better to wait for nightfall, but the entire journey to the south Wicklow mountains will take a day and a half, so you need to choose your time to leave and places to hide along the way."

"But we need to be exposed for Fiach's patrols to find us?"

"We have to balance the risks. We are better off exposed the further we penetrate the mountains where Fiach is strong."

They walked down the last high mountain of the Wicklow mountains before descending into the foothills. To their right-hand side was a significant drop. Seamus looked down and then stared at Art ahead of him.

"Art?"

"Yes?"

"I need help."

Art shivered when he saw the seriousness on Seamus's face but stopped all the same.

"Thank you for bringing us this far," said Seamus, and Art could feel the coldness in his voice as Seamus advanced towards him.

"We have a long way to go yet," said Art, trying to state his importance.

"This is no time to trust traitors. I have to go on this journey on my own."

Art went for his dagger hidden beneath his jacket, but Seamus had long predicted this move. A swift blow to the head, but gentle enough not to lodge his axe in Art's skull, had Art tumbling down the rock face and onto the rocks below.

"Forgive me, Dervella," said Seamus as he bent over to clean his axe on the grass.

* * *

Seamus knocked on the door of the hideout several hours later.

"Who goes there?"

"Do you have to relive minor victories in faraway countries at every available moment?"

Sean opened the door.

"We've got to have some security," he protested.

"Shut up and get your things. We have no time for horseplay. We need to leave."

"Where's Art?"

"He gave his life in service of his country for once."

"You only get one life."

"Then he gave it better than he lived it. Are we ready to go yet?"

The men hurriedly packed their thing.

Hugh Boye was most displeased.

"Did he tell you where he hid my baggage?"

"He was otherwise engaged receiving an axe to the head. Put your baggage down to casualties of war."

Hugh Boye howled in mourning for his baggage. He was an itinerant rebel once again.

22

Becoming his own man

On the mainland by the shore of the lake was Eunan's horse and a guide waiting to take him to the Maguire and his forces. The horse looked plump and content; the guide looked stern and impatient. Hugh Maguire had taken to the forests of western Fermanagh once more to evade detection by the Crown's forces. The trees bent their naked limbs and greeted Eunan as he rode through the familiar countryside. The puddles seemed shallower that appeared, and the muddy paths beckoned him forward. The cold barely penetrated the blanket sent by the Maguire, and even the grey inflated clouds appeared as a comfort rather than the bringer of rain and cold. Eunan was ready to return.

Once in the camp, he got directions to the men of south Fermanagh. Eunan ignored the camp of the O'Cassidys, for he knew his welcome was as worn out as their few tents. Óisin was waiting for him in the disorganised camp of the men he had recruited and assembled in Eunan's absence. He ran and clasped Eunan by the forearm.

"It is good to see you again, lord."

"I am your friend, not your master," replied Eunan. "But it is good to see you too."

Óisin extended his arm to show the village of tents that surrounded them.

"Let me show you what a good job I have done for you in your absence. Men! Form a line and meet your constable!"

Curious heads popped out from the slits of tents and faces stacked together as heads peered out from behind each other.

"Form a line, not a gaggle of geese," Óisin shouted. "And bring your weapons!"

Men and boys leaned into and behind the tents and picked up whatever implements they had brought with them, which they thought, or hoped, could yield English blood. An age elapsed before Eunan could witness his men form a crooked line. The occasional man stood in line with three or four boys on either side. Some axes, mainly of the wood-cutting variety, the occasional sword, but mainly hay forks and the sporadic long-sharpened stick impersonating a pike, made up Eunan's new arsenal.

A sarcastic laugh came from behind him as Cillian O'Cassidy, in free chain mail and helmet, smirked at him. Cillian slapped the shoulder of a newly recruited Galloglass, who stood beside him and joined his master's smirk.

"I see you are planning to run away from the next battle as well," called out Cillian before he disappeared behind the tents in his own campsite.

Óisin looked at Eunan and decided he needed some reassurance.

"We were all naïve farm boys once."

"But we had time to grow up before the next battle," grumbled Eunan.

Eunan sat by the campfire that evening and caught up with all his old comrades. Óisin told him they expected Cormac MacBaron to re-enter Fermanagh any day now and link up with the Maguires. Eunan soberly accepted the news, much to the disappointment of

Óisin. That night Eunan retired to his bed, weary from travel, ale and disappointment. As he pulled his blanket over himself, among the turmoil of a sleepless night, he thought to himself:

"What would Seamus do?"

* * *

In the days after, Eunan organised training for his shambolic group. Óisin had done his best to recruit as many men as possible, but had neglected to apply a selection process that involved sifting for readiness, never mind suitability for combat. As long as they were from south Fermanagh and would accept Eunan as their leader, they were in. Eunan selected a periphery field, away from prying eyes, especially those of Cillian O'Cassidy, to begin his selection process. Sixty men and boys followed Eunan and Óisin to the field.

Eunan ordered them to surround him in a circle, and he threw down a long wooden axe shaft with no head in front of him. He stood ten feet back and placed a similar shaft in front of himself.

"Men of south Fermanagh. You have come here to fight the English for the Maguire. You are here to defend your way of life and your homes. But we only want those who are willing and able to fight, for it will give me no pleasure to tell your kinsfolk we had to bury you from fatal wounds in your back. Therefore, each one of you will take up the shaft on the other side of the circle and come and fight me. I will then assign you a role based on your performance. Does everybody understand me?"

There was a general silence.

"Does everybody understand me?!"

"Yes," murmured the circle.

"Right then, who's first?"

Nobody moved.

"Óisin, if you would, please."

"Eyes forward!" said Óisin.

Óisin crept along the outer perimeter of the circle behind all the men and boys who faced inwards. He pushed a random man in the back and into the ring, which then closed behind him. The man stood terrified in front of Eunan.

"Well? Battles don't wait. Pick up the shaft!"

"I don't want to hurt you."

"Pick up the shaft!" ordered Eunan.

The man reluctantly picked up the shaft. Eunan went for him. One shift blow from the butt of the shaft, and the man was down.

"Baggage train!" shouted Eunan.

"What?" answered the man as he sat up and held his head.

"Baggage train. You now work in the baggage train."

"But?!"

"I told you the rules. Get out of the circle before my men drag you out. Next."

The man walked out of the circle, and Óisin told him where to sit. Óisin patrolled the perimeter again and selected Eunan's next victim.

The boy fell into the arena, picked up the shaft and swiftly dropped it again.

"Baggage train."

Another came and soon dropped the shaft.

"Baggage train."

Some parried his blows.

"Kern."

Some even exchanged a few blows.

"Galloglass."

The morning went quickly, and Eunan remained standing. When the last of his men had been assigned a group, Eunan dusted himself down and dabbed his bruises with water from his bottle. Óisin apologetically approached him.

"It'll be some baggage train we'll be guarding."

Eunan could not contain his fury.

"They can't all be this bad. Surely these men know how to defend themselves? I cannot go to the Maguire with results like this. Let us see how good the baggage train guards are with the bow. Óisin, fetch some bows."

Eunan's trusted men brought back bows from the camp and set up some targets. One by one, the men assigned to the baggage train queued up to show what skills they had with the bow. Those that passed inflated the ranks of the kern until they became the largest group. Eunan now permanently split the men up into their assigned groups and forced them to lodge together to foster comradeship.

As they marched back to the camp, Cillian and his Galloglass sneered at them.

"Don't bother with the axe or bow; just teach them how to run."

Eunan ignored them, but Óisin went to face them off.

"One day, O'Cassidy, there is going to be a reckoning in south Fermanagh."

Cillian laughed.

"I'll ask my father to extend the cemetery in Eunan's former village."

Eunan turned around to Óisin.

"Leave him. First, we deal with the English."

* * *

Eunan spent the next few weeks training his men, begging and borrowing as much armour and weaponry that he could, considering its general scarcity. He almost groaned with disappointment when he was told that they were moving out, as he was making some progress. However, they only marched for two days and took up residence in their campsite of the previous year, where the siege of Enniskillen had taken place alongside Cormac MacBaron and his O'Neill soldiers. Eunan settled into a routine of training and scavenging as he waited for the instructions of the Maguire.

The Maguire army reassembled its strength of the previous year as men flowed in from Fermanagh and the surrounding territories after the crops were planted.

One morning, a group of twenty young men armed with bows and axes walked into Eunan's camp. They walked with a youthful bounce more attuned to the spring than the current depths of winter, so they were immediately out of kilter in both looks and spirit. Instantly drawn to such enthusiasm, Eunan recognised the faces but could not recollect where from.

"Good day, sir," said the young man who led the group's approach. "We have come to serve under you again."

"Again?" exclaimed Eunan, for they did not resemble any O'Cassidy cowards.

"Devenish Island?"

Eunan leapt from his seat and stuck out his hand.

"Welcome!" he exclaimed as he greeted the young men who, in return, stuck out their hand. "I am honoured that you would come and seek me out when I am in such esteemed company."

"We asked the Maguire, and he directed us here. You led us when most had abandoned the cause. When we heard you were in the camp, we came straight away."

"We are mainly kern here, and we are training to harass and harry the enemy. I also train Galloglass, but that is a privilege to be earned if you perform well enough."

"Few would provide us with such an opportunity, so we are glad to join. Do you have any accommodation for us?"

"The men will help you pitch tents. Be ready for the next morning when training begins early."

"We look forward to it."

Eunan smiled as his recruits went and assimilated themselves with the men who were already there.

* * *

Hugh O'Neill had retaken to his horse and travelled to Dundalk to arrange negotiations. The Irish Council invited the individual lords of the north to make submissions of their grievances to the Queen. The Crown claimed not to know of any maltreatment by her officers and let the lords know their assertions would be investigated, and if found to be true, the lords would be compensated. Donnacha O'Cassidy drafted a submission that Hugh Maguire duly signed and submitted.

While these submissions were being made, O'Neill's subordinate captains and lords carried out a series of raids in Leinster along the borders of the Pale as a show of strength before the talks started. What remained of the English allies in the north had their lands raided alongside those of Sir Henry Bagenal. With the garrisons in Enniskillen, Monaghan, and the Blackwater Fort surrounded, Lord Deputy William Russell was under pressure to act.

23

Departure

They travelled by day and by night, fearing every crack of a twig and rustling of a bush. The wind proved more foe than friend; she heightened, and in her strength caressed the tops and bodies of trees, fanned the paranoia of the men below, and masked the sounds of the forests. They penetrated further and ran into the patrols of Fiach MacHugh O'Byrne somewhere in the central Wicklow mountains. There was no need to declare themselves to Fiach, for the men immediately recognised Seamus and welcomed him back. It was a stroke of luck as some men in Seamus's party were seeing through the bluff that he knew where he was going. Hugh Boye complained all the way, but Seamus had long since given up listening to find out if he saw through the deception, for he no longer cared.

It delighted Fiach to host the legendary Hugh Boye MacDavitt and wanted to hold a feast in his honour. Still, Seamus advised against it as he wanted to keep Hugh Boye's presence a secret. He knew the outlaws of Wicklow were riddled with spies and persuaded his compatriot to stay hidden. Fiach was furious.

"What's the point in bringing me Ireland's greatest tactician if he has to stay hidden in his tent?"

"I didn't bring him for you. He is merely sheltering here as I work out how to smuggle him north," replied Seamus.

"What about the alliance? What's theirs is mine and all that?"

"He will make a massive difference to the much larger armies up north and only a minuscule one to you, for you are already the greatest ambusher in Ireland!"

"Flattery will get you nowhere. I still want his help."

Seamus could see how determined Fiach was and that he would have to appease him somehow.

"I will speak to him and see how he can help you. But he has to remain hidden."

Fiach bit his lip.

"Agreed, but I want to see some results from this so-called strategic genius of yours," and Fiach stormed off.

* * *

Hugh Boye remained confined to a grand tent in Wicklow terms, but a hovel only fit for prisoners or a brothel for a man used to being a renowned officer in the Spanish Grand Army. Fiach posted some of his best guards (and least susceptible to bribes) around the tent, which drew almost immediate attention to it. They drove away anyone who lingered. Those who attempted subterfuge and offered bribes decorated the trees around the camp the next day. Yet Fiach soon abandoned this policy because of the damage it was inflicting on an already fragile camp morale.

Fiach craved his peers' respect as a military leader. That one of Ireland's greatest living military strategists in his camp was too much for him to preserve both his dignity and decorum. Fiach smuggled himself into Hugh Boye's tent at convenient times to discuss strategy and ordered his most trusted men to keep him abreast of the thoughts of the renowned Irish strategic genius, hoping that some of it would rub off on him. At first, Hugh Boye found it hard to be polite as he was frustrated with his living conditions and the fact that nobody had retrieved his lost baggage. But Fiach generously ladled the flattery out and sent every luxury he could lay his hands on. Soon they had the maps of Wicklow laid out before them, and they would spend hours discussing the strategic scenario. Fiach got some fine wines from the merchants of the Pale and regaled Hugh Boye with dinners of the finest Wicklow deer. Meanwhile, Hugh Boye retold tales of the Dutch wars and how much he thought of himself. Only occasionally did Fiach find the length of these stories challenging. He was even persuaded to send out some men to look for the baggage.

Seamus disapproved of Fiach's fawning. But he concerned himself with the continental veterans, restoring them to their previous health and fitness, and turning them into a formidable fighting unit. The slow but steady progress pleased him.

* * *

The return of Walter Reagh and Turlough O'Byrne disrupted the temporary lull in the war. They came up the mountain, with their followers reduced from twenty to fifteen. Fiach stood at the top, waiting for them.

"I see you've swapped my warriors for farm boys and adventurous young fools. The tall tales you've had to tell to recruit them haven't even been elaborate enough to replace what you lost. I've heard of what you've done, burning farms and homesteads of the English settlers. Commendable, but it only made me a more hunted man. Come in and tell me why you didn't return sooner."

Fiach pointed towards his tent.

195

Walter and Turlough's hopes of being hailed as heroic rebels fell flat on their faces, but they followed Fiach, who signalled to Seamus and Rose to join him.

The arriving men stood before Fiach like a pair of naughty boys caught thieving by a neighbouring farmer and sent to their father, resigned to their punishment.

"So what have you to say for yourselves, those who have brought upon us the English's wrath harder than ever?"

Turlough stood forward.

"We brought the fight to the English, father. That's what we did. The Crown detained us, but we fought our way out. We hid out in the lowlands, lived off petty crime and assembled ourselves another gang before deciding enough time had passed before we could safely return. The English have seemed to diminish in numbers, and there appears to be growing an appetite for rebellion in Leinster."

Fiach composed his response.

"Your mother-in-law and I have noticed that the old Gaelic lords of Leinster seem more willing to talk about alliances and are less stringent in their demands. However, you disobeyed me by going off and attacking Crumlin without my permission. A stint taking orders from your younger brothers should soon cure your rebellious streak, or at least hone its effectiveness!"

"What! You cannot do that!"

"I can, and if you wish to remain here, you will obey my instructions. The same goes for you, Walter. Now leave me before I change my mind and think of a punishment that I would give to someone who disobeyed me and was not my son!"

They both looked displeased but bowed and left the tent.

Clouds of concern creased Rose's normally pleasant completion.

"Those who escape the custody of the English unaided usually come back with a dagger beneath their cloak," she whispered in her husband's ear. "The son returning to topple his father for English gold, a coat of arms, and the protection of the Queen is a well-worn story."

She nodded knowingly and left the tent to tell her sisters' husbands the news.

Seamus sensed it was time for him to return to Tirconnell.

* * *

Several days passed, and jealousy and rivalries stewed in the camp. Fiach stuck to his own tent and wondered whether he had done the right thing, only going to Hugh Boye's tent in moments of greatest doubt, hoping again that some of the man's genius would rub off on him. Such visits only added to his disappointment. But things never stayed the same for long in the O'Byrne camp.

"The English are retreating! The English are retreating!" shouted a messenger as he scrambled up the mountain to give Fiach the news.

Fiach ran out of his tent and stood astride the entrance to the camp.

"I heard you the first time wailing like a banshee. So will any spies hiding in the bushes or the bottom of the valleys. What has you so excited, boy?"

"The English are retreating, lord. They are abandoning the valleys and going back to Dublin."

Turlough walked over and joined his father.

"Surely this is just a ruse? We follow them and then they spring their ambush?"

"What about Ballinacor and their new fort?" asked Fiach of the boy.

"I couldn't see that far. But they seem to retreat from everywhere."

Fiach turned to Turlough.

"Send scouts to find out. I must know before I make my move," said Fiach, as he shook with excitement. "Ballinacor, I am coming for you!"

Turlough left to make the arrangements, and Seamus replaced him by Fiach's side.

"I have forgiven him for his previous follies, and he stands at my side again as my firstborn. But I need to protect him from his younger brothers and their O'Toole wives. He is the only one I can trust as being capable of keeping our fragile alliance together when I pass. That is if he can survive the pit of vipers that is clan politics."

"If I succeed in my mission, that could all be a thing of the past," replied Seamus.

Fiach barely recognised his friend.

"What has you so optimistic? Have you been at the drink again?"

"I had a decision forced upon me and took it. If I die, may it be for a cause, a reason more than a couple of coins and some cattle."

"You'll be spouting religion at me next, and the tales of St Colmcille fighting monsters!"

"I'm not that bad."

"Well, I've never seen you like this. So where does this mission of yours have you going next?"

"Back north to work out an escape route for Hugh Boye and the veterans. I have to go alone, for the mission is both important and top secret. You can look after my men for me."

"You'll have my blessing if the English are gone."

"I must make my preparations."

Fiach nodded, for he knew it was time as well. Even he was growing tired of Hugh Boye.

* * *

The scouts returned several days later and confirmed that the English had left, but they still garrisoned the fort in Ballinacor. Seamus went to gather his things. Sean O'Toole waited outside his tent. He had the benefit of several weeks of food and rest and regained the energy that Seamus would have expected from a veteran of the Dutch revolt. Seamus slung his bag over his shoulder and set out to leave. Sean made his presence known.

"Can I come with you?" asked Sean.

"Come with me where?" replied Seamus.

"Up north, to the O'Donnells?"

"News certainly spreads fast in this small camp. I wish to remain inconspicuous. Therefore, I travel alone."

"It is much easier to fight off bandits if someone has your back. If there are two of us, there is twice the chance that one of us makes it to Tirconnell."

Seamus saw the determination in Sean's face.

"Are you fit to fight?"

"Yes."

"Then get your bags."

Seamus and Sean went to Fiach's tent. Turlough and Hugh Boye were also waiting for them. Fiach handed Seamus two letters.

"Here. There's one from me and one from Hugh Boye. Only give these to Red Hugh. Part of my letter is requesting that you return to collect Hugh Boye as I trust you, but few others as the rebels' ranks are riddled with spies.

"If the O'Neill and the O'Donnell could see their way to giving me some more soldiers or raid the Pale to draw some English soldiers away, then I could rally together south Leinster and rise with my allies."

Seamus took the letters and put them in his bag.

"I'll see what I can do. Goodbye, old friend. Try not to get killed while I'm gone!"

"Try not to die before you reach Tirconnell!"

They warmly embraced.

Hugh Boye gave a grunt that Seamus generously interpreted as a goodbye. Fiach provided Uaithne O'More and some guides to escort them out of Leinster and as far as Maguire territory.

* * *

After a long two weeks of travel, Seamus and Sean finally arrived back in Donegal town. The journey took twice as long as expected, for the countryside was in chaos, and the letters in Seamus's possession needed to be protected from the English and bandit alike. Once in Donegal town, they were directed straight to the court of the O'Donnell.

The court was in session, and busier than Seamus remembered. Red Hugh seemed to attract every rebel and never-do-well, expelled from either Connacht or Leinster, looking for glory, spoils, or the resolution to a long-held grudge, whether real or imaginary. He had been vocal in his submissions to the Irish Council, calling for the return of tanistry to Connacht and the restoration of O'Donnell land and levies in Connacht. Probably the strongest rallying call for the rebels of Connacht and Leinster was that the lords of Connacht were to be pardoned and restored to their former positions. While Hugh O'Neill had a disciplined and well-trained army, thanks to the English sheriffs and the Spanish survivors of the Armada, the O'Donnell had the motley crew of Irish rebels with a spine of O'Donnells and MacSweeney Galloglass, albeit all highly trained in killing other Irishmen.

To all in the court, Red Hugh seemed to be the rising power in Connacht and Leinster. Ineen Dubh used her contacts in Scotland, and many a well-to-do redshank constable lingered at the back of the hall, costing the job and waiting for the war to start. But such preparations needed cattle and money, and as Seamus and Sean entered, the walls reverberated with the O'Donnell's plans to raid Connacht. Seamus worked his way through the crowd and past the guards to whisper in the ear of Eoghan McToole O'Gallagher.

"I have urgent messages for the O'Donnell from our friends in Wicklow," and Seamus opened his bag to show Eoghan the letters.

"Wait 'till he's finished, and then I'll get you a personal audience."

Red Hugh finished his speech with promises of help from the Spanish king and told everyone to prepare for Connacht. The men loved it, as it paved the way to their apparent fortunes. Red Hugh rose and lapped up the applause. He walked out of the court, beaming from ear to ear. Eoghan McToole O'Gallagher approached him as he left the room with Ineen Dubh and their bodyguards.

"Lord, Seamus has returned from Wicklow with urgent letters."

"Come to my room and let us read them."

Seamus was invited to follow, but Sean was directed into the court to refresh himself after his long journey. Red Hugh did not look back to greet Seamus until the door of the room was closed behind them.

"So what news do you bring me from the south?"

"Fiach MacHugh O'Byrne still resists after all these years but is under heavy pressure from the English. I don't know how long he can hold out."

"He shall have all the help that I can give him. If it weren't for him, I would have ended up back in prison in Dublin or frozen to death in the hills of Wicklow. I have been putting his case forward to the Irish Council for a pardon."

"He is also hiding Hugh Boye MacDavitt from the English."

Red Hugh looked elated.

"Come to the meeting of the O'Donnell leaders tomorrow. We have plans that may provide a suitable distraction for both our friends."

24

Raids in Connacht

Seamus and Sean made their way through the camp outside Donegal town. The depraved pit of mud, drunkenness and lawlessness that had blossomed in their absence suited its occupants well.

"What these men need is a good battle," said Seamus and Sean nodded his agreement.

He sought directions from a man in rags wrapped around a bottle. The man was sitting alone amongst a group of tents and did not recognise Seamus, but gave him directions all the same. Seamus arrived at where he thought he once camped but recognised neither man nor panorama. Shea Óg was nowhere to be found, or his son Sean, or their three remaining companions from Enniskillen. Seamus wandered a little further to where he thought the overseas veterans were camped, but they too were nowhere to be seen. He slapped his thigh in despair.

"Just what you'd expect of a bunch of never-do-wells with nothing to do."

Seamus walked on and saw a face he recognised, looked bored by a campfire whose only companion was a bottle.

"Hey! Where's the man with a bag on his head?"

"That troublemaker went back to his clan," and the man pointed to his right.

"The O'Rourkes?"

"That'll be the one," the man nodded and returned his attention to the fire and the bottle.

"Damn."

The O'Rourkes were one of the larger clan contingents in the camp. Shea Óg was gathering allies.

"Are we going to look for your friend?" asked Sean.

"No, and he's not my friend," came the curt response.

"Then?"

"We go find some of your fellow soldiers, the Munster boys from the Netherlands."

They walked through the camp, and from the way the men sat in their own circles enclosed by their own tents, it was apparent the soldiers had broken down into their clan rivalries.

"They need someone to fight, and fast," remarked Seamus.

"Yes, the war can't come quick enough," agreed Sean again.

After seeking directions several more times in the chaotic camp, they finally came across the men from Munster. There were only about twenty, but fifteen were veterans while the rest were farm boys they picked up on their trek north. However, in Seamus's absence, the men had proved themselves to the O'Donnell as good, loyal fighting men and subsequently joined the small but growing O'Donnell shot.

They warmly greeted Seamus and Sean, for those who did not know the former in person knew him by reputation.

"I'll make you eejits good MacSheehys yet! So what do you boys do for a good time around here?" roared Seamus.

The men cheered and raised whatever vessels they could lay their hands on that contained beer or other alcohol. Seamus led them to Donegal town, where they knew him well in all best alehouses and brothels. Given his standing with the O'Donnell, he could get them in anywhere. They spent three days idling away, drinking and bonding.

"Sure, what's the point in training you for three days when we could drink for three days instead," said Seamus as he raised his mug for the umpteenth salute.

The men roared back their appreciation and emptied their cups. The rowdy crew was one of many that littered the streets of Donegal. However, if anyone ever objected or complained about them, the men would point to Seamus. He would tell the complainant to make their objections about Seamus MacSheehy to Red Hugh himself, for he was the only person he answered to. Nobody went to make known their gripes. But he remembered he had responsibilities that went with his connections, and eventually they had to return to their tents to sober up.

News of his return soon spread around the camp. Seamus lay in the communal area of the veteran's tents, contemplating training when Shea Óg and his son came within earshot.

"Oh damn!" and Seamus covered his face with the nearest cloth within reach.

"Hells bells."

He chose the wrong one.

He bolted upright, overwhelmed by the smell, and straight into Shea Óg and Sean.

"I see you're doing well for yourself these days," smirked Shea Óg.

"When was the last time you washed your mask? I can smell it from here."

"You've been gone a long time. The captain has been looking for you," said Shea Óg, ignoring Seamus's last comment.

"Well, he knows where to find me, and he knows what he has to do. Now excuse me, I've got work to do. May your last days with the O'Rourkes be pleasant ones," and Seamus waved Shea Óg away.

"What's that supposed to mean?" and Shea Óg felt for the axe in his belt.

The commotion attracted the veterans, and they surrounded Shea Óg.

"I would leave while you still can."

Seamus smiled at Shea Óg, who growled and turned tail.

"Who's he?" asked Sean.

"No one. Just a shadow from the past."

* * *

Several days later, Seamus was summoned to attend the meeting of the military heads of the O'Donnells as the representative of the veterans. Spirits were high and Red Hugh did not disappoint when he announced they were going on a massive raid into Connacht. Hugh selected Seamus to lead a unit of men on the raid alongside a force of rebels assembled from those who had fled Tirconnell from Connacht and Leinster. They were to be stiffened by MacSweeney Galloglass and redshanks.

There were still shortages of modern weapons, so they were only to be allocated to men who had already been trained in their usage. Most of the veteran shot were sent off to join a unit of recently trained MacSweeney shot, and those that were skilled with pikes enhanced the MacSweeney pikes. Despite his extensive knowledge of the art of warfare, Seamus always preferred the axe and stuck with a unit of traditional MacSweeney Galloglass. Sean joined him, and Shea Óg stayed with the O'Rourkes. The O'Donnells departed in high spirits, especially Red Hugh since he knew that Hugh O'Neill was co-ordinating raids on the other side of Ulster to draw the English away from Connacht.

The raiders spread out on columns to avoid detection from Sligo Castle, the main English base in the area which controlled easy access to Connacht from the north. Once past the castle, the columns spread out. Renegade clan members from Connacht advised each column regarding the clan territories they passed through. They were supposed to identify local farmers and chieftains sympathetic to the O'Donnell and identify the collaborators with the English. However, the guides were not always impartial and also took revenge on their enemies and rivals.

The stream of cattle being redirected to Tirconnell pleased Red Hugh. Some of the local people moved too. They were encouraged to go north to Tirconnell as long as they swore loyalty to Red Hugh. The rebels met little resistance, for the locals expected the raids to continue until the English defeated the O'Donnell in battle.

Once Red Hugh heard the English were rallying their forces in Connacht, he called the retreat. Sir Richard Bingham and his army of raw recruits tried to intercept Red Hugh as he returned to Tirconnell, but the latter easily evaded him. MacSweeney Galloglass gave cover to the raiders, expertly herding the cattle and covering the retreat, so the locals or the English recovered very little of what was taken. They spent the next couple of days counting cattle and dividing the spoils between the O'Donnell lords and their allies. The mercenaries and allies in the camp were treated to an endless supply of beef and ale to celebrate their success. Red Hugh ensured he had a considerable surplus, and when he knew what was set aside, he sent his mother to Scotland once more to bring back redshanks.

He was further encouraged by news that O'Neill raided the lands of Sir Henry Bagenal, and the counties of Meath and Louth, even penetrating as far as the Pale. Encouraged by the successes of the Confederacy, Red Hugh ordered another raid into Connacht.

Seamus enjoyed the successes of the raid, and his men had performed well. His band of veterans had attracted other experienced soldiers with no fixed or firm allegiance to any clan swelling their ranks. He promoted those with leadership skills and assigned them with men to lead. The rest were trained to fight like a traditional Galloglass. He was acquainted with Spanish methods from his time in the Netherlands and could mould his men to operate effectively with the pike and shot, both enhancing his reputation and his usefulness to the O'Donnells. He was rising through the ranks and catching the eye of Red Hugh.

* * *

The next day Red Hugh summoned Seamus to meet him in one of his private rooms. Red Hugh stared out the window with his back to the door as Seamus entered. Eoghan McToole O'Gallagher stood in the background. The table was awash with maps, and Eoghan's face was a prelude of seriousness.

Seamus stood and announced himself, and Red Hugh acknowledged him with a brief nod before getting straight to business.

"Seamus, things are looking up for the confederation of the North. But we need to expand it into Connacht and Leinster to have any hope of a strong Irish army before the Spanish army arrives," Red Hugh puffed his chest out to show that he would lead this Irish army.

"Is there news from Spain?" Seamus asked.

"The archbishops of Ireland put our case to the king at any opportunity. They have told us that the Spanish king will send a mission soon."

"Hopefully, that will lead to something this time," replied Seamus.

"Indeed, but the more we prepare, the stronger our position we will be when they arrive, and the English are defeated. You can play an important role."

"Thank you, lord, for such high praise. What would you wish me to do?"

"Our next raid will be deep into Connacht. I have assembled some men that know Leinster well. Break off with these men when we reach the lower Shannon. Go to Wicklow. Use these men to beef up the resistance. Then return here with Hugh Boye MacDavitt. We need him to help train our armies so we can take on the English in the field. I cannot stress the importance of your mission. Eoghan will bring you to meet your men."

Seamus bowed.

"Thank you for entrusting me with this. I will return with Hugh Boye as soon as it is safe to do so."

"The O'Donnells, the northern Confederation, indeed Ireland no less, needs you to succeed."

"I bare this burden for the glory of the O'Donnell and the good of Ireland," and Seamus bowed and left, inwardly unmoved by such histrionics.

Seamus secretly hoped that being the O'Donnell had not gone to Red Hugh's head.

* * *

Following Eoghan McToole O'Gallagher through the network of corridors and out into the field behind the castle, Seamus noticed a ragbag of men in a disjointed line looking for their new leader. He was delighted to find Sean O'Toole amongst them. However, another familiar face awaited Seamus.

"I'm not taking him! How are we supposed to remain inconspicuous with a man who has a bag on his head?"

"Sorry, Red Hugh thought you might object. But he knows Leinster better than anyone. Besides, Red Hugh has done a deal to support Brian Óg O'Rourke, and part of it is to take some of his men. But you never know, he might die on the way," replied Eoghan McToole.

Seamus scowled, for he knew he was stuck with him. He inspected the men and did little to disguise how unimpressed he was with them. It certainly was not like the days when he served the Fitzgeralds, but they were long behind him. But he had to make do.

* * *

The next day, the O'Donnell army set off for Connacht. Again, it was a united enterprise comprising the O'Donnells and their supporters from Ulster, Connacht and Leinster. Their mission was to defeat whatever opposition they came across and steal all the cows and any transportable victuals they could lay their hands on. Unbeknown to Seamus, Red Hugh invited Hugh Maguire to join him in the raid. Maguire could not resist the offer of potential loot, and he also had mercenaries and soldiers that required paying. He took some of his best men away from the siege of Enniskillen, leaving the conduct of the blockade to Cormac MacBaron. Eunan O'Keenan Maguire would be in their ranks.

* * *

Shea Óg proved useful during the raid at first, as his knowledge of the land was extensive. However, his true talent for cruelty and greed was wasted on the local population. Not only did Red Hugh wish to dispossess the most prominent landowners who supported the Crown, he also wanted to invoke the local population's sympathies. Impartiality was therefore required, something which Shea Óg lacked. As Seamus reprimanded him and tried to constrain his actions, their already frayed relationship collapsed.

Red Hugh was about to penetrate deeper into Connacht when he called a halt to the advance. They directed the herds of captured cattle to Tirconnell and word spread that he was waiting for Hugh Maguire. The rain pelted down, and the day became increasingly darker. Seamus summoned Shea Óg for advice, where he was directed to a hill to survey the land overlooking Breifne. He gave Shea Óg the slip, for he did not want him to follow him and learn what he was planning. He returned to his unit and then issued his orders. As they climbed the hill, visibility steadily worsened. Seamus and his men were on high alert, exercising caution with every tread.

* * *

Maguire summoned Eunan to his tent, along with other senior Maguire men. He told them to rally their men for a raid on Connacht. The Maguire's financial and victual needs became more pressing since the siege had caused considerable disruption to food production and the roaming of the cattle herd in Fermanagh. Also, Red Hugh did not supply his redshanks for free.

Eunan relished the opportunity to forge his men in battle, for there was only so much training that time, weather, morale and insufficient supply of weaponry would permit. Cattle rustling would be an easy and familiar introduction to the art of war for those farm boys who needed the experience.

The men of Hugh Maguire marched south in high spirits, eager for the successes of Red Hugh to rub off on them. Neither fog nor rain could deflate their spirits. Maguire ordered Eunan to climb a hill on the flank to scout for the English and the O'Donnell. They did so with a spring in every boggy step.

* * *

Eunan's men reached the top of the hill amidst a blanket of dreary fog. They walked to each visually impaired vantage point on the hill but could not lay sight to the land beneath. His men rested and laid their weapons on the ground, searching their pockets for stale bread stolen from an unlucky farmer in Breifne, whom they declared to be 'a whore of the Crown'. The man was spared his life, but only after his livelihood had been stripped from him.

Eunan sat in the centre of his men, proud of the marauding beasts they had become, their tentacles spreading across the land. They had dispensed the justice of the Maguire and the O'Donnell to those waverers and traitors that stood in their path. They had stripped the unworthy of their ill-gotten gains obtained by siding with the English or standing idly by whilst the English crushed their fellow Irishmen. Those same ill-gotten gains were then redirected northwards where they could be put to work for the cause of the rebellion. Sure, some of their victims were innocent, but the clans were innocent and English justice was imposed on them, regardless. Eunan was the leader of men; the leader of men with a purpose. Every action they took was for the Maguire, the rebellion and the impending arrival of the Spanish king's men.

The sound of voices and the clinking of armour alerted Eunan that a body of men approached through the fog. He immediately ordered his men to pick up their weapons and prepare to defend themselves.

"To whom do you serve?" Eunan shouted at them.

Seamus did not recognise Eunan's men, for their shambolic assortment of chain mail, arms, and armour did not reveal them to a force of professional standing. Still, they could have been a collection of local farmers who had dug up what arms they could to defend their homestead. Usually, Seamus would merely order his men to charge, and such a ramshackle force would dispense anything of weight and run like rabbits to their burrows. But he had no wish to risk injury with such thick fog and treacherous ground underfoot. He barked instead.

"I am here on the business of Red Hugh O'Donnell. If you are friends, make yourselves known. If you are foe, take this opportunity to run. We have buried enough of our enemies this day. The O'Donnell wishes no harm to the gentlefolk of Ireland but desires them free. His enemies, however, can rest eternally in this bog."

Eunan did not recognise his voice, for he considered Seamus to be in some other faraway place.

"We are the men of the Maguire, and we have come to join the raid of the O'Donnell. Let us join forces so I can send word back to my master about the location of the O'Donnell so he can co-ordinate."

Seamus considered the proposal and decided this could be an opportunity to ditch most of his men and set off on his mission to Wicklow.

"Stop your men where they are, and we will come and join you."

The two groups of men joined, and they embraced and exchanged stories about how they got there and the lands of Connacht that lay open before them. Eunan searched for the O'Donnell commander, who was not leading his men. The soldiers opened their ranks, and there before him stood...

"Seamus!" Eunan growled, and his body became rigid.

He raised his axe.

Óisin, who stood beside him, threw his arm across Eunan's axe. Even he had kept a sense that they should not be engaging with the forces of their allies, especially if those forces could easily carve them up into little pieces.

"Eunan," said Seamus, almost monotone. "I see you have sought to make something of the life I saved. I see the anger still burns in you.

There are plenty of foes for you to throw your little axes at rather than avenge imaginary grudges against me."

"Imaginary? YOU KILLED MY MOTHER!" Eunan raised his axe and, in a blind fury, ran towards Seamus.

Óisin saw the snarls on the men's faces from the north and knew that if Eunan reached Seamus, they would all die. Eunan tripped and fell face down in the mud. Óisin retracted his foot then went to cover up his treachery by helping Eunan up, but he refused the hand of help.

"Your friend has more sense than you," said Seamus. "Come back to me when you have the guts to admit you're a MacSheehy. Then we can talk or clash axes. I'll leave the choice to you."

Seamus walked away. He saw the humiliation of Eunan's face, a reminder of the fragility of his ego. Eunan was losing his men. Whatever of his many faults, he was still his only living relative, the last in a line of MacSheehy Galloglass. Everyone had old dreams and myths running through their heads and driving them towards the battlefield. Seamus's tale was that the MacSheehy Galloglass would rise again and return to their lands of Munster. Everything would be like it was in the days before the Desmond rebellions and the endless spiralling feuds between the MacSheehys and the Munster MacSweeneys. Sean O'Rourke stepped out of the ranks, and Seamus noticed the lust for blood and revenge in his eyes. He saw an opportunity.

As he walked over to Eunan, he extended his hand and helped him to his feet.

"Get up, you are a chieftain of the Maguire, and we are allies."

Eunan could barely lift his head, and he wiped the blade of his axe in his trousers. Seamus noticed the men from both sides smirking at Eunan in front of his face.

"Whatever grudge you hold against me, we should settle now. You want to fight and kill me? I am an agent of the O'Donnell, a commander of men, and bestowed with a mission. By Brehon law, you would owe my master a debt if you kill me - a debt so large, you could never repay. You would also sully your master's reputation with mine. My death would be the only consolation you would have as a broke and humiliated outcast roaming Ireland. Therefore, it would be better for both of us if you lay slain on the ground.

"However, that is a proposition you may not be agreeable with. So I propose a solution: I will elect a champion to fight in my place. If you kill him, our issues are resolved. If he kills you, then I shall mourn for the death of the last of my kin. I will give you one of my very best men so that you will know if you kill him, you will have done damage to me. Let all of you who stand here and watch that this fight witness the resolving of our issues. I nominate as my champion, Sean O'Rourke."

Eunan cocked his head.

"A champion!?"

He looked at the faces of his men and knew that if they were ever to respect him again, he had to accept the challenge. Sean strode out of the ranks, drooling at the prospect of gaining revenge for his father's maiming and family's humiliation. Seamus stepped back to adjudicate the fight.

"I assume we follow the Galloglass way and fight with axes?"

"We can fight any way you want, but it'll end up with me splitting his head open," exclaimed Sean.

"Hack the little bastard to bits," screamed his father.

Eunan took his axe and looked at Óisin for reassurance. Óisin nodded back.

"Then let us begin! To the death!" cried Seamus before melting back amongst his men.

Sean raised his axe. The rain pelted off the freshly sharpened blade. His grip was firm and his gaze steady.

"Come on then. Raise your axe!"

Eunan gripped the shaft of his axe and psyched himself up for battle. He gripped the ground with his feet, as he was unsure how he fell in front of Seamus. It was slippery underfoot, but he had fought in a bog before, standard fare for a trainee Galloglass.

"Quit praying for your Mammy and come on," shouted Sean.

Eunan charged like a bull. Sean skipped aside like a matador. Eunan rolled around in the mud like a pig ripe for slaughter.

Seamus tapped Sean O'Toole on the shoulder.

"Gather the men. Our mission awaits."

"Are you going to leave your only living kin to die in the mud?" exclaimed Sean O'Toole.

"If we stay, the O'Donnell may die in the mud, too. The boy has to learn. If he lives, he will be wiser for it. The characters of men are forged in the fires of war or the mud of a bog. Let us go, or you can stay and be the champion for him."

Sean O'Toole directed the men down the opposite slope of the hill.

Sean O'Rourke raised his axe above his head to go in for the kill. Eunan tried to push himself back in the slippery mud but only spend energy and panicked. An idea flashed into his mind.

"What would Seamus do?"

He reached for his axe and thrust it up from the mud. The spray blinded Sean and allowed Eunan a moment's respite to get back to his feet.

"Don't let him up! Kill him!" screamed Shea Óg.

Óisin's heart warmed when he estimated they were cheap deaths under Brehon law as per Seamus's previous threats.

Sean was a hulk of a man, with excellent technique and a steady balance on his feet. He was, however, impatient and went for the knock-out blow each time instead of waiting for an opportunity to present itself. He swung for Eunan again, who by now found his feet. Eunan parried Sean's blows, inviting him forward, retreating slowly and feeling the ground as he did so. Sean jabbed and swung, advancing. The men surrounding the fight bellowed their support for their favoured side and expanded the circle as Eunan retreated. Eunan watched Sean's feet, along with his swinging axe.

"Finish him!" cried Shea Óg, and Sean thrust forward.

As he did so, he placed his foot in a hole in the bog that Eunan had carefully avoided. Eunan had not wasted his time as the mud rolling pig. Sean collapsed, his axe fell to the ground, and Eunan's axe fell on him with such force Sean could merely whimper until a second blow put him out of his misery. Eunan raised his hands in triumph and wiped the blood and mud from his face. He looked around for Seamus so he could lord over him.

"He is gone," said Óisin as he saw that victory rapidly deflated from Eunan's face.

Indeed, Seamus was now a mile or two across the bogs toward Wicklow. The rest of his men disappeared to link back up with the O'Donnells. Meanwhile, Shea Óg and a couple of O'Rourkes made good their escape in the post-victory commotion and departed back to Breifne.

25

Return to Wicklow

Every man who could bear arms and would take the Queen's shilling was sent to Connacht or the northern Pale border, leaving Ulster to fend off the strongly rumoured rebel invasion. Red Hugh and his spies provided Seamus with the perfect cover to slip into Wicklow. He hoped it would be this easy on the way back and hoped he would not die in a hangman's noose. With such a stream of people on Ireland's dirt roads, nobody noticed a couple of strangers with a place to go. He soon found himself in the foothills of the Wicklow mountains, and Fiach's agents brought him to the rebel camp. Once there, Seamus sent Sean O'Toole to find out what happened since they had departed. Seamus did not have to wait long for news.

Fiach looked pained when Seamus went to see him in his tent. He lifted his head from his hands as he sat in the makeshift wooden chair of the O'Byrne.

"I am so glad you are back, my friend. You may have brought me few reinforcements, but at least you brought some."

"Where is my greeting? Why am I not bowled off my feet with the great bear hug I crossed Ireland to receive?"

"I would be a hypocrite to hug you and then tell you that my underlings wasted the lives of your men."

"Tell me what happened?"

"You haven't heard?"

"I have been in the field for weeks."

"Walter Reagh proved to be as uncontrollable, but as charming as ever. Your men craved action and soon fell under his spell. Walter was.."

"Was?"

"Was… Walter was always determined to retake the lands of his forefathers."

"Every Irish lord is the prisoner of his past, and the past gives birth to many a foolish thought."

"Indeed. We are all trapped in a loop of imagined past glories and spend our lives trying to live up to them. Anyway, Brian O'Byrne, a well-known turncoat, came under the vengeful spotlight of Walter Reagh. Walter gathered his men, including your own, and went to take out his vengeance. His men were no match for the O'Byrne castle walls, but Brian's ego was weak, and he fell for Walter Reagh's goading and came out to fight him in single combat. As dexterous a swordsman as he is, Walter Reagh was no match for Brian, a once valiant fighter for the rebellion until the Crown bought him off. Walter was wounded and dragged to the hills. He was placed in a cave for safekeeping while some men came back to fetch us. In the meantime, Brian alerted the garrison of the Pale, and they took to the mountains to find Walter Reagh. I raised our men to form a rescue party, and the survivors of the raid led us back towards the cave. We kept running into English patrols, who were increasingly suspicious that they were close to Walter Reagh.

"Our men had left Walter in the capable hands of a young physician charged with ensuring he could travel. Every day the physician gathered herbs so he could apply fresh medicine to Walter's wounds. But one day he was caught by the English patrols. By fair means or foul, they persuaded him to betray his patient. Walter was captured and imprisoned in Dublin Castle. A swift trial followed, and he was found guilty of treason, hung, drawn and quartered. His head was placed on a spike outside the castle for all to see."

Seamus hesitated as Fiach's hand juddered.

"I am sorry for your loss. Walter Reagh would have made a good rebel if he was capable of any control. But you realise that many heads of your family will decorate the spikes of Dublin Castle, maybe even your own before we see any progress."

"You have a hard heart Seamus MacSheehy, a perceptive brain for war and its surrounding horrors and a sharp tongue to administer advice. If ever I needed counsel, I would wish for you."

"My advice will always be available for as long as I am around. However, we must still get down to business, even in a time of mourning. Where is Hugh Boye, and how has he been?"

"When he is not complaining, he has proved himself to be of much use. His reputation is deserved. We have waged a more effective campaign in the mountains, draw more allies to our cause, and if it were not for the various hotheads I attract, we would do well."

"You will attract every rebel bard in the country wanting to write songs of your glories!"

"Hmm, they would also want to be great poets to edit out all my errors."

"Come, lead me to Hugh Boye. The O'Donnell raid will last at least another two weeks. I need to leave while there is still cover provided."

Fiach rose, and they left the tent. He had sent word, and the sons and leaders of his ragged alliance were outside waiting for them.

"Is Hugh Boye still in hiding?" asked Seamus.

"Yes, but it is pointless. Every man and his wife knows him and where he is. The English must've paid a pretty penny for his location for their patrols get nearer every day."

Once outside, Seamus looked out at a sea of faces. They were worn, tired, unhappy. Not an ounce of joy. They had been chased relentlessly from pillar to post without a victory or rest. But at least they were still here. However, he could ride a coach and horses through the divide in the camp. It was visibly much worse now between O'Byrne and O'Toole. For all his talents, the return of Turlough O'Byrne had brought the alliance to breaking point. The English would at least save some money, for it would take fewer bribes now for someone to give up a brother or sister-in-law or a soon-to-be-former friend.

Fiach called a council meeting in the tent of Hugh Boye.

"Walter Reagh may have united the bards together to sing his praises to melt down his foolishness and forge a heroic memorial for him, but all he has done is bring the English to our door," said Fiach.

"He was a courageous man, a great patriot, a true Irishman," said Turlough in defence of his friend. "We should use his death as a call to all good Catholics of Leinster to rise up and rid the land of our heathen English oppressors."

"Are these the words of a wise Catholic lord confident of victory, or those of a man who wants to bring us out into the open and get slaughtered? A man with a dagger beneath his cloak and English coin in his pocket?" replied Redmond O'Byrne.

Turlough went for his dagger but was restrained by his brother Phelim. Turlough shook him off.

"The daughter of the Welsh whore must be good in bed if she can turn you against your own brother! How can you trust these O'Toole women, the descendants of a Welsh pastor? How can they come in and take over a good Irish family and say they believe in the one true faith? Look at us. We are still brothers in blood. We spend our time these days with our knives to the other's throat!"

Fiach slammed his knife on the table.

"Enough! We are nothing if we are not united! There will be no more of this fighting between my sons. If there is, you may force me into considering a more permanent solution.

"For now, we must consider the penetrations the English have made into the Wicklow mountains. We are no longer safe here. We must move south to a new camp I have been preparing."

"But father," said Turlough, "if we continue to retreat, we'll run out of mountains. We need another Glenmalure to send them packing back to the Pale."

"We no longer have the strength to launch such an extravagant ambush. If we had, I would have done it long ago. Our friends in the north have kindly provided us with cover so we can lick our wounds. We should accept the opportunity they have given us."

The room was silent.

"I take it we are agreed. We leave at first light."

The tent cleared except for Seamus, whose face had become less friendly.

"We had an agreement. I take Hugh Boye up north at the first opportunity."

"Be at ease, my friend. The mountains are no longer safe. You will be released at the first opportunity."

Seamus left the tent, furious that he could not leave immediately. Sean O'Toole was following him.

"Master, I have news of the O'Tooles."

"Let it be good, for that is all the news I could bear."

"The camp is more divided than ever and rife with spies. We are in great danger here."

"We cannot leave without Hugh Boye, and Fiach knows this. We shall leave at the first chance we get, but only with Hugh Boye."

"I will keep my eyes open and my ears to the ground."

"Now, let us get some sleep, for I fear that it'll be in short supply soon."

* * *

The opportunity to escape with Hugh Boye was elusive. Lord Deputy Russell sensed he had Fiach on the run. He sent more men into the Wicklow mountains to flush him out. Fiach and his men spent six weeks being chased around the mountains eating into their stock of safe houses as one by one their houses were given up by traitors, who were tired of the fight and wished to retire and be on good terms with the English or succumbed to greed. Death, debilitating wounds and sickness also depleted Fiach's numbers. The alliance broke down into the family groups, with Seamus and Hugh Boye sticking with Fiach, Turlough and the O'Byrnes, and Rose went with Phelim, Redmond and the O'Tooles.

The latter went north to their traditional lands to save the rapidly diminishing number of O'Byrne safe houses. Rose went to a cousin of hers, an Irish Catholic with a good-sized plot of land, but an excellent reputation with the English, for he had remained peaceful over the years and had not openly joined the rebellion. She was to hide with him until summoned back by Fiach.

* * *

By now, Hugh Boye mapped the mountains of Wicklow and was planning a series of ambushes to drive the English back from the Pale. Fiach was quietly confident but wished for his wife to be safe and entice some of the lowland chieftains into the rebel confederation.

Fiach reunited with Turlough's men and executed the first ambush of their new campaign. They were in a self-congratulatory mood.

"Those English won't be leaving Wexford soon," laughed Turlough. Fiach grabbed him by the shoulders.

"It is good to taste success again. It has been a long time. We should send out bands of raiders across Leinster and rally the chieftains of old!"

Hugh Boye was allowed out in the open now. Fiach felt more secure with the reduced numbers of men, most of whom he was familiar with for a considerable time. However, Hugh Boye would always remind Fiach of the other reason he remained in seclusion.

"They were a small patrol, Pale irregulars. They would have run if a wild boar had run from the trees at them," he said.

"Give the men their victory. They have precious little else to hold on to as they endlessly roam the woods," and Turlough dismissed the critique with the wave of an arm.

Tension had grown between Seamus and Fiach since the former had arrived back, and Fiach was reluctant to let Hugh Boye go, fearing the loss of his greatest asset and leverage with the northern lords.

"Hugh Boye is wasted here, Fiach," said Seamus. "Your problems would be solved quicker if he could go north and train the northern armies. They would draw the English away from here and allow you to retake Ballinacor and reestablish your alliances."

"Hugh Boye is no good to anybody dead. What will the Hughs say to me if he dies under my care? He can go at the first good opportunity, but it had to be an obvious opportunity. I have responsibilities to more than just you."

Seamus was about to reply, but his words got stuck in his throat as they saw Phelim and Redmond emerge from the trees.

"Father! We must speak with you alone."

Fiach directed them to a secluded part of the wood. Seamus grew immediately suspicious. After several minutes later, Fiach returned alone. His eyes burned with a fury worthy of hell. He called his eldest son.

"Turlough, may I speak with you, please?"

Heated words were exchanged between father and son. Phelim and Redmond sat in silence by the fire and helped themselves to some food.

Turlough stormed back.

"Men! We are leaving."

The O'Byrne supporters of Turlough left in confusion but obeyed the summons all the same. Fiach walked back slowly, lost in his thoughts.

"What just happened?" asked Seamus.

"We shall speak of this later. For now, I need to keep my thoughts to myself."

They sat for what seemed like an age, all staring into the fire and not speaking. At last, Fiach got up.

"Come, we'll speak now," and Fiach signalled to Seamus and Hugh Boye to follow him. They walked to the same secluded patch.

"The English have taken Rose," he muttered.

"What!? Who gave her up?" asked Hugh Boye.

"Let him tell the story before we jump to any conclusions," said Seamus, trying to calm things down. "What happened?"

"She went to her cousin as arranged, the one who gave her residence of an abandoned house on his small estate. She awoke after her first night to be surrounded by English soldiers and is now a prisoner of Russell himself."

"Will she talk?" asked Hugh Boye.

"She'd never give me up."

"You never know what a torturer can do to a person until they experience it," said Seamus as he rubbed some old wounds.

"She won't talk," said Fiach firmly.

"So who gave her up?" asked Seamus.

Fiach paused.

"The O'Tooles say it was Turlough," and Fiach looked away, ashamed that his son could be associated with such treachery.

"They would say that," said Seamus. "You've got to look at it sensibly. The most likely person to have given her up is that cousin of hers. Have you sent men to speak to him?"

"It is a delicate situation. Phelim and Redmond have taken the O'Tooles' side. They say that Turlough became a traitor the day the English imprisoned him."

"And you believe that?"

Fiach paused again.

"I believe that the brittle alliance that I have so long held together is now falling apart. I need Rose as a man needs his wife but also as a king needs his first minister to hold everything together."

"However, you must follow the truth. You must discover who the traitor is, and if it is not Turlough, you must see that he is acquitted. Only then can the healing between the two families begin."

"As you can see, I require counsel. If you leave now, I fear the Leinster alliance will collapse."

"Then I insist you listen to counsel and establish if your son is guilty."

"My investigation results will be open for all to see," replied Fiach.

* * *

Turlough returned with O'Byrne supporters three days later. He also acquired on his travels another rebel of minor repute, Maurice Fitzgerald. Upon arriving back at the camp, Turlough was immediately summoned to meet with Fiach, who asked that Seamus and Hugh Boye join them as observers. Turlough stood defiantly before his father.

"You burned the house of your mother-in-law's cousin to the

ground?"

"I avenged the O'Byrnes against the traitor who sold your wife to the English, just as you should have done."

Fiach did not fall for the provocation.

"The O'Tooles say that the traitor is you. That you were so consumed by hatred for your mother-in-law that you had her followed, and when you knew where she was residing, you went to your English masters and gave her up for gold. You then returned to the scene of your crime and burned all the evidence."

The anger seared down to Turlough's clenched fists.

"Do you believe that of your firstborn son and heir? I did what the strong must do to maintain the alliances. I dealt with the traitor the way traitors should be dealt with. Those O'Toole harlots entrance my brothers, those daughters of the Protestant minister were sent to infiltrate and destroy us! Can you not see that they are tearing us apart with their lies? They just want to take over these lands and sell them back to the English."

"I realise you are angry, son, but I have got to be seen to be fair. The O'Tooles believe these things are true, and I need someone who can hold the alliance together if I die. You have been uncontrollable these past months, yourself and Walter Reagh. All your follies heaped upon us are miseries, and now we are but outlaws in the forest, no better than the wild pigs."

Turlough could see that his father's mind was made up.

"Do with me what you wish. However, be prepared for the consequences when the truth emerges."

Fiach paused again. He did not look at Seamus and Hugh Boye.

"I have little choice, son. If I side with you, though you may be right, the O'Tooles will leave. If I side with the O'Tooles, Phelim and Redmond may bring some O'Byrnes with them, and the alliance remains intact. You are to remain under house arrest until I can discover the truth. I am sorry, but that is what needs to be done. Take him away."

Two O'Toole men took an arm each and led a protesting Turlough to an outhouse where he was placed under guard.

"Be careful what you do, Fiach," warned Seamus. "That boy may be headstrong, but he is the best of your offspring by a distance. I would have torched the cousin's lands myself if Turlough hadn't done it. By looking weak, you attract every traitor who was previously too cowardly because there would have been no fear of reprisals."

"It is hard to condemn me if you don't walk in my shoes. You can go north and leave the hard decisions and consequences to the O'Donnell. I have no such luxury."

Seamus took his friend by the arm.

"I will defend you, but don't make it so difficult that you drive me and everyone else that wants to help you away."

Fiach took his arm back.

"I must alert my spies and get news of what has happened to my dearest Rose. Please leave me while I make my plans."

Seamus and Hugh Boye swiftly left such foolishness behind.

* * *

Maurice Fitzgerald turned out to be the latest potential rebel that Fiach could not control. Upon hearing that Turlough was placed under house arrest, he gathered together the dwindling band of Turlough's supporters and rode towards the Pale. To all observers, it appeared as if the O'Byrnes were about to implode.

26

The gift

Hugh Maguire called his best warriors to meet with him in his tent in search of volunteers for the fresh assault on Enniskillen Castle. Everyone gladly volunteered, and he chose forty warriors for the mission. Eunan was one of the first to be selected, such was his standing in the clan.

Hugh and the selected men assembled at dawn the next day in the woods near the castle. They still had quite a distance to travel in open country to the walls of the castle, since most of the trees had fallen victim to the forays of the garrison. Hugh, in his speech to his warriors, singled Eunan out for praise.

"Since you have been such a brave warrior and fought valiantly for me, especially when I was down on my luck, let me give you a gift."

Hugh snapped his fingers, and one of his servants strained at the shoulders as they brought forward and held out a new set of chain mail.

"It may not be a musket or a pike, but you fight in the traditional way. Eunan, take this chain mail and lead the attack. But never give up our traditions for the falsehood of English modernity. Make sure you are not the last of the Galloglass."

Eunan combed his hair back with his hand, for he was embarrassed and did not know what to do with himself.

"I am truly grateful, lord, and may this chain mail protect me and protect the Maguires."

"Serve well and honour your clan. I leave you in the capable hands of my captain, Caolan Maguire. Follow his instructions to the word, for it is a dangerous mission on which I send you. Take back Enniskillen for the Maguires or, failing that, provide me with the means to take it. Let this night and each of your names be remembered in song."

The men saluted Hugh, who then retreated to the safety of the camp. The specially selected warriors stole off into the misty morning.

They crossed no-man's-land and got to Enniskillen Castle's moat without being detected and saw the occupants had not repaired the castle walls properly since it initially fell. The men split into small groups and swam across the moat at various points where the gaps were easily accessible. They crept through the damaged walls until a clumsily placed foot gave away their positions and intentions. The garrison rushed out to light up as much of the castle yard as their limited amount of torches would allow. The first couple of guards succumbed to the anger to the Maguire axe blades, and the slaughter continued until the defenders could accurately fire their muskets. They took out a few of the attackers, but were forced back into the castle tower.

Eunan and the remaining axemen huddled beneath the tower's walls, seeking shelter from the bullets and boulders hurled from the roof. Caolan tapped the bottom of his axe against the north door four times.

"What are you doing?" asked Eunan, crouched beneath the walls on the other side of the door frame.

"The Maguire made me keep it secret, but there is a traitor in the tower who upon our signal will open the doors," said Caolan.

They waited a couple of minutes to no response.

"Maybe he can't hear you?" said Eunan over the noise of the battle. The rocks showered from the roof. The brutal thud on the impact on the ground sent shivers through the attackers. Sunlight came over the ramparts of the castle, and with that, the element of surprise evaporated. A scream came from overhead. A man fell to his death and lay mangled in the courtyard.

"I think we know what happened to the spy," said Eunan.

Caolan gave the signal to retreat. Eunan followed him as they made their way through the courtyard, climbing over rubble and debris, dodging bullets and arrows. A few of the Maguires fell, but most made it to safety. Eunan crouched in the gateway to the piers in the river. Bullets peppered the surrounding walls.

"If we can't take the tower, at least we can steal their boats!" said Caolan, and they smashed down the door to the pier with their axes.

Once through the gates, they stole the three boats the English used to patrol the river, which also provided their primary means of escape.

They gathered all the survivors and sailed downriver to Hugh's camp. Guards alerted Hugh when the English ships were spotted on the river, and he and his men waited on the shoreline to bombard the boats with missiles. Caolan, conscious of a hostile reception, raised the Maguire's standard from the leading boat and was met with cheers when they disembarked to tell the Maguire of their failure to retake Enniskillen.

"With no boats and no walls, we'll soon starve them out," said Hugh, and he retired to his tent to dictate a letter to Red Hugh and Cormac MacBaron.

The Irish confederacy settled in for a siege.

Hugh assigned Eunan to a section of the river to watch over so that the English or Connor Roe from the south could not get past the siege works and smuggle supplies into Enniskillen Castle. With the time the siege granted him, Eunan trained his new men and cast feelers to the old lands of the O'Keenan Maguires to see if he could return and reestablish himself.

* * *

A month passed until Hugh met with Red Hugh and Cormac MacBaron to plan the final assault on the castle. After agreeing to the strategy, Eunan was summoned to see Hugh, who raised a smile when his colleague broke through the sunlight door of the tent.

"Eunan, how has your training of our recruits gone?"

"Steady, but slow. We seem only to get farm boys from down south. The cream is already in the army."

"Well, I have spoken with our allies and secured the privilege of the Maguires leading the assault to relieve their own castle. I would like you to lead that assault."

Donnacha O'Cassidy Maguire entered the tent and grinned at Eunan.

"It is a great privilege the Maguire offers you to enhance both your own and the Maguire's reputation and unite the people of Fermanagh behind him. It is especially a privilege for you to lead the men of 'south Fermanagh' into battle. The O'Cassidys will merely have to wait behind and then follow in your gloriously trodden path."

Eunan ignored him, for he remembered the warnings Desmond had given him about Donnacha. He bowed before Hugh.

"It would be a great honour for me to lead the assault. I trust I will have ladders and other equipment to take the tower?"

"Trap the English in the tower, and our allies will do the rest."

* * *

There were no axes and chain mail presented this time. Eunan assembled his men with whatever protections they acquired and whatever weaponry they possessed before. It was a mob of farm boys being led by young warriors to attack professional soldiers defending a castle. The sea of faces were eager, and the axe felt good in Eunan's hand. They set off on their mission.

The men advanced through the forests between the Maguire camp and Enniskillen until they reached the siege lines of Caolan Maguire.

"Who sent you to attack during daylight hours?" asked Caolan.

"Donnacha."

"If you survive this, I'd watch your back!"

"And he his. What is the plan?"

"You tell me. I assume you are to take the brunt of the fire from the garrison and drive them back into the tower? If you get bogged down, I'll attempt an amphibious assault."

"We will see this day through and ensure in the future the Maguire is properly advised."

"Humpf! See you on the other side!"

Eunan waved his men forward. When they reached the open fields, he contemplated Donnacha's words and Caolan's opinion of the assault. He finally realised the O'Cassidys wanted nothing to do with him, and they would prefer him dead. Eunan cursed his relatives.

"On my mother's grave, I will avenge how her family has treated the both of us. There will be only one O'Cassidy standing after this war, and that will be me!"

His thoughts wandered to Seamus and how this was precisely the type of situation he relished.

"What would Seamus do?"

A bullet whizzed past his head.

* * *

Enniskillen Castle had a commanding view of the surrounding lands, and they could see any attackers coming from miles away. The Maguire needed a distraction, and Eunan was it.

His men huddled together to cross no-man's-land. Eunan and the more experienced men stayed in the middle, so they would be more likely to survive the crossing than any of the inexperienced boys. If they thought before becoming overwhelmed by fear, they would realise there was nowhere to run. They were better off seeking shelter under the walls of the castle, as it was the only cover around. Bullets whizzed over their heads, and the sounds frightened some of the green boys who yelped and pissed their pants. However, Eunan and Hugh, who watched from afar, came to the same conclusion simultaneously. The castle was running out of ammunition.

Hugh quickly rallied his men and charged towards the moat. On the Maguire's instruction, bands of kern made their way towards the castle from multiple directions. Shots rang out, but not a Maguire man fell. The musketeers stopped firing until the attackers came within a certain range. The O'Neills and O'Donnells then took to the field, and their shot advanced to take up positions where they could provide covering fire for the assault on the castle.

Eunan and his men reached the moat. His men peppered every head that appeared over the parapet with arrows. Soon they surrounded the castle on its three land-bound sides. But all the attackers could do was pin down the defenders. They could not penetrate the castle. Then the Maguire took to the river.

Eunan and his men came out under the cover of arrows and swam the moat. The defenders resorted to casting down blocks from the tower. He scrambled up the muddy slopes and sheltered under the castle walls. His men struggled, unwilling to brave the crossing. He reached out to one poor fellow who, neither by foot nor hand, could get a solid grip to pull himself out of the moat.

"Here! Grab my hand!"

Boulders crashed all around. The man extended his hand, and Eunan tugged as hard as possible, but lost his grip. His hand was not a help, but a hindrance. He landed on top of the fellow, and they both crashed under the water. The man thrashed his arms to break the skin of the water, for his lungs needed air. The boulders fell around them, demon spawn from the castle tower. Eunan swam once more toward the shore. He looked back and saw his companion drowning. He scrambled over and pulled with all his might. Like a beached seal, he dragged the man upon the shore. Yet Eunan was not greeted with gratitude but by a hail of arrows, and what was once a seal was now a hedgehog. The life he tried so hard to save drained into the moat.

"Eunan! Eunan! Come on!"

Now was no time to mourn. Óisin called him to the wall. Eunan picked himself up and pulled his axe from the strap on his back. Óisin and several men crawled beneath the walls, with Eunan in hot pursuit.

"We must penetrate through the gaps and take the courtyard. Then the Maguire can cross no-man's-land unhindered," said Eunan.

"They have resorted to arrows. They must be nearly out of ammunition," replied Óisin.

"Indeed! We must get to the gate on the other side of the courtyard and open it up for the boats."

They crawled along the bottom of the walls, over boulders, bodies and blood, until they were below the gap in the wall. Two muskets protruded over the top of the broken wall, providing a small amount of resistance to the Maguire's advancing kern. Eunan and Óisin positioned themselves beneath the guns.

"One, two, three!"

They both reached up and grabbed for the gun muzzles.

"Ow!" and Óisin burnt his hand and fell back below the wall, nursing his wound.

Eunan was wiser and deflected his muzzle before dispatching his man with a flying axe to the forehead. Óisin's opponent suffered a similar fate, thanks to Eunan's quick thinking. He now had an excellent view of the courtyard.

"Óisin, can you fight?"

"I'll do my best," he croaked from the other side of the wall.

"For the Maguire men! FOR THE MAGUIRE!"

Eunan charged across the courtyard with bullets screaming around him. His men clambered in behind him, led by Óisin, and the few remaining defenders scattered and ran for the tower. Eunan did not pursue them, but ran to the recently repaired gate by the pier. Finding it locked, he smashed it open. His men followed him and joined his assault on the door. The defenders rallied at the entrance to the tower and reloaded their guns. The ships of the Maguire came around the river bend.

Bullets ricocheted off the walls.

"Óisin, give me cover! I need some time."

Óisin tore off some of his tunics and wrapped them around his hands so he could get some solid grip on the shaft of his axe.

"For the Maguire!" Óisin led the charge, but some bullets were absorbed by his men, which frustrated his planned charge.

Eunan smashed away at the gate, Óisin drove the defenders back to the tower. The door to the tower flew open, and the English soldiers sallied forth with a blood-curdling roar. Óisin fell back, Eunan smashed at the gate once more. The pain in Óisin's hands seared so that he could barely hold his axe up to defend himself. His men were outnumbered.

"Help Eunan! It's now or never!"

Eunan summoned the last of his strength and crashed his axe once more into the door. His initial reward was splinters, then a hole, then a friendly face.

"Get back!" the face said, and the men from the boats who had now landed smashed through the door.

Eunan turned and charged to save Óisin. The defenders fled into the tower.

* * *

With the courtyard in rebel hands, the tower running out of ammunition, and the Maguire in command of the river, the siege quickly petered out. The Maguire men brought bails of hay and bundles of sticks and placed them below the tower. The inhabitants were offered terms: their lives, bags and baggage or be burned alive. They swiftly surrendered, filing out of the tower and into the courtyard.

Shortly afterwards, the Maguire arrived. He spoke to the ward of the castle, and the English who could still walk returned to the tower to retrieve their bags and baggage. They lined up once more in the courtyard and gave what they carried out for the wounded to them. The castle prison was emptied, and the prisoners directed to the rebel camp for water and provisions. Red Hugh and Cormac MacBaron surveyed the ruins, which had cost so many lives and much of their time and energy over the past year. Both were elated and congratulated Hugh. Hugh claimed both Enniskillen and the prisoners for himself, with no objections from the other two commanders. Red Hugh and Cormac MacBaron retired to the camp to organise the celebrations. Hugh informed his captains of their next task. Some were ordered to clean up the castle, some were sent to the camp to prepare the celebration, while the rest escorted the prisoners.

* * *

The prisoners were a sorry lot, stripped of their weapons and armour, all of which remained in Enniskillen Castle for the northern confederacy to fight over. They barely seemed like men to Eunan, these dirty beasts who had not for a long time felt the cleansing water of the Erne on their skin. The remains of their once-proud uniforms were just rags, the blood and dirt of battle etched into every crevasse, and the discernible smell of smoke battled the unnameable concoction of other foul odours. Eunan was confused about how their opponents could have resisted them for so long.

"What men are these that would let themselves fall so low? To suffer such deprivations, only to humiliate themselves so by surrendering. What men are these that should deserve our mercy when all they have done is come to Fermanagh to cause misery?"

They reached the shelter of a wood, and Caolan ordered the column to stop. The men of the Maguire stopped shoulder to shoulder with the prisoners. The Maguires stood upright and proud, buoyed by their victory. Conversely, the prisoners were stooped and broken, with pleas for mercy etched on their faces, but had not as yet descended to the depths of their lips. Eunan gulped, for he did not know what would happen next, nor did he want to imagine.

Caolan turned and raised his axe.

"You English have been a blight on the lands of Fermanagh. You stole our land, money and food, left us to starve. Then you took our town and mercilessly slaughtered the defenders. Now it is time for our revenge. By order of the Maguire, I condemn you to HELL!"

The Maguires raised their axes. The wind went cold, for Fermanagh did not want this blood. Only one man knelt in his rags, shielding his head with his hands after his comrades had been felled. Eunan stood over him with his limp axe. One by one, the men of the Maguire stared at him. Óisin nodded towards Eunan's prisoner, the nod to signal what Eunan must do if he was to be one of the Maguire's men. Eunan did not want to be this man. This was his birth father—the father who raped his mother.

"Eunan!"

The axe fell. The blood and brains splashed all over Eunan's face. On his chain mail, the gift from the Maguire, the gift that ensured Eunan did his dirty work. On his axe. On the axe of this new family, the one he wanted to join so badly to cleanse his past, to cleanse his soul. It was now soiled with the blood of the slaughter of the defenceless hidden from the sight of the world in a dark forest. With one flash of adrenalin, did two souls die?

"Eunan!" Óisin put his hand on Eunan's shoulder, but he brushed him off and ran into the forest.

27

The forest

E unan went into the depths of the forest, not hearing the shouts, calling him to return. In his head swirled memories of his mother and father, Seamus and his brother. In his veins swirled Odin, Loki and Badu. He had joined the Maguire and wished to be a Galloglass to free himself and his clan, not to plunge his axe through the head of a broken man, once his former enemy and a proud soldier, even if the man served the crown.

He got away from the external voices and found a clearing in the forest with a blue sky for a roof, somewhere where he could do ultimate battle with the beasts in his head and banish them to the skies. Sitting on a broken log, its fissures filled with buoyant green moss, a haven for ants and other insects until he invaded their space, and upon their home, he invaded with his broken soul. It was an apt choice. It was like one of those places the priests would drum through his mind where the saints of old retreated to free their souls from sin and the trappings of the world.

Eunan picked up his axe, pride and misery in wood and iron. The blade still dripped from its latest victim. Red and white fragments sought the solace of the grooves of the wolfhound emblem. He wiped it on the moss the burial ground for the remains of the man's brains.

"God forgive me," Eunan cried out to the heavens. "I did it for the Maguire and my clan. If I had spared him, I would have lost all that I worked for, and someone else would have taken my place. My father, my birth father, would have gleefully committed such an act, but not me. I am a good man trapped in a body filled with bad blood."

Eunan hung his head, for the shame would no longer permit it to be held aloft.

"The coward you killed will not be here with me in Valhalla, but you could. Alongside your father!"

Eunan flung down his axe and screamed at the sky, but Odin laughed in his mind's eye. He collapsed in a heap on the log, the weight of the world compressing his brain, closed his eyes and prayed through the tears. But soon, tiredness overcame his anger, for he could keep up the rage no more.

"I'm even a failure at being possessed by bad blood."

He fell asleep.

* * *

The sound of voices disturbed Eunan from his sleep. They were coming his way with sounds of joy and relief. He saw there was a pathway nearby and hid behind a boulder with a commanding view of the path. A huddled mass of dirty faces and rags came towards him with a couple of Maguire men for guides. The stooped shoulders of the escorted men gave way to extended arms that pointed the way to the cloud strewn sky. Their faces shone with their newly found freedom. Eunan did not want to be reminded of the siege and what he was forced to do. He turned to leave until he heard what he thought was a familiar voice. Turning back to peer over the boulder just as the last of the group was passing by, the voice was confirmed.

Eunan leapt down from his hiding place as the last of the stragglers cowered back.

"Eunan!"

"Get back. No matter if you are not innocent, I don't want to kill a woman."

"Innocent of what? I've been imprisoned for months."

"You know what Seamus did to me. But it is not you with whom I have a score to settle. Stand aside Lorcan and Manus. I'm not the boy you can exploit. Come! Fight and feel the wrath of my axe."

Lorcan and Manus were much diminished by their months in prison and could barely raise a run, less so a fight.

"You would scythe us down like stalks of wheat. We are not the warrior you remember. The guards gave up feeding us long ago. We can offer you an apology, the rags off our backs and the prayers off our lips, for we have nothing else. If you want to fight someone, fight Seamus, for it was his orders we were following," said Lorcan.

Eunan could not see the skeletons before him through his rage. All he saw was Seamus and his brother, taunting and teasing him.

"Has captivity made you cowards? Remember, once a Galloglass, always a Galloglass. Raise your weapon and fight."

"We have no weapons to raise! But we are sworn to protect Dervella until Seamus returns. If you kill us, you kill Dervella, and you will die, no matter what you are to him."

The Maguire guards came down from the front of the group.

"What is going on here?" said the guards as they parted the travellers.

"These men are traitors. They should die as our foes did from the tower. Arm them, and I will give them a respectful death."

"Who are you to say they are traitors? What evidence do you have? For all, we know you could be a robber from the woods."

"I am Eunan Maguire commander from south Fermanagh and

the emblem you see in my axe marks me out as nobility from the O'Cassidy family. But it is my deeds that make me known, not my face. How could I carry out the actions with the stealth required by the Maguire if everyone knew my face and said, 'there goes Eunan Maguire'? Now arm these men and let me give them an honourable death, not for their sakes but for the reputation of the Galloglass."

The guards were aware of of Eunan Maguire's reputation and owed the refugees nothing. They did as he asked. Lorcan and Manus stood with the axes of their guards, but refused to raise them. Eunan was confused. Then he remembered:

"What would Seamus do?"

He swung his axe towards his foes.

"Have you no shame?" *"You call yourself a Galloglass?"* *"There is no honour in murdering the unarmed."*

Where there should have been the glory of striking down a foe, there was an empty hole, where there should have been glory and pride, bitterness and resentment, where there should have been the closure of a searing wound on his soul was…

"Eunan!"

A hand from behind grabbed his axe. Eunan snapped to.

"You do that, and we're both dead," cried Óisin.

Eunan wrenched his axe back from Óisin's hand and saw what he had done. Two barely recognisable corpses, blood haemorrhaged from their cavernous head wounds. Before him, Dervella knelt, her arms raised, pleading for her life.

28

Clontibret

Lord Deputy Russell was shocked at the fall of Enniskillen, for he believed that it could have held out for several more months as he resupplied it only nine months previously. Having received reinforcements of veterans from Brittany, he was feeling more confident about subduing any rebellions. Already engaged in Wicklow, he asked Sir Henry Bagenal to resupply the besieged garrison at Monaghan. Sir Henry assembled a massive force of fifteen hundred men and two hundred and fifty horse made up of Brittany veterans and recruits from the Pale. During the preparations, the captains complained of the potential shortage of ammunition, but Bagenal waved them away. He considered he had such a powerful force the rebels would not be brave enough to engage him. He set out from Newry to relieve Monaghan.

* * *

Eunan found himself outside Monaghan, laying siege to the town. He reconciled himself with Óisin for his behaviour in the forest and got his agreement that he would not disclose what happened to the men. It had all happened so quickly. When they got back to camp and had sobered up from the celebrations, he was called into the tent of the Maguire and given the news that they were to join campaigning with the O'Neill. Eunan was elated. He could think of nothing better to clear his troubled mind. A proper campaign with a proper army. The most impressive force he had ever seen, which included all the English troops he had encountered, was that of Cormac MacBaron, and the main army of the O'Neill was supposed to be far superior. But the O'Neill was somewhere in the distance as he was stuck in a siege which meant they were part of the inferior quality of soldier.

The order soon came to abandon the siege as word spread that Bagenal and the English forces were coming. Eunan was viably disappointed when summoned by the Maguire, but Hugh told him to have faith. He temporarily sent them back to Fermanagh to wait for further instructions.

In the meantime, Red Hugh returned to Tirconnell with his forces to counter amphibious raids being launched along his coastline. That left the O'Neills, Maguires, MacMahons and an assortment of minor allies to face the English army.

Sir Henry had suffered some harassment on the way to Monaghan town but replenished and reinforced the garrison. The next day he set off on a different route back to Newry. However, Hugh O'Neill planned for this eventuality. He summoned the Maguires back and northern rebels lined themselves up on either side of the route and prepared an ambush.

* * *

Eunan returned from the tent of Hugh Maguire. The bittersweet reality of fighting openly with the entire O'Neill army sank in. They sliced the Maguire forces up into different sections depending on the level of sophisticated weaponry and, to a lesser extent, experience. They took the limited number of pikemen and shot in the Maguire army to support the equivalent O'Neill units. Hugh Maguire's calvary joined O'Neill. They left Eunan with his men, boys, and farmers from south Fermanagh and their pitchforks, old swords and axes. Even the MacCabe Galloglass, traditionally armed due to lack of weaponry, were grouped with the traditionally armed soldiers from the other minor lords of the north. These so-called inferior men were designated to play a lesser role by merely harassing the enemy in the battle. Eunan bitterly ordered his men to gather as many javelins, darts, bows and arrows and other throwing objects as they could, and they took up positions on route to Clontibret just south of Monaghan town.

Bagenal and his men marched in formation, split into three sections. Each section had a core of pikemen. Their ten-foot pikes bristled on the cloudy but dry day, and their steel helmets and breastplates shone whenever the sun snook out for behind the clouds. Drawn in squares, the hedge of pikes was enough to drive away even the most heavily armoured horsemen. They feared for nothing.

On the flanks rode the calvary, again with their shining helmets, breastplates and the addition of slashing swords. They struck fear into the hearts of the most resolute Irish, for even the O'Neills had no match for them.

The army also had two sets of shot. One group was armed with heavy muskets, the latest gun technology not widely available to the rebels. They supported the pike squares and were deployed in sleeves or lines on the flanks of the squares or out in front. The second set of shot was armed with lighter caliver guns and was deployed as sleeves or lines alongside the marching columns to offer protection from attack.

All the English soldiers were armed with weaponry and armour the rebels could only pick up from the battlefield or, if they were lucky, get in limited amounts from Scotland. Only the O'Neills had weapons of this calibre. The rebels were no match for the veterans of Brittany and could only hope the men of the Pale would run away and leave their equipment behind.

Eunan gathered his men on the other side of a small hill and waited for the English army's front section to pass. Óisin lay beside him as they hid in some bushes and observed the army pass by below them.

"How many do we let pass us by?" said Óisin impatiently.

"Enough so they can't escape. Our job is to make things difficult for them. The O'Neills do the actual engaging."

"One day, you might grow up to be an O'Neill!" laughed Óisin.

"Fat chance of that. Why would they waste one of their ladies on a layabout like me?"

"Well, if you had your uncle's wealth! Then again, if you had that, you'd take his daughter too."

"Just concentrate on the enemy, please."

"Look!" and Óisin pointed north. "We want to avoid them. Let them pass."

A unit of English cavalry rode below them.

"We need to wait for the signal now. Cormac MacBaron will charge down his hill, and we will distract the English in the middle from helping their trapped comrades."

"You mean use us as target practice while the O'Neills grab all the glory?"

"We wouldn't even be on this hill and contemplating this if it weren't for the O'Neills. Just keep your eye on them and tell me when they pass Clontibret church."

Óisin saluted him, and Eunan ignored the sarcasm. Eunan went back to compose some stirring words for the men that would give them courage when facing bullet and arrow.

He waited over the other side of the hill, just out of sight, until Óisin waved excitedly, and then led his men to the top of the hill. While not the highest piece of ground, it had a commanding view of the English column. To the south of Clontibret church, Cormac MacBaron and his O'Neill pike slammed into the front of the column once it reached a narrow section of the road. To the rear, Hugh O'Neill did the same. On the hills to the left and right, rebel shot made their way down the hill to open fire on the column. Eunan raised his axe. Forgotten were the words composed, so he relied on what stirred his own emotions.

"THE CRY OF THE MAGUIRE!"

The men of south Fermanagh followed the words of Eunan down the hill. The English skirmishers saw them coming, loaded their guns, and bullets whizzed past Eunan's head. But he was not afraid, for this is what he waited for. He ran down the hill and charged on Bagenal's right. To the left was a bog. A thin line of rebel skirmishers who laid down withering fire on the column occupied it. The bog was impassable to both pike and horse, and Captain Brett ordered his caliver shot into the bog to drive off the rebels. He turned his pike to face the charging insurgents.

Eunan was almost at the bottom of the hill when the English skirmishers unleashed their last volley before retreating behind the squares of pike. Even his single-mindedness could not block out the bodies dropping. Eunan pulled up when he saw the hedge of pikes in front of him.

"Discharge your weapons and RETREAT!" he ordered to anyone who could hear over the din of battle.

The pike wall swallowed a meek volley of javelins, darts, and arrows and stood no less diminished. Eunan could see the shot rushing out from between the pike and reloading.

"RETREAT!"

Eunan turned and ran up the hill. Bullets hurtled past his ears.

Midway up the hill, some O'Neill shot replied in kind.

"The battle's that way," and one of the shot pointed to where Eunan had run from.

"I've just got to go for a quick shit in that bush over there. Save a couple for me," and Eunan winked and ran past them.

He made it to out of range of the English shot and rallied his men. He tried to hide the disappointment from his men that he had failed to get into close quarters with the enemy and could not wield his six-foot-long battle axe. Óisin caught up with him, and they counted their losses. Ten men were missing. Not that bad. Eunan looked down and saw that the English army was trapped and was being assaulted from all sides.

"Men, we go back once again into the cauldron of battle. Take up what weapons you can find on your way down and pelt them with it. If we cannot engage them hand to hand, we will charge up the hill and charge down again until we can. This army will break. We have to apply enough pressure. Now take up arms again, and I will make the cry."

They charged again and threw what they could find. The English bullets were discernibly less in volume than before, but the hedge of pikes held. They climbed the hill once more. Eunan counted his men. Fifteen more missing. He saw his men were exhausted, so he sat them down, and they watched the battle unfold. The English forces were being squeezed from the north and south, taking substantial losses. Rebel forces fought them to a standstill from the morning until the afternoon. The English cavalry charged Cormac MacBaron's men and cleared a path in the pass where the ambush was first sprung. They passed through the gap towards Newry. However, unblocking the passage led to a breakdown in the English discipline as the men tried to force their way through the gap. The pike squares collapsed in their rush to get through the pass.

"This is it, men! The cry of the MAGUIRE!" cried Eunan.

They charged down the hill accompanied by the Maguire cavalry. This time pickings were slim, and the main missiles hurled at the enemy were rocks. The central column broke, and Eunan's men pursued their opponents until the rear column came up behind them. This column kept its discipline, and the marauding rebels fled as it fought its way through. The O'Neill shot ran out of ammunition so Hugh O'Neill called off the attack. The English army retreated, bruised but intact. Eunan withdrew to the hilltop to gather his men and salute their glorious victory.

29

The offer

The glorious victory at Clontibret brought a new sense of hope to the beleaguered Irish in Wicklow. Fiach was injured in a failed raid on the Pale. Turlough was released yet stayed. But that only heightened the tensions between the O'Tooles and the O'Byrnes. Seamus was given temporary control as Fiach recuperated, but Seamus wished he had not given him such an honour. It absorbed all of Seamus's energy and self-control to prise the O'Byrnes and O'Tooles apart. He hoped that the victory at Clontibret would provide sufficient cover for himself and Hugh Boye to escape back north, but he could not leave Wicklow in such a state, for he knew that if he left, the situation could rapidly collapse.

Fiach regained his strength and gradually took back some responsibilities from Seamus. Not long passed before Fiach heard Rose was in Dublin Castle, being attended to by no less than Lord Deputy Russell himself. She had a swift trial and was sentenced to be burned as a witch. Fiach howled with pain and quickly dispensed with Seamus and Hugh Boye's counsel. He sent Redmond to Dublin under a flag of truce to negotiate terms for his wife's release. When Redmond returned a week later, he was sent straight to Fiach's tent.

"Here, father, I have two letters for you. One is from Lord Deputy Russell, as you can see from the seal. I know not what it contains. The second is from your wife that was smuggled to me when I was in Dublin Castle waiting on the lord deputy. While it is not sealed, I could not resist looking upon its contents to see if it was from your wife's fair hand. I believe it is. Read it yourself, but I believe it confirms the doubts we already had in our minds."

Fiach snatched the letter purportedly from his wife and devoured it. It contained only pain. He took the second letter with less vigour, broke the seal and refolded the letter.

"Please fetch me, Seamus and Hugh Boye."

* * *

Darkness fell, and Fiach positioned his guards twenty yards from the tent, as he knew the sensitivity of the subject to be discussed and he did not want friend or foe to overhear. Seamus entered, followed by Hugh Boye. He was curious why he was summoned, for his friend's decision making had become more erratic since his wounds healed. For Seamus, the walls closed in, and the guards seemed increasingly less friendly. When they entered, Fiach was pacing the floor.

"Gentlemen, come in. I have received two letters from Dublin. One of those is from poor Rose.

"She is still alive, awaiting her sentence to be carried out. Russell taunted her with stories that her own son-in-law gave her up. She said that Turlough was in league with Russell since the day he was captured by the English. Russell struck a deal in which Turlough agreed to give me up. In return, he would be granted an English title and inherit both my lands and the lands of the O'Tooles. I was supposed to be in that same cousin's house where Rose was captured but was drawn away by events at the last minute. She says that she has proposed an alternative deal by offering Turlough and Uaithne O'More and I agree to retire and pass along my titles to Phelim and Redmond, then Rose will be freed and Wicklow left in peace to heal."

"And the second letter?" said Seamus, the lines on his face pointed to his concern.

"The second is from Lord Deputy Russell and confirmed that he has Rose. He outlined what her sentence is and when it will be carried out, along with the details of the bargain Rose described in her letter. He says I have until the first of June to decide, and if he has not heard from me by then, Rose will be burnt alive."

Fiach was almost moved to tears by the trap he found himself in.

"I need your counsel before I have Turlough and Uaithne arrested. I have my doubts about the former, but Uaithne? He has been like a son to me, a better warrior than most of my sons and more obedient than any. They want me to hand over my two sons to die."

Seamus stroked his beard as a distraction to give him time to think.

"If you took up this bargain, which I am not advising you to do at this stage, what would you do after? Would the great Fiach the Raven of Wicklow retire peacefully with an English title and farm the land like a lowly tenant? I don't think so!"

"I would rebuild the rebellion with Phelim and Redmond. Rose would be the glue to rebuild the alliances. We would be nothing without her."

"I know you ask for my opinion because you value it and know there is always a large element of truth and straight talk to it. I'll do the same as always, even though it may not be what you want to here and place my position in jeopardy here. The rebellion would die on a stake outside Dublin Castle if you sacrificed Turlough and Uaithne."

"I still have my other sons," protested Fiach.

"While able, neither alone nor combined do they have the talents of either Turlough or Uaithne. Russell would cut the head off the snake of the rebellion, and Wicklow would slip into the Pale."

"I have been in worse positions in the past, made compromises and then reneged on them. Why would now be so different?"

"You are old and no longer have the energy."

"That is why I need Rose and the O'Tooles. Now, are you with me or against me?"

"I am the representative of the O'Donnell and am ultimately here to represent his interests."

"So be it. Then stand aside while I act."

"You are the lord and master of Wicklow," and Seamus bowed, departing with Hugh Boye, who followed him.

"What are you going to do now?" asked Hugh Boye of Seamus.

"Go back to your tent. You have far more important battles to fight than this. Do not get involved," and Seamus disappeared into the dark.

* * *

Seamus searched the outer perimeters of the camp. He searched the illuminated faces around every campfire and asked for directions from anyone he could trust. At last, he found the lit face he was looking for. Seamus barged past the drunken men in his way, knocked the drink from the man's hand, and lifted him to his feet.

"Get out of here! Run! Men are coming to give you to the English!"

Uaithne pushed Seamus back.

"What are you doing, you mad, drunken fool? Have you come here to fight me? What have I done to deserve this?"

"Rose O'Toole has done a deal with the English: you and Turlough for her own life. Run while you have the chance!"

Uaithne shook his head in disbelief.

"Fiach would not do this to me. He is like my father."

The light of the fire illuminated Redmond at the head of a body of men, striding purposefully towards their campfire. Seamus pointed at them.

"Do you believe me now? Redmond is coming to arrest you, not refill your drinks. Get on your horses now and ride away."

One of Uaithne's men got up to stop Redmond and ask what he was doing, only to receive the butt of an axe to the face.

"Have you enough proof now? Better to ride and ask questions later. You can thank me one day."

Uaithne looked at Redmond, and how he brushed aside Uaithne's men to get to him.

"Goodbye. What will you do?"

"Go. Worry about yourself."

Uaithne fled, and some of his men escaped with him. He reached his horses to witness Seamus being placed under house arrest.

* * *

Fiach needed someone else besides Turlough to offer the English in exchange for Rose. He chose Maurice FitzGerald, whose crimes retold and embellished by Fiach, increased his value to Russell. After some persuasion, the Lord Deputy accepted. It broke Fiach's heart, but with a little more persuasion he arranged the switch. He feared it was a trap and sent Redmond to the Wicklow lowlands to perform the exchange at a carefully chosen point, the residence of an O'Byrne relative who had remained neutral. Russell kept his forces away, and it all went off without a hitch. Rose was escorted back into the Wicklow mountains, and when Redmond was sure that he was not being followed, he led Rose to Fiach. It was a tearful reunion in a camp shorn of any confederates. Turlough's arrest had destroyed their fragile alliances.

Rose wept as she showed her husband her injuries from being tortured. Fiach cried but could not match her physical scars. They both swore that they would rebuild what had been destroyed, and they retired to the house Fiach had occupied so they could convalesce.

* * *

Weeks later, Fiach summoned Seamus and Hugh Boye to his tent. The weeks had been filled with silence and frustration on both sides. Fiach sent the guards away, but Seamus was impatient, for he grew tired of Fiach.

"Well? What is to be done with us? We are tired of pacing around a tent or being unwilling participants in your mournful procession around the Wicklow mountains. Release us now so we can return to the O'Donnell."

The exhausted creases on Fiach's face became inflamed.

"I should have you killed for the insolence you showed me."

"You don't frighten me, Fiach MacHugh O'Byrne. I feel sorry for you now. If you were going to kill me for insolence, you should have done it. Your hesitation just showed weakness and allowed the O'Tooles to consolidate their positions. Your only hope now is if the northern lords allow you a pardon, but they will not do that if you kill their envoy and don't hand over Hugh Boye. Release us now so we can return to the north."

Fiach turned to him, almost tearfully. He had the remains of a letter in his hand, which he scrunched upon reading its contents.

"I brought you here today, for we have been friends for years. The letter is from my most reliable spy in Dublin Castle. Everything he has told me in the past has turned out to be true, and he has been by far my most dependable source. He told me that Turlough and Maurice FitzGerald have now been executed."

Seamus's anger subsided.

"I am sorry for your loss. He was a credit to the Irish Catholic cause everywhere," said Hugh Boye.

"Accept my condolences also," said Seamus.

"That is not the worst news."

Seamus became concerned for his old friend and placed his hand on Fiach's forearm, hoping it would console him.

"My son absorbed every torture they performed on him, declined every bribe. He refused the option of assassinating me or give me up. I killed my own son, for I thought him a traitor," Fiach bellowed as the tears streamed down his eyes.

Seamus did not know what to do, but he wrapped his arms around Fiach's shoulder as his distraught compatriot slumped to a seat with his head to the wall, crying.

Eventually, Fiach's tears dried, and he sat at the table with Seamus and Hugh Boye.

"Your only hope is with the lords of the north. Let me go, and I can get you help. Make me stay, and we'll all die together."

"Go, go!" and Fiach waved them to the door. "I now know why you saved Uaithne. I will have word sent to him of your journey."

"Thank you. I will return with help."

They clenched hands, and then Seamus and Hugh Boye went to pack their things.

Sean O'Toole and the survivors from the northern missions to Wicklow waited for Seamus outside his tent.

"It is good to have you back, Seamus," said Sean.

"It is good to be a free man again. I would request that you stay to help Fiach rebuild, but I would fear for your life. What do you say to a return up north with me?"

"It would do my clan better as your right-hand man in the arm of the O'Donnell than getting stabbed in a petty squabble in the Wicklow mountains. Let's go while we still have the benefit of the dark."

The O'Byrne scouts led them to a safe spot in the lowlands of Leinster. Waiting for them in a cluster of giant boulders at the edge of the foothills was Uaithne, a band of men on horseback and an abundance of spare horses.

Uaithne smiled at the sight of Seamus.

"I wished to put an axe to your head that night, for I feared a drunken fool accosted me. It was only after I made my mistake that I realised what you did. I owe you my life, and my first down payment will be to escort you back to Tirconnell safely."

"You have a heavy burden on your shoulders now that Turlough is dead. The rebellion rests with you."

Uaithne's face visibly drained.

"I had not heard of my half-brother's death. It is indeed a tragedy to which I will dedicate my life to getting revenge."

"You will be the scourge of Leinster. Now let us depart, for the journey is long."

30

A sort of homecoming

U aithne was true to his word and escorted the party to the borders of Tirconnell.

"The O'Donnell will not forget the favour you have done him today. I will make sure that he hears of it and sees you as being one of his most important allies in all of Leinster," said Seamus as he put his hands on Uaithne's shoulders.

"I do it all to avenge my brother and half brother and to free the traditional O'More land from the English settlers."

"Red Hugh will soon sweep down through Connacht and into Leinster. Be sure to be aware of his movements, for there will be plenty of advantage to be gained when he comes."

"I will return home and begin preparing for that day."

They embraced, and Seamus and his entourage rode towards Tirconnell.

* * *

Seamus and Hugh Boye made straight for Donegal Castle. The banners from the towers told him the O'Donnell was in residence there. Sean O'Toole, in the meantime, brought the men back to the camp. When Seamus revealed who his esteemed guest was, they were immediately ushered to the O'Donnell's private rooms.

Red Hugh rushed to embrace him, much to Seamus's surprise. He had never met Hugh Boye MacDavitt before, so Seamus introduced the two men.

"I have heard so much about you. Your reputation precedes you! I will draw up what forces are around the town tomorrow morning so you can inspect them. Then you can assess my fighting capabilities, and you can tell me what I need to do to field an army worthy of gracing the best battlefields on the continent."

"It would be my honour, lord," replied Hugh Boye, but he looked dubiously at Seamus as if to ask him to step in.

"Unfortunately, we have had a long and dangerous ride, lord," interjected Seamus. "He would be happy to inspect the men tomorrow, but he also needs to sort out his past and those men who may hold the past against him."

Red Hugh looked confused, but Eoghan McToole O'Gallagher, Red Hugh's only adviser in the room, whispered in his ear. Red Hugh nodded and instructed Eoghan to leave the room to carry out his instructions.

The awkward silence that followed Eoghan leaving the room was interrupted by Hugh Boye pulling a letter from his pocket. Seamus knew nothing of this letter.

"I received this while I was in the Netherlands before I arranged passage to Ireland," and he handed the letter to Red Hugh.

Red Hugh read it and put it in his pocket, much to Hugh Boye's irritation.

"We'll see to that later. Let us take one day at a time. Today, let us fix the past."

Eoghan ushered Niall Garbh O'Donnell into the room.

"My lord," said Niall Garbh before frowning when he saw Hugh Boye.

"Eoghan has told me what happened between you in the past," said Red Hugh, "and he also told me how sorry he was for killing your relative in a duel. Isn't that right, Hugh Boye?"

Hugh Boye did not respond until Seamus nudged him.

"It is, lord, a regret."

"Under Brehon law, the death can be compensated through payment. Hugh Boye would like to offer you…" And Eoghan whispered in his ear. "The equivalent of fifty cattle."

"Fifty cattle!" said Niall Garbh, not disguising his disgust.

"Eoghan, please would you take Niall Garbh aside and make sure he is happy," said Red Hugh.

Eoghan and Niall Garbh went to one corner of the room for a heated negotiation, and Hugh Boye took Seamus by the arm for his own mediation.

"They can name any price they wish, and I cannot meet it. Whatever wealth I have is hidden near some beach in Wicklow."

"I will sort it," said Seamus. "What was in the letter?"

"An invitation from Hugh O'Neill to marshal his army."

"Is that why you came?"

"That is the arrangement I had before I came."

"It will be difficult, but leave it to me."

Eoghan and Niall Garbh returned, with faces that expressed agreement over a tough compromise. The former whispered the result in Red Hugh's ear, who looked displeased but did not argue the result.

"We have agreed that Hugh Boye will pay two hundred cattle in compensation."

It was Seamus's turn to whisper in Red Hugh's ear. Red Hugh called Eoghan over again, and after some deliberation, he concluded.

"We have decided that I will pay the two hundred cattle, and Hugh Boye will pay off his debt by working for me."

Niall Garbh looked delighted with his bargain, alongside Red Hugh. Seamus had to signal to Hugh Boye not to protest.

"Thank you for resolving that, lord, but may we now retire so we can be fresh for the morning?" replied Hugh Boye, hiding his urgent desire to leave.

"Yes, and Eoghan will take you to the accommodation I have arranged for you. Something that fits a man of your stature."

Eoghan arranged for Hugh Boye to stay with him.

31

Connacht opens up

Time did not give Seamus long to rest, for Red Hugh was determined to sow division and unrest throughout Connacht to persuade the Gaelic lords to side with him. Mostly, he appealed to devotion to one faith, some for their wish for the return of the supremacy of Brehon law, the offer of support to become the head of their clan, and if all else failed, he lured them with money. To prepare for Red Hugh's plan, Hugh Boye was put to the fields to work off his debt. Red Hugh gave him the support of the survivors from the Spanish Armada to assist him in his preparations. Hugh Boye did what he could with those in the army who aspired to be soldiers that could stand alongside those that graced the fields on the continent and ignored the rest. Seamus still stood with those who followed the traditional way of fighting and wished to perfect the art of the ambush.

The ease with which the seeds took root was primarily because of the excessive repression of the chief commissioner of Connacht, Sir Richard Bingham. Sir Richard had been successful. He implemented the composition of Connacht, crushed the dominant clans of O'Brien, Burke, MacWilliam Burke and O'Rourke, and made the province self-sufficient. However, he treated Connacht as if it were his fiefdom, doling out jobs to his relatives and siphoning off as much money as he thought he could get away with. The local lords made continuous protests to the Irish Privy Council, asking for restitution for the lands that were confiscated or stolen, and murdered clan members. As long as the money kept rolling in, the Irish Privy Council ignored any protestations. However, as Lord Deputy Russell came under more and more pressure; he requisitioned the experienced soldiers and replaced them with raw recruits.

* * *

George Bingham, son of Sir Richard Bingham, was stationed in Sligo Castle, the most northerly castle held by the English. It was of great strategic importance for the confluence of rivers in the area and hampered Red Hugh's access into Connacht. George shared his father's disdain for the native Irish, even though he commanded a mixed force of raw recruits from the Pale and men from the lords of Connacht. He gained infamy in Connacht for conducting the amphibious raids on Tirconnell and the islands off it. Two monasteries dedicated to St Colmcille were desecrated and looted. The effect it had on the O'Donnell was to draw him away from Clontibret. However, it left a bitter taste with Bingham's native Irish troops. Even though they fought for the Crown, they held St Colmcille in higher esteem.

George, a slender man, more brave than intelligent, called his captains together. He gave them a small share of the spoils which belittled their efforts, and when they protested, he berated them and threatened to hang them as traitors. One of his captains, Ulick Óg Burke, was determined to get his revenge and seized his opportunity by murdering George when he was poorly attended. Ulick declared for the O'Neill and the O'Donnell, albeit with the proviso that they give him support against his uncle, the Earl of Clanricarde. Word was sent north to Donegal and Dungannon, where Red Hugh was in conference with O'Neill and Maguire. Red Hugh immediately left for Donegal town, rallied his forces and took Sligo Castle.

He took up residence there, and over the summer, the disgruntled lords of Connacht who had not already taken up residence in Tirconnell declared their allegiance to him. Red Hugh sent Ineen Dubh to Scotland and the many islands to recruit mercenaries. She was again successful, and her connections still carried significant weight. Six hundred Redshanks landed near Lough Foyle, and Red Hugh, Seamus and Hugh Boye set off to Tirconnell to inspect, train and organise the new men. However, this was only part of the success of Ineen Dubh's mission. Another three thousand Redshanks landed on an island off the Ards Peninsula. For some unbeknown reason, put down to error or folly, they were a long way from the safety of Lough Foyle or the Scottish colonies of Antrim. The English detected them as they made their way towards Ireland, since they were attempting to open diplomatic negotiations with the King of Scotland and use sea patrols to cut off the rebels' supply of mercenaries. These new Scottish mercenaries had little stomach for a fight. After a brief skirmish with the English and no sign of O'Donnell or O'Neill's forces, they set sail back to Scotland. English diplomatic efforts bore more fruit as James VI of Scotland banned the export of weapons to Ireland, and Scottish mercenaries were never to be seen in such numbers again.

Despite this setback, Red Hugh was ready to invade Connacht. He rallied his men and his newly recruited Scottish mercenaries and targeted the castles in northern Connacht that had not pledged to him. While some of his forces besieged castles, the rest marauded around Connacht, stripping their enemies' assets and sending all chattels back to Tirconnell. O'Donnell's men roamed freely from the top to the bottom of Connacht. Chief commissioner Bingham gathered his forces to counter the threat of O'Donnell. O'Donnell evaded direct battles, extricating himself from anything bigger than a skirmish. Bingham then settled in to besiege Sligo Castle.

* * *

Despite the success he enjoyed, Seamus was forlorn. Sure, his men had done well. They were on the way to being wealthy men, for experienced men knew how to exploit the scenarios of war. But with Shea Óg gone, he had lost contact with Captain Williamson. While that was good for him in a professional capacity, he could no longer be deemed a traitor; he knew nothing of what happened to his wife and presumed she was dead. He vowed to avenge her and took enthusiastically to Red Hugh's cause. He was positioned in western Fermanagh, ready to strike at Bingham's rear should he be required. He sat, as instructed, and waited for the forces of Maguire. Then one fateful morning, he heard the cry: "the Maguire is coming!"

It had been over a year since he had met Hugh Maguire, and Seamus did not know what to expect.

"Seamus," Hugh shouted as he embraced him. "It has been too long! I should never have hired you out to Red Hugh, for he always covets my best men. At least I protected Eunan from his clutches."

Out from the entourage came Eunan, wearing a mask of seriousness, the only face he could show to both Seamus and Hugh at the same time. His blood boiled, but he controlled himself for the time being. Seamus and Eunan shook hands and muttered a greeting at each other, hoping that Hugh would not notice the resentment between them.

"You both look like you were greeting Governor Bingham," said Hugh Maguire. "We cannot have such animosity between two such important men. Seamus, your protégé has done so well in his service to me. He could only have done better if you were there to guide him. When are you going to come back to the fold? The Maguires have a great need for men of your talents."

"Thank you for such kind words, but as you said, it would be very difficult to persuade the O'Donnell to part with me."

"No matter. We shall see what happens. The tides of war are so unpredictable. Anyway, we are here to see if Red Hugh needs us, so we'll pitch camp and wait. I'll leave yourself and Eunan to get reacquainted."

Hugh left along with his men, leaving Seamus and Eunan, but Sean O'Toole and Óisin stayed, just in case it got violent. Tension drove Seamus to break the silence.

"So you won the duel then?"

"Was he someone you wanted to be killed? What were the O'Rourkes doing in your company anyway? The last I remember of them is you slamming one of their faces into a pot of boiling water."

"We are both valued assets to our respective masters. There was no point in wasting our own lives over some petty squabble. Anyway, I knew you could take him."

"So you wanted him killed."

"You were the very man to do it. I'm sure you've become more acquainted with such methods since you have risen in the esteem of the Maguire?"

"I would never lower myself to such base methods. The Maguires are men of honour with a noble cause."

"I see you still have much to learn, or should I dig your grave now?"

"Do nothing for me. Despite our differences, you are useful to an ally of the Maguire. May you give your life bravely on the field and make up for some of the many crimes you committed during your life."

"Don't be such a pompous ass all your life. Have you accepted the circumstances of your birth? That you are at the end of a long and proud line of Galloglass?"

"Tell him!" interjected Óisin, for he saw the conversation only leading to violence.

"Tell me what?"

"Go on, tell him! Put an end to this bitter feud now."

"If you have anything to say, say it to me now. I am ready to tell the world I am your uncle and your only living relative and I say that despite your resentment of me and all your other faults."

"Tell him!" insisted Óisin.

"Your Dervella.."

"What!? You have news of her?" and Seamus tensed with anticipation.

"Enniskillen fell a couple of months back."

"I heard, as did the whole of Ireland and maybe the entire world."

"There were a certain amount of prisoners held within the tower who were released after the garrison was killed. Amongst them were the remains of your Galloglass families. Not all of them survived the aftermath of the siege."

Seamus gripped his axe's shaft in anticipation that he would not like the rest of the tale.

"However, Dervella had taken to the road and did not know where to turn."

Seamus fixed his gaze on Eunan.

"I took Dervella in and brought her to the islands of Lower Lough Erne for safekeeping. She is with a great friend of mine and my mentor, Desmond MacCabe."

Seamus sat back and released the grip on his axe.

"So this is what it has come to. Is there a bargain to be made?"

Eunan was a little taken aback.

"Dervella made her bargain with me a long time ago. Without her kindness during the time we spent creating the village, I don't know how I would have coped."

"So she is not leverage?"

"No! How could you say such a thing?" Eunan thought for a minute. "Hey, was she… She told me that the O'Rourkes took her prisoner and that she was held there by an English captain who would visit her occasionally to threaten her."

Seamus went red and gritted his teeth.

"I feel I owe you a great debt, Eunan. Take me to her, and all on my part will be forgiven. I will grant you my service to fulfil your greatest desire as repayment for a kindness I did not deserve. But chose wisely so you will not regret your choice."

"The island is but two days travel from here at most."

"Then let us go while there is a lull in the battle. Sean, look after my men and Óisin you do likewise."

They embraced, got on their horses and set off for Lower Lough Erne.

32

Reunion on the lake

They reached the shores of lower Lough Erne and left their horses with a farmer sympathetic to the cause of the Maguire. He was willing to help while equally fearful of retribution if he stole their horses. They hired a boatman and sat at the back of the boat, and reacquainted themselves with one another. Now that Eunan was more experienced and had a more worldly view, they could speak more as equals rather than as mentor and pupil as in the past. Seamus found Eunan more likeable than before, even if the naïve edges still needed considerable honing. Eunan found a much greater appreciation for Seamus's battle-hardened wisdom, and a form of mutual respect grew.

They reached the island and saw only Desmond dangling his feet in the water, holding his fishing rod in such a manner as to suggest he had long given up any pretence he was going to catch anything. Eunan jumped off the boat.

"Desmond!" and he ran to his father figure.

Seamus almost felt a pang of jealousy at the warmth of their embrace. It was like his last grip on the MacSheehy Galloglass legacy was being slowly ripped away. There saw no sign of his wife and therefore felt no urgency in leaving the boat. He unloaded the bags, paid the ferryman, and arranged for him to return the next day. He carried the bags up to Eunan and Desmond.

"Desmond, this is…"

"I well know who this is. Welcome to my humble abode, the mighty Seamus MacSheehy!"

Their handshake reeked of begrudging respect.

"When was the last time we met? Was it the Netherlands? Enniskillen some time?"

"So much time has passed and so many things have passed. It is hard for me to remember with precision. Am I to say you have gone up in the world?" asked Seamus.

"It may not look like much, but how many men like us can say they achieved peaceful retirement instead of dying in horrible pain at the hands of one of our many enemies?"

"Your skills are wasted pretending to fish alone on a little island."

"There you go trying to reunite me with my deserved horrible, painful death again! Who said I was alone? Arthur! Dervella! We have visitors!"

Arthur was first to appear from the other side of the island.

"Eunan!" and he ran to greet his old friend.

Then from the doorway of the house appeared Dervella. Seamus dropped his bags and weapons and ran to greet her. Eunan did not think Seamus was capable of such emotion.

"You'll squash me to death if you hug me so hard," and Dervella prised herself out of her husband's arms.

"Let me look at you. Well, you haven't been eating properly, I can tell that straight off."

But his eyes held a brightness that was otherwise a stranger to his otherwise weather-ravaged, battle-hardened complexion.

"You could do with a good feed, a bath, change of clothes, and a rest.

The usual state you normally show up in. Come on in and let's get started."

Seamus followed her in. She kept the same cheeriness as he remembered, only slightly diminished given her recent experiences. She certainly seemed overjoyed to see him. He reached out to her waist to embrace her again.

"Tell me what happened? What did they do to you?"

Dervella shied away.

"Can we not just enjoy the moment? We have so few of them let us make the most of what we have got," and she led him into the kitchen. "You sit there now and let me give you a good feed and then we can think about washing you."

* * *

Eunan and the others left Seamus and Dervella to have the run of the house for a couple of hours while they sat outside, fishing and talking. Desmond was up to date with the rebellion but waited for Seamus before discussing anything further. Eunan spoke of his relationship with Seamus.

"We can make this right, leave it to me," said Desmond as Seamus finally emerged from the house and came down to join them by the shore.

Seamus seemed rather calm to Eunan, in a peaceful state never witnessed before.

"I haven't seen her in a long tie," grunted Seamus in response to Eunan's grinning. "I thought she was dead."

"No matter," interjected Desmond. "This island is a place of peace. A place where weary souls can come and rejuvenate from the war. Seamus, Eunan has something to say to you."

"I do?"

271

"Say it."

"Seamus, I owe you my life. You could have slain me on Enniskillen tower, and you would have had every right to do so. Yet, you saved me and risked your own life. I am grateful and I owe you my life."

Seamus bowed his head, conspicuously touched by Eunan's admission.

"You are my kin and, like it or not, I am yours. We are the last of our line, the last of the MacSheehy Galloglass. If we do not stand up for each other, then we are forever lost. Just as I saved your life, you saved mine. Dervella is what is good in my soul, what makes me carry on. You may not bear the name, nor come into the world in ideal circumstances, but I am proud of you all the same. I said I owed you a debt when you saved my Dervella, and I still do. Desmond is nothing if not wise and I know I sit here for a purpose and will be told how I can repay my debt. So, Desmond, an arch schemer wasted sitting on a tiny island, tell me of your plan."

* * *

The next day the ferryman arrived and Arthur waved him into the small harbour as Seamus and Eunan prepared to leave. Everyone gave Seamus and Dervella space to say their goodbyes. He grasped both her hands and held them up to his chest.

"Desmond says you can stay here for as long as you like."

"He already told me that, my love," and Dervella smiled as the rays of sunshine penetrated deep into the chasm of Seamus' heart.

"You make me soft, I have to go back to war, remember?"

"But you can come and visit?"

"I would wish for more privacy."

"You wouldn't have me live on an island all by myself just waiting for you, would you?"

"I have just got you back from the dead. Am I not given the allowance of a slice of selfishness?"

"I'll look after Desmond and Arthur on condition they make scarce when you come to visit. Is that a sufficient compromise?"

"At least I know you'll be safe. For the first time in a long time, I'll know who to fight for, if only to keep you safe."

"It is good that purpose has returned to your life Seamus MacSheehy. I know there is good in you, even though you bury it deep."

"You are the good in me and give me purpose," and Seamus kissed her tenderly on the lips.

"Come on, it's time to go," called Eunan as he threw his weapons into the boat.

Seamus hugged his wife and walked down to the shore to join his compatriot.

Desmond and Arthur were there to see them off.

"You smell of… flowers!" and Desmond smiled at Seamus.

"Only you would have the balls to make a joke like that," and Seamus looked back to wave to his wife. He turned to Desmond again. "If she dies, so do you."

"Oh sure, I take that as a given. But as long as she stays here, I have the protection of the mighty Seamus MacSheehy!"

"That you do, Desmond, that you do. You'd better watch out, as I may find you some gainful employment in Enniskillen. That toe rag O'Cassidy may vacate his position soon."

"I am happily retired pretending to fish on my little island, thank you very much. Goodbye and I'm sure I'll see you soon."

"You will, and look after her."

"And you Eunan."

With that, Seamus and Eunan boarded the boat and rowed away.

* * *

They returned to their men in western Fermanagh, staying together for a week as Governor Bingham made futile assaults on Sligo Castle. The arrival of the Maguires and O'Donnells from the rear made it unsafe for Bingham to continue the siege, so he retired back to his more secure bases in Connacht. Once the siege was over, O'Donnell ordered the destruction of Sligo Castle, for he did not want to defend it indefinitely and desired free passage between Tirconnell and Connacht. It was time for Seamus and Eunan to part.

They now shared a sense of purpose. Seamus embraced Eunan before setting out for Tirconnell.

"Just send the word to me if you need my help. I am assembling the finest, experienced fighting men in all of Ireland, of which you'll find no equal. They'll be at your disposal."

"Thank you, Seamus. I may call on you sooner than you think."

"Goodbye nephew," and Seamus set off back to join the army of the O'Donnell.

33

Mullabrack

R ejoicing broke out across the north after the brilliant victory at Clontibret, and it breathed confidence into the rebel confederation that the English could be beaten. Many a letter was filled with stories of the glories gained that made their way to potential allies and sponsors in Ireland and the continent.

However, Lord Deputy Russell did not let the lords of the north rest on their laurels, and in June 1595, he gathered his forces and marched north. He reinforced the Monaghan garrison and established a fort in Armagh, hoping it would be a lance in the side of the rebellion. O'Neill, in return, levelled his castle in Dungannon, depriving the lord deputy of a potential base in O'Neill territory should he continue his offensive. O'Neill refused to give battle, and in July, Lord Deputy Russell withdrew once more to the Pale.

In August, Sir John Norreys, a veteran of the Dutch revolt and in command of a sizable force, including a large contingent of veterans from Brittany, was given command and marched north to add to Russell's foundations. Again O'Neill refused to offer battle and instead made proposals for a ceasefire. But September came, and two significant events changed everything.

First, Turlough O'Neill finally died, resulting in Hugh O'Neill taking the Irish title of O'Neill which he used instead of his English title of the Earl of Tyrone. This confirmed in the eyes of the English his commitment to the rebellion.

Second, English spies intercepted a letter in which O'Neill and O'Donnell promised Ireland to the king of Spain and restore it to the Catholic faith in return for his military assistance. The crown had always believed the rebels to be in league with Spain, but this was the first definitive evidence. All of O'Neill's pleas for a ceasefire were subsequently dismissed.

* * *

Eunan had made much of his men's vigour for the fight at the Battle of Clontibret. He returned to Desmond's island and delighted Desmond with tales of his bravery and leadership and his contribution to the victory. Desmond polished and embellished these stories and dictated the revised tales to Arthur, who converted them into letters. He then went to his trunk and handed a fist full of coins to Eunan.

"Offer these to your men. Give a coin to each man who can go to a different town, village or marketplace in south Fermanagh and have them read aloud the tales of Eunan Maguire. I guarantee you, you will have at least double the men to replace those who you lost."

Eunan was sceptical, but he waited a couple of days for Arthur to make as many copies as he physically could. By the time the Maguire recalled him, he had one hundred and fifty men and had collected enough weapons to arm them all. The legend of Eunan Maguire was spreading.

When Norreys came north, Eunan was sent with the Maguire contingent to join the O'Neill. Before they left their camp outside Enniskillen, Caolan Maguire came with men from the MacCabe

Galloglass. They placed two large wooden boxes in front of Eunan.

"Another present from Hugh Maguire. He must like you," said Caolan.

Eunan took one of his throwing axes and cut the ropes holding the wooden boxes together.

"Guns! What am I supposed to do with them?"

"He'll tell you," and Caolan pointed to a man who came from behind the Galloglass.

"Arlo!" cried Eunan to receive back a nod and a grunt.

* * *

They arrived in Monaghan and found themselves in the O'Neill camp, sitting out the stalemate as O'Neill refused to engage Norreys. Arlo and Eunan did not waste the time the lull in fighting granted them. They caught up, for they had not met since Eunan and Desmond 'rescued' Arlo from the wreaks of the Spanish Armada.

Arlo told how he did not like the cold, the wet, the food or the quality of the men they gave him to train, but the women seemed to find his accent appealing, which was some compensation for being held prisoner. Eunan said that the Lord in heaven had many missions for his people, and we would not always appreciate what we were asked to do. Arlo grumbled, but Eunan said he should be grateful he was still alive, unlike many other of his comrades.

After enduring Arlo's grumbles, Eunan set about training the men to use the guns he had been fortunate enough to receive. Arlo again proved himself a deft instructor and turned the men from south Fermanagh into a unit that could, under the lightest of scrutiny, pass as a unit of shot. Hugh Maguire was obliging enough to apply such scrutiny as to let the obvious deficiencies of the men bypass him either by passive or deliberate negligence and committed the unit to battle.

* * *

O'Neill waited to set his trap as Norreys, the great English general who was supposed to inspire fear in the rebels, reinforced the garrisons in Armagh and Monaghan. Norreys turned south to return to the Pale, but O'Neill was determined that he would not get away unmolested. He set a trap for his adversary with his own men as the pincers for the ambush and his allies, the glue to hold Norreys in place.

Eunan and Arlo took up positions on their assigned hill as part of the ambush, conscious of their subordinate role. Eunan was in two minds, for he doubted the potency of the guns as weapons, in the hands of his men at least, and considered that they would be a poor substitute for an axe should they find themselves in hand to hand combat. It was a fortunate Maguire indeed who had a gun and a sword or dagger. They went around and gave each of the men a handful of bullets and told them to use them prudently. Spirits were high, given the result of their last ambush, and the men were eager for battle. They took up their positions and rehearsed Arlo's instructions in their minds.

Norreys was wise to what had previously happened to Bagenal and spotted where the potential ambush could occur on the road home. He changed route and forced his baggage over the ford at the Cusher River and prepared for a fighting retreat. O'Neill manoeuvred his forced to catch the English before they got away. He struck with his cavalry only to be pushed back. Eunan's men had to abandon their hilltop positions to pursue the enemy and joined the other Maguire shot who stood alongside O'Neill's shot in the woods and bog to the left of the retreating English. The rebels laid down a withering fire. Eunan had taken a caliver to set a good example to his men. He joined the crooked line of his men and stood ankle-deep in the waters of the bog and fired his weapon. Arlo wished he stuck to his axe.

"No, no, no!" he howled. "You cannot hit them shooting from there. Move closer! Move closer!" and he waived Eunan and his men forward.

There was a collective scowl, but they moved forward all the same. They cursed the smoke of the battle, for in their confusion and determination to obey Arlo's commands they now found themselves shin-deep in water. The men fiddled with their powder and bullets whilst around them the O'Neills let off round after round. They fired again and created another cloud of smoke. The smoke hung in the air as even the normally reliable breeze had abandoned them. They shivered and loaded their guns again.

Beyond the smoke, O'Neill ordered his primary force of shot and pike forward. They charged, but the veterans of Brittany were too much for them and forced them back. The English shot came out from behind their pike to skirmish. Their sleek lines and smooth loading and reloading action proved a source of jealousy for Eunan, as he could only wish for men as proficient as them. But Eunan felt he was not made for this kind of war.

"Curse this thing," he said, as he threw his gun to the ground. "Barely can I get three shots away before it jams. And if it does not jam, it burns my hands with the heat. All of this to shoot into a cloud of smoke. Give me the bow and axe any day!"

"And every day, you will be condemned to defeat. As you charge with your axes and your pitchforks, the well-trained gunners will shoot you down with one volley," replied Arlo over his shoulder.

Eunan reached down for his gun. But it was now spoilt, for it had landed in one of the bog's many puddles. He took up a position behind his men so he could guide their volleys. However, one by one, Eunan's men stopped firing and held out their empty hands.

"We may as well use our axes, for we have no bullets left," said Eunan. He felt embarrassed as to both his flanks the O'Neills continued to fire volley after volley. Arlo saw the look on his face.

"Come! Let us leave this bog, or you will all catch a chill. We pull back and wait for the instruction from the O'Neill. You were given fewer bullets, for you are inexperienced as today showed and wasted most of, if not all, of them. Come speak to me," and Arlo beckoned Eunan forward.

He put his arm over his shoulder and walked up the hill with him.

"You need to show better self-control in front of your men. The day of the Galloglass is dead. There will be no more great clashes of armour, no more battles decided with the axe. If you want to get ahead and be a battle commander, the gun is the way forward. Heed my words, or you'll be only good for guarding the baggage train."

"I trust you, Arlo, and your knowledge. I can promise only to think about what you said."

They reached the top of the hill, but Eunan was finished for the day. There would be no drawing of axes, no last great charge. They sat and witnessed the dying embers of the battle as little puffs of smoke below signified that the skirmishing continued until both sides ran low on ammo. When the smoke had died down, they saw that the English had slipped away.

34

A time for peace?

Both sides claimed victory in the stalemate of Mullabrack: the rebels for propaganda and the English to save face. Both played to their audiences.

The rebel letters proclaiming the second victory in a row for the O'Neill were well received by the Catholic monarchs of the continent and the Pope. However, the north had been devastated by a failed harvest, something that blighted them frequently in the past decade, and the people were starving.

O'Neill was also running low on ammunition and needed to find alternative sources of supply. The king of Scotland had banned the sale of arms to the Irish lords as he was trying to advance his claim to the English throne should the elderly Queen Elizabeth die. Troubles in the Highlands, the defeat of the Scottish landing party in July and King James's ban on mercenaries going to Ireland also added to the confederacy's troubles.

They now had to turn to the continent more than ever to seek help for their cause. But that would take time, given their most significant source of support, the king of Spain had been taken gravely ill. Even after the two greatest victories ever by Irish rebels over the

English, the insurgents were vulnerable. Therefore, O'Neill pressed his advantage and sought a ceasefire.

However, after suffering two defeats and large numbers of desertions of their Irish recruits, the English were suffering severe manpower shortages. What soldiers they had could barely be fed. The Crown was in financial trouble and could not readily supply adequate resources. Therefore, they duly agreed to a ceasefire when it was offered. The onset of winter and a further deterioration of supplies led to a truce and formal negotiations.

When the peace negotiations started, the Irish lords tried to play a double game. The northern lords sent priests to Spain and Rome to plead for help while O'Neill played for time in Dublin and Dundalk. He insisted that both he and Red Hugh had to be present for the negotiations, and there was always some excuse why one of them was not present.

The double harvest failure hit the Maguires hard, and Hugh was eager for peace. No matter how much he wanted to continue the war, Donnacha would remind him he did not have the resources to continue. Donnacha promised he could negotiate good terms, and it would not affect whether the Spanish would come. The more the talks ground on, the more he wanted to shut out the Maguire captains and others who may persuade Hugh to reach a lesser deal or even to continue fighting, both of which options Donnacha disapproved. Donnacha sent out his agents to move the negotiations forward.

* * *

Eunan returned to the island to discuss his experiences at the battle of Mullabrack with Desmond and get advice on what he should do next. With assurances from the latter, he spent the autumn in the fields around Enniskillen, using up valuable bullets, training his men the art of musketry. However, before that could happen, he had to fix any lingering friction with Arlo, as Arlo was the best trainer in modern warfare under the employment of the Maguire. After much persuasion, he came to an understanding with Arlo. If his colleague made the men of south Fermanagh the best shot available to the Maguire, Eunan would help him escape back to Spain. Arlo agreed, thinking little of the bargain for his hope had long since sunk into the bogs of Ireland. Eunan's men were no worse than most of the farm boys he was asked to train, and at least Arlo found Eunan to be pleasant company. The Maguire shot at Mullabrack had much room for improvement, so it would not be hard to show progress.

The second rock in a river of obstacles Eunan had to cross was the domestic positions of his men. He had to battle with the prospect of continuing war and the need for the men to go home and feed their families. He kept a core of men together who did not have the burden of a family, and the Maguire agreed to take on the strain of feeding them. The rest trained when they were available. Improvements were slow and steady, but a constant irritant to the impatient young man.

* * *

The depths of winter came, and through the darkness and sheets of rain, a loan cart came and sought entrance into Enniskillen Castle. A rider led the way and called to the gate. Eunan watched from a window high in the tower, for the cart was more entertaining than the rain. One guard at the gate went to the tower. Out rushed Donnacha, which piqued Eunan's interest. MacCabe Galloglass surrounded one man from the cart and the rider, who appeared to have one arm and rushed them into the tower. Eunan could not contain his suspicion and went to investigate. He could hear the strangers being ushered in, and so followed the commotion to the private room of the Maguire.

Caolan Maguire appeared from the doorway and stepped in his way.

"This is a private meeting. No one else but the Maguire and Donnacha are allowed in."

"Who are his guests? You can tell me that at least."

"Why don't you go back upstairs and mind your own business. If the Maguire wants you to know, he'll tell you!"

Eunan could see that he would get nowhere with Caolan, who had not forgotten about the instance in the forest and disliked the perceived favouritism shown to him. Eunan turned around, for he knew a trick from his youth shown to him by Desmond when he wanted to know what Cúchonnacht was up to.

He fetched Óisin to stand guard while he went into a small room used for storage. It shared a wall with the Maguire's private room and smelt of deceit. He removed some loose mortar from the wall and placed his ear upon the hole.

"...you're not negotiating directly with the Crown. I represent the king of Scotland, an interlocutor meaning to bring about peace between the kingdoms of Ireland and England. War in Ireland damages us all. We can sound out your demands in Dublin and London without getting them mixed up with the demands of the O'Neill or the O'Donnell, who I can guarantee you are having their own private negotiations on the side with the Crown."

"No one will sign any treaty without the nod from the Queen. Now I know who you are, who are you?"

Eunan guessed Hugh was addressing the other guest.

"I am a special envoy for her Majesty that allows my friend to travel the land unmolested. I can get you the approval you seek. Her Majesty is prepared to grant you a full amnesty and other favourable terms, but you would need to show her some goodwill."

"What kind of goodwill?"

"Change sides and fight against your former allies."

Eunan slipped from his perch, and some of the dry mortar tricked out of the other side. There was a momentary silence, but he did not know if he had been rumbled. He wanted to believe that they had not caught him, for he wished to hear Hugh Maguire's reply. He crouched beneath the hole and prayed.

Donnacha spoke next and louder than the previous voices.

"Let us meet again in a week, and we will give you an answer then. My brother's daughter is to be betrothed to Connor Roe's son, Art. Go to Derrylinn and enjoy my brother's hospitality, and we will meet you there before the wedding to give you our answer."

Donnacha smiled when he heard the faint noise of the hole he so frequently used himself being refilled.

Eunan ran out of the room and grabbed Óisin.

"Have men watch the tower. I want to know when our guests leave."

* * *

The two guests left the castle at daybreak. They left their cart, which was full of foodstuffs, as a goodwill gesture because of the famine, and set off on horseback. Eunan was a half-hour behind them, leaving Óisin with instructions to get Seamus if he had not heard from him within a week. Seamus had the ear of the O'Donnell, and if he proved what was happening, the O'Donnell would be in the best position to do something about it. Eunan declined Óisin's offer to accompany him and only took two men with him.

He rode as fast as he could towards Derrylinn, the direction the two guests had been seen riding. Eunan rode full pelt into one of the many forests along the way. He tore ahead of his guards, eager to catch the emissaries from Scotland and the Crown. He was determined to catch the strangers unescorted before they made it to Derrylinn and so dug his heels into the side of his horse. This was it. His big chance.

Save the Maguires, save the rebellion. No more living under either of his father's shadows; Odin and his cronies banished forever. Eunan the her….. Everything stopped.

Out of nowhere he was suddenly wrenched from his horse, and his head hit the ground, leaving a trail of blood. A rope vibrated between two trees on either side of the path.

His next memory was seeing the clouds in the sky, hurting all over and dying of thirst. He raised his head to see the mask of Shea Óg.

"You're gonna wish they let me kill you after what they are going to do to you, ya little bastard!"

The last thing Eunan remembered was the butt of an axe rapidly coming towards his face.

* * *

"No!"

Eunan awoke to a bucket of slops thrown over him. The cold floor pushed up its slime into his skin. The cell stank of excretion and death. Eunan grabbed onto a nearby wooden stool and hauled himself up to sit on the ground. Two guards and the grinning face of Shea Óg appeared in the doorway.

One guard took a letter from his pouch and moistened his lips.

"By order of Sir Richard Bingham, governor of Connacht, and the law courts of her Majesty Queen Elizabeth, you have been declared a traitor. The crimes you have committed are rebellion, killing the Queen's agents, raiding and theft of goods rightfully belonging to her Majesty's subjects and any other crimes we may discover before you are tried. You will appear before the court in due course and, if found guilty, be hung, drawn and quartered. You will remain in jail until you appear in court. May God rest your soul."

"I told you you'd wish I killed you," sneered Shea Óg.

The door slammed shut. It sucked out life, light, and hope. Eunan fell to the ground.

"Is this to be the end of me?"

He noticed one little window with bars towards the top of the wall. It was a light to the outside world. But on that sill sat Odin, Loki and Baku. They leapt down towards him.

35

A phoney war

The months grew colder as the year slipped into December. Famine once again blighted Ireland as the ever-present threat of harvest failure became a reality for the second time in a year.

The ceasefire seemed not to affect Connacht, for it had become overrun with would-be rebels, and the lack of experienced men crippled the governor's ability to act. Therefore, the English and their allies had taken to hiding behind the walls of their towns and castles.

While O'Neill had concluded a ceasefire in Ulster and the east, Red Hugh did not consider that it applied to him in Connacht and continued to support his allies and subordinate clans in the province. He sent Seamus to the province along with other captains of the O'Donnells. Their mission was to sow the seeds of rebellion in those clans who had not yet sided with Red Hugh and reinforce with men and equipment those clans that had. They were to disrupt the rule of the Crown through raids, kidnap, and assassination.

In early October, Tibbot MacWalter Kittagh Burke (known as Kittagh) won a notable victory when he ambushed an English column near Belleek, County Mayo, after the English tried to relieve a castle he was besieging. Red Hugh made much noise about this for propaganda in order to persuade other clans and chieftains who wavered on the sidelines and declare for him.

The next significant event was the assassination of Captain William Fildew by his men and the commandeering of his galley. Captain Fildew was the leading English naval commander. His death meant that Bingham could no longer conduct amphibious raids along the coast of Tirconnell.

The third was the death of the MacWilliam Burke. The two leading powers in the province were the MacWilliam Burkes and the Earl of Clanricarde, from another branch of the old Norman Burke clan. This gave Red Hugh the opportunity to stamp his authority on the province and place someone loyal to him as the MacWilliam Burkes leader. The tanistry title of MacWilliam Burke had recently been abolished, and Red Hugh was keen to reinstate it.

The Lord deputy became convinced that the troubles in Connacht were no longer solely motivated by the resentment of the native population to Governor Bingham, but that they had joined the rebellion in Ulster. Because of the restriction in men, equipment and supplies, the Lord deputy could do little but launch small expeditions into the province and strong-arm minor lords on the periphery into renouncing O'Donnell and declaring for the Crown. By December 1595, most of Connacht was under the control or influence of Red Hugh. He decided it was time to reintroduce tanistry to the province, a culture that Governor Bingham had done his utmost to destroy.

* * *

Into this maelstrom rode Seamus, as he emerged from the dusk in front of the gates of Galway town with several carts strung out behind him. He had five men with him, including the ever-loyal Sean O'Toole.

"Who goes there?" exclaimed the guard from the tower.

"A travelling merchant responding to a summons by the Earl of Clanricarde asking for supplies of food to be brought. I understand the famine has bitten that Galway town hard?"

"Aye, that it has. I hope you've not come armed, for no weapons are allowed on the orders of Governor Bingham."

"I thought the Earl of Clanricarde ruled these lands?"

"That he does, but the governor resides here as well."

Seamus already knew these facts, but he sought to play dumb to make his role more believable.

"Are you going to open the gate, then? Can I pass?"

"As soon as we search your wagons and are satisfied you are who you say you are, then you can go."

The man waved to his men to leave the safety of the walls and conduct their search.

Seamus expected as much, and his party was unarmed. He waited patiently and was soon on his way to refresh the town stores. It was a slight loss to the Confederacy, but given the aim of Seamus's mission, potentially very worthwhile.

* * *

Meanwhile, down at the docks, a mysterious ship cut its way through the night, moored, and unloaded its cargo. The guards picked up their weapons and went down to investigate. They illuminated the dock.

"Who goes there? Who permitted you to unload these barrels?"

The captain of the ship walked over from his position of supervision and handed the guards a letter.

"These are a gift from the MacWilliam Burkes to the governor and his men. It looks like an early Christmas present for you as these barrels are full of wine!"

The leader of the guards took the letter from the man's hand.

"It is what you say it is, but why would the MacWilliam Burkes give us this?"

The captain laughed.

"You must be a poor man indeed if you are in charge of the docks and never received a bribe? How should I know why Theobald Burke is trying to bribe you or the governor, nor do I care. Maybe it's for the spanking they gave you last October? Maybe they wish to make peace? Now, are you going to take this wine, or what?"

But the captain's chance to decide was taken away from him when one of his men took an axe to a barrel, and the wine spilled out over the dock. The guards cupped their hands and drank what they could hold from the wine fall.

"It's real, and it's good!" called the men, and a couple of them ran off to find mugs.

"That's the last," said the captain as the final barrels rolled onto the dock. "I'll be out of your hair in the morning if it does not displease you."

But the guards no longer cared. They were too busy dragging the remaining barrels back to their barracks to share the spoils with their comrades. The captain laughed and went back onto his ship.

⁎

Seamus and his men cautiously advanced through the winding streets and into the town. The streets only benefited from sporadic pools of light, so he had difficulty spotting who he was supposed to meet. However, the unidentified man recognised Seamus from the halls of the O'Donnell.

"Come this way and leave the carts in this alleyway," said the man as he pointed to a dark shadow squeezed between two houses.

The stranger sported a dishevelled appearance with an air of mischief, not a look that would win the confidence of Seamus.

"I warn you now, man, if you endeavour to perform some mischief upon me and my men, you'll wish never to meet the light of day again after we are done with you!"

"It is I, Damien Burke, who you were sent to meet. It is for the harm that you can do to others that I wish to meet you," came the reply.

"You should have said so earlier. Lead the way."

The man led the men to a small house neatly tucked away in a large sheet of darkness near the harbour. Seamus placed his hand on the door frame to prevent Damien from entering, for he still feared a trap.

"Have you got everything we need?"

"Yes, but we need to go inside to get it."

Damien brought them into the main room of the dreary house and pulled a blanket out from under a table which was pushed to the sidewall. The dust lifted from its resting place, an unwanted intruder in the nostrils of the men.

"There you go. All the weapons we'll need. The captain has done his job and is waiting for you."

Seamus bent over and prodded the weapons with his finger so he could give them a superficial inspection.

"Good. Are you also our guide?"

Damien nodded.

"That I am. We must wait for the signal before we make our move."

They were situated close to the barracks and sat in the darkened house as the chaos of the gift of the wine unfolded. The English soldiers and their Irish lackeys rolled the barrels up the hill to the barracks gate, which was by now flung open with eager hands and greedy eyes embracing the barrels. The English officers had by now lost all control, and they all but gave up. Their cups battled with those of their men to be overflowing with the free wine.

The drunker the men got, the more they wandered off in different groups to find or create some mischief in the town.

"It is time," said Seamus. "We still need the cover of the night, no matter how inebriated they get."

Damien nodded and pointed the way towards the barracks.

"How many prisoners are there?" asked Seamus.

"Around thirty or forty. It changes in number, but since the rebellion in Connacht burst into flames, they have mainly been locked in the jail rather than distributed around the loyal local gentry."

"Do we have enough weapons for all of them?"

"If we get into a scuffle where they all need weapons, then we would all surely die. This was only ever meant to be a quick raid. The aim is the bring them back alive, not make up stories about a supposed glorious death."

"You're a good man. You see through all the crap. I always need good men," said Seamus, who expressed his admiration and appreciation through a good slap on the shoulder.

"Honoured that you would think of me so, but let us survive the mission first. Here, I assume you want an axe?"

"You read my mind!" Seamus took the axe and assessed its quality. "This will do nicely," he said with a pleased glint in his eye.

They crept towards their objective, sticking to the shadows and avoiding the pools of light from the drunken revellers' fires. On the occasion they ran into opposition, where someone would ask them why they weren't drinking, Seamus made his best officer impression, and they would soon scurry away.

They came to the gates where two dutiful men remained on guard. Seamus resorted to the more conventional espionage method of silently slitting their throats, stealing their keys and hiding their bodies where they would remain hidden until at least the morning.

"This way. I used to work here," said Damien as he unlocked the door and led them into a courtyard. Several guards sat around the fire warming themselves and complaining that they had to remain on duty while the biggest party in years was happening all around them. Seamus pointed to the dark shadows that draped the walls and ordered some of his men to use the cover to surround the guards. He went for the direct approach and walked up to the campfire with two of his men.

"Who goes there?" called a guard as they grabbed their sword and stood up.

"We're here to transport the prisoners to a safe place," said Seamus in his most authoritative voice.

"On who's orders?"

"Hugh O'Donnell's!" and Seamus plunged his previously concealed dagger into the man's guts.

The other guards jumped up and took hold of their weapons, only to be set upon by Seamus's men leaping out from the dark. Soon the guards were all dead, with nobody noticing any commotion. Damien searched the bodies for the keys to the prison door.

"Got them!" he cried in jubilation and ran over to a door hidden in the darkness.

"Can you do that a bit quieter!" hissed Seamus as Damien struggled to open the door.

The door clicked, and Damien smiled back at him. It swung open, and a shaft of light in the shimmying dust brought the men inside what they had forgotten: hope.

"Shut up!" Seamus whispered into the doorway as the shaft of light was greeted by moaning and the rattling of chains.

"Get some light in there," and one of his men thrust a torch of fire into the darkness of the prison.

"Sorry," muttered Damien as he slowly backed away. "They took my family once they found out I was a spy for the O'Donnell."

The interior of the prison lit up with fire torches to reveal the Earl of Clanricarde's men.

"I'm not leaving without getting what I came for." cried Seamus, as he raised his axe and sliced off the hand in which Damien held the keys.

The Burkes charged towards the prison door.

"Hold them here," ordered Seamus, and several of his men ran up to thrust their swords into the doorway, preventing the Burkes from spilling out into the yard. He grabbed Damien by the collar as the latter tried to nurse the stump of his wrist beneath his arm.

"If was laying this trap, I would have your family in the prison, so if anything went wrong, they would be the first to die. But it is not my trap, and drunken English soldiers roam the street. So my guess is that the earl got greedy and organised this ambush all by himself. Would that be correct?"

Damien nodded and shielded the stump of his arm.

"Are the prisoners still there?"

Damien nodded again.

"What about the captain? Is the boat ok?"

"The boat should have been taken. But I expected more men to be here at the prison. They should have come from behind you as well."

"So, we still have a chance. You! Guard him!"

One of Seamus's men ran over and held a sword to Damien's throat.

They still held the Burkes in the doorway. Seamus gestured to Sean O'Toole, and they took one side of the doorway each. He waved his hand, and his men retreated. The Burkes spilt through the opening in pursuit. When the last man emerged, Seamus's men found were heavily outnumbered. He nodded to Sean, and they charged with their axes at the rear of the Burkes, caving in two mens' skulls, which evened the odds. Seamus started swinging. The Burkes were not expecting an attack in the rear, and in a few moments, whoever was not dead had fled.

"Pick him up!" and Seamus pointed at Damien.

"If you help us now, we'll give you and your family safe passage to Tirconnell. If not, your head will join your hand, rolling around in the dirt."

Damien needed no more persuasion.

"I will lead you to the prisoners and your boat, but we'll probably all die before we get there."

"You lead the way and leave me to worry about the rest."

Damien got to his feet, and he was offered him some dirty rags with which to wrap the stump of his hand.

"The prisoners are in there," Damien said, pointing to the door from where the guards poured forth. "The one you are looking for is at the back."

"Will this set of keys cover all the cells?"

Damien examined them.

"Nothing a sharp axe wouldn't fix," came the reply.

"Then hurry through the door. If I find guards that you should have alerted me to, then contemplate your family's slow death."

Damien entered and soon returned to wave them in.

They found themselves in a dark, dank dungeon and the prisoners rattled their chains to welcome them in.

"How do I tell the hostages of the Connacht gentry from the criminals?" asked Seamus, the darkness and the neglect the men endured disguised friend and common criminal alike.

"Just let them all out and see who follows us. The rest can act as cover," said Sean O'Toole. "But hurry. We need to make the tides."

Seamus inserted the key into the lock of the first cage. The prisoners stared expectantly at him, clawing at the bars, giving him the benefit of the doubt that he was their saviour. He unlocked the door and got out of the way. Some prisoners made straight for the door.

"Let them go," said Seamus, for he was convinced they were the common criminals.

"Give us weapons so we can fight," said one who remained.

"Pick clean the bodies of the guards outside. That is all we have to spare. We'll get more on the way."

Sean directed the men out into the yard.

"I hope you've put something in that drink, for they'll easily find this rabble trying to get to the harbour," said Sean.

"First we get Eunan, then we worry about getting to the harbour. I've got out of worse scrapes than this."

Seamus went to the next cage and tried the key. The key clicked with a bit of coaxing, and the men were freed. There was one more cage, but Eunan was nowhere to be found.

"The special prisoners are behind that door," said one prisoner and pointed to a black monstrosity of a door at the end of the hall.

Seamus looked at his one remaining key.

"You better be it," and Seamus turned the key in the lock.

No click. The door did not budge.

"We have to go, now!" shouted Sean down the corridor.

"The door won't budge."

Sean ran down to help.

"Give it here," and he took possession of the key and caressed the innards of the lock with the sides of the key.

"You've got to treat the lock like you treat a woman!" said Sean.

"Just get the door open before you see how I treat my axe!"

"We need to go," came a cry from the doorway to the courtyard.

The lock clicked.

"There you go," said Sean. "All she needed was the gentle touch."

The door creaked open to reveal two guards with the points on the tops of their axes at the ready.

"Leave this to me," cried Seamus, and he swung his axe into the doorway.

The two guards were no match for Seamus, and Sean was soon picking the dead guards' pockets for keys while Seamus banged on all the cell doors, calling for Eunan.

"I am here," called out Eunan, in such a state of neglect that he was unsure whether he was in a dream.

"Bring the keys here, and be quick about it," commanded Seamus.

Once the keys were in his hands, he fumbled with the lock as Eunan approached the door from the other side.

"We've got to go," came a familiar but, by now, more distant refrain.

"Which is the damned key?" cried Seamus.

"Give them here," and Sean took the set of keys off him.

Sean logically eased each key into the lock, waiting patiently for the click.

"Hurry!"

The click eventually came, and Seamus brushed past Sean.

"Look at the state of you!" said Seamus as he stood in the doorway and set eyes upon Eunan, wallowing in his punishment pit. "Sure, the rats can grow better beards than you."

* * *

Eunan huddled in the corner of the boat, wrapped in a blanket, trying to get life back into his frozen bones. The sea gently licked the side of the boat, and the beauty of the Galway coast to the starboard was smothered under his blanket of melancholy. Seamus walked towards him with a vague air of concern.

"Here, have a wet cloth and get some of that blood off you. We have to scrub you down to make you vaguely presentable for when we meet the O'Donnell," said Seamus as he leant over and offered Eunan a cloth from a bucket of fresh water.

Eunan reached out his hand.

"Thanks," he muttered and cleaned his face.

"Well, your brief incarceration has not dimmed your skills with an axe," said Seamus to brighten Eunan's mood.

"I am honing my skills for when I wreak my revenge on the O'Cassidys."

"Oh, your day will come soon, I'm sure of it. Now you rest up. It may take us a couple of days to sail 'round to the MacWilliam Burkes. Try cheering up as well. The jail rats would've been more grateful if I'd rescued them instead of you."

"Thanks," and in a mumble, Eunan expressed all the gratitude he could raise.

He reached over and dipped the blood-soaked cloth in the bucket.

Sean O'Toole came over to Seamus.

"I'll leave you be, Eunan," and Seamus turned his back so he could speak in private.

"That was a close call," said Sean.

"The captain deserves the generosity of the O'Donnell when the proceeds of this season's raids are distributed out, and I'll make sure Red Hugh is told. If those soldiers hadn't so much drink on them, they would have slaughtered us like a couple of calves. We lost a few men when they tried to spring a trap upon us just before the harbour, but the boy has not lost his prowess with an axe."

"He needs to recover and quick, for Red Hugh sent word that he would be in Connacht in a week."

"That soon? Sure there's nobody to stop him judging by the state of the English and the Burkes in Galway town," said Seamus. "How's the haul we got?"

"Most of the prisoners made it back to the ships. We also picked up a couple of criminals since their identity is not credible."

Seamus slapped his comrade on the shoulders.

"The O'Donnell will be pleased. Now rest up for the rest of the journey, for I fear this could be the only break we'll get for a long time."

"I'll rest when I'm dead!" replied Sean.

"You need to recuperate to avoid becoming dead. Now, do as I say, for I'll need you fully alert for what is coming."

Sean nodded his head and took up a blanket that sat on top of one of the cargo boxes. He then sat beside Eunan, for there was no more space on deck with all the human cargo they had picked up. Sean attempted to banish the faces of the men he had killed that day and tried to sleep while the sea was calm. He knew he would have disturbance enough when he awoke.

36

Kilmaine

The time had come for the election of the new MacWilliam Burke. Red Hugh was determined that he would impose the old O'Donnell rights and be the one to confer the title. Governor Bingham would indeed have been informed of the impending ceremony, so the O'Donnell brought the largest army he could muster with him. Along the way to the inauguration in Mayo, he broke down the castles of all of those who either opposed him or would not pledge to him.

Red Hugh's march to Mayo and the inauguration of the MacWilliam Burke was to be a display of power with a large and varied audience. The most conspicuous target audience was Governor Bingham to show the Crown that tanistry was alive and well, and that both he and they were powerless to stop Red Hugh from appointing who he wanted to lead the Irish clans. The lesser lords of Ulster were among the invitees, including Hugh Maguire, so that the O'Donnell could show them he was the rising power in Connacht. Finally, Cormac MacBaron came with a sizable force to remind O'Neill that Red Hugh was an equal and not a junior partner. It was a powerful statement that he could match what O'Neill had done to eastern and southern

Ulster.

Kittagh MacWilliam Burke, a candidate for the title and a favourite of Red Hugh, secured the area around the village of Kilmaine, County Mayo, and waited for his esteemed guests.

* * *

The two ships that escaped Galway moored into a small harbour on Clare Island in Clew Bay after enduring two days of terrible storms on the Atlantic Ocean. During one tumultuous episode, an O'Malley prisoner claimed to have much sway with the O'Malleys because he was a close relative, and the family would shelter them in gratitude for his safe return. Since the worst outcome would be death postponed, Seamus agreed to change course and follow the man's directions. The O'Malley ships intercepted them once they entered the calmer waters of the bay. The freed prisoner was as good as his word for when the O'Malleys boarded their ship he was recognised straight away. They were taken to the harbour beneath the castle the O'Malleys built to command the bay.

The matriarch of the family was Grace O'Malley, mother to the leading contender to the MacWilliam Burke, Theobald ('Tibbot') Burke. Grace was a woman of formidable reputation, which had spread much further than her fleet could travel. She had grown old, but that did not affect her standing, for the bards and poets had committed her legend to the ages. Grace was stout of stature, with a face of a woman who would not suffer fools. Her MacSweeney Galloglass escorted her down to the dock. Seamus went to greet her as soon as he disembarked. He was full of admiration and respect, as he was well acquainted with her legend.

"Seamus MacSheehy," and Seamus put out his hand for Grace to leave it hanging in the air. "Thank you, Ma'am, for the port in a storm, so to speak. The Atlantic winds had us in her grip and would not let us go."

"I, for one, are glad to see you, Seamus, for you brought with you sons of the Burkes and O'Malleys that we thought we'd never see again."

Seamus resisted a self-congratulatory smile, for Grace's stony face said it was uncalled for.

"I'm glad that you can benefit from the work that I do for my master, the O'Donnell. Has he arrived yet?"

"Word has it he will arrive in the next couple of days for the inauguration of the new Lower MacWilliam Burke. My son Tibbot is the firm favourite to succeed to the title, having already amassed the pledges of most of the local clan leaders and was given the earldom by the Queen as part of surrender and regrant not even two years ago. Who would vote against that?"

Seamus bowed his head.

"It's not for me to say, Ma'am, I'm merely a lowly Galloglass doing his master's bidding. I'm sure your recently released sons and nephews etc., are looking forward to celebrating their newly found freedom at the inauguration feast."

The disembarking of Eunan and his ex-prison mates rudely interrupted Seamus's attempted pleasantries. All of his efforts to make Eunan look presentable were in vain, for he had acquired a fresh collection of bruises and was caked in vomit after being thrown around the ship like a sack of potatoes. Seamus ordered some men to pick him up and help him off the ship.

"That's a fair party of land lovers you acquired," remarked Grace.

"I apologise for their appearance, Ma'am. We need to get them washed up and give them some new clothes if it wouldn't be too much trouble," said Seamus, slightly embarrassed.

"That can be arranged. I will see you at the dinner I have organised to welcome the long-lost souls home. Get some rest for we feast tonight and set off for the inauguration on the morrow. My son will meet us on the way there," said Grace.

She snapped her fingers and her bodyguards turned and set off back up the hill to the castle.

Seamus was almost relieved she was gone. He wanted to get out of Connacht as soon as possible, for the December lashings of rain and bitter piercing wind disagreed with him and his men. It was praying for a miracle that they could be well at the same time in such conditions. But he needed one person well by the next day and went to see if Eunan was feeling any better.

Eunan had not left the modest dock. The mere sight of the hill to the castle had drained the energy from him. He had taken up residence on a barrel and was not for moving.

Seamus went to talk him off it. He tugged on Eunan's arm, his barrel side manner more goading than sympathetic.

"I'll be ok. You don't have to mother me!" said Eunan as he freed his arm.

Eunan appeared to be in a daze, having said little since they freed him from the jail.

"What's wrong with you?" said Seamus. "Merely my presence was enough to have the arguments leaping off your tongue in days gone by. Now, I can barely get a peep out of you! You haven't gone all soft on me, have you?"

Eunan's eyes glazed over and swirled with the dark clouds that gathered in the sky.

"I just need to be left in peace for a while. Maybe I'll go back to the island and convalesce with Desmond. You don't know what it's like being locked up like that."

"You'll do no such thing! I could compare my multiple lengthy stints in jail to what little experiences you have had in your sheltered life, but I fear embarrassing you will only lead to further delays. You need to look presentable to the O'Donnell, for we need to garner his support to become the next O'Cassidy Maguire as we talked about."

"But there already is an O'Cassidy Maguire?"

"Don't you worry about little details like that. Your uncle Seamus will sort you out. You just concentrate on getting better and being able to string polite sentences together."

"Please don't call yourself that," whispered Eunan.

Seamus signalled for one of the local men who had been on the mission to come and join him.

"Feed him, clothe him, make sure he has a shit and a shave. I want him coherent for the inauguration tomorrow."

The man nodded and took Eunan by the arm and walked him up the hill to the valley.

* * *

The next day they set out to the harbour and boarded ships destined for the mainland. Last night's feast had been a strange affair which Grace did not attend, giving the excuse she had things to arrange for the upcoming inauguration. The atmosphere was subdued, except for a few young men reacquainting themselves with alcohol after a forced abstention because of incarceration. Most of the guests retired early, for they knew that the next few days would be long and taxing. Others were forced to retire because of illness, having been deprived of such rich food and alcohol for so long. Seamus stayed until a reasonable hour, for he could not turn down such a valuable opportunity to gather information, but Eunan was one of the first to retire early.

When they landed on shore, they began the trek to Kilmaine, the traditional Lower MacWilliam Burke inauguration site. There were a limited amount of horses, and Seamus ensured Eunan got one, for he was only marginally better after a night of rest. The party picked up several minor clans along the route and met Tibbot Burke and his entourage several miles away from the ring fort of Kilmaine.

Grace was determined to put on an early show of strength to ensure her son got enough votes for the election. They marched into Kilmaine in full battle order. Still, she was disappointed to see that, except for dignitaries from other minor clans from around the region, only MacWilliam Burkes of the major clans had arrived. Grace and her entourage were directed to a patch of land where they could set up camp. Seamus and his men pitched camp beside the O'Malleys, for they were there as their guests.

That evening seven MacWilliam Burke candidates came to Grace's tent. Some naively asked her for her vote; the cleverer ones opted to open up a friendly dialogue to be on good terms if they beat her son and create an alliance if he beat them. Everyone knew the amount of influence she held in the region and over her son, so it was always better to be on her good side. Grace was gracious to all and told them she would tell her son that the candidate was willing to make an alliance, no matter the outcome. Most of the parties exercised restraint, both in diplomacy and alcohol, for they knew that whatever happened, this was only the prelude.

The next morning, the candidates counted their pledges and consulted with their advisors for their chances of getting elected. The more powerful candidates discussed fetching more of their armed supporters to force the issue but, upon consultation, thought better of it. They were all waiting for Red Hugh since it was he who facilitated the reintroduction of tanistry to the Lower MacWilliam Burkes.

By midmorning, word came to the camp that Red Hugh was on his way. By midday, the O'Donnell marched in with an army of 1,800 men. It dwarfed the size of the forces available to the candidates and was immediately apparent to all those present that he was here to impose his will.

Red Hugh was directed to the ancient ring fort as it was the traditional site of the MacWilliam Burkes' inauguration. He and his advisors made camp in the middle of the ring fort, for none of the candidates were brave enough to object. Surrounding him were four rings of men, the inner ring were men of O'Donnell, the second were men of O'Doherty, the third was the MacSweeney Galloglass, and the fourth were Connacht allies who joined him on the march south. He also brought many of the leading nobles of Tirconnell. Cormac MacBaron came to represent O'Neill. It was a show of strength to the lords of the north and the mobile court of the O'Donnell to the lords of Connacht.

Seamus sat in Grace's tent, waiting to see what would happen.

"The O'Donnell shows up as if a conquering lord, as bad as any Englishman," complained Grace. "I hope he will not interfere in the election of the MacWilliam Burke today?"

"You can't expect him to come to Connacht unescorted, Ma'am. Governor Bingham still has a formidable force and is far from beaten."

"You defend your master well, Seamus. However, all I have seen him do is remove the wealth of Connacht and transfer it to Tirconnell."

"I have no wish to wear out my welcome, but he needs to deprive his enemies of the means to wage war and punish those who do not join him in resisting the English."

"You are right, Seamus, but don't wear out your welcome."

Seamus nodded and knew it was time to be silent.

One of the O'Malley men stepped into the tent.

"I have a messenger from the O'Donnell outside with a message for you and Tibbot, Ma'am."

"Well, don't just stand there. Send him in!"

A captain of the O'Donnell came in, dressed in the latest breastplate and helmet from Spain, still covered in the mud from the roads of

Connacht. He nodded at Seamus, for he knew him from the court of Red Hugh.

"The O'Donnell would like to meet Tibbot Burke so that he can put forth his case to be the MacWilliam Burke."

"Would he now?" sneered Grace. "What if my son wishes to declare himself the MacWilliam Burke of his own accord?"

Seamus saw he needed to diffuse the tension.

"I will come with you. I know the O'Donnell well, and I have advised him frequently."

"And is declaring himself king of Connacht part of your advice?"

"I will prepare myself and be back here momentarily."

"You do that!" and Grace called one of her captains in. "Go fetch my son, so we can meet the O'Donnell."

Seamus sought after Eunan.

* * *

Eunan was sitting beside a fire in the O'Malley camp, looking more forlorn than when Seamus had left him. Seamus pondered why as he walked over to him until he heard a noise. He looked to his right to see Óisin pissing beside a bush.

"How did he get here so quick?" asked Seamus of Eunan. "You aren't even a week out of jail?"

"He came here seeking you, in order that you could free me. You beat him to it," replied Eunan. "He came here with this," and Eunan handed Seamus a letter.

Seamus read it. He held it down by his thigh as he contemplated its consequences.

"She can't marry him. It is against all decency," squealed Eunan.

"He's a crafty one, Cormac O'Cassidy, but what is he willing to do to win?"

Óisin came back after he finished relieving himself.

"I see he's free now. I have one hundred men ready to act on his, or your, command. What'll it be, Seamus?"

"I have important business here to settle first. You may think me a heartless bastard, but I owe my loyalty to the O'Donnell and need to ensure he sees past his foolish pride before I can sort your woes, Eunan. We have a week. Óisin, you will return to Fermanagh and assemble your men in the forest below Eunan's village. I will send Sean O'Toole northwards to fetch my men. Eunan and I will depart as soon as we finish our business here. Óisin lay low and do not reveal your intentions before I arrive."

Seamus stood between Eunan and Óisin, and they both realised their reunion was over.

"Eunan, get yourself together and pick up your things. Before we save Fermanagh, we need to save Connacht!"

* * *

Seamus and Eunan arrived at the ring fort with Grace, Tibbot, and their entourage. Eoghan McToole O'Gallagher greeted them, for he was acting as the gatekeeper to the O'Donnell.

"Hello, Seamus. Sorry, candidates and their select advisors only are allowed in."

"He is an adviser," hissed Grace, and she walked in, only for her way to be blocked by the axes of the O'Donnell's Connacht supporters.

"Is your master here to start a war?" asked Grace.

"No," Eoghan replied. "He is here to free Ireland."

"Why do I then feel as if I am his prisoner?"

Eoghan saw that arguing was futile.

"Go on in the lot of you, but no bodyguards."

They made their way through the four rings of soldiers until they reached the centre of the fort. Red Hugh sat in the middle, and as he said his goodbyes to the entourage of Kittagh Burke, Seamus, Grace and their entourage were told to stop and wait.

"If I knew I was in for this power game, I would have stayed at home," whispered Grace.

They were beckoned forward to meet the O'Donnell.

"Tibbot Burke, lord of the Lower MacWilliam Burkes, by arrangement by my dear mother, Grace O'Malley, 'the Pirate Queen', with Queen Elizabeth herself. But I am not the Queen's man, having rebelled against her twice and merely awaiting your good self before I make it a third," and Tibbot bowed as low as it was polite to do so given the circumstances.

Red Hugh smiled.

"Your fame almost rivals that of your mother. Now, why should I make you the clan chief of the Lower MacWilliam Burkes?"

Both Tibbot and his mother were taken aback.

"Surely we are having an election if we have returned to tanistry?"

"Indeed, we have tanistry because of all of my efforts to persuade the Gaelic lords of Connacht to stand up for the old ways. But yet, here am I sitting with the largest army as lord of Connacht. Connacht was once under the O'Donnells and soon will be again. So, therefore, I ask again, why should I make you the MacWilliam Burke?"

"I have most of the votes, most of the warriors and most of the ships. If not me, who do you have that has the power to oppose me?"

"Will you help me fan the flames of the rebellion in Connacht and rise against the English?"

"How little you know us," said Grace. "The tales of the rebelliousness of the Lower MacWilliam Burkes can be heard as far away as the fields of Flanders, the court of the king of Spain, and the halls of the Vatican itself. You must be sorely mistaken if you do not realise we will support you if you have a just cause."

Both Grace and Tibbot bowed to signal this was the end of any case they may have wanted to make.

"Thank you for your words. I will gather the votes for the election and inform you of the results. Eoghan will escort you out," and Red Hugh pointed to the line of O'Donnell soldiers who created a gap.

"May I have a quick word, lord?" enquired Seamus.

"You cannot influence the matter in favour of Tibbot, so I would forget what you are about to say," replied Red Hugh.

"It is not about this. I have another matter to discuss. It is urgent."

"More urgent than the consolidation of Connacht? My Seamus, you have risen in the world."

"May we speak briefly?"

"We may speak here. You may go, Tibbot."

Tibbot bowed, for he did not know what to do. He was unused to being spoken in that way.

Tibbot, Grace, and their advisors walked through the gap in the soldiers.

"Here, lord? But what about spies?"

"Come and whisper in my ear. We need to be quick for the next MacWilliam Burke is already on his way."

Seamus walked up to Red Hugh, who was the only person seated, and the surrounding advisors moved out of Seamus's way.

"Cormac O'Cassidy is about to marry his daughter to a son of Connor Roe Maguire. Both these men are supporters of the Crown. If they unite, the bottom half of Fermanagh could cede to the English. Indeed, I have it on good authority that Donnacha O'Cassidy Maguire has persuaded Hugh Maguire to open up separate peace talks to yours with the Lord deputy. I wish to return to Fermanagh at once to remove Cormac O'Cassidy and have Eunan take Cormac's place. Do I have your permission and protection to act, and may I leave now?"

Red Hugh paused, and one advisor whose face Seamus could not

311

see bent down to whisper in Red Hugh's ear.

"I care not for Cormac nor Connor Roe Maguire but do not start a civil war, especially one that can be traced back to me. I need evidence of this purported treachery by Hugh Maguire. The O'Donnell cannot take action without evidence. As for leaving now, Connacht is much more important right now than some petty land squabble in Fermanagh. Stay with the O'Malleys and Tibbot and make sure they agree with my choice of MacWilliam Burke. That is your principal task for now."

"But Lord, the wedding takes place within a week."

"Then you must act fast with Tibbot MacWilliam Burke. Quick, be off with you! The next candidate is here."

Seamus stepped back and saw there was no talking to Red Hugh. The soldiers parted, and he went to find Eunan.

* * *

Seamus returned to the fire where he left Eunan but found him gone, replaced by men of the O'Malleys in his place.

"Where's the man that was here? He was with his friend from Fermanagh."

One man who recognised Seamus looked up and shrugged.

"He went somewhere with his friend. Back to Fermanagh?"

Seamus cursed.

"How long ago?"

The man shrugged again.

"He left as I sat to eat my midday meal. So the answer must be midday."

"Thank you," grunted Seamus as he saved the curses for under his breath.

"That foolish boy has at least a couple of hours on me."

Once he reconciled Eunan was gone, Seamus noticed who else was missing.

"Where are the Lady O'Malley and Lord Tibbot?" he asked again of the man by the fire.

"I do not know, nor would I look for them after their fury following their meeting with Red Hugh. If I were to suggest, they would have gone to speak to their allies. I'm sure you'll find them at the inauguration ground if you want to."

Seamus grunted his thanks again and strode off with a purpose.

* * *

Most of the Mayo gentry gathered outside the entrance to the old hill fort and were denied entry by the soldiers of the O'Donnell. The lords and ladies had given up attempting to petition the soldiers to let them in and turned inwards to their group. Seamus overheard discussions of their grievances with the process imposed on them by Red Hugh, or trying to find out how the other lords voted, what their impressions of their meeting with Red Hugh were, and then assessing whether they still thought they were in with a chance or not. Seamus picked his way through the crowd and found Tibbot and Grace, who were less than pleased to see him.

"I hope you put in a friendly word with your master when we were dismissed," said Tibbot. "Red Hugh would be sorely mistaken not to appoint me the Lower MacWilliam Burke. I've got the votes, and I've got the muscle. He would be a fool to make an enemy of me!"

"Nobody is making a fool out of anyone else. If nothing else, Red Hugh has a sensible head on him. He's got to show consideration for everyone so that everyone goes along with the process. He has a heavy weight on his young shoulders, being the O'Donnell. I think everyone is getting a bit overexcited. Imagine if Bingham showed up to break up the ceremony. You'd be glad of his army then!" replied Seamus.

"We trust you, Seamus, for you brought back the cream of our youth to us," said Grace. "However, spend that trust wisely and don't use it on a false hope that could evaporate into the wind," advised Grace.

She and Tibbot turned their back on Seamus when the next minor lord left the ring fort. They wished to base their assessments on how their clansmen spent their votes. Seamus knew he had no time to waste. He went to fetch some men to ready themselves so they could depart to Fermanagh when the opportunity arose.

* * *

The deliberations went on throughout the day, and since it was Christmas Eve, night fell early. However, Red Hugh was determined to wrap everything up before Christmas Day. He ordered his men to light three massive fires to illuminate the ring. They invited the disarmed nobles of the Lower MacWilliam Burkes in to hear the result. They congregated around whichever fire reflected their confidence in being elected. The flames of the central fire reflected in Tibbot's eyes as he stood before the empty seat beside Red Hugh. Grace stood behind him, her face as impenetrable as the cliffs of Clare Island. Seamus, again, got in under the pretext of being an adviser to Tibbot and Grace. He stood nervously behind them, hoping that they would settle the outcome by the end of the evening and he could saddle up for Fermanagh.

Red Hugh appeared to the address the Lower MacWilliam Burkes with Kittagh Burke smiling beside him. The speech was a blur to Seamus. As he heard the air punctuated with the words 'loyalty and 'the O'Donnell' he could only play out in his head the scenarios of how long it would take him to get to Fermanagh, given the numerous disastrous outcomes he imagined the speech would bring. He missed the simplicity of swinging his axe to solve his problems. The only alleviation of seeing the crimson fury of Tibbot Burke was that Tibbot was taking it in silence. That did not last long, however. A cry came from the other fires.

"How can he have won? He is an attainder!"

"Who said that?" shouted Eoghan McToole O'Gallagher. "That is English law! It has no jurisdiction here."

"Attainder!" came the shout again.

"The O'Donnell has no jurisdiction here!" came another shout.

"SILENCE OR I WILL HAVE THE FORT CLEARED!" cried Red Hugh.

It finally dawned on Tibbot that O'Donnell's soldiers surrounded them, and Red Hugh could massacre the nobility of the MacWilliam Burkes with ease while his own soldiers stood idle outside.

"Listen to the O'Donnell," he pleaded with his fellow nobles. "We should accept Kittagh as our leader, for he is the O'Donnell's choice."

With those that protested, he whispered in their ears that if they did not accept it, they would not see the end of the day. Silence extinguished the rippling protests in the crowd.

Red Hugh sat down in his chair.

"Good. Now we have silence and you can listen. Many of you have served the rebellion well and have received my generosity. However, Kittagh came to me at an early stage as he was treated so unjustly by the Crown, as was I. You insult both him and me when you condemn him with the English term 'attainder'. It is a branding of our oppression by the Crown that we use this term to curse each other. Kittagh has my full confidence, and when Christmas is over, we will bring the war to the English. Come and join us. Connacht is a rich province. The supporters of the crown are rich, so there are plenty of rewards for all. Come and hail the new MacWilliam Burke and join us outside for the celebratory feast!"

There was a half-hearted cheer from the crowds gathered around the two fires to the sides.

"But first, we must have the pledges and hostages from the MacWilliam families. Eoghan, line them up and have my scribes ready to note down their hostages and what soldiers they pledge."

The various branches of the Lower MacWilliam Burkes were lined up and forced to pledge to Kittagh and Red Hugh. Three of the losing candidates were taken hostage there and then, and as the other families named their hostages, men were dispatched to take the unlucky relatives into custody.

"'Tis a bitter irony that my son exchanges an English prison for an Irish one, all in the name of freedom," muttered one of the minor clan heads as he queued to add his son's name to the register.

Red Hugh then named four of his supporters as heads of four of the minor clans in the region. Taking hostages for those clans then began.

They forced the nobles of Mayo to part take in the celebratory feast to show their loyalty to the O'Donnell. Seamus tried in vain to speak to Red Hugh but was rebuffed at every attempt. Neither Grace nor Tibbot appeared to want to have anything to do with him, so he went to drink with the men from the Galway mission. At least they seemed to be happy, if only because they were given free wine.

* * *

Seamus awoke in his tent the next day with a thumping headache. It was eerily quiet, which let paranoia get the better of him. The inside of the tent was covered in mud, but the clothes and the contents of the pockets were his, so he reckoned he had slept in the right tent. He stuck his head outside. There was a large hole in the campsite where the O'Malleys and Tibbot's men once were.

"I really shouldn't get so drunk!" he muttered to himself, wondering how he missed or could not remember them leaving.

He got dressed and wandered through the camp, and noticed other gaps of varying sizes.

"How could O'Donnell have been such a fool, and am I a fool for following him?"

Seamus now heard the noise of drunken men and looked over to the camp of the O'Donnells. The celebrations continued with the odd priest dotted around the camp, not shielding their disgust at the blasphemy as they prepared to hold mass for Christmas Day. Seamus knew he had not got long. The wedding would take place on New Year's Day, and it would take several days to get there. Eunan already had twenty-four hours on him.

"But the boy needs far less than a day to destroy everything through his own stupidity. Why am I continually surrounded by fools?"

Seamus decided his mission with the O'Malleys was over. He went to get his men and left for Fermanagh.

37

New Year's eve

After several harrowing days of travelling blighted by wind and driving rain, avoiding random bands of men, and not wanting to find out if they were friend or foe, Seamus got back to familiar territory. He had been here many a time in his life defending and springing ambushes in the woods of south Fermanagh. The woods felt like home, as if they embraced and protected him, every clearing offering a potential ambush spot to rid himself of his enemies.

He felt that the local population had been ungrateful for all the persistent efforts he had made to defend them, even though he was well compensated for his time and loss of men. He thought that what he was about to do was for the good of the Maguire, and they would be no less ungrateful this time. The boy's gratitude was another matter, but as long as he reestablished the Munster MacSheehys as a force, that would be all the gratitude he would need. First, he had to find out what kind of mess the boy had gotten himself into in his haste to get back to Fermanagh.

Arriving at the location where Seamus had arranged a meeting, there was no one there. It was a half-day ride to Derrylinn at the best of times and longer if you needed to avoid the O'Cassidy patrols and invitees making their way to the wedding. He sent one of his men north, towards Enniskillen, to look for Sean O'Toole. The second man was told to wait where he was in case anyone came along, and Seamus, knowing how prone Eunan was to sentimentality, rode towards the old village.

It was midday when he arrived, and the sun came out from behind the clouds depriving cold of its companion, rain. The grey of the sky compounded the grey of the land for famine even blighted the garden of Fermanagh. The remains of the village clung onto the shore, refusing to accept its destiny of being forever doomed. This backdrop made a familiar home to its on/off leader - Eunan O'Keenan Maguire - the man whose fortunes and inward toil fluctuated as with the fortunes of the village. Eunan had returned to revive his fortunes, as much as he had buried the O'Keenan part of his name in the village cemetery. He held court with those who remembered him with any fondness outside the building positioned over the ruins of his father's old house. He held court by the shore, just as his father did.

In Seamus's eyes, Eunan had returned to revel in the past and was foolish to potentially reveal his position when they still had to formulate their plan. He had to extricate Eunan without revealing he was there. The hood could only hide Seamus's identity for so long. He knew that if he waited long enough, a spark of luck would come along. That spark was Óisin's weak bladder. Óisin got up from his seat and walked between the houses.

"What are you doing here, you bloody fool?"

Óisin stumbled around in a circle, searching for the voice, and then looked to the heavens as if his judgment day had arrived.

"If I was your enemy, I could have slit your throat, set the village on fire and be helping myself to your cows by now."

"Seamus? Is that you? Reveal yourself and don't be a phantom of the shadows."

"Young, reckless and lucky to be alive, that's what you are," and Seamus stepped out from behind one of the wooden houses.

"We were wondering when you were going to show up," replied Óisin.

"So you went back to the place that Eunan was more or less thrown out of and announce your presence the day before the wedding?"

"He wanted to see how much support he had if he was going to become the O'Cassidy."

"He has all the support he needs from my axe. You should have hidden out in the forest and waited for me as I told you."

"Eunan is his own man, he…"

"Quit your blabbering and just get him."

Óisin was taken aback.

"What do I tell him?"

"That it is time to go, but do not mention me."

Several minutes later, Eunan came around to the back of the houses.

"Seamus!"

He looked glad to see him, but that feeling was chased away by the scowl on his compatriot's face.

"Where are your men?"

"They are coming from Enniskillen. I thought they would be here by now. However, the men of the village said they would support me. They hate Cormac."

"Connor Roe will make quick work of farm boys. We need proper soldiers. Óisin, get the men and bring them to Derrylinn and hide near the site of the wedding. Wait for my signal and then attack. The farm boys can also attack on the signal. Eunan, you are coming with me."

The expression on Seamus's face meant there was no room for arguing.

* * *

The two men rode down towards the rendezvous point. Eunan rode with renewed vigour, as if the village had revitalised him and given him fresh blood.

"What has you in such high spirits?" said Seamus, still seething with anger in the wake of Eunan's petulant actions.

"I have a certain confidence again, after everything that happened."

Seamus was nonplussed.

"What? Giving away your position has you more confident?"

"Going back to the village reminded me of what I was fighting for. It all seems abstract in some wet and windy bog in Connacht."

Seamus shook his head.

"That's what war and being a Galloglass is all about, splitting some man's head open in a wet and windy bog so that the person giving the orders can gain revenge, feel more important, or gain more cows. I thought you'd seen sense and put all this youthful idealism behind you?"

"I still fight for the Maguire!"

"Even as he tries to make a treaty selling you out to the English behind your back?"

Eunan, tired of such needling, whipped his reigns hard and rode ahead of Seamus.

They approached the forest, where they were supposed to meet their comrades. Eunan pulled up so Seamus could catch up. The two men entered the forest and broke into a trot but proceeded slowly, for Seamus knew how productive this forest could be for bandits. Having reached a stretch of the pathway with uncommonly good visibility, Seamus spied a party ahead of them. He signalled to Eunan, and they left the path with their horses tied up. Slipping further into the wood, but not far as they could not see the path, they ran through the trees to get ahead of the strangers. Both were adept at running while creating the minimum amount of noise, for it was a skill that kept one alive in the warfare of Ireland. The three figures were on foot as they escorted a cart behind them. Eunan and Seamus crouched behind a rock.

"They are monks. Leave them," said Eunan, and he turned to go.

Seamus grabbed him by the arm.

"Sit down," hissed Seamus. "They are perfect. With those disguises, we can sidle into the wedding without being noticed."

"We cannot murder monks!"

"Did you bring your little 'Maguire' throwing axes with you?"

"Of course, but I am not throwing them at the monks!"

"Calm yourself. Just follow my lead."

Seamus snook ahead and looked for the perfect ambush spot. He jumped onto the road from behind a tree.

"Excuse me, men of the cloth. I have an urgent need for your clothes. I'm sure it will give you great pleasure to endure the hardship of nudity and to kneel beside the roadside and pray for the deliverance of new clothes."

These insults disgusted Eunan, and he remained hidden, refusing to take part.

"You're way too fat for my habit and my knees far too delicate to kneel by any roadside," and the lead monk pulled out his axe and pulled down his hood.

"Sean O'Toole!" exclaimed Seamus.

"Great minds! Great minds!" and Sean ran over and embraced him.

Eunan came out from hiding, his soul relieved.

"When I asked you to get some men, I meant more than two," said Seamus.

"I got you many more than two. I have fifty men, Galloglass and veterans, for your unit making their way down separately, maybe a couple of hours behind me. They know where to go. I thought I would come with these two gentlemen to scout ahead."

"Well, you didn't let me down, and it sounds like a good plan. But we have no time to waste. Let us press ahead to the meeting place and see how many men we have."

"You might need these." Sean went to the cart and pulled out two other habits.

Seamus beamed from ear to ear.

"Sean, you think of everything!"

38

New Year's resolutions

Seamus, Eunan and their men sat in a wood in the cold and dark with only the wild animals, fairies and ghosts for company. They had been warm and had the benefit of light until Seamus returned and pissed on the fire.

"Are you stupid? That light can be seen for miles," he hissed at Eunan.

Seamus was extremely agitated, for he had gone to inspect the wedding venue, but Connor Roe turned up in force.

"He has at least one hundred men with him, and O'Cassidy has at least fifty of his own and twenty of those are Galloglass."

"Do we have to call it off?" asked Eunan, who was seated beside Seamus as they discussed with Sean the plan for the next day.

"No, it is now or never. If the O'Cassidys marry into the senior line of the Maguires, any claim that Eunan could have will be dead. We must strike tomorrow."

"What are our chances of success?" enquired Eunan.

"How many men do we have now?" asked Seamus.

"Three, two, and us, er, eight?" replied Sean.

"We have one hundred and fifty on the way?" suggested Eunan.

"If they are not here, they are as good as a fairy tale. Eight means we are dead in five minutes. We need more." Seamus's words had the same dosing effect as his piss had on the fire.

"The men of the village?" suggested Eunan.

"They are only meat for the Galloglass axe. We would have an extra five minutes before we die. We need something more, a lot more."

"Let us sleep on it," said Eunan. "I, for one, am dead to the world."

"With the dice in the air, we don't know how they will fall until the morn. Let your men take first watch, Sean. The rest of us will retire. At first light, we'll set in motion our plan once we know the circumstances of the day."

Seamus felt a drop of rain in his head.

"We are all to sleep in our tents tonight. No one is allowed to die of the fever when they could die on the Galloglass axe tomorrow."

Eunan grimaced at Seamus and then retired to bed.

* * *

Memory played a cruel trick on Eunan. For what lived in his memory as the evenhandedness and benevolence of his father were remembered by those who survived the original destruction of the village as tyranny and toil. Those who remembered the reign of Eunan remembered folly and destruction. The child of the Galloglass was deemed to be a curse that needed to be eradicated before he destroyed them all. The men of the village sent their hunter blessed with the greatest skills of stealth to find out where Eunan and Seamus lay. He now returned to the village to fetch the rest of the men. The heads of Seamus and Eunan would bring a bounty not seen in these parts in many a year.

* * *

Seamus's guards wrapped up well. It was a well lit night, and they were tired from the long march from Tirconnell. They died in mute resistance, causing the villagers no more bother than their largest pigs as their throats were slit and their lives gushed out onto their blankets and tunics. The village men gathered around the modest tents and ensured they observed no movements inside or out before they tried to guess which tents belonged to Seamus and Eunan.

* * *

Óisin had little of the discipline needed to become a proper soldier. His recklessness and disregard for orders signalled him out to the Maguire officers that he might make a good kern, scout or maybe a bandit. But he was too much of a free spirit to stand in line and wait for the enemy or be expected to cover for his comrade when he could lead a reckless charge instead. Óisin was a street urchin from Enniskillen. His father served and died for the Maguire, and his mother killed shortly after in one of the many raids that blighted Ireland. When his parent passed, he was far too young to remember what clan he was from, so once orphaned, he took to the streets. He found in Eunan a kindred fellow lost spirit, so Eunan absorbed any bonds of loyalty and comradeship Óisin could give.

Óisin fulfilled his mission and positioned one hundred men hidden but within striking distance of Derrylinn. He then got bored and took a handful of his companions to seek his friend.

They made their way up the hill and saw the tents just where Seamus said they would be. He noticed the villagers around the tents. Óisin smiled. That many recruits bode well for the mission tomorrow. He waved his men forward. One of them grabbed his arm to caution him and pointed to the suspicious behaviour of the men as they congregated around the tents. Óisin signalled to make silent haste.

* * *

Seamus was a paranoid creature of habit, as cautious and as cunning as any beast that lived to a ripe old age in the woods. When he heard the twig snap, that same twig he positioned outside his door every night, his hand crept from its warm abode and took into its warm cave a dagger, an aerodynamic and sharp blade equally adapted for stabbing and throwing. Seamus rolled over to appear asleep but could spring into action. In the distance, he heard "THE CRY OF THE MAGUIRE!" but it did not stir the patriotic duty or the adrenalin in him. The feelings that such calls to arms inspired were better expressed as:

"What foolishness has the boy embroiled himself in now!"

Seamus cursed. He knew stealth was no longer required, and picked up his axe. Only by swinging his old faithful would this problem be resolved. He cut through the tent door, for the time spent picking through the door string knots could be the difference between life and death. Seamus burst out onto the crest of the hill. The villagers still had the upper hand, trying to cut through the roof of Eunan's tent to release themselves and be free of his curse. Óisin's men charged up the hill, a couple having been cut down by the arrows of their foes. Seamus got to work.

His axe cut through the air as efficiently as any scythe that had ever graced the fields of the village. Not armour, blades, bones or pleads for mercy could stop its trajectory once it had fixated on a target. Seamus honed the smooth, sharp edge to such perfection that it sliced through anything in its way without getting stuck. Óisin's men reached the top of the hill, and the reckless charge had drained the lungs and legs of some, and their fall became a short-lived victory for their foes. It was short-lived because to achieve their victory, the men became static, the swinging of their arms like the swaying of the barley in the wind. They merely lined themselves up for the sweeps of the axe.

Seamus raised his axe above the pleading body below, only to stop upon hearing a familiar voice. He looked down.

"Taighe Maguire!" Seamus exclaimed and lowered his axe. "I took you in and trained you. Now you come back to kill me as your repayment? Tell me why you are here and why I should not dash your head off with my axe right now?"

"Please have mercy," said Taighe as he feebly raised his arm to defend himself, knowing full well that the only defence it would do is blunt the descent of the axe and maybe prolong his death. "Soon after you left, the O'Cassidys asserted their authority over the village and promised a cow per head of Eunan and his men should he ever return."

Seamus looked around the hill, at the bodies strewn across the hillside and at the remains of the villagers fleeing.

"If I remember correctly, you are a man who can spread much honey with his tongue. I have an ear I wish you to pour honey down. Does the O'Cassidy know your face?"

"He surely does, for I would meet him often at the market at Derrylinn."

"Then deliver the heads of Eunan and his companions you shall do!"

39

New Year's Day

Eunan, Seamus and their mixed party of volunteers and the conscripted travelled to a secluded wood well known to Eunan, just north of Derrylinn. Taighe Maguire sat on the back of the cart with a sack beside him which rested in an ever-expanding pool of blood. But it was not the sack that concerned him. Rather, it was whose side should he be on to ensure that he and his family would be alive. He bitterly regretted bringing his boy on the doomed mission the night before. The boy may have been thirteen and of fighting age, but Seamus's men snared him as if he were a rabbit. Now his son's life was in his hands.

They pulled up before reaching the wood to send Taighe on his way with two of Eunan's men as an escort. Taighe got down off the cart and took hold of the bag. Seamus came up behind him and grabbed his ear.

"Remember what to do. Do nothing stupid like you did last night. Never bring your boy to do a man's work. What actions you take today will be reflected in what clemency I give to the boy and your village, if I give any."

Taighe nodded, and for his compliance, received back his ear. He set off with his escort to find Cormac O'Cassidy.

Eunan was getting agitated.

"Why did we have to leave the boy back in the wood with a knife to his throat? You know how I feel about such things having been used as a bartering tool for most of my youth."

"Such is the way of the world to persuade a man to do something he doesn't want to. These things are required of Galloglass and men of power, so get used to it."

Sean reached into the cart and handed Seamus and Eunan each a monk's habit.

"I hope it is not beneath you to disguise yourself as a monk?" sneered Seamus.

"Such is the way of the world and the requirement of men of power and Galloglass!" replied Eunan.

"That's it," laughed Seamus. "You'll need good spirits for today. Now, where's that reprobate commander of yours?"

"Óisin!" Eunan called.

Óisin came scampering from the woods like a hound dog called back from seeking a fox.

"He wants you," and Eunan pointed to Seamus.

Óisin presented himself before Seamus and saluted him. "Ready for orders!"

"That is the state I want you in, but fear you take the whole thing in jest. Are you ready to obey orders today and follow the plan?"

"I know exactly what you want me to do."

"Does that mean you are going to do it, though?"

"I will be there to rescue you, should you need it or not."

"There's no talking to you," Seamus turned to Sean. "Where are the rest of your men?"

"They will be in position by the time you arrive."

"Even I am nervous, with so many things held captive by chance.

But it is time to go. I salute you men, and if we are successful, by nightfall, Eunan will stand in Derrylinn as the O'Cassidy Maguire."

Óisin's men saluted Eunan, who saluted them back. They pulled the hoods of the habits over their heads, and Eunan, Seamus and Sean set down the road to Derrylinn, hoping that fate had not set a trap.

* * *

As they came towards Derrylinn, the dirt track that impersonated a road became more crowded. They joined a caravan of well-wishers heading down from eastern Fermanagh, laden with a wedding gift of cows to welcome Caoimhe into the senior line of Maguires. Sean posed as the head monk, for he had slightly greater knowledge, but definitely more respect for religion than Seamus, with a story that they had been sent from a monastery on an island in lower Lough Erne and the other two had taken a vow of silent prayer only to be broken when the happy couple were married. They were invited to join the rear of the caravan.

They got to within sight of the O'Cassidy house in Derrylinn before being stopped by an O'Cassidy patrol. The patrol spent several minutes interrogating the leader of the caravan before testing the truth of his explanations by searching the carts, one by one. Eunan's leg twitched as the soldiers made their way up the caravan. He fiddled with his 'Maguire' throwing axes, pondering whether to use them and seeking the one with the notch on the lower shaft, a mark created so that he would not forget which axe he blamed for his father's death.

The soldiers found nothing contraband or concealed in the rest of the caravan.

"Sorry, fathers, but we're going to have to search you for weapons," said the lead soldier.

Sean stepped forward, as Seamus had planned. He held out his arms as a sign of no resistance.

"You can search me all you like, but my two brothers have taken a vow of silent prayer until the happy couple are betrothed. I would not like any blame to fall on you if the happy couple is cursed, suffer bad luck or cannot conceive because you were so mistrustful of some priests that you would disturb their prayers."

The lead soldier hesitated and then turned towards the front of the caravan and shouted: "Let them pass!"

"Bless you, son," said Sean.

"Say a prayer for them from me," replied the soldier.

Sean saluted him, and they followed the caravan along.

In the fields to their left, they saw a herd of cattle being driven along by Galloglass.

"I recognise them," said Seamus. "Men of Connor Roe. That must be the dowry. We must make that dowry our own if we are alive by the end of the day."

Eunan gulped.

"Would you not have thought to paint such a bleak picture before we set out so we could plan accordingly?"

"If I had, you would have stayed in the village and had your throat cut as you tried to convince yourself how wonderful your parents were. You are far better off here with me with at least a fighting chance of becoming the next O'Cassidy Maguire. It is not a time for weakness and dreaming."

Eunan tensed his arms and tried in vain to conjure up his bad blood. Nothing. He dreamed of Odin, Loki and Badu. But the characters did not come to life and haunt him as they used to. Eunan then considered a drastic measure.

"Odin, give me strength."

But the only thing he gained was a sense of guilt for uttering blasphemies. It was no good. He was that scared little boy again, fearing his father pushing open the front door again and returning home or the shrill call of his mother, calling him to attend to her again. He was no O'Cassidy Maguire.

* * *

It was a cold and cloudless day by the time they arrived in Derrylinn. The air had a certain chill that could penetrate cloth and armour alike. The wedding was to take place outside on the grounds of the O'Cassidy house, for it was a long tradition that O'Cassidys got married outside, and Cormac wished to carry on with the tradition.

"Everything must be ready by midday," he shouted at his lackeys.

But everything was far from ready, and they expected Connor Roe within the hour.

Cormac spent long hours debating with Donnacha what form the wedding should take. On the one hand, he had only two children: Cillian was the heir under English law, but under Brehon law and tanistry, Eunan was his greatest rival. Cormac was unsure of Eunan's whereabouts, still in the Galway jail or Fermanagh with his accomplice, the cunning Galloglass Seamus MacSheehy? Cillian was in peril taking part in the rebellion, but appearances demanded that he be seen to support Hugh Maguire. Otherwise, Cormac feared he would be ousted. Therefore, for appearance's sake, Brehon law seemed the right choice.

However, Connor Roe was both a knight and an ex-sheriff. Under English law, Cillian would inherit, but if the worst were to happen, and he died, Connor Roe's son would inherit through marriage. Once Caoimhe conceived, the bloodlines would be mixed. Even if the O'Cassidy line was broken and then erased, his relatives would be in the senior Maguire line and a hereditary English lord. Thus, once the couple were married by Brehon law, they would be whisked off to the

Pale to have a wedding that the Crown would definitively recognise. This is what Donnacha advised and what Cormac had set out to do that day.

Cillian was called into his father's presence, for he had returned from Enniskillen the day before. He dutifully bowed before his father.

"It is a blessed day and a great one for the O'Cassidy clan. Soon you will soldier with Connor Roe and hopefully bring forward the day he becomes the Maguire."

"My men have spotted him in the distance. He brings with him a healthy entourage and a generous dowry."

"How many men did you bring back from Enniskillen?"

"Unfortunately, most of your men were released back to the fields once the peace negotiations started. But I have fifty men of fighting experience. They cover the roads into Derrylinn seeking those who may create mischief."

"Any word on Eunan Maguire?"

"None of yet. He may be dead or still languishing in a Galway jail for all I know."

One of Cormac's staff entered.

"Your brother Donnacha has arrived, lord."

"Good, good, send him in."

Cormac reserved a warm embrace for his brother.

"How goes the negotiations in Enniskillen, my brother?"

"The biggest barrier is the Maguire's pride, swiftly followed by the refusal of the English to show pragmatism. Maguire refuses to accept a sheriff and an English title, and the negotiator insists the Maguire show loyalty and turn and fight his former allies."

"When will we return to a simple world of commerce? The O'Cassidys can be great but only when the Irish give up the savagery of cattle rustling and feuds and settle on the genuine power of money and commerce. There is a perfectly good trade to be had with the towns of the Pale, but all my compatriots want to do is ape some myth about a great ancestor who had the most cows in the biggest field and cudgelled to death all those with whom he festers a grudge."

Into the cynical discussion on politics danced the young Caoimhe, dressed in the finest green from the port of Dublin and a faraway land beyond that. Her flowing black hair was decorated with white flowers the womenfolk had spent the best part of the day before collecting. She spun around before her father, radiating youth and beauty to all who set eyes upon her, and the cynicism was cast away with each ripple of her dress.

"Oh, my beautiful daughter! I wish your mother were here to see you today. 'Tis a truly bittersweet day for me."

"Oh father, why bitter?" she said and took both his hands and his heart melted in the sadness on her face, as if she had disappointed him.

"I am the proudest I have ever been to see you all grown up, and the most beautiful woman in all of Fermanagh is my very own daughter. But bitter for I know that such a moment will pass and you will be gone away to greater things with your husband. I will feel so proud but also deep with loneliness. My little girl will be gone."

"Father, I may be grown up, but you will always have me as your daughter. You will also become a much richer man than you are already with the future Maguire as my father-in-law."

"You are worth more to me than all the gold in the world," and he took his daughter by the hand to lead her from the house. On his way out, he turned once more to Cillian. "You are responsible to ensure that this wedding goes ahead without interruption."

Donnacha nodded to Cillian and departed with his brother and niece, leaving him to contemplate the size of his task to defend his beloved sister.

* * *

Connor Roe arrived and, not having been greeted by an O'Cassidy of any stature, immediately took charge. He instructed his MacCabe Galloglass to form a guard of honour for the bride and groom and protect the wedding party before, during and after the ceremony. He gave a curt nod to both Cormac and Donnacha when they finally came out to greet them, for he still had reservations about marrying off his second son to what he saw as a lowly family. It had taken much persuasion by Donnacha, not that he trusted Donnacha much, but he knew he had to build up alliances if he wanted to become the Maguire.

"So where is the groom?" asked Cormac.

"One of your men directed him to some local house to get ready. Lucky that, since the bride walks around free as a bird," replied Connor Roe.

"I hope she remains free as a bird when your son Art takes her into his house!"

"I'm sure you hold the same yearning for grandsons as I, for I hope she provides plenty, and soon," replied Connor Roe. "Now my men and I need food before we start. We have travelled far and will set out soon again. What provisions have you laid on for us?"

"You are not staying?" said Cormac, trying to hide his disappointment at the offhandedness of his soon-to-be new relative.

"You would need to convince me that this is friendly territory. You have not laid on too much security, so I presume you think it is?"

"Think of it as your second home," said Cormac, doing his best to ingratiate himself to his guest.

Connor Roe laughed

"Many a Maguire wish my second home as a cell in the jail of Enniskillen Castle, so I will decline your offer and set up my own security."

Connor Roe turned to Donnacha.

"What news of the promise of peace? That would be the best wedding gift you could give me. I so wish to remove the yoke of the O'Neill from my back."

"No news as yet. Being it the middle of winter and the famine biting again, nobody is interested in anything more than writing letters to delay what they can until the spring."

"What news of Spain? Do the wise lords of the North still pander after a Spanish ruler rather than an English one?"

"Therein lies their great hope! The O'Neill and the O'Donnell recently wrote to the Spanish king suggesting that after he liberates them, they will become his vassals and that he should make his cousin Archduke Albert prince of Ireland."

"Who's he?"

"A royal person who has the perfect balance of piety and laziness, specially chosen by the Irish clergy in Spain for having enough gravitas to deserve an army but also the same quantity of laziness to let the Irish lords rule as they please."

"They can pray all they like to the good Lord for salvation, but the Crown will always be the primary route to power in Ireland. Remember our bargain, Donnacha. I am here giving my son because when the Maguire dies in some bog in Connacht trying to rob some cows for his master, the O'Donnell, you said you will support me and make sure I am made the new Maguire, the title that is rightfully mine!"

"That is why we are here today," and Donnacha nodded solemnly.

"Good. As long as we are straight with that. I don't want any tricks. I want to get the wedding done and get back to Lisnaskea. Now, where's that food we asked for? Let us eat and get this day over with."

Donnacha hurried off to make arrangements. Cormac went back

towards his house to see what they were doing in the kitchen. One of his Galloglass approached him.

"Lord, one of the local villagers says he has news of bandits and seeks a reward."

"Get Cillian to deal with it. He is in charge of security," and Cormac waved the man away.

The Galloglass looked bewildered and then went off to find Cillian.

* * *

Cillian O'Cassidy felt the weight of responsibility on his shoulders. He was the second born but the only son. His father had been surrounded by tragedy, with the death of his wife and the death of his sister. Caoimhe, according to his father, encapsulated the best parts and the beauty of both, and his father had only to set eyes on her to be visibly moved. Cillian had no great skills in the art of war or agriculture nor any great intelligence nor skills with people that would make him in any way noteworthy. The role he took was that of the head of his father's underlings, but even then, he was overlooked when the task required a particular deftness or skill. He was given the tasks that required an O'Cassidy, jobs that his father did not want to do. Listening to tall stories from the local peasantry was just one of those tasks.

Taighe Maguire and his companion were presented to Cillian around the back of the O'Cassidy house. The meeting was arranged out of the sight of the wedding party so that the O'Cassidy and his guests would neither see nor hear anything unpleasant. They picked up their sacks and emptied the contents in front of Cillian. The numerous heads rolled on the ground until they settled in whatever divot on the ground, or in the skull, brought it to a halt.

"I'm here to claim the reward for Eunan Maguire and any bandits that may have rallied to his cause that once lurked in the yonder woods. The villagers elected me to collect the reward. Eunan returned to the village of his birth and tried to rally us against the O'Cassidy cause. When he left with no more followers, we set upon him and behead him which lays before you now."

Cillian did not want to dirty his wedding clothes and did not recognise the head of Eunan from what was visible before him.

"Bring his head to me before I consider any reward."

Taighe searched the heads until he found one that was sufficiently mutilated.

"That is him," said Taighe as he showed the face by rolling the skull under his foot.

"Pick it up! I can't see it properly under your foot, and it's covered in blood and mud. If you want a reasonable price for it, pick it up and show me properly."

Taighe grabbed the skull by the hair and held it up in front of Cillian.

"That is not him. It may be the most battered face you could find, but it is not Eunan. I served with him for the Maguire, you know? I know his face well, and it is not his. Do not take me for a fool. How do I know you are not a bandit and killed these men yourself and try to sell their heads to me as if they were those of someone else?"

Taighe saw the anger boiling in Cillian's eyes.

"You have me mistaken, sir. I come to you for I know you as a great man who can make things happen."

Flattery floated easily into Cillian's ears. Anything to raise his esteem and make him look like the next O'Cassidy Maguire in his father's eyes.

"What, pray tell, can I make happen?"

Taighe leaned into him so they would not be overheard.

"I bring you a message, but it is for you alone."

Cillian contemplated the risks and rewards from hearing this message. But a great man should not be afraid. He waived his two guards away.

"I bring you a message from a great warrior by the name of Seamus MacSheehy, a man of influence and stature in the court of the O'Donnell."

"I know of him," replied Cillian, who by now was most intrigued.

"He has noticed you and how you lead men. He has also seen that you go unnoticed by those in your own clan. Probably motivated by pure jealousy because of your esteemed service for the Maguire."

"Humph!"

"He wishes to enlist your help in a scheme to assist you both."

"Why should I trust him?"

"If you don't, your father will give away your inheritance, and you'll never be the O'Cassidy Maguire."

* * *

As the caravan travelled past Derrylinn, the O'Cassidy soldiers withdrew to form a ring around the house and wedding venue.

"Good on you, Taighe," exclaimed Seamus as he grabbed and shook Eunan's arm to absorb his own delight. "If you weren't such a snake, you'd make a great Galloglass!"

"I would have thought that being a snake was a prerequisite for being a Galloglass?" sneered Eunan.

"A different type of snake, there are loads of types of snakes," and Seamus dismissed his nephew's sarcasm.

"Don't celebrate yet," said Sean. "We've still to get into the wedding itself."

The caravan was ordered to disburse in a field in front of the O'Cassidy house.

"Where do we go now?" said Eunan, whose fit of nerves had not dissipated.

There was a group of monks kneeling beside a pond, praying.

"I hope you've got sturdy knees, boys. Keep your eyes out for Taighe!" exclaimed Seamus.

They walked over to the monks whilst rubbing their knees to warm them up, each hoping their knowledge of Latin was sufficient for them not to be found out.

* * *

Connor Roe was slightly more pleasant now that he had been fed and interfered in the wedding arrangements by ensuring that everything was up to his exacting standards. He was sorely disappointed.

"Where is that incompetent boy of yours?" he demanded of Cormac.

"May I remind you that you are a guest in my house!" came the heated reply.

"I beg your pardon, but as pretty as your garden is, I don't want it to be my grave, which is what it will be if your boy does not get the security right. Where is he?"

"My men will fetch him," and they obeyed as soon the words as they were parted from his tongue.

Cillian came with his breastplate and helmet freshly polished.

"Boy, you look splendid. Fitting to grace the finest courtyard in all of England!" said Connor Roe. "But alas, it is not your skills as a mannequin that are required today but your organisational ones. My newly arrived men rode all the way here from the lake and only encountered your men once they got past Derrylinn. Where are the patrols you agreed to and the perimeter you said you would create?"

Cillian smiled.

"Because I had good news! My agents killed our major rival, a certain Eunan Maguire, along with many of his fellow bandits.

Therefore, with him dead and the Maguire and the famine calling more of our men away, I concentrated our forces in a smaller area. Nothing will get past them."

"That is splendid news! Now let me get into this joyous occasion of seeing the evidence of the death of our foe so we can all join in your relaxed mood."

"My men brought me the head of Eunan."

"That is most excellent. Now bring it here."

"It has been badly mutilated. They took much frustration out on his head, for it cost them many of their comrades before he was slain."

"Hmm, stop me when I err. Your men bring you a badly mutilated head, one no doubt that had a large bounty on it, and you no doubt paid this bounty? Show me the record of the payment."

"Er, I have not had time to discuss it with my father yet and gain approval for the payment."

"Well, at least one of you has some sense. Your enemy is not dead! He is on his way here if not among us yet."

Connor Roe turned to his own Galloglass.

"Constable, protect the bride and groom, throw a cordon around the wedding venue and prepare our horses and carriages to leave at a moment's notice. We leave when this wedding is over."

Mouth agape, Cormac grabbed the arm of his witless boy to give him a piece of his mind. They had ousted him in his own house.

* * *

Seamus got suspicious when Connor Roe's men appeared to be taking control of the security arrangements. He shook the sleeve of Sean's robe.

"We need to go now!"

Sean nodded and poked Eunan, who finished his prayer and blessed himself.

"You'll definitely be needing some luck today," said Seamus.

They slipped away from the other monks, and Eunan led them around the side of the house.

"You know where you are going, don't you?" whispered Seamus to Eunan.

"I have been here many times. The door is this way."

"I thought that you only knew the front door and the dirt that laid before it, for they would throw you out each time you tried to enter?"

"I have been here enough to know my way around," growled Eunan.

"It's funny, but don't wind him up now," said Sean to Seamus.

They made their way around the angles of the house to the door of the kitchen where a steady stream of kitchen hands was going back and forth preparing the wedding feast. The door was on the other side of the kitchen door. Unfortunately, there stood before it two of Connor Roe's Galloglass, who had replaced Cillian's men. Sean looked pensively at Seamus but was waived on. He led the way and stood before the guards, and bowed his head.

"We are here to bless the bride before her wedding. The master of the house has directed here us."

The guards looked them up and down.

"No one told us. Come back with the master or a letter from him."

"Do you know the consequences of disobeying a priest?" Sean bellowed.

"I know the consequences of disobeying my master, and it may not be the same thing, but both would be hell all the same. Come back with the master of the house if it means so much to him."

Seamus signalled to his companions to leave. They walked back to the front of the house and straight into more of Connor Roe's men.

"Monks over there," and the constable pointed towards the newly concentrated brethren of monks to one side of the wedding venue.

"I can't sing!" protested Eunan, for he knew the monks would provide suitable religious musical accompaniment.

"Just mouth along," hissed Seamus. "At least you'll know the words!"

They walked over to the monks and took their places. The monks began their chant. Eunan knew enough to make the right sounds and not draw too much attention to himself. There was always at least one young monk that found difficulty in learning Latin. But there was a gaping hole of silence in the middle of the choir. They soon drew attention to themselves. A senior monk made his way through the crowd to them.

"What is going on here? Why aren't you singing?"

Seamus gave Sean a swift kick in the ankle.

"They have taken a vow of silent prayer until the happy couple is married. As soon as the tying of the hands is completed, they will express their joy in song."

"This is highly unusual. Why was I not told?"

"They are relatives of the bride, here by special request of the master of the house."

"Hmm. They really should have sat somewhere else, but it is too late for that. It is about to start."

* * *

Cillian had been suitably admonished by his father and told to retake charge of the outer security. He left the inner ring around the wedding to Connor Roe. In his fury at being humiliated, he sent out patrols to the countryside, hoping that such measures would both impress and reassure his father that he had made the right decision to leave him in charge.

He returned to his rooms to change once more, for mud spoilt his breastplate, and he wanted to look his best as he avenged himself upon Connor Roe. Climbing the stairs with his men, the risk of the bargain he made with Taighe Maguire played on his mind. He would rush down the stairs and announce that Caoimhe had been taken, the victim of a vicious kidnapping attempt, all of which occurred when Connor Roe's men were supposed to be in charge. His father would be so furious with Connor Roe that he would send him packing back to Lisnaskea, and the wedding cancelled forever. With Connor Roe banished, he would gather his most trustworthy men and fake rescue his sister from the clutches of Seamus MacSheehy, and return to Derrylinn as a hero. His father would be so grateful that he would name him his heir. Then he would return to service with the Maguire, Seamus would put a word in for him and he would get a high-ranking position. He would then lead the men of south Fermanagh on the most successful raids the bards of Fermanagh had ever had the pleasure to sing about. But first was the matter of his side of the bargain.

He put his hand on the door and turned the handle.

"Be patient, brother, I'll be ready momentarily!" came the voice of his sister.

He nearly vomited.

Meanwhile, the bows of Óisin's men made quick work of the isolated O'Cassidy patrols. Once the outer perimeter was cleared, they made for the O'Cassidy house and the wedding.

40

Who is the O'Cassidy Maguire?

A bitter sorrow came over Eunan as he observed the wedding venue. The tying of the hands was supposed to take place under an enormous old oak tree, supposedly seeded a thousand years ago, before Christianity came and before the stories of the Maguires in Fermanagh. It was the traditional wedding ceremony location of the O'Cassidys. His mother was supposed to have got married there, had events worked against her wishes. He could have been married there too, and he wished it was him marrying Caoimhe, instead of Connor Roe's son.

It was a rather low key event, all things considered, for neither side wished to draw attention to the wedding from the wider clan. What should have been a joyous occasion was stiff and stern, a competition of polished breastplates, helmets and swords, of pride and jealousy instead of being filled with the mischief of children and smiling relatives. Connor Roe had only brought two of his sons, one to get married and the other to command the guard. He was so paranoid that he left his wife back in Lisnaskea. Cormac only brought his captains of commerce and constables of his guard. Meanwhile, the priest was from the local parish instead of a bishop or archbishop.

No one was supposed to know about the new alliance until it was all over.

All of this was hidden from Caoimhe. Her father considered her rather delicate and frivolous, and she would not appreciate how he saw the occasion. After a quick tour of the grounds in the morning, she was hidden away in her room until her brother was sent to fetch her. When she arrived outside, she returned her father's smile until it melted away at the sight of all the soldiers.

"Is my wedding to be a military parade, father?" she asked, hoping he would notice her subtly disappointed tone.

"Alas, dear daughter, while sometimes marriage is a fairy tale, mostly it is duty."

Duty brought a tear to her eye.

"Do I not even get one day of the fairy tale?"

"You get a financially secure life with one of the most prominent families in Fermanagh and the chance to sire the next generation of Maguire leaders. What more could a girl ask for? If you don't appreciate it now, you'll thank me in the future. Now wipe your tears and think of how proud your mother would have been."

Caoimhe did as her father asked, except the tears multiplied no matter how much she wiped them away.

"That is what a veil is for, dear. Allow me."

One lady in attendance helped her hide her tears with her wedding attire.

Her father turned and took her hand, and the small smile of reassurance died when he saw smiles did not flower on Caoimhe's face. He led her out to the old oak tree she used to sit under as a child, now a rainbow of ribbons and flowers tied to every branch. The men formed a guard of honour, all shiny and new, and the few female relatives that were there all gathered to one side with their best shawls to protect them from the bitter wind. Art stood at the top of the guard, waiting, smiling, for his new bride. Even the finest clothes imported from the Pale could not lift Art above being unremarkable in mind, body and spirit. He was definitely Connor Roe's spare son. If she were to be a sow, surely they could find a better boar?

The monks sang, except for the pocket of silence. The finest bards her father could hire scribbled notes trying to add sheen to the solemnity of the occasion. If Caoimhe could not have the wedding she wanted, at least she could read a decent poem and dream. Then her father's money would have bought something of value even if it were just an illusion. Cormac passed Caoimhe's hand to Art. Art put on his best smile, and Caoimhe looked at the ground.

"Can we get on with it?" said Connor Roe to the priest.

Eunan's dreams were disintegrating before his eyes. He turned tearfully to Seamus.

"What are we to do? She will soon be gone and the O'Cassidys too. Help me, Seamus!"

Unfortunately for Eunan, Seamus had already planned ahead.

"Where are your throwing axes?"

"Strapped to my leg."

"You know what to do to end this."

Eunan's hand trembled. Kill Connor Roe? Revenge for his father? How would he escape? Where was Óisin and would he get here on time?

"Hurry!"

Eunan stuck his hand under his habit and fumbled with the knife belt around his leg.

"Ow!" he pricked his finger on his blade.

"Hurry!"

He picked out the first string knot, then the second, then the...

"Got it!"

Eunan held the shaft of his axe in his hand beneath his habit and jutted it out within his habit as if he was symmetrically pregnant.

"Don't just show it to me, throw it!" hissed Seamus.

"I cannot get good aim," whimpered Eunan as Connor Roe's helmeted head bobbed and ducked behind the heads of his men.

"I can see him perfectly well, and so should you. Throw it!" Eunan panicked. His childhood flooded back. Death, death, death, bad blood, 'it's all your fault', 'your poor mother', 'you'll never be the O'Cassidy Maguire…'

Seamus shook his arm.

"You'll never be the O'Cassidy Maguire if you don't throw that axe!"

Eunan meekly lifted the axe from beneath his habit and brought the clan chief maker out into the open. His hand shook.

"Now it is time for the tying of the hands," said the priest, as he smiled at the soon-to-be betrothed couple.

"Now or never!" hissed Seamus, only to receive the meekest of smiles.

"Pass me the tie," said the priest.

Seamus snatched the axe from Eunan's hand, paused momentarily to take aim and then…

"Fly straight and true."

The axe spun in the air. Eunan's world imploded.

"What if it missed?"

But Seamus's aim was true. It spun and flew straight into the back of its intended target. The back of Art Maguire's head exploded and blood and brains spattered all over Connor Roe's breastplate and Caoimhe's veil and dress. Caoimhe screamed.

"AMBUSH!" came a male voice.

The wedding party and guests scattered in all directions. Moments after the ambush cry was made, a hail of arrows rained from the sky. The monks tried to flee, but Seamus grabbed the nearest one by his habit hood and the monk became a cushion full of arrows, blood gushing from every pore.

Eunan tried to hide amongst the scattering monks, but Seamus grabbed his arm.

"Óisin is nearly here. I can hear them charging. Lose the habit and grab an axe. Here we stop Connor Roe for good."

"Why did you kill Art?"

"So that he couldn't marry Caoimhe. That was the plan all along. Now grab an axe!"

Arrows whistled down again and "the cry of the Maguire" was heard in the distance. Seamus went down to the old oak tree amongst the fallen O'Cassidys and Maguires and selected a battle axe. Eunan discarded his habit, only to be immediately recognised. He threw his two remaining axes to stop O'Cassidy's men from surrounding him.

* * *

Meanwhile, Connor Roe recovered from the initial shock. He fled the wedding site and was now at his horses, which were set up for his escape.

"Rally the men, constables," he shouted at his bodyguards. "We must have my son's body and the bride back at Lisnaskea! I'll remain here until you bring me news."

Ten Maguire Galloglass were dispatched towards the old oak tree.

* * *

Cormac fled back to his house after the first volley of arrows.

"Cillian! Cillian! WHERE IS Cillian?" he screamed to anyone who would listen, but most had scattered into the fields.

Little did he know Cillian was forever ingrained into the tree roots of the old oak tree he enjoyed playing under as a boy. The shiny parade armour was no match for a determined volley of arrows that pinned him to the roots of his beloved tree. The blood of Eunan's greatest rival seeped into the ground.

Óisin had discharged two volleys of arrows and was too impatient to wait for the third to be loaded before he had the honour of hollering 'the cry of the Maguire'. He gathered the best part of a hundred men whose chief strength was their archery skills, but Óisin preferred the adrenalin of hand to hand combat. With most of the O'Cassidy patrols picked off, they more or less had an unobstructed charge from the woods to the house.

Cormac desperately tried to rally his men from the remains of the wedding ceremony. Donnacha stood behind him and concluded all was lost. He turned to leave, but Cormac spotted him.

"The Maguire will hear about this abomination and the perpetrators will hang for it!" exclaimed Donnacha.

"Good to hear, but what are we going to do in the here and now?"

"Where is that boy of yours? He is skilled with the sword and axe, but this is not the place for me, a man of words. My skills are better deployed elsewhere. Troops will be dispatched as soon as I set foot in Enniskillen! To me, men!"

Donnacha and his two bodyguards ran towards the stables.

"Curse you, brother!" and Cormack shook his fist at his brother, but Donnacha was long gone. He picked up a sword, gathered as many men as he could, and prepared to defend the house.

* * *

Óisin's men gathered around the house and sheltered from the sporadic gunfire and the occasional arrow. He wanted to burn the house down and would have done so if he only had Eunan to contend with. The men then spread out and mopped up the dying as they robbed or beheaded those they could find that had coins in their pockets or a price on their head. That is, until Connor Roe's men counterattacked. No match for the disciplined Galloglass that Connor Roe could afford to train and hire, Óisin's men were soon on the run.

* * *

Seamus and Eunan found themselves alone beneath the tree, encircled by the men of the O'Cassidy. They were both armed and prepared for one last stance.

"Well then, what are you waiting for?" shouted Seamus. "If you don't close now, fifty Galloglass of the O'Donnell will be here to cut you into little pieces. However, you may also choose to drop your weapons and run, just like your masters did."

The men looked at each other until one of them said, "I don't want to die today," and he dropped his axe and ran. The rest were straight behind him. Eunan put down his axe.

"Our day is nearly done here," he said as he sat on one of the large protruding roots from the oak tree.

At his feet lay the body of Art Maguire. The arm twitched.

"He's not dead!" exclaimed Eunan.

"He soon will be," replied Seamus. "Do you think his head is worth anything or is that a sensitive subject with the politics and all?"

Seamus raised his axe.

"Do that and it'll be the last thing you do!" came a voice.

Connor Roe's men had arrived back to retrieve the body.

* * *

Óisin's men ran back to the woods.

"RALLY HERE! RALLY HERE!" he shouted.

He hid behind a massive boulder and peered back over the fields to the O'Cassidy house. No one pursued them.

"There can't be that many of them!" he murmured in his despair of staring defeat in the face.

Óisin ran around the wood, gesticulating with his axe in the direction of the battle.

"To me, men! To me!"

He gathered as many as he could find: sixty men sat or stood around him after heeding his call.

"We have about equal numbers, but at the very least we need to rescue Seamus and Eunan. How many of you have bows?"

Óisin counted about half who raised their hands. He found himself a stick and made a crude drawing of the house and its surroundings.

"We will drive a wedge between the house and the wedding venue. The bowmen will pin down the men at the house, the others will attack the wedding venue. The aim is to rescue Seamus and Eunan and then we see what happens. Are you with me?"

The men raised a reluctant nod.

"Then let us charge once more."

They lined up in two groups.

"FOR THE MAGUIRE!"

The earth appeared to shake as they charged for the Maguire once again.

* * *

Seamus and Eunan stood over the body of Art Maguire, being careful so that they did not create an obstacle for their feet. Connor Roe's men circled around them until Connor Roe appeared before them.

"Men, you get him," he said, pointing to Seamus, "and leave the other one to me!"

They prised Seamus and Eunan apart.

"An axe!" cried Connor Roe, and one of his men obliged.

"I know who you are," said Connor Roe. "That fool O'Cassidy should have taken care of you long ago, but I'll just chop you in two." He thrust his axe forward only for Eunan to parry.

They circled around each other and jabbed with their axes until Connor Roe heard the cry of Óisin charging over the field again.

"Do you think I'm a fool to fight a young warrior like you? Men, help me finish him!"

Three of his men broke off fighting with Seamus.

"EUNAN! RUN!" cried Seamus as he fended off the men attacking him. But Eunan was already surrounded.

* * *

Óisin's bowmen rained arrows down on the men in front of the house. The defenders scattered, as they had little response to the new assault and sought shelter in the house and its surroundings. The bowmen pinned them down in the house, reducing the threat of their opponents to Óisin's flank. Óisin commanded the rest of his men to charge to the wedding venue. But to their left appeared heavily armoured, fresh Galloglass charging towards the oak tree. Óisin hesitated.

"If they are not with me, I lead my men to get massacred, but if I hesitate, then Eunan and Seamus could die."

Óisin raised his axe.

* * *

Eunan swung his axe in a semi-circle around himself but Connor Roe's men closed in like a pack of vicious dogs. They took it in turns to thrust from different directions, and Eunan parried each time. He began to tire. Seamus had some early success and downed a couple of his opponents, but he also found himself surrounded. Connor Roe broke away.

"Constable! Bring me some archers!" he cried to the men guarding the horses, and two archers duly obliged and ran to his side.

"That one," he said, pointing to Eunan. "Cripple him, then I'll finish him myself. Kill the other one!"

The archers loaded their arrows and pulled back their bows.

"For the Maguire!" the Galloglass charging the field had changed directions and descended onto Connor Roe and his men. The bowmen were forced to defend themselves, and their arrows were loosened into the mass of charging men.

"Stand your ground," Connor Roe shouted before signalling to his constable to bring his horse.

The men who surrounded Eunan and Seamus backed off to form a wall for a fighting retreat. The new Galloglass ran past Seamus and Eunan.

Sean O'Toole slapped Seamus on the back.

"Where on God's earth have you been?" exclaimed Seamus.

"When all hell broke loose, I sneaked under the cover of the monks. I remembered the men from Tirconnell were only a few hours behind us so I took a horse and went and found them."

"So from deserting me, you ended up my saviour?"

"I just got lucky. Unlike the O'Cassidy," and Sean pointed to the house as it became engulfed in flames.

Seamus pointed in the other direction. Connor Roe had mounted his horse and rallied his men.

"Hold you ground boys and do a fighting retreat. You will be well remembered whether you get back to Lisnaskea!" and he turned his horse around and galloped away.

* * *

The fighting between the two sets of Galloglass lasted another ten minutes before the rest of Connor Roe's men broke away and fled. Eunan collapsed onto the roots of the oak tree and stared at the sky. The adrenalin pulsating, he noticed Art Maguire still twitched. He put him out of his misery. Óisin came over with his men, or at least those who were not trying to loot what they could from the burning house.

"Look what I found!" Óisin said as his men threw Cormac O'Cassidy to the ground. Cormac crawled on his knees and grabbed for the edges of Eunan's breeches.

"Please don't kill me, I'll give you anything you want," he pleaded.

On the day that was supposed to catapult his family into being Maguire royalty, he was now reduced to a penniless beggar.

"Why should I not just kill you here and now?" asked Seamus.

"I renounce the title of O'Cassidy Maguire, the boy can lead the clan. Just leave me with a few pennies in my pocket and point me in the direction of the Pale and my daughter and I will sail away to a far away land and you'll never hear from us again."

"But if I just kill you now, then the boy can become the O'Cassidy Maguire and I'll never have to worry about you coming back."

"But my daughter will…"

The words choked in his mouth. He covered it with his hand, for he felt he had given too much away. Behind him now was Caoimhe, the priest who was supposed to marry her, several monks and servants from the household, all surrounded by Óisin's men. They had been rounded up in their attempt to flee the burning house.

Seamus suppressed the smirk as a plan dawned upon him. He walked over to Caoimhe and took her by the arm. Her tear ducts were now dry, so she could only sniff and shudder.

"Eunan, do you wish to become the O'Cassidy Maguire like you always dreamed of? I give you your bride to seal your claim!"

"NO!"

Caoimhe howled as she found more tears and pulled herself out of Seamus's grip.

"We can always do it the other way if you find the idea so repugnant," and Seamus lifted his axe towards her father's head.

Caoimhe ran and threw her arms around her father's shoulders to protect him from harm. She looked at him, but he could only whimper and nod. She stood up; the blood and brains of her previous husband-to-be had barely dried on her dress.

"Well, Eunan? Destiny awaits!" and Seamus smiled and pointed his axe at the cowering Cormac.

Eunan froze. Confusion overpowered him and left his mind blank.

"Here, take this." Óisin placed his hand on Eunan's shoulder and handed him the wolfhound axe.

Eunan paused and looked at the axe.

"Let's make Teige decide, shall we?" and Eunan took the axe, picked a side, and threw it in the air with a bit of spin before it fell to the ground

O'DONNELL
BANAGH CASTLE
CASTLE
DONEGAL CASTLE
DONEGAL TOWN
TURLOUGH LUINEACH O'NEILL
TIRCONNELL
TERMON MAGRATH
O'NEILL
OMAGH CASTLE
ATLANTIC OCEAN
BALLYSHANNON CASTLE
HUGH MACNEILL
MAC COSNE O'NEILL
AUGHER CASTLE
BELEEK CASTLE
LOWER LOUGH ERNE
CORMAC MAC BARON O'NEILL
BUNDROWS CASTLE
DEVANISH ISLAND
ENNISKILLEN CASTLE
TADHG OG MAC CLANCY
SHEE OG O'ROURKE'S VILLAGE
HUGH MAGUIRE
MAGUIRE
CONNOR ROE MAGUIRE
CASTLE SKEA
LISNASKEA
HUGH ROE MAC MAHON
SIR BRIAN O'ROURKE
O'CASSIOS HOUSE
EWNAN'S VILLAGE
MONAGHAN
DERROLINE CORMAC O'CASSIOS
WEST BREIFNE
BRIAN ORIEL HUGH OG MAC MAHON
HUGH MAC HUGH
OMOS O'ROURKE
SIR JOHN O'REILLY
O'REILLY
PHILIP O'REILLY
MOYLURG
WILLIAM O'FARRELL BANE
CAVAN TOWN
EAST BREIFNE
MAGHERY CONNAUGHT
ANNALLY
MAEL MORA O'REILLY

CASTLE
TOWN
LAKE

MAGUIRE — LORDSHIP
HUGH MAGUIRE — PRINCIPAL LORD

WOODS
HILLS

FERMANAGH AND SURROUNDING DISTRICTS 1590s

359

About the Author

C R Dempsey is the author of 'Uprising' and 'Bad Blood', two historical fiction books set in Elizabethan Ireland. He has plans for many more, and he needs to find the time to write them. History has always been his fascination, and historical fiction was an obvious outlet for his accumulated knowledge. C R spends lots of time working on his books, mainly in the twilight hours of the morning. C R wishes he spent more time writing and less time jumping down the rabbit hole of excessive research.

C R Dempsey lives in London with his wife and cat. He was born in Dublin but has lived most of his adult life in London.

I would be grateful if you would leave a review of the book at the vendor where you purchased it. Please click here.

You can connect with me on:
- https://www.crdempseybooks.com
- https://twitter.com/dempsey_cr
- https://www.facebook.com/crdempsey
- https://www.instagram.com/crdempsey

Subscribe to my newsletter:
- https://www.subscribepage.com/c4m9k5_copy

Also by C R Dempsey

★★★★ **"A new piece of Irish historical fiction that pulls you in through its protagonist, and is full of plenty of action. - Reedsey Discovery**
https://books2read.com/u/mKyJR9
What would you do to save your clan?

Ireland 1585. Eunan Maguire lives in a small village in Fermanagh and wonders why his parents hate him and his neighbours shun him. When his village is raided by the English, he flees to save himself, his parents are killed and he blames himself for their death.

When he meets Seamus MacSheehy, the head of a wandering band of Galloglass, Seamus encourages him to take his father's title of the head of the village even though everyone in the village is dead. Eunan goes to the election of the new leader of the Maguire clan to claim his father's voting rights. With Seamus' guidance, he sets out to ingratiate himself with the new Maguire. But all is not well for Eunan is wracked with guilt because of the death of his parents and Seamus is not all he appears. The English invade Fermanagh, and he is called to fight.

Will Eunan find out the secret of why his parents hated him so much and the circumstances of their death? Will Eunan discover who is Seamus MacSheehy and why he has taken such an interest in him? Or will the clan fall and perish under the English onslaught?

Bad Blood is the first novel in the 'Exiles' series of Irish historical fiction novels. If you love fast-paced action and adventure orientated historical fiction then you will love this book.

Click here for store links.

Printed in Great Britain
by Amazon

80200117R00210